A Kiss
From Death

Line/Copy Edits: The Fiction Fix
Cover Design: Wavy Hues
Formatted by: Brady Moller
Map Design: Alexis Morgan
Character Art: Salooch Art

A Kiss From Death

Alexis Morgan

Content Warning

LUNARIA IS AN ADULT ROMANTIC FANTASY THAT EXPLORES MATURE AND dark themes. It is **intended for readers 18 years and older**. This book contains scenes and situations that may be distressing for some readers.

If you are comfortable with heavy content and prefer to experience the story without spoilers, feel free to continue on and enjoy the ride.

However, if you have specific triggers or sensitivities, please review the content warnings below before diving in.

Here is a list of possible triggers: Murder, Death, Blood, Gore, Grief, Violence, Torture, Drugging, Dismemberment, Profanity, Alcohol Consumption, Sexually Explicit Scenes, Death of a Child, Weapons, and Hallucinations.

Playlist

For the full playlist, check out the link!

Survivor – 2WEI, Edda Hayes
Crazy – Tell Me Lies
How Villains Are Made – Madalen Duke
Paint It, Black – Ciara
Jealous – Labrinth
The Night We Met – Lord Huron
Can't Help Falling In Love – Tommee Profitt, brooke

Listen now on spotify!
https://open.spotify.com/playlist/5vdr4JaV2sB6WICcA2e5KW?-si=_IEmBRXdRtSPOZ4G0P5d2w&pi=u-veDnq8hzQKSt

To the girls who are afraid to be their true selves—
Lay yourself bare to the world,
and watch every soul who dared stand against you
burn alive in the heat of your success.

Pronunciation Guide

- Lunaria: *Loon-area*
- Nyxi: *Nix-ee*
- Hade: *Hey-d*
- Airestol: *Air-eh-stall*
- Rayah: *Ray-uh*
- Odessa: *Oh-des-za*
- Moji: *Moh-jee*

Fallout Sectors

- Command: Law makers and enforcement.
- Enlightened: Scholars and teachers.
- Visionary: Creatives and healers.
- Sweat: Farmers and constructors.
- Vagrant: Outcasts.

Magic Guide

- Enhancer: Amplify voices and sounds.
- Illuminist: Broadcast events witnessed.
- Migrant: Teleport location over great distances.
- Scorch: Fire manipulation.
- Fib: Detect lies.
- Dash: Fast.
- Float: Fly.
- Luster: Enhance beauty.
- Stretch: Lengthen body and limbs.
- Soak: Water manipulation.
- Fabricant: Create objects.
- Manipulant: Coercion.
- Death: Speak to the dead, command death, shadow manipulation. (Full depth of power is uknown)

FALLOUT

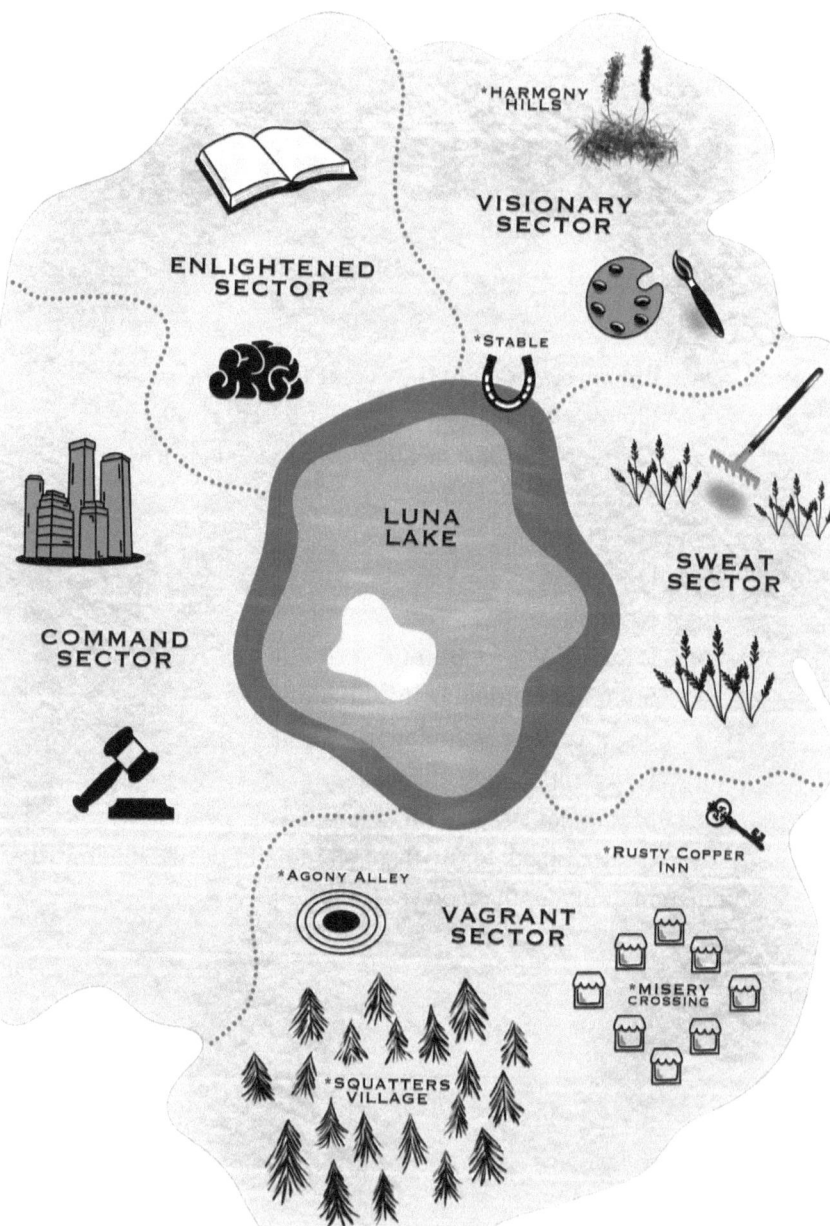

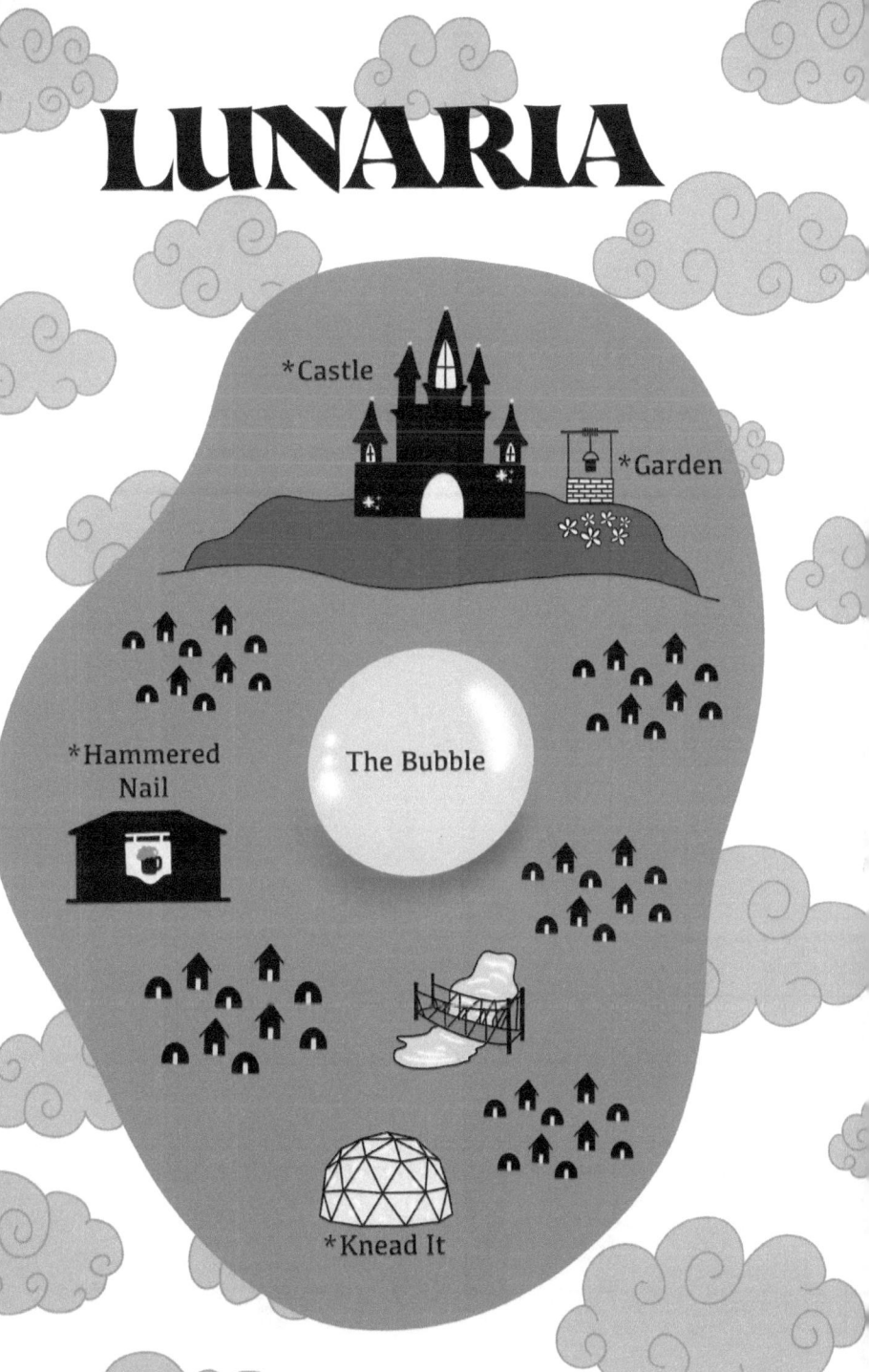

Prologue

CROUCHING BEHIND A THIN CANVAS WALL, I YAWN WHILE LISTENING to the conversation unfolding inside the makeshift tent. Honestly, after hiding here for the past two hours, I'm beyond bored, ready to take all the gossip I've learned home to Theo so we can sell it to the highest bidder.

I know what you may be thinking: sounds like slimy business to be in. While you might not be wrong, to survive living in Fallout, you must do whatever it takes. 'Whatever it takes' to me is being the best hired spy in all of Fallout's five sectors.

My boyfriend, Theo, is the brains of the operation while I'm the brute. He finds people looking for information, and then I weasel my way through the sectors, spying from the shadows and learning what I need.

This little operation we have going on makes us enough money to stay alive, but not much above that. That's the norm, though, when you're stuck living in Vagrant Sector—or "Misery", as I like to call it.

They call our sector where everything comes to die. People, will, sanity, and most importantly, *dreams*. We are the misfits and outcasts of Fallout, full of poor and troubled souls. Poverty, crime, you name it—we've got it.

It's not all bad, though. Some of us, including me and Theo, are good people who were just dealt a bad hand. Well, Theo is what I consider a good person, the best, actually. Me, on the other hand…I could still use some work.

He embodies everything that encompasses a warm cozy summer day, and I'm like the thunderstorm that rolls in at night, except when it comes to *him*. He is the only person capable of stripping my thunderclouds away, the only person I can trust and be my authentic self around. I guess when you grow up in an abusive orphanage with no knowledge of your family, it kind of makes you a closed off, heartless bitch or something.

I met Theo in the orphanage, and I instantly clung to him like a lifeline. Theo is the first person to ever show me love and compassion. He protected me when no one else did.

It is a miracle to me how he can stay so positive and happy with his traumatic past. Most people would wither away to nothing if their mother and sister both died during childbirth. Then tack on your father passing away less than a month later of what they called "a broken heart" and one would assume you would be scarred for life. Not my Theo, though. He is kind to everyone, charming and bubbly in a non-annoying way. Most people like that get under my skin, but never Theo.

His smile is the first thing I see every morning when I open my eyes. His boisterous, infectious laugh is always running on repeat in my head when life gets tough. But most importantly, he wears his heart on his sleeve and lets those he cares about know without a doubt that he will love you fiercely until his last breath. He is a miracle—no, he's *my* miracle.

Slowly sinking into the shadows, I make sure the black scarf wrapped around my face and hair is hiding my features then start my trek back towards our "home" before I get caught and blow my whole cover. My usual all-black getup helps me blend in, sitting snugly against my skin like a glove, weapons strapped with while buckles encompassing me. You don't get labeled the best spy in all the sectors if people know what you look like.

I'm an expert at blending in and fighting my way out of sticky situations, which has happened a time or two. I wish I could say I feel sorry for the poor souls I've had to take out, but as we've already established, I'm a heartless bitch, and I like it that way.

Gripping the tiny dagger hanging from my throat, I weave through the bustling streets of Misery's Crossing, all the shops in full bloom trading or selling various goods for the day. Crumbling buildings surround me in every direction, selling items from dried meats, pastries, and weapons, to clothing and contraband.

All the potent smells of Misery's Crossing hit me at once, assaulting me with its sticky, pungent air that seeps up from its rotting streets. I easily weave my way through the packed streets, taking shortcuts I've learned over years of walking this same route.

Still gripping my dagger necklace out of habit, my thumb glides over the indent I've rubbed into the handle, and I'm reminded of the day Theo gave it to me.

He pressed the tip of the tiny black metal dagger into my palm, the necklace chain dangling off the side of my hand, and told me to always wear it so I will never forget he always guards my heart.

I don't know how I got so lucky to have caught his eye in the orphanage all those years ago, but I thank the Empress daily that I did. He is my chosen forever family, since my biological family wanted nothing to do with me, and I wouldn't have it any other way. Having Theo as family for the rest of my life sounds pretty fucking good to me.

Once out of Misery's Crossing, I walk the dirt road leading to Squatters Village, where all the housing for Vagrants Sector is located. It's nestled deep in the forest, surrounded by thick pine trees, a running stream, and dangerous creatures, and I keep my eyes peeled for any danger.

The walk from Misery's Crossing to Squatters Village isn't too long, but it's still enough time to get yourself into a sticky situation. Deadly creatures prowling from above as well as Vigilantes are known to frequent this area.

I learned how to fight and defend myself from a young age. You learn quickly when you grow up in the sort of place I did, and I have the scars to prove it.

Rounding one last corner, I approach our shack of a house nestled right in the center of our village. It's not much more than a rotting roof covering four questionable walls, but Theo makes it feel like a home.

Gripping the rusty door handle, I fling open our front door, and I'm immediately tackled to the ground by a six foot tall, lanky ray of sunshine staring down at me. His large hands bracket each side of my head, caging me in.

Peering up at him, I take in his warm, sun kissed skin peppered with freckles. His shaggy and disheveled auburn curly hair flops messily over his forehead, and his piercing hazel eyes remind me so much of the pine trees surrounding our shack, which happen to be wide with excitement.

I grab a lock of his unruly hair and give it a firm playful tug. The side of his lip tugs up in a smirk that warms my heart. "You know, most would think twice before tackling me to the ground for fear of losing their life," I scold playfully.

He just winks while casually breathing over my lips, "Good thing I'm not most people then, princess."

He pulls my scarf down and pecks me on the cheek, which makes me giggle like a schoolgirl. Pushing Theo off, I right myself again. Striding across the room, I plop down on our makeshift couch, which is just a bunch of giant pillows shoved together in a pile against the wall.

"So, fill me in, Nyxi girl. How did it go?" Theo prods while wiggling his eyebrows and plopping down next to me.

"Same old, same old." I sigh, plastering my best overdramatic bored expression on my face. "I swear, these people get less and less secretive as the days go by. It's like they want me to hear all their dirty secrets and pass them along to their enemies."

"Or, hear me out. Maybe, just maybe, you are too damn good at your job, and they have zero idea a dangerous creature is even lurking in their shadows," Theo whispers, grazing his lips against the shell of my ear.

Chills run down my spine, and I shove my shoulder into his before he continues. "I mean, half the time, even I have no idea you're home." He stops to tap his chin thoughtfully, and a smile splays his lips. "At least not until I hear your ear-splitting belting you like to call... What is it again? Singing?" he teases, and I just roll my eyes in return.

"Ha-ha, real funny, mister. I seem to recall you asking me to sing to you every time you get sick because it helps you heal faster," I deadpan, making air quotes with my hands at him.

He rolls his eyes at that, but he still can't help the smile slowly taking over his face as we both shatter into a massive giggling fit.

"I swear to the Empress, that voice of yours has special healing remedies, and I will die on that hill." Crossing his arms over his chest, he pretends to play dead, and I tackle him before we both fall into a fit of laughter again.

The rest of the evening, we sit on our "couch" while I relay all the important information I learned from today's outing. I leave out all the boring nonsense I had to sit through and only tell him the important parts worth money. Only one of us should have to suffer through the vulgar, brain-melting conversations I sat through today.

Tomorrow morning, Theo will take the information I learned and sell it to the highest bidder. Afterwards, he will scout through Misery's Crossing for new job opportunities and pass any leads my way. This is how we've filled every day since turning eighteen, when the orphanage kicked us out two years ago. I wouldn't have it any other way. It will always be me and him against the world.

Theo and Nyxi.

Sᴜɴ ʀᴀʏs ʙʟᴀᴢᴇ ɪɴ ᴛʜʀᴏᴜɢʜ ᴛʜᴇ ᴡɪɴᴅᴏᴡ ᴀᴅᴊᴀᴄᴇɴᴛ ᴛᴏ ᴏᴜʀ ʙᴇᴅ. Iᴛ cascades through perfectly on my face, alerting me it's time to wake for the day.

Slowly peeling my sleep-ridden eyelids open, I roll over to snuggle deeper into Theo's warmth before it's time to get up for the day. Feeling around, all I find is a cold, scratchy flannel sheet. Theo has most likely already been up and going for the day for quite some time.

He always has been an early riser, so it doesn't surprise me the least that he's already out scouting for the day.

Blowing a breath out, I scoff to myself. "Overachiever."

Hopping out of bed, I slide on my favorite long sleeve, black cotton shirt and matching leather pants that hug my lean limbs. They make it easy for me to blend in with the shadows of Misery's Crossing while working.

Quickly, I run a brush through my long, thick curls, the inky strands covering my back. I decide to tie it back into a slicked low pony to keep it out of my face. I finish off by sliding one dagger into my waistband and another into my right boot for easy access.

Grabbing an apple off the counter, I sink my teeth into it while striding out our front door towards Misery's Crossing. I hightail straight to our meet up spot on the outskirts of town, crouching around the abandoned tent that used to sell the best mouthwatering pastries.

It's a real shame a fire started out of the blue two years ago, forcing them to pack up and move shop. I giggle at the memory.

Theo still holds a grudge against me for that one, but we needed a private meet up spot so no one would learn my identity, and I found a solution.

Picking up the giant rock nestled behind the back of the tent, I find the piece of parchment Theo left for me like always. In simple, clean handwriting, it reads:

Princess,

Got a fun one for you today. Rumor has it, some of the healers in Visionary Sector are smuggling illegal drugs from above. A few of the higher ups aren't happy about it, I guess. Something about not wanting it to lead to overpopulation in Fallout due to its excellent healing abilities. If you can confirm a drop off time and location for me, it would score us a few pretty coppers. I know Visionary Sector is your favorite, so enjoy yourself today and don't work too hard. I'll bake your favorite strawberries and cream cookies and have them waiting for you when you get home. Maybe tonight, we can finally paint the walls that obnoxious bright purple shade you've been asking for the past year. Stay safe for me, Nyxi.

Location: Healer's Haven/Visionary Sector

Love you now and in every life to follow,
-Your Theo

Folding the parchment back up, I slide it securely into my waistband and place the rock back where I found it. Just as I'm about to head out, I notice the handpicked arrangement of flowers carefully placed next to the rock.

When I pick them up, my eyes are assaulted with a rainbow of colors, from bright yellows and deep blues to pastel pinks and purples, all wrapped tightly together by one long clipping of tall grass.

Flowers this vibrant and fresh cannot be found in soul sucking "Misery", which means Theo must have set off early this morning to gather them for me in the luscious Harmony Hills, located deep in Visionary Sector.

While it's not illegal for people in Fallout to wander into different sectors, it also isn't highly appreciated by members in the higher ranking sectors. Just thinking about the heart attack it would have brought one of the Visionaries if they caught Theo clipping all their precious flowers brings a genuine smile to my face as I tuck the flowers gently into my sack.

Visionary Sector is by far the brightest sector of the five, housing the most creative citizens of Fallout. The day goes by in a blur, taking in all the vibrant buildings covered in murals and the sweet aromas lingering from nearby cafes. Live music and singing fills each street I turn down on my journey towards Healer's Haven.

Everywhere I look, there are people dancing and laughing, and jealousy starts to creep up my neck as I take in how genuinely happy they all are. If I could choose any of the sectors to live in, Visionary would be at the top of my list.

Shaking the intrusive thoughts from my head, I approach Healer's Haven by midday and set up camp on the stucco roof right above an open window.

I spend three hours camped on the hard, uncomfortable roof until I have enough concrete information to bring back to Theo. Rushing home, I smile to myself at the thought of Theo agreeing to live in a bright purple house with me. That man would rearrange the moon for me if I asked.

My smile immediately runs off my face—the bloodcurdling screams coming from Squatters Village make my ears ring. Panic sets in as I turn my leisurely walk into a full blown sprint towards our home.

The village is in utter chaos, people running in every direction with ghostly white faces full of panic. A body catches me off guard from behind, plowing me to the ground as people stomp frantically around me.

I take two calming breaths, regaining my bearings and wedging myself back into the chaos around me. My heart stops altogether when the deafening scream of a Necroshriek flying above me shatters all the windows of the house to my left.

Shit. Shit. SHITTTT.

Flying around the last corner, I rip open our front door, nearly knocking it off its rusty hinges. I throw my body inside, looking for him, hoping and praying he's okay, while the smells of freshly baked cookies wrap tightly around me.

I don't know what I expected to find when I walked inside, but nothing, not even the Empress, could have prepared me to see Theo, *my* Theo, my *only* family, my *only* person, staring lifeless back at me.

I trail my eyes across the river of blood leading me to him. His once-floppy auburn hair is now painted bright red and slicked against his forehead. His once-inviting hazel eyes still lay open, entirely unseeing, soulless. His lifeless body is littered with deep gouges across his face, throat, and abdomen, and he's still protectively curled around a tiny pail of lavender paint he just purchased, guarding it with his life while dragging his body inside.

9

My entire existence is over in a flash of an eye, and all that is left behind is red hot *rage!* My brain is drained of every thought except one: *revenge*. I know exactly how I'm going to get it. They already think of us as monsters down here, so I might as well show them exactly what kind of monster they just created.

I'm going to enter myself in The Reaper Crucible, hosted above in Lunaria. It's time to unleash the monster they just created. Make no mistake—I will burn everything to the ground in my wake.

They messed with the wrong Vagrant, and now, it's time they learned who I am.

Death Reincarnate.

Chapter
ONE

8 Months Later

I WILL CHEAT, FUCK, OR KILL ANY PERSON WHO COMES BETWEEN ME and my revenge. And make no mistake—I will have zero regrets doing it. My body is just a vessel to use at this point, and I will take advantage of it in any way possible. I will burn this world to the ground, ashes to motherfucking ashes, even if that means *burning* with it.

Which leads me to my current sticky situation of sneaking over 200 extra entries into Vagrant sector's raffle selection for entering the deadly Reaper Crucible.

It was easier than I thought to knock out the pathetic guard half-dozing off instead of keeping watch of the bowl. Just a quick silent headlock, and he was out like a light. Maybe I punched him in the face as well, just to make sure he was out. Broken noses don't take too long to heal, so I would call myself a saint of a lady today.

I wasn't lying when I said I would do whatever it took to get my revenge, and that starts with cheating my way into being picked as one of two slots from Vagrant's Sector. It blows my mind why anyone would enter the Crucible of their own free will when your odds of survival are a whopping 10%...but I guess that didn't stop me.

Citizens of Fallout train their entire lives to be prepared for the off chance they are selected to enter the blood bath games. Two members from each of the five sectors are chosen at random for the year each summer by the Empress up in Lunaria.

Each year the Crucible looks a little different, making it next to impossible to prepare for—all done by design, of course, to give our lunatic of an Empress the grandest show. Her wicked mind comes up with the cruelest ways to test each participant's physical and mental barriers, all for her enjoyment. Each round ramps up in difficulty and deadliness, leaving a single survivor in the end.

No member of Fallout is required to enter themselves into the Crucible, but that doesn't mean there's a shortage of willing participants. Quite the opposite, actually.

Each year, the number of participants increases, making it next to impossible to get chosen. Even with the knowledge of two contestants being sacrificed each round until one winner is chosen during the fifth and final doesn't slow the influx of people risking it all for a chance to play.

Members of Fallout are greedy and power hungry, which is exactly why so many of them are willing to risk their lives for the chance of winning the ultimate prize.

Magic.

Not a single soul living in Fallout possesses the ability to wield magic except the Empress and her Vanquishers, who are tasked with guarding and protecting her when she is down here, living in the smaller version of the castle above. It's a phenomenon.

Empress Gwyndolyn Seraphine is an Impart, meaning she can harness magic from the Earth and gift it to whomever she deems fit. One's own soul decides what magic it can harbor and wield and is not decided by the Empress. Some can take on elemental magic, like controlling water or wind. Others can emerge with rarer magic, such as telepathy or invisibility. Most victors of the Crucible end up with some sort of elemental magic, which is the most common.

If you are lucky enough to withstand all five rounds of the Crucible and come out as the victor, Empress Seraphine hosts a huge party in your honor, where she performs the blessing ceremony to grant and announce your new magic. In winning the Crucible, each victor is also granted a letter of acceptance to move up to Lunaria to live among the magically blessed, or magicals.

Down here, we like to call Lunaria the "dreamland"; every person living there is blessed with magic, wealth, and happiness. I mean, I would be happy too if I had the ability to wield magic and got to live on a floating rock in the sky. I'm not sure what's in the air up there, but I wish we could breathe that air down here too.

Stories have been passed down through the generations of the wonders of Lunaria. Some say the colors are brighter, smells are stronger, flavors more potent. Others say there's no crime or poverty, and everyone is friendly. Rumors spread through the orphanage that even their fashion and looks greatly differ from ours and contain colors that aren't even visible in Fallout.

The kicker is, no one really knows the truth, since no one from Fallout is allowed to visit or live there unless they win the Reaper Crucible. Magic is the key to a better life that most here will never get the opportunity to obtain. Real buzz kill, I know.

I have never been one to hang on impossible dreams of a better life for myself in hopes of living there one day. All I need is Theo, and I'm a happy girl—or needed I guess. Now, the only thing that matters is entering and winning the Crucible to get my lucky ticket up to Lunaria. They won't know what's coming for them until it's too late.

The one thing we do know about Lunaria is its shitty Vanquishers and their bonded Necroshrieks that have terrorized Fallout for far too many years. Vanquishers can command their bonded Necroshriek through mind control, and they have fun doing it.

Most Vanquishers live and patrol up in Lunaria to ensure peace. A select few live in Fallout to Guard the Empress, who lives part time below with us. She governs our land and her word is law. I guess when you're the only person who possesses magic amongst a bunch of nobodies, it's hard to be overthrown.

Yuck.

Thinking back to the day the rogue Necroshriek terrorized our village and took Theo from me gives me the shakes. Necroshrieks are even scarier and uglier than they sound, which is saying something. They feed off human souls and can scent fear from miles away. They thrive off it. Legend says their piercing screeches are the combined screams of every soul they have devoured, now trapped within them. Their giant, black, batlike skeletal wings make them impossible to out run. They can melt a person, bones and all, within seconds with the black acidic clouds they spew from their vicious beaks.

Their hollowed out eye sockets will haunt my nightmares for the rest of eternity. I can still smell its rotting flesh like it's right in front of me. It's safe to say I am no longer a fan of birds in any form, especially giant, black, rotting ones that literally look like death on wings. Don't even get me started on their nasty horns.

Double yuck.

Tomorrow, each sector's representative from Fallout's council will host the drawing ceremony by picking two names out of the sector's participant bowl, and then publicly announce the lucky winners. Once your name is pulled, there is no getting out of it. So, you better be more than sure you know what you're signing up for. Two sundowns later, Vanquishers will come to collect the ten "lucky" contestants to commence the annual Reaper Crucible.

I send a prayer to the Empress that my name is chosen tomorrow and hopefully chosen only once. That would be an ugly situation to deal with and talk my way out of. I'll worry about that if the time comes, but for now, it's time to sneak back home and get some much needed rest before tomorrow's adventures.

Looking down at the bowl one last time, I am reminded exactly why I'm doing this.

"Love you now and in every life to follow, Theo," I whisper.

Chapter

Two

So much for a good night's rest. Nervously tossing and turning the entire night was not a part of my ten step plan for revenge, but I guess you win some, you lose some.

After I stare out the window for several hours, sun is finally starting to stream in, casting a warm glow on the living room. I take that as my cue to get up and going for the day.

Grunting, I peel myself up off the lumpy "pillow couch" and make my way to our room to get ready. I haven't been able to bring myself to sleep in our bed, using the couch as my makeshift sleeping spot. This room and bed holds too many good memories with Theo, and I want it to stay that way forever.

I grab a corner of the comforter that sits on Theo's side of the bed and deeply inhale. It still smells like sunshine and fresh air and reminds me of his warm, infectious, toothy grin he would shine down at me every morning we woke tangled in the sheets together. I fear the day that smell disappears.

Forgoing my usual attire, I stride over to Theo's pile of clothes and dig through it. I need all the extra strength I can get to get through this day, and having a part of Theo with me is just what the healers ordered.

I find my favorite plain white tee and leather jacket he flaunted often, slipping them on. They engulf me, hanging way past my hands and waist, since they were made for a six foot tall man and not a woman a whole eight inches shorter.

I tuck his tee into the waistband of my trusty leather pants and start cuffing the sleeves of his leather jacket. I don't want to have a safety hazard if I get jumped on my way to Misery's Crossing for the drawing ceremony.

Drawing ceremonies tend to get rowdy, so I make sure to strap extra daggers to my body, totaling four weapons I have access to: one in each boot, and two in my waistband. You never know what a Vagrant might do to survive. I've quite literally seen people's shirts torn from their backs like it's nothing. It's every man for themselves in our sector.

Planning out my day, I decide my best plan of attack is traveling to each sector to watch their individual drawing ceremonies. That way, I can size up my competition and get a couple extra days to dig around Fallout for weakness in my opponents.

Drawing ceremonies go in order of sector rank, meaning Vagrant's will be last. That should give me enough time to make it back to ours before they announce the winners.

I walk towards our front door, our old floor boards creaking with each step of my dirty boots. Flinging open the door, I step out into the crisp air and start my trek towards Command Sector for the first drawing.

Command Sector is top of the food pyramid in Fallout, housing our lawmakers and Enforcers. Even though the Empress has final say on what goes on in Fallout, she is too busy to keep up with the government structure of our sectors, hence the creation of Command Sector.

They create and uphold all laws in Fallout—trading goods, curfew times, education laws, sector transfer requests, anything you could imagine. The Empress then filters through each law created and approves the ones that fit her liking. Breaking any law in Fallout, no matter how small, is punishable to death by the Empress. She has a very creative imagination that is not to be messed with.

Most citizens of Fallout stay within the sector they are born into. On the rare occasion someone shows great strength or knowledge of another sector, they are allowed to submit a sector transfer request to the Command Sector at eighteen. These rarely get approved, but it's not unheard of.

My breathing is elevated from the trek to Command Sector. I keep my eyes peeled for Enforcers and make sure to weave around them when spotted. Even though Enforcers aren't as dangerous and scary as Vanquishers, they still aren't to be messed with, especially since they are not the biggest fans of Vagrants.

"Yeah, well, we aren't the biggest fans of you either," I mumble under my breath.

People are already starting to gather in the center of town. Excitement and nerves bleed into the crowd as everyone waits.

I've only traveled to the Command Sector a handful of times, so I make sure to take in the rare scenery. It is opposite in every way to Vagrant's Sector. Where we thrive on chaos and danger, they thrive on purpose and structure. The colors of the buildings are neutral and bland, all by design. Everything has harsh, straight edges and serves a purpose. It's clean and so boring. I would never want to live here.

Even their citizens have zero personality and are painful snobs to be around. I guess you can act that way when you're a member of the top sector.

Weaving my way through the growing crowd, I hear excited whispers of people swearing this is the year they will finally get picked. I find it odd how everyone is so excited for the chance to basically sacrifice themselves to the Empress solely for her entertainment. That's not how they see it, though. They see it as their ticket to a better life.

Pfft, losers.

The crowd hushes when a burly, cruel looking man approaches the makeshift dais in front of us. I assume he is the Command Sector's council representative. I have never seen him before; I make it a habit to keep my nose out of the politics of Fallout, but by the way he commands the crowd's respect and attention, I can assume so.

All eyes fall to the man standing slightly above us while a small woman walks beside him, holding a giant glass bowl full of folded pieces of paper—lots of them. This has to be a record year of willing participants, and it sets me a little on edge.

Attempting to calm myself, I recite Fallout's motto and pray somewhere in the castle, she hears my call. "Submit to your Empress, and you will be blessed. Stand in her way and be forever in duress," I whisper over and over again until my lungs breathe easier.

I jolt back up when I hear the deep baritone casting over the crowd. "Citizens of Command Sector, it is my great honor as your council representative to announce this year's nominees for the great Reaper Crucible!" The crowd buzzes to life with ecstatic screams and shouts.

I just roll my eyes.

Empress save us all.

"I have great faith that this year's victor will hail from our sector and prove to all of Fallout once again why we are number one," he belts out with unwavering certainty.

The crowd erupts in unison, chanting, "COMMAND SEC-TOR, COMMAND SECTOR, COMMAND SECTOR," while stomping their feet to a steady beat.

Jeez, it's like they are brainwashed cattle.

The man turns and dips his hand deep into the oversized bowl, swirling around the papers until he plucks one. The crowd goes eerily silent, waiting.

"The first nominee from Command Sector is…Sierra Foster."

The silent crowd parts when my eyes snag on bright crimson hair bobbing through the masses towards the dais. She confidently stomps up the few steps and juts her hand out to shake the man's outstretched limb. She turns to face the crowd with a blank expression and waits for the second name to be announced.

My eyes roam over my competition. I take in her straight, fiery red hair that flows down the entirety of her back. Her eyes look as if gold rings have been shoved inside them, trapped for eternity. Her warm skin is speckled with a field of freckles like the ones that dust my cheeks and nose, and she wears zero emotion on her face. Her body is warm, but the scowl she wears is anything but.

I tuck the information about my opponent safely in my brain for later and focus my attention back on the councilman. He doesn't pay Sierra another glance as he dips his hand back into the bowl. They really are stone cold in this sector.

"Our second and final nominee from Command Sector for this year's Reaper Crucible is…" The councilman pauses for dramatic effect, gaining everyone's unwavering attention. I can feel my heart beating out of my chest in anticipation, and this isn't even my sector.

It feels like an eternity passes before the councilman clears his throat and announces hesitantly, "Aeron Gavis."

The crowd gasps, sharing shocked faces, which I find odd. Aeron must be widely known in this sector, which isn't a good sign to have in a competitor. It's common knowledge that the last couple rounds of the Crucible are heavily influenced by both Fallout and Lunaria to gain advantages. If he already has reach within his sector, that is terrible news for me.

It isn't hard to spot Aeron making his way through the stunned crowd towards the dais. I have to crane my neck to catch his tall, bulky frame towering over most he walks by. The crowd erupts in whispered gossip.

"I can't believe he entered himself," one woman whispers to her friend. "Do you think Councilman Gavis knew he entered?" another man says to my left.

That sentence has me snapping my head back toward the councilman as it all clicks. Taking in his deathly pale face, one would assume he, in fact, did not know his son entered himself in a very deadly game to win magic. Things just got a whole lot trickier.

Shit.

My heart sputters as I turn my full attention back to the barbarian of a man walking up the steps of the dais towards his *father*. He has to be at least a couple inches taller than Theo, with the same golden skin. His shaggy, dirty blond hair bounces as he swaggers up the stairs, almost reaching his shoulders in length. He grips his father's hand in a firm, almost authoritative handshake, then turns, dismissing his father without saying a single word so he can work the crowd.

All eyes are on Aeron as he raises both arms above his head, waving and winking to the crowd with a shit eating grin. I just found his weakness, and I'm going to exploit his flirtatious behavior for my benefit. Any alliance I can secure early on is one step closer to winning the Crucible.

I'm coming for you, Aeron Gavis.

Confidence and cockiness radiates off him as he works the crowd like it's his profession. Suddenly, his eyes lock on mine, and I feel like I'm drowning in his icy blue gaze. He holds my attention like he's daring me to submit to him to assert his dominance. I'm up for the challenge, though, so I hold his gaze without blinking until he chuckles to himself, breaking contact to bat his long eyelashes at pretty girls in the crowd.

What am I getting myself into?

Councilman Gavis shakes out of his trance-like state and takes back control of the crowd as if nothing happened. "Well, there you have it, folks. Congratulations to this year's nominees from Command Sector for the Reaper Crucible!" he shouts out to the crowd, plastering on the fakest smile. Clearly, Aeron entering the Crucible has Councilman Gavis all worked up and caught off guard, and he's doing a terrible job at hiding it.

Rushing through the crazed crowd, I make my way towards Enlightened Sector to catch the start of their ceremony. I make it just in time to hear their councilwoman announce, "Cartwell Hart" and "Yazi Mintz" as their nominees.

Making my rounds to the remaining sectors, I learn the names of the rest of my future competitors. "Rayah Wixx" and "Hudson Beckett" from Visionary Sector, and "Briar Ellis" and "Tank Finnegan" from Sweat Sector.

I am exhausted down to my bones from today's outing, but there's still one more piece of the puzzle to get through. It's arguably the most important of today's tasks. My entire plan for revenge falls apart if I don't succeed in this. I honestly haven't stopped to think what I will do if I'm not picked. It just isn't an option in my mind.

My nerves kick up as I reenter my sector that feels more like home than the others I traveled to today, even if it is a literal dump. I like that I can be whoever I want to be here, never having to conform to certain sector standards. Vagrant Sector may not be a lot of things, but we let anyone do as they please. I'll take that any day of the week.

"PLEASEEEEEE!" a woman pleads between sobs, and I startle out of my thoughts at the haunted emotion in her voice. She isn't close to me, but her screams are so loud, it's as if she's standing right next to me. Her voice travels from the west side of Misery's Crossing, which can only mean one thing: Agony Alley.

Agony Alley is where one is sentenced to gruesome death at the hands of the Empress for breaking the law, no matter how small. Vanquishers carry out her chosen punishment, always ending in loss of life. The sunken arena is carved out of stone, seats circling the entirety of the stage in the center. Members are allowed to watch punishments for their entertainment.

Sick fucks.

On occasion, the Empress requests an enhancer for punishments. Enhancers amplify voices or sounds with their magic, which must be why I can hear this poor woman's screams from across Misery's Crossing. They like to make sure everyone in Vagrant Sector can hear what happens if you go against the Empress and her laws.

I've accidentally walked by Agony Alley a few times while punishments were being dealt and had to rush to empty my stomach. I've never stayed long enough to see them meet their end, and I'd like it to stay that way.

Picking up my pace, I blend into the massive crowd already fully packed around Councilman Scar making his introduction. It is hard to see him over the crowd, since our sector is gruesomely poor to the point of not having access to a makeshift dais.

Squeezing my slim body through the over-packed crowd, I make my way to the front to see better. I catch Councilman Scar removing the first slip from the bowl right as I make it to the front. I think I can literally feel my heart beating out of my ass with anticipation. If my life depended on staying calm right in this moment, I would be dead as a doornail.

Breathe, Nyxi. Theo would make fun of your ass right now if he could see you. Yeah, well, this is all for you, Theo, so you can shove it—with love, of course.

Councilman Scar's gravelly voice punctures my ears as he reads off the first nominee's name. "Your first nominee from Vagrant Sector is…" He grunts, coughing and trying to catch his breath. "Jade Huxley."

A blonde little thing practically skips up to the front to greet Councilman Scar. She's at least a couple inches shorter than me, basically the size of my pinkie finger, but she looks around the same age as me. If I thought I was malnourished, then she looks like she hasn't eaten a meal in weeks. Her tan skin is evidence that she spends most her time outdoors, maybe even lives on the streets. She wears a confident smile that borders on evil while shooting daggers with her vivid green eyes at the crowd. I will be keeping my distance from *her*.

Well, I guess they are saving the best for last—if Councilman Scar lives long enough to finish this ceremony. The old man is half kneeled over, his back arching at an abnormal angle that makes me wonder if he's been sleeping on the same stack of pillows for a bed like I have. His nonexistent hair must have all fallen out prior to the Empress being born, and what's left behind is a wrinkled bald head that reminds me of another part of male anatomy. That thought makes me giggle.

There is no way my name won't get picked with the amount of slips I sprinkled with my name into the bowl…right? Now is the time for positive thoughts only.

Theo, if you're listening, help a girl out, please!

Tap. Tap. Tap.

Councilman Scar's nails drag along the bottom of the bowl while he swirls the remaining names around. "Vagrant's final nominee for the Reaper Crucible is…Victoria Bronx."

All the air is knocked from my lungs by two simple words. My vision blurs, and I start to sway on my feet. I think I actually might faint.

This can't be real life.

Chapter
Three

NOTHING HAPPENS. NO ONE MOVES. THAT'S WHEN I HEAR FAINT SOBS coming from the back of the crowd.

"Sh—sh—she isn't…she won't be able…" The woman breaks out into hysterical sobs, unable to finish her sentence.

The crowd is eerily silent; I can hear my own heartbeat thundering in my chest. It feels like I just ran for an hour straight as I struggle to keep up with my rapid breaths.

The woman goes to speak again but is cut off by Councilman Scar. "It seems like Miss Bronx has gotten herself into a little trouble with the Empress and is no longer with us. Pity." He says it so casually, like her life has no meaning. That's Vagrant Sector for you.

"In that case, I guess we will redraw for our second slot in the Crucible." He shrugs, looking bored out of his mind and wanting to get this over with.

A dull pain draws my attention to my hand, which has a death grip around the dagger necklace hanging from my neck, a habit I partake in absentmindedly when I'm nervous.

My nerves are shot, but deep down, I know this is meant to be. There has to be some kind of meaning behind Theo's death. I need some small meaning behind it to keep the heart in my chest beating while I'm stuck down here without him.

Theo would want a better life for me. He would want me to thrive and find purpose, have the chance to gain something invaluable for once in my life, something to give me the upper hand and a fighting chance at survival.

"Ah, let's try this again." Councilman Scar's monotone voice carries over the crowd. "The official final nominee from Vagrant Sector is…"

It's now or never, Theo.

"Ummm…Nyxi? Just Nyxi, I guess." He shrugs and mumbles to himself. "Works for me."

I'm frozen. My heart is at a standstill. Did I hear him correctly, or am I officially at the stage of delusion from stress? Surely, I'm not imagining this, right?

I frantically look around to see if anyone is making their way towards the front. No one is moving as they all mirror my own actions, looking around for 'Just Nyxi'.

Truth be told, I don't know my last name, growing up an orphan and all. The orphanage said they found me one morning, crying in a small woven basket with a piece of parchment tucked inside containing a single word.

Nyxi.

My "DNA donors", as I like to call them, didn't even have the decency to leave me with my lineage. They wanted zero chance of me being able to track them down one day. Parents of the year, lucky me.

I started going by Theo's last name, Adler, when I became old enough to understand I was different. My wound was too deep to keep explaining. It's one thing to grow up in an orphanage, but it skyrockets in severity when family-less kids can make you feel lesser.

It didn't feel right to put Theo's last name down for this, though. I have to do this one on my own, for him. It is my time to emerge into the woman I dreamed about as a child, the woman whose life had played out differently. It's time to show the world the woman who's been hiding in the shadows, waiting for her moment. For this moment.

My *awakening*.

I take in a shaky breath, attempting to calm myself before I slip past the few people standing in front of me. I already feel more at ease in the open air instead of being pancaked between sweaty, stinky Vagrants. Many Vagrants live on the streets without running water, and my nose is paying the price for it right now.

Clearing my throat, I stand eye level with our hunchbacked Councilman. Reaching out, I shake his boney hand. "Just Nyxi," I state in a firm but borderline bored voice. I cannot let anyone find weakness within my exterior for their own leverage, especially with all eyes on me.

Let the games begin.

Chapter
Four

I'M WELCOMING THE PAIN WITH OPEN ARMS TONIGHT, ALONGSIDE A
bottle of the cheapest and shittiest moonshine I could pawn from
Misery's Crossing. It's my last night in Fallout before I'm rushed
away to compete in a game to the death. Honestly, what the hell
was I thinking?

*You were thinking you need to weed through every member up in Lunaria
until you find the scumbag that let their Necroshriek loose on a killing spree.*

Ahh yes, revenge is a convincing bitch.

I spent the last two days hauling my ass all over Fallout, learning
details about each of my competitors—their daily routines, habits,
personality traits, weakness, and most importantly strengths. Anything to give myself the upper hand in this competition, the better,
putting my professional spy skills to the ultimate test.

Unlike my competitors, I did not grow up training my entire
life for this opportunity. They grew up mastering swords, daggers,
and bows, testing the limits of their endurance and intelligence.

I grew up blending into the shadows of the orphanage, avoiding beatings or worse—private "lessons" with our leader.

Now, I'm staring down at the one thing I have yet to conquer since Theo's death: our bed. I've been standing in the doorway of our room for the last 30 minutes while chugging moonshine straight from the mouth of the bottle.

My bare feet feel heavy and rooted to the floorboards just outside the barrier of the room. The traitorous things act as if the floor is lava and they are not brave enough to test the waters.

Sleeping in this damn bed tonight is a necessary evil, one I need to put my big girl panties on for and get over with.

I haven't had a good night's rest in far too long, and that is top priority in preparing for the Crucible. It's also the last night I will be spending in this little place I called home with him. This place and bed are my last memories of Theo.

After tonight, I will either be dead or win the Crucible and be welcomed into a world that has shunned me my entire life. I need this one night snuggled up in the place I use to find the most comfort in. My happy place, where I felt safe. One last night to be with him.

An owl hoots in the distance, and it's the final push I need. I've always felt a comforting pull to owls, seeing my abandoned past in their lonely residence, and this one gives me the strength I need right now.

Peeling one shaky foot off the ground, I take my first unsteady step into our room. Following suit, my other foot makes the leap and lands next to the first. I take in a deep breath, centering myself and my raging emotions, and continue walking the few feet left to the edge of our bed.

I take in every inch of our untouched bed. The blanket lays exactly how we last left it months ago, his pillow forever frozen in time with a slight indent where his head would rest.

Suddenly, I feel something wet land on my foot, and it's then I realize the steady stream of tears flowing from my eyes, cascading down my face to the floor.

Theo, you're turning me soft, you little devil.

A slightly hysterical giggle erupts from the back of my throat at the thought of Theo seeing me all emotional like this. He would for sure tease me and then tackle me into the bed with him, pulling me tight into his warm chest.

I miss him so damn much, it physically hurts.

I drag the backs of my hands over my eyes to wipe the tears away and cannonball jump into bed. It makes a creaking noise, and I swear, I see dust puff up around me. That's when it assaults me: *him.*

I *feel* him all around me. His gentle but sure touch. His infectious laugh. His smell of fresh air and sunshine. I'm engulfed in a cloud of him until it's too much to bear. It's all consuming, devouring me whole.

It's devastating and beautiful all at the same time because it's him. The man who took me in like a lost and injured stray. The man who protected me in the orphanage against bullies and threats. The first man—no, *person*—to ever love me unconditionally.

He was too good for this place. Now, I only pray that wherever he is, he's happy, and eventually proud of me. All that matters is him. It hits me then that I've never been surer about anything in my life than I am with entering myself in the Crucible. That brings me immeasurable peace.

I hope I can make you proud, my love.

Gulp. Gulp. Gulp.

I hiss at the burn festering in the back of my throat where the moonshine I'm guzzling leaves a trail of fire. I might need a little extra shove to help me fall asleep tonight, and this is just what the healer ordered.

My head feels like it's floating in Lunaria, and my thoughts have slowed to a tolerable speed. My muscles are relaxed, and for the first time in months, I feel content.

Dropping the bottle off the side of the bed, I flop onto my back and let it absorb me.

Ouch.

Something firm pokes me from under Theo's pillow I'm snuggled up on. Reaching under it, I feel a smooth, cool surface and drag it out from under the pillow.

It's a weathered, deep brown leather journal, with the letters T.A. carved into it. It's Theo's personal journal he always had his nose buried in but never let me look at. There's a small feather wedged in the center.

Sliding my fingers between the marked page, I open the journal and gasp. Scribbled at the top is *Reason 274 why I love Nyxi.* Below, he's written *Her unwavering strength after everything she's been through. She is my rock, and I cannot wait to make her Mrs. Adler for real one day.* He's drawn two wedding bands overlapping in the center next to it.

He wanted to marry me, make me his forever. Me, the person whose own family didn't even want her. He chose me, not because of blood, but because of *who* I am. This is the greatest gift Theo could possibly give me.

Even in death he takes care of me when I need him most. I didn't realize how badly I needed to hear that; somehow, it has healed a small corner of my heart I didn't think was fixable.

I skim through some of the pages, and sure enough, it's full of reasons why he loves me, or beautiful portraits of me, along with his favorite memories we've shared. This journal is us, stitched and bound together by leather. It's pieces of our story, creating a map of us.

I would have been honored to be Mrs. Adler.

My heart aches but feels full at the same time, like I've been stabbed straight in the heart but with a sword carved with love. A pain stokes my fire until it's raging flames. *Whatever it takes* is the only thought running through my head as the world fades to black and sucks me under.

Chapter
Five

BANG. BANG. BANG.

WHO IN THE EVER LOVING FALLOUT IS MESSING WITH MY BEAUTY sleep at this hour? My eyes are sealed shut with no plans on opening anytime soon. My brain is running at half speed as I float in the in-between of sleep and consciousness.

"Just Nyxi!" a loud and very angry male voice yells somewhere in the near distance. "I'm here to escort you up to Lunaria." His tone carries an edge.

Lunaria?

LUNARIA!

"Fuck!" I bolt out of bed as reality slaps me across the face. This man is here to take me for the start of The Reaper Crucible.

My head spins, and I'm not sure if it's from rushing out of bed or the obsessive amount of moonshine I used to numb myself last night.

"Just a second!" I shout towards the front door, where I can sense the mystery man is losing patience by the second.

He grumbles something under his breath about not getting paid enough for this shit. "You have five minutes before I knock this door down and forcefully remove you myself." His tone is final.

Someone woke up on the wrong side of the bed, *jeez*. This man could bring death to all things fun in Fallout with just the tone of his voice.

"No need to get your underthings all in a bunch, *Death Reaper*. I only need three," I spit back, an edge to my tone. An amused grunt travels through the door, like there's an inside joke I'm blind to, and then he yells at me to hurry up yet again.

It takes me no time at all to make myself presentable and gather the few belongings that have any meaning to me, including my new favorite, Theo's journal. Taking one last look around the house, I commit it to memory, then stride to the door.

"That's it, I'm coming in," he grumbles just as I turn the knob, opening the door. My face is immediately acquainted with his rock hard fist flying towards the door to knock. Instead, it assaults me straight in the nose, making a crunching noise as I'm launched backwards.

Lightning fast, he reaches out his other arm, catching me by my neck before I go toppling backwards on my ass.

"OUCH!" I glare up at him with a look I know can kill, as Theo told me many times. "Is that how you treat every woman who ignores you? You're mighty full of yourself."

Narrowing my eyes at him, I rub my throbbing nose. He better not have broken it, or I'll have to give him a matching one in return.

He stands there staring daggers into my soul, and I think I might faint from the intensity they hold. He may have knocked me senseless, because now, I'm the one hypnotized as I take in the beast in front of me.

He towers above me, casting a large shadow from his sheer size. He has to be at least a full foot taller than me, and I am positive this man was sculpted by the Empress herself, carved and sculpted to perfection.

Every square inch of him is packed with muscle and then more muscle on top of those. They're the kind of muscles you aren't born with but build over time with immense training and dedication.

His shaggy, wild obsidian hair reminds me of the darkest night sky. He looks like he just ran his hands through it out of frustration, but it still looks effortlessly edible. The tips of his hair curl in every direction in a chaotic but still presentable manner.

I drag my eyes down his body, where they snag on his piercing eyes, which are complete opposites. The one on the right is an identical twin to his midnight black hair, as if every color swirled together inside to create a twinkling, iridescent black. It's all contained inside a halo-like, glowing silver ring.

Trailing over to his left, I'm taken back. He sports a jagged white scar running from his hairline across his eye to the side of his nose. It reminds me of a lightning bolt cascading through the night sky.

That's not what catches my attention, though. It's the contrast of this eye compared to his other. It's as if they represent day and night, light and dark, right and wrong. It's almost like this one was black at one point, but all the color has been sucked out, leaving a speckled light gray in its place. Somehow, it looks even more deadly than his black one, which shakes me to my core.

There is nothing pretty or soft about this man's face. It's all sharp, carved edges and screams *man*, with dark stubble that peppers his jawbone. His fair skin is tanned from the sun, warming his sculpted features. He's somehow devastatingly beautiful in a rugged way.

His brown leather pants hug every inch of his tree trunk legs, paired with a simple white cotton shirt strangling the life out of his swollen biceps.

My eyes bulge out when I take in the chaotic tattoos covering his entire left arm—abstract shapes, swirls, and landscapes, all blending together in unison to create a sleeve. The same arm still has a death grip firmly around the entirety of my dainty neck.

Blinking out of my trance, I cast narrowed eyes aimed right at him. "Are you going to let go of my neck, or do you choke out every woman who defies you? No shame here—I know some people are into that sort of thing—but there's a time and a place, and *now* is definitely not it." I add a hint of annoyance to my tone to get my point across.

He glances down at his hand, just now realizing he has a death grip on me, and releases quickly, like his skin burns where we connected.

"Where is your stuff?" His deathly low growl sets my temper ablaze.

"One, are we just going to skip over the fact that you just punched me in the face and possibly broke my nose?" Taking a step closer to him, I shove my finger into his chest, making me wince as my finger bends against his unyielding brick wall of muscle. "And two, everything of value to me fits in this bag." I point at the bag previously strapped over my shoulder, now thrown across the room.

"Is your nose broken?" he deadpans.

"Well, how should I know? I'm no healer." I fold my arms across my chest, jutting my chin up for dramatic effect.

"You look fine to me. Now, let's go. We're late as it is since you wanted to sleep in." He turns and starts to walk away without another glance.

"What?" I stutter. "Are you a certified healer or something?"

"Or something," he shoots over his shoulder as he continues to walk away from me.

"Are you even old enough to come to that conclusion?" I say, more to myself than him, but of course, he has super hearing, because why wouldn't he?

"I'm twenty-one. Now, keep up."

Men—they really have the audacity, I swear.

I've never met someone who could get under my skin as easily as this man has in less than five minutes. My exterior is normally an impenetrable force of nature, resulting in people running when they see me. Theo called it my superpower. For some reason I can't place my finger on, this man makes my insides crawl with fire. The flame inside me that's long since extinguished sparks to life again in an instant. He makes my skin itch like my whole body is ablaze, and I don't like it one bit. Two can play at this game, though, and I fight fire with fire.

"Are you at least going to apologize for ruining my pretty face with your fist?" I pretend to throw daggers with my eyes at the back of his unknowing head.

"Sorry," he says bluntly.

"Do you mean it?"

"No. Now keep up," he grunts.

"You really are a real charmer, you know that?" I spit the words like venom, hoping they strike true.

"Not interested."

My eyes widen in shock. "Ha. As if I would ever touch you, even if we were the last two citizens left to repopulate the lands, you…you brute!"

"Likewise. Is that seriously as fast as those tiny things you call legs can go?" he grumbles to himself in annoyance.

"Sorry, not all of us are blessed with legs the size of mountains and feet the size of small livestock." I roll my eyes at him and clench my fists to keep from hitting him across the back of the head, which I'm honestly not so opposed to at the moment.

"Blessed, huh?" His voice raises an octave in question. I almost pick up on a hint of a smirk, but it's gone just as fast.

"Pig!" I scoff.

"Better than Death Reaper," he mumbles under his breath.

"Death Reaper it is then, sir." I add extra umph to the word sir, dragging it out longer than necessary.

"Don't call me sir." His voice turns deathly serious.

"What shall I call you then?" Thinking to myself, I excitedly raise my hand. "Ooo, I know. His royal pain in my ass? No, even better: the bane of my existence?" I'm shocked at my outburst, my temper getting the best of me, which rarely happens. I just can't help it around him, though, and this annoying shit knows exactly his effect on me and is wielding it like a bloody weapon.

"My name is only for people of importance, which you are not." Giving me no time to respond, he adds, "Why don't you have a last name?"

"My last name is only for people of *importance*, and I'm afraid you just missed the cut." I throw his exact words back at him as punishment, adding my signature glare.

He growls under his breath, sounding more animal than human. "Hade," he states.

"What?"

"My name. Now, why don't you have a last name?" he pushes again.

"Why do you care so much?" I scoff.

"I don't." He throws back defensively. It's then I realize I may be equally getting under his skin, which I don't think he's particularly used to.

I raise my eyebrows in mocking. "Then why ask at all?"

"Just answer the damn question, Nyxi! How does one have no last name?"

I can feel his temper growing short, like a fuse ready to blow. Hearing my name roll off his tongue in a sharp tone makes my skin break out in full body hives. I'm playing with fire here, but for some reason, I can't seem to stop myself from poking.

"Seems a lot like you do care." I pair the statement with my fakest smile for good measure.

"NYXI!" My name smokes out of his mouth like a dragon breathing fire.

"Yes?" I ask innocently, batting my eyelashes at him.

"I have zero patience for games. You can learn that lesson the easy way or the hard way. The choice is yours. Now, tell me," he seethes.

"Admit you care, and I will." I'm testing his limits right now, and I can feel the end nearing.

"Hard way it is." He turns around so fast, I crash into the brick wall that is his body. He grabs me with ease, throwing me over his shoulder like I'm a sack of potatoes, and continues walking.

"Put me down!" I scream, slamming my fists on his back. Holy Empress, this man is a solid wall that physically hurts as I continually assault him.

"I told you, I have zero patience for games. Now, you have to live with your choices. Plus, you're slower than watching paint dry." He sounds like a rabid animal trying to remain in control.

Shit, maybe I took it too far this time.

"PUT. ME. DOWN. I'll scream louder if you don't," I threaten.

"Don't care."

"You're insufferable," I huff against his back.

"And you are an annoying fly that won't leave me alone," he throws back.

"Uggghh! Fine. If you let me down, I'll tell you," I plead in defeat.

"Too late. You had your chance."

"Please?" It comes out as a whisper. Being this close to another man who isn't Theo is overwhelming my senses, and I think I'm starting to hyperventilate.

As if picking up on my sudden change of emotions, he gently sets me back on my feet, in harsh contrast to his brute personality. He stands there with his arms crossed, staring at me with raised eyebrows for an answer.

"I don't know what my last name is," I say honestly.

"Lies."

Glaring, I take a step closer to him. "I swear on the Empress' life."

"Explain."

"Do you know how to respond with more than a single word, or are you illiterate?"

"Yes."

"Yes, you're illiterate?" I snap back.

"No," he grumbles.

"You could have fooled me," I sing.

"Do you want a date with my shoulder again?"

This man is insufferable, so I glare back at him. "Aren't you supposed to buy me flowers before a date?"

"You are my own personal *nightmare*, woman. This is the last time I will ask before I wrap something around that feisty mouth of yours so you can't talk at all." He sounds more on edge somehow, if that's even possible.

Nyxi, what the heck did you get yourself into?

It's so easy to push all his buttons, but I would rather not be acquainted with his shoulder again so soon.

"I don't know who my parents are, hence my lack of last name. Are you happy now?" I raise both arms out with dramatic flair.

"No," he grunts.

"I'm gonna go out on a limb here and gamble you've never been happy a day in your life, Death Reaper." Judgment seeps from my pores, and I can tell I've hit a nerve there.

He ignores my comment. "Who raised you then?"

"Now *that*, we are not diving into. Strictly off limits." I tense at the mere thought of the orphanage.

He must sense my change in mood, because he doesn't continue to push the subject, and for once I'm thankful. We walk in mutual silence the rest of our journey.

Chapter
Six

A GIANT LAKE MARKS THE CENTER OF FALLOUT, OPENING WIDE IN front of us. Each sector wraps around it in a circle, encasing it.

This used to be our favorite spot to sneak to on late summer nights. The calm blue water stretches as far as I can see, wild grass surrounding it. It's so smooth, it looks like you could walk right across it. It smells fresh and earthy and instantly calms my raging emotions.

This place has a way of making everything else disappear and lets you live in the moment. We didn't have to carry labels around here like orphan, spy, or Vagrant. We were just Theo and Nyxi, one soul shared between two vessels. Just *us*.

The ache in my heart draws to the surface again, and it takes everything in me to shove it far down into the depths to deal with later. Right now is not the time to display any signs of weakness.

There's a small, wooden dock jutting out towards the center of the lake, where the rest of the contestants are gathered. I take in each sector's nominees spread out as far as the small docks allows, glaring at each other with threatening looks. Seems the games have started before the Crucible has even begun.

This is the first time my competitors are getting a glance at their competition. Me, on the other hand, I've already done my due diligence. I've learned each of their personalities and strengths I can use to leverage my game. I know who might make sound alliances and who I should definitely stay away from.

As if on cue, I spot Tank Finnegan from Sweat Sector talking with Jade Huxley from my sector. I knew they would become quick allies. Both lack empathy and tend to choose violence as the only answer to any situation. They are definitely on my 'no chance in hell as allies' list.

Tank towers over Jade's small frame, a sinister smile slapped across his face. He is easily the biggest man here in terms of pure size, his giant, tanned arms on full display. I have to crane my neck to take him in entirely, and he's even bigger than I thought while standing this close, light blue eyes shining with mischief. He has to be at least seven feet tall, standing almost a full two feet above me. His hair is bleached by the sun, making it so blond, it almost appears white. I feel sorry for his mother, who had to push out that monstrosity.

Ouch!

Scanning the crowd, my eyes snag on Cartwell Hart from Enlightened Sector standing alone at the very edge of the dock. This is exactly where I would expect him to be. From what I've gathered, he is very much an outcast and sticks to himself and his thoughts.

What he lacks in size and muscle, he makes up for with his brains. The man is a certified genius. While others may underestimate him, I know he will be a fierce competitor.

"Don't embarrass me," Hade whispers under his breath, which draws me back to reality.

This man really has the fucking audacity.

"I was just about to tell you the exact same thing." I whisper back snidely. "Unlike you, I have to make a good first impression around my competitors for the sake of my game. So, don't *fuck* with me," I growl.

"So she does have brains. Hmmm; could have fooled me." He says it mockingly, and I can't help the way it rubs uncomfortably against my skin.

"I'm not religious, but you bet your ass I will be praying to the Empress tonight that I never have to see your insufferable face again." I shove a shoulder into him, and of course, he doesn't move an inch.

"Hate to break it to you, *Nightmare*, but unfortunately, you are stuck with me for the time being. And trust me, I would rather be shackled to anyone in existence *but* you," he states. "So, you better rein in that nasty temper of yours and behave. I don't give second chances, and unfortunately, you've already used up all of yours in record time." His temper flares back to life.

Who the hell does this man think he is? A self-proclaimed god, if I had to guess.

I'm about to make a snarky retort when his words replay in my head. "Wait, what did you just say?"

"I threatened you to behave. Does that word exist in your vocabulary, or do I need to spell it out for you?"

"First off, kindly go eat a bag of oranges. Second, I meant before you let your brute-ish tendencies take over and threatened me to behave. What did you say?" I pray to the Empress I heard him wrong.

"That you're stuck with me," he says bluntly.

"No," I reply in a clipped, final tone. "Not happening. Why do I even need to be shackled to anyone?"

"Trust me, I'm not happy about it either. Each contestant is paired with their own personal Vanquisher during the entirety of the Crucible," he states. "They are responsible for escorting you around and keeping tabs on your whereabouts at all times."

"I don't need a babysitter," I seethe.

"I beg to differ, but this isn't about you. In past games, contestants have tried to escape to live in Lunaria off the grid. The Empress was not pleased," he says plainly. "Trust me, I have way more important things to be doing with my time than being your glorified babysitter." He pins me with his hard gaze, but I don't back down.

"More important things like what?" I hold up one finger. "Stroking your giant ego?" A second one. "Putting your nose into people's personal business?" A third. "Oh, or maybe handing out nose jobs to women who don't bow to your every waking demand?" Now, I'm the one glaring.

"Do *not* push my buttons right now. I will not tell you again." He steps closer, his chest against mine while glaring down at me. "You *will* obey me, or I will lock you in your room like a prisoner for the entirety of the Crucible. At this rate, I don't believe it will be very long with that obnoxious mouth of yours. Got it?" He waits for my compliance with raised eyebrows.

"Crystal clear, Death Reaper. Killing the mood, as usual. I really nailed your nickname on the head." Taking a calming breath, I look up at him with pleading eyes. "Can I at least choose who my guard will be? Maybe someone with less of a temper and easier on the eyes?"

I know damn well this man is *extremely* easy on the eyes, and it infuriates me to my core. I'd sooner die than admit that to him, though. I will, however, take any jab I can to knock his giant ego down a peg or two...or eight.

"Lucky for you, I am only your *temporary* guard. As I said earlier, I have more important things to do with my time than babysit a child."

"Me, a child? Says the one who literally punched me in the face and didn't have the balls to apologize. Are you lacking in that department? I know a good healer who could help you out," I taunt.

A fed up grunt is his only response.

"If you aren't my guard, why come here at all?" I ask honestly.

"Your prick of a guard partied a little too hard last night and failed to show up to his post this morning. Seeing as I am the Empress' personal guard and right hand, I took it as my duty to get the job done by any means necessary." He sounds annoyed.

"Personal guard..." I repeat, trying to make sense of them. If he *is* Empress Seraphine's right hand, that means... No, it can't be.

Shit.

My eyes turn to saucers as I gaze up with understanding, and I wish I could wipe away the smug smile spreading across his face at my realization.

"You're the Cardinal," I state rather than question. Everything suddenly makes so much sense—his bluntness, his hard exterior, his all together 'I don't give a damn' attitude towards everything and anyone.

This man sports a god complex, but for good reason. Tales of the ruthless Cardinal spread all the way to Fallout, the great warrior who could shatter a man's mind with a single look. His full depth of powers are unknown, but it is rumored he can control anything to do with death. It makes sense he's tasked as the Empress' personal protector.

"You've heard of me?" he asks smugly.

"I'm not gonna answer that and feed into your overflowing ego," I say plainly. Now I know why he laughed when I called him Death Reaper. "So, when do I get my original guard back? And are we going to stand here all day, or do I finally get to see what all the fuss is about with this giant floating rock they call Lunaria?" I counter.

His face turns serious at my mention of returning to my previous guard. "You will have me until I find someone capable of taking my spot." There is no arguing with his tone.

Every time I feel like I'm starting to understand this man, he makes my head spin. I don't want to piss him off after learning who he is, so I keep my mouth shut for now.

One of the other Vanquishers clears his throat in an attempt to gain everyone's attention. "The Empress has a message for you all," he states, masking his face in neutrality.

He raises his palms face up in front of his chest, facing the sky. Closing his eyes, he concentrates while flexing his hands in a claw-like shape. What forms in front of my eyes is one of the most breathtaking things I've ever seen: a baby blue orb of light exploding from his palms, casting a globe floating in the air. Staring straight at us, in perfect detail, is our Empress.

Illuminist.

Illuminists can replicate anything they've seen by creating light illusions out of thin air. They can create stagnant or moving shapes from their imagination or replay events that have unfolded in front of them, including sounds. This illuminist must have listened to the Empress earlier and is now relaying it for us in exact detail.

"It is with great honor that you have been chosen to represent your sector in this year's Reaper Crucible. You should all know the great sacrifice you are making with your life by entering yourself in this fight to the death. But with great risk comes great reward. In my opinion, there is no greater reward than the possession of magic."

The Empress carries an unmatched elegance. She is poised in every meaning of the word, commanding attention like a true deity. She is the epitome of regality, and her words pack a mighty punch.

"This game will not only test your strength, but your wits. Every moment of your life leading up to this will either make or break your gameplay. Keep your guard up, alliances strong, and play with your head, not your heart. Make no mistake—every person here is not friend, but foe. The greatest advice I shall give you is this: keep your cards close to your chest, but your enemies even closer."

And just like that, the illusion is gone as fast as it appeared.

The Vanquisher drops his hands back by his sides. "You will travel in pairs with one Migrant to assist your travel to Lunaria. There are only a couple Migrants here as guards, so it will take them a few trips to get you all there. You may now pair up." He joins the other Vanquisher guards as my competitors pair off anxiously.

I make to walk away, but Hade abruptly grabs my wrist, halting my advance.

"Where do you think you're going?" he says with brute force.

I stare up at the wall of a man, both in confusion and caution. Does he expect me to walk with him? Maybe he wasn't done drilling me with an unnecessary amount of personal questions? Or maybe, he just wants to keep fucking with me? Either way, I do not want to stay and find out.

Putting up my armor, I mask my face in pure, unyielding steel and pray to the Empress it's believable. "I was going to find a competitor to pair off with—then this pain in the ass of a man stopped me."

I narrow my eyes in an attempt to look fierce, even though my pulse is raging and ready to burst. Hopefully, he can't feel its growing ascent under his deathly grip on my wrist.

"I can take you," he says matter of fact, which is the last thing in Fallout I want to do right now. I'd rather not stay and learn whatever strange magic this brute possesses to transport us to Lunaria.

No fucking thank you.

"I think I'll take my chances over there…with someone else." I hike a thumb over my shoulder, and my voice raises in weariness at his overbearing presence.

"I actually was just about to pair off with…" I hesitate, trying to think of the name of one of my competitors. Before I get a chance to finish my sentence, a seductive male voice brushes past my ear.

"Me," the male purrs, finishing my sentence for me, and I've never been more grateful.

I slowly turn my head, locking eyes with an equally intense pair already familiar to me. I'm taken back to the standoff I had with this man during Command Sector's ceremony.

Aeron Gavis blinds me with his perfectly white teeth and his signature wolfish grin. Most women would faint at the sight, but I see past his charm for what it truly is: a weapon.

Aeron Gavis is in my gray zone. I'm not sure whether I should keep distance between us or play into his flirtatious behavior. Both directions are a gamble, but for now, my best bet at survival is to play the naive girl falling into his flirtatious trap.

My biggest weapon to yield in this competition is being underestimated, and if I have to play a lovesick puppy, then so be it. I just hope it doesn't come back to bite me in the ass.

Forgive me, Theo.

Regaining my composure, I straighten my spine and yank my wrist from its detainer. "Exactly. I was just about to go find Aeron." My tone turns harsh as I glare at Hade.

Aeron's smile somehow grows, taking up more real estate on his face, which I didn't think was possible. I may be trading one devil in disguise for another, but I'll take my chances with the one who isn't known to shatter people's minds with just one look.

Hade doesn't move a centimeter. I think I start to see steam pour from his ears. I'm just thankful that look isn't directed at me for once.

"I'm sure you have more important things to do with your time than babysit us, hmm?" Aeron holds his ground, showing no signs of intimidation as he recites Hade's words from earlier.

Shit.

The sly fox must have been listening to our conversation earlier. I need to start being more careful and observant from here on out, but that all goes out the window when Hade's personality is choking the life out of me.

Both men stare each other down for what feels like a lifetime before Hade grunts and walks off without another word.

"Well, that went well." I release a harsh breath. The tension from the walk slowly starts to subside the more distance I put between me and that hellion.

"Swell, I would say." Aeron smirks, walking around my body to face me. "Aeron Gavis," he states, grabbing my hand and brushing a feather light kiss on the top. "But it looks like you already knew that, didn't you, little mink?"

This man oozes cockiness from every pore. I would bet all my coins he's never been rejected a day in his life. He's the epitome of sex appeal, and unfortunately for him, that's the fastest way for me to lose interest.

Today is not that day, however. Today, I must play the part of the innocent damsel in distress in need of saving from the big, bad wolf.

I force a blush to my cheeks while shyly tucking a loose curl behind my ear. His eyes follow every movement, like a predator tracking its prey.

You can do this, Nyxi. Play the part.

"Oh, well, I overheard you introducing yourself to another contestant," I say innocently, a submissive tone to my voice.

"Really?" he drawls. Stepping forward, he drags his calloused palm down the side of my face to cup my chin, tilting it up. "Funny, because I could have sworn I've seen you before today. I could never forget these beautifully unique eyes forged from steel." He pauses while staring intensely into them. "Beautiful," he whispers.

I smile up at him, ever the doe eyed girl I'm trying to portray. This man thinks with his dick before his head, and I'm going use it to my advantage.

His look takes on an edge as he pinches my chin with a little more force. "Ahh yes. Maybe I'm recalling seeing you sneaking into Command Secor for the drawing ceremony. You are a troublemaker indeed." His grin turns devilish as he sets his trap for me to fall into.

This man knows exactly what he's doing, and he's smarter than he lets on. I need to play these next moves very carefully.

"Y-yes," I stutter. "I was there getting some fresh produce. Food in Vagrant just doesn't compare to other sectors. I honestly didn't think you would remember me," I say innocently while fluttering my eyelashes, praying he buys it.

"It's kind of hard to miss a woman such as yourself. You stick out like a diamond in the rough, with your long curls that remind me of the galaxies I fall asleep under every night. Don't get me started on those foggy doe eyes of yours. *Perfection*. And this porcelain skin I could run my hands over all night... I've never come across someone who even comes close to comparing to you." He leaves no room for argument or question. "What's a pretty thing like you doing in Vagrant Sector?"

He leans in closer so our noses are practically touching. I can feel his even breaths brushing against my lips. His words slam into me like water breaking through a dam, and I'm stunned into a frozen statue.

If he's trying to weasel into my head to make me drop my guard, he's going to have to try a lot harder. He doesn't need to know I'm onto him, though, so I play the part and ignore his question.

"I'm sure you have an ocean of women at your feet daily. I don't think highly enough of myself to snag your attention among the masses of beautiful women living in Command Sector." I tug one side of my lip up in a half smirk.

He drops my chin and flicks his towards our competitors, signaling me to walk with him. "You can drop the innocent girl act. It doesn't flatter you. I know a mink when I see one, and I prefer my women to be self-assured." His voice takes on a level of cockiness I loathe.

"Who says I want to appeal to you at all?" I retort with a slight edge, accidently fading back to my true colors.

"There she is," he states, taking my hand like it's a natural instinct to him.

What is it with these men and thinking they can own my body?

"If you're used to women falling to their knees for you, you're in for a rude awakening," I retort.

"Quite the opposite, actually. I prefer a good challenge, and I always get what I want." His confidence is unnerving, and I want to claw the stupid grin off his face.

"Let the games begin then. Oh, and make no mistake, Aeron: I always win." I drop his hand and walk over to the remaining Migrant waiting for us.

He grabs each of our hands, creating a connection between the three of us. In a blink, the world around me transforms from open lake air to a stuffy smelling vintage dark corridor. I blink a few times, trying to make sense of my new reality.

The corridor is lined with black metal sconces holding floating blue orbs that barely light the space around me. Black damask and charcoal wallpaper lines the walls, giving it an eerie feeling. The narrow corridor feels bigger due to its ribbed, vaulted ceiling, giant, stained glass windows lining the entire right side. For Lunaria to be described as bright and magical, this place is the complete opposite.

"This is where you will sleep and spend all your time unless you are training, eating, or summoned by the Empress. These two are your rooms. Rest up before the commencement dinner tonight. Your handmaids, who will assist you throughout the Crucible, will be here shortly." The Vanquisher poofs into nothing, leaving me and Aeron standing alone in the dark corridor.

I take a step towards my door and slam into the wall. No, not wall—man. Specifically, the man I've been trying to avoid.

"Nyxi." Hade's deep voice drags down my skin, begging for my attention.

Nope, not happening. I will not be trapped in this small hallway with the two men I despise.

"Wait!" they say in unison, then glare at each other as I turn my door handle and slip inside.

I feign a dramatic yawn and toss over my shoulder, "Sorry, so tired from today." Then, I slam the door in their faces and collapse onto the bed, drifting off to sleep immediately.

Chapter
Seven

A CHEERFUL, HIGH-PITCHED WHISTLING SLOWLY DRAWS ME BACK TO reality from the deepest slumber I've had since Theo passed away.

"Ahh, perfect. You're finally awake," a bubbly girl, maybe a couple years younger than me, sing-songs as I blink her into focus. Sitting up in bed, I take her and my surrounding room in. I hadn't spared a glance at when I first entered,

The room is a perfect twin to the corridor outside my door—wrapped in matte black floral wallpaper and adorned with a single glowing sconce by the door. A gothic black metal chandelier hangs in the center of the room, drooping black melanite crystals hanging from its branches.

I'm currently sprawled out in a king-sized, black wooden four-poster bed with matching black sheets and throw blanket. Obsidian velvet strips drape across the top, connecting each corner before cascading to the floor down each post, gathered together by black silky ribbon.

Light streams in through the single stained glass window depicting a flying Necroshriek, green curvy hills in the background.

The room's only other decor is a black vanity pushed against the wall, a vintage oval mirror hanging above it. It's accompanied by a black velvet throne-like chair with black angel wings jutting off each side. Continuing the theme, a simple black wooden armoire, that I'm sure houses the few pieces of clothing I bought, is wedged in the other corner. Next to the vanity stands a black and white floral folding screen to change behind. Not sure why anyone would change behind that when I have my own personal washroom, but like everything I've seen so far, this place is a little over the top.

"Have you even been listening to anything I've been saying, girl?" The woman from earlier somehow has crossed the room, now shaking me by my shoulders.

"Huh?" I reply with a bewildered look.

"Ugh, you're killing me," she groans. "It's a good thing I like talking so much and you weren't paired with Hanz as a handmaid. That old hag is the queen of grouchville. No, thank youuu." She drags out the last word with dramatic flair.

"Any whoosies, like I was saying before you so rudely ignored me..." Words pour out of her mouth in a single breath. "I'm Odessa, but everyone calls me Des. I'm basically a fashion prodigy and, like, the coolest ever, but that's beside the point." She laughs to herself.

"Basically, my job is to make you the hottest bitch out there so you can score some bonus points with the crowd to help your game. You want everyone to either want to be you or be envious of you." I can see the wheels turning in her head and internally cringe. "So I guess I can call you my blank canvas. Ahh, this year is going to be so much better than last year, since I was paired with a guy. Snooze fest, am I right?" She fake-yawns for dramatics.

"Hello, Earth to Nyxi! Don't tell me I need to repeat myself." She huffs, and I think it's the first breath she's taken.

"Do you always talk this much?" I question her with vivid concern etched on my face.

"It's my specialty." She grins back at me with the warmest smile. "So, do I need to repeat myself for a third time?" She scrunches her face in an attempt to be serious, but it just comes off looking like a pouting child.

"Hanz is an old hag. Des for short. Hottest bitch. Make everyone jealous. Snooze fest, and you never shut up. Does that cover everything?" I teasingly smile back at her, and I find it odd how easy it is to do around her.

Snapping her fingers at me, she states, "I knew I was going to like you!" She turns to walk towards the vanity and starts giggling to herself again.

Theo, what have I gotten myself into?

I use this moment to take in Des in all her glory. She is one of the most stunning and naturally beautiful women I have ever laid my eyes on. Is this what everyone in Lunaria looks like? They definitely don't make them like her in Vagrant Sector.

Her skin is a rich, glowing mocha, warm freckles painting her face, neck, and arms. Her hair falls in silky, light gray curls all the way down to her butt. Pink and yellow monarch butterflies are clipped throughout her hair, pairing perfectly with her bubbly personality. She has a cute button nose covered with blush, making it look rosy. Her eyes remind me of bright fern leaves, and her pink lips are full and puffy.

Her small frame sits at least a few inches shorter than me, covered in a white cotton dress with puffy short sleeves. The round neckline swoops low. Layered on top of her dress is a green and brown floral corset that tightly laces up the back, giving her an hourglass frame. She's paired her outfit with black lace up platform boots.

Stumbling over to the vanity, I plop down in the oversized chair fit for a queen. "So, where do we start? I need all the help I can get in the fashion department. I go more for practicality over style. I only brought a few things with me, but I'm sure we can muster up something presentable...right?" I look over at her anxiously, and for some reason, I want to make a good first impression. Normally I couldn't give two shits about what I look like or how people perceive me.

Des smiles back at me, and it's the first genuine emotion I've felt since Theo's passing. I've known Des for only five minutes, and I can already tell she has a heart of gold.

"Let's take a peek at what we're working with." She winks at me, all the anxious nerves inside me draining away to nothing.

She flings open both doors to the armoire and gasps, dramatically throwing the back of her hand over her forehead. "What in all Lunaria is this, Nyxi?" She turns around to face me with raised eyebrows.

"So we may be a little more limited with options than I initially let on...but you did call yourself a fashion prodigy, did you not?" I make an innocent face and pray this girl lives up to her bold accusations.

"Limited... Girl, there are four things in here, and half of them have holes. Not to mention, you don't have a single dress. This all has to go. It's decided: we are starting fresh and holding a sacrificial ritual to purge these monstrosities." She goes to snatch my clothes up, but I whip my arm out, halting her in her tracks.

"Wait, you can't take that... It's my boyfriend's." My voice cracks, and the darkness starts to dig its nails into my battered heart again.

"Boyfriend!" Des wiggles her eyebrows in a playful manner. "Please tell me he's an absolute hunk. I mean, who am I kidding—this jacket is massive, so of course he is. Do you have to climb him like a tree? Is his branch big? Just tell me when to stop." She starts slowly moving her hands out in a measuring motion. "Tell me when to stop because this is starting to get into 'needing to see a healer after' territory."

A single tear slides down my face, and I'm shocked at my raw emotions taking hold of me in front of this stranger. Des doesn't feel like a stranger, though; she feels like Theo. She feels like home.

"Shit, what did I say? Was it the tree climbing part? Hanz always tells me I'm too forward, but who has time to live a boring life, right?" She grips my hands and wipes the single tear I shed off my face in a motherly gesture.

"Do you want to talk about it?" It's a simple sentence, but it holds so much power. I know in my heart she truly means it. Theo is the only person who has ever cared for me in that way, and I never thought anyone else would fill that void.

I let out a long sigh through a wobbly smile and squeeze her hands back. "Theo, he *was* my boyfriend. He, uh—he passed away recently. He was my only family, and now, all I have left of him are these scraps of cloth." I release a massive breath from the depths of my soul.

It feels like a heavy weight has been lifted off my shoulders at this admission. Sharing this burden with someone makes it a little more bearable.

Trust is not something I give lightly or easily, and for some reason, I have this deep rooted feeling that I can trust Des. I think she might even be my very first friend.

"I am so, so sorry, Nyxi." Her voice is filled with raw emotion, speaking from similar pain, as if she has an intimate relationship with loss and heartache.

"I know what it is like to lose someone who made you, *you*. There is no getting over it, just through it, one day, one smile, and one regained laugh at a time. That is all we can hope for—a better tomorrow."

She speaks with such wisdom, like she's lived a thousand life times, and maybe, mentally, she has. I know right in this second, Des and I are cut from the same coin.

"Thank you, Des, truly. That means more than you will ever know." I smile at her, and I think it's the first true smile I've openly given in a very long time.

"Okay, now that the waterworks show is over...do you think you will be able to help me find something presentable to wear to dinner tonight? I know it might sound silly, but I think I would like to feel beautiful. Maybe wear a dress? If that's possible... I don't want to be too much trouble." I fidget with my hands, and my palms start to sweat.

A childish squeal assaults my ears. "Oh my Empress, we are totally breaking out the rainy day closet. This is just perfect!"

"Umm, what exactly is a rainy day closet?" I ask, hoping I haven't gotten myself in too deep.

Her immediate response is a smile that could rival the devil's in mischief. "First, let's work on your face and hair, and then, we will get to your wardrobe."

"Problem: I have no makeup, and I'm not sure there's any luck of turning this bird's nest I call hair into anything suitable for an Empress." I lay the news on thick.

"Hush, child. Let the professional work her magic. I was made for this." She smiles at me while lifting her hands. Little white glowing orbs dance off her fingertips.

What the heck?

"Have you ever heard of a Luster?" She prods me while simultaneously moving her hands in front of my face like she's conducting a symphony.

"No. Should I know what that means?" I ask wearily.

"I'm gonna pretend you didn't just say that to keep my fragile ego intact. But, any whoosies, Lusters can enhance someone's natural beauty, basically making them glow brighter," she states with sheer certainty.

"A swipe of my hand here, and suddenly, your eyes are lined a little darker, making the gray pop brighter than any star could." She slides her hand lower. "A dip of my hand here, and your lips soften to a brighter pink, making your porcelain skin brighter against them. A flick of my wrist here, and your lashes darken and curl. I like to call myself an artist." She's beaming at me, and I can feel the pure joy and passion radiating off her.

"I can tell you love what you do, Des."

"It helps keep my demons at bay...so yes, it is my everything."

"Well, I might just be your hardest canvas yet. Give me your best, Des." I wink, giving her carte blanche to do as she pleases.

She licks her lips and claps. "I love a good challenge."

Her hands take on a life of their own, moving so fast, I find it hard to keep up with them. Her face contorts as she focuses on turning me into a masterpiece. The air around us feels charged and begins to warm with the presence of magic.

She finishes up with my face and moves to my hair that falls in long curls down my back. "I have just the perfect idea for your hair. We will keep it simple tonight to start, since this is just the welcome dinner. We don't want to set the bar too high this early in the Crucible." She puts both hands on her hips with a smug smile, like she never doubted herself in the slightest.

"Stay put. I'll be right back. Don't touch a thing, or I will filet you like a guppy." Even her threats come off childish; I'm certain Des couldn't hurt a fly even if she tried.

Empress help me.

"HOLY EMPRESS…" I WHISPER AS I TAKE IN THE WOMAN STARING AT me in the mirror.

"More like a hot piece of meat," Des coos over my shoulder as she admires her handiwork.

I've never felt so…so…beautiful in my entire existence. Des truly earned Luster title as I take in my reflection.

She's left my hair in long, obsidian curls, but she opted to French braid the top half down the center of my part before tying it in a knot so the curls continue down my back.

To bring it all together, she's speared it with a silver miniature dagger to hold the knot in place. The handle depicts silver vines with flowers growing around it, adding a touch of beauty paired with the symbol of death. A symbol to represent myself.

My pale skin sparkles like I'm being lit up in harsh sunlight. She's smoked out my eyelids in a gradient of charcoal and gray, painted my lashes in a black glitter, and added tiny gemstones on them, turning them into a starry night sky. She's added shine to my high cheekbones, and they catch the light in a blinding manner. To finish the look, she's painted my round lips a deep plum.

What emboldens me the most, though, is the simple, classic dress she's picked out for me. It fits me like a glove, as if she's been holding onto it for this exact moment.

What transpires before my eyes can only be compared to the saying opposites attract. My pale, glimmering skin takes on a godly glow against the midnight satin dress. The simple thin crystal straps hold up the low, swooping neckline, showing off my small cleavage. The satin hugs my middle and sucks in around my round hips. One side is ruched, supporting a high cut slit that exposes most of my thigh and leg. The hem is adorned with teardrop crystals that dance as I move. It's paired with clear glass, open-toed slippers.

"You, my friend, are a one of a kind masterpiece." Des beams at me, unwavering admiration in her eyes.

"Thank you, for everything. This is the greatest gift you could ever give me. I feel beautiful for once in my life. I will cherish this for the rest of my days." It's then I notice the twin smile to Des' shining on my own face. "I would like to add one more thing to my outfit, if that's okay." I ask nervously.

"Of course. This is all for you, my friend."

I reach into my small bag of belongings and pull out my weathered dagger necklace, holding it up for Des to take as I turn around and lift my hair for her.

She claps it around my neck, the dagger nuzzling the center of my exposed cleavage. I take a deep breath in and use the necklace as a place of comfort to hold all my nerves.

Knock. Knock. Knock.

I smile at Des. "Let the games begin."

Chapter
Eight

Swinging my door open, I'm greeted by a tall figure I think is deathly allergic to smiling. "Death Reaper," I spew in greeting. "Whatever have I done to be graced with your positively joyous presence?" My tone straddles on the line between mocking and disinterest.

He ignores my snarky comment and gestures his arm out for me to join him. I stride past him, and I'm about to drop another attitude-filled remark just to get under his skin when my arm is abruptly swept up into the crook of someone else's, wedged against their body.

Turning my head, I'm greeted by an icy blue gaze and wolfish grin. I'm tugged along down the hallway, and behind me I can hear what could only be described as an animalistic growl from Hade.

Sheesh, someone needs to let off some steam.

I make a mental note to bring up his growling problem the next time he gets under my skin. Tucking that away for later, I focus my attention back on the other thorn in my ass: *Aeron*.

"You clean up well for a Vagrant," he utters.

"Ouch!" I screech. Aeron's eyebrows raise the faintest amount in question. "Just wounded from you being such a pain in my ass." He blinks at me rapidly in confusion. "What? Were we not stating facts?" I shrug nonchalantly.

He chuckles to himself. "She's a fighter."

"Fighting implies there is a chance of me losing. I do not partake in child's play. I simply win...at everything." I throw him a feral grin, granting him full access to my pearly whites as I fake bite at him.

"Calm down. You don't want to injure my fragile male ego now, do you?"

"That would imply I have a scrap of care to give you, and would you look at that, I just ran out," I coo.

Hade grumbles under his breath. "If you two are done pissing on each other's shoes, hurry up and follow me. I'm going to be late a *second* time because of your childishness."

"Am not!" Aeron and I both shout at his accusation.

Sighing, he motions us down a connecting hall that opens into the grand entrance of the castle. It is spacious and bright, with light filtering in from the stained glass windows on each side. The ceiling is vaulted, a grand chandelier hanging in the center. Sun bounces off the black and white checkered tiles. A white grand piano nestled in the corner that practically screams *expensive*.

Hade takes us down another hallway that leads us to giant black double doors adorned with black metal handles. Hade grabs a handle at the same time Aeron's Vanquisher, tasked to watch him, grabs the other. In perfect unison, they open the doors, revealing a long wooden table splattered with delicacies I've only seen in my dreams. Every one of our competitors stare at us with wide eyes as Aeron and I stride in, arm in arm.

So much for trying to stay under the radar.

I try to tug my arm away from Aeron's, but as soon as I tug, he only grips harder, digging his fingers into my bare skin.

"Play the part. Make them fear us," he whispers next to the shell of my ear, sending chills down my spine.

"And what if I don't want to play the part with you, hmm?"

"Then you will be walking to your own downfall."

His considerable lack of confidence in my abilities only fuels my fire to prove them all wrong. This man thinks he's playing God. I picture my knee slipping up towards his manhood and showing him exactly what I'm capable of, but that little thought in the back of my mind keeps me from carrying that dream out.

My weapon.

My most advantageous weapon to wield here: make them underestimate me. Let them think I'm hiding behind the strength of a strong, bold man. Let them see my 'weaknesses' before I pounce.

With that in mind, I play the part of the dainty girl in need of rescue by the big, brawny man, if only for the time being. Donning my mask, I lean in a little closer to Aeron's body and stride in time with him to the remaining two seats at the end of the table. Aeron steps in front of me, pulling my chair out, playing the part of the perfect gentleman.

Puke.

Pinning him with a feline smile, I blink up at him sweetly. "Such a gentleman," I purr, as if I'm awestruck he has taken interest in me.

Double puke.

Aeron pushes my chair in for me, rounding the table to sit directly across. My competitors chat amongst themselves, getting a feel for their competition, while I sit silently, taking it all in—the people, this place, and most importantly, the food.

Half the food in front of me, I couldn't name even if there was a dagger pressed to my throat. I look down at a plate lies decorated with desserts with pink, bubble-like clouds floating out between the cracks. Tracking one of the bubbles with my eyes, I watch it burst, freeing the pink fog within.

The fog hits my nose, but I'm shocked it carries no smell. Then, as if hit by a galloping horse, my tastebuds explode with an array of flavors. Sweetness spreads across my tongue, sweet but tangy at the same time, with a hint of something I've never tasted before.

It's magic encased in food, letting me get a glimpse into what the delicate pastry sitting in front of me tastes like, and it has me drooling for a bite. My only mission right now is seeing if the pastry lives up to its name.

I go to snatch up a bite when a delicate hand closes around mine, giving it a soft shake.

"Rayah Wixx, but you can call me Ray." The girl beside me shakes my hand in forced greeting, stealing my hand from its mission.

"I'm Nyxi." I shake her hand back just as gently as I trail my eyes over the girl sitting next to me. Her hair is what steals my attention first. The brightest shade of pink is coiled into tight curls bouncing around just above her shoulders. Her tan skin is smooth like honey, with faint freckles here and there as if they were an afterthought when creating her. Her features are youthful compared to mine, but she's still filled out in areas, making me assume she's only a couple years younger than me.

"Your eyes." The words slip from my mouth on their own. "I've never seen anything like them."

She shyly tucks one of her pink coils behind her ear. "Mama told me it's a birth defect. Told me something made me all kinds of funny, from my bright pink hair to my sunflower eyes."

"They are beautifully unique." They remind me of running through a field of sunflowers while a lover chases close behind, giggles floating up in the space between.

"Mama wouldn't agree with you. She would say they make me stick out like a sore thumb and will hinder me from ever being wedded off. That's why I'm here." Her once-cheerful face sinks an inch at the reminder of her future.

"And why is that?" It's an honest question. I want to know because I'm interested, not simply to gain information on an opponent for once.

"To finally rid myself of them if I lose. Or, to finally add meaning to my existence in my family's eyes if I win." She states it so plainly, as if it's been ingrained in her head since birth. Maybe it has.

"I still don't understand."

"And here I was, relying on you to bring brains to the game as a potential ally." She giggles shyly to herself then abruptly slaps a hand over her mouth in shock. "Sorry, I didn't realize I said that out loud." She shakes her head like she's mad at herself. "Flowers, Ray, already making enemies for yourself." She talks to herself in a whisper I can barely hear.

Here I am, making friends with another psycho who talks to herself, Empress save me. This one seems a little shyer than Des, though.

"Anyways, long story short, my family has forced me to enter my name in the Reaper Crucible. Well, if I wanted to keep living under their roof, that is. Never thought I would get picked, though. Guess that's just one more thing about me to add to the difference list—"

"Unique," I cut her off.

"Huh?"

"You are unique, not different. They are two very different things."

"Hmmmm…" She ponders the thought like it's never occurred to her. "Maybe in another world, but not this one." She
huffs. "Anyways, either I die and they have one less mouth to feed,
one less daughter corrupting their household, or I win and finally
bring honor to our family. I dream of the day they talk about my
bravery rather than my difference." She looks mesmerized by the
thought.

"Ahh, yes, *dreams*. What a terrible motivator for hope that is."
The woman's haunting voice slithers up the back of my spine, skit-
tering into my ears like snakes. No, not a woman—the *Empress*. I
steel my spine, and the flowers and butterflies melt away as reality
comes sweeping back in.

She storms in, commanding the room with a snap of her fingers. All eyes are trained on her as we stand, the symbol of our
very being, the hand that feeds and commands our every move.
She gives us what she wants and takes as she pleases, a force to be
reckoned with.

She glides across the floor like a wind storm to the head of
the table, where her larger-than-life chair is perched, awaiting her
arrival. Either she has more than one throne, or she had her work-
ers drag it in here for the occasion. I wouldn't doubt that; she has
always been one to show her wealth and power when possible.

Straining my eyes, I peer down the length of the oversized
table to where she now stands beside her throne, awaiting our
gratitude. She's draped in all red, twin to her flaming red locks
floating down her back. Her hair reminds me of the brightest
embers floating about a fire. She has it styled in long, loose curls
reaching her hips.

I try to stray my gaze from her in submission, but her glowing
orbs are like magnets for mine. They glow a bright orange, like
twin flames swirling inside them. Her features are sharp to match
her disposition. Her skin is warm in tone to match the rest of her.
Freckles dance about her skin like sparks igniting across it.

The room has raised in temperature by a few degrees from the outfit accentuating her every curve. Blood red leather is sucked around her in a skin-tight, strapless, floor length dress. It hugs her body before it flares out from her knees to the floor. Every inch of her dress is lit by flames licking at the air.

I assume this illusion is due to magic, since she isn't screaming in pain, but it still radiates slight heat in warning. She clears her throat in greeting. "Welcome to the start of your destiny, however short or long it may be. Let the annual Reaper Crucible commence."

I imagine an evil laugh ringing through her head at the prospect of fresh blood being spilled for her entertainment. She is sick and twisted, everything I do not want to be in life. Once I take out my competitors, maybe I'll take her out as a victory lap. Let the hand that feeds us poison get a taste of her own medicine.

We all bow, and she smiles at our compliance. "You may be seated."

The sound of chairs dragging across the floorboards ring out around us as we all shuffle back into our seats. "Feast and celebrate tonight, but tomorrow, your training and ranking begins. Oh, and one more thing: I *hate* being disappointed." She claps her hands, and servers flood in from every direction, carrying more trays laden with smoky meats, colorful fruit, and potent-smelling drinks.

My eyes track every new slice of heaven. I stack one of everything on my plate like a starved stray saving rations for the future. I guess, in a way, I am; I have never seen this much food in a single area at one time. It makes my stomach turn in guilt and fury that all this food is being thrown around for party tricks while innocent people and children are starving on the streets of Vagrant.

Suddenly, I have no appetite at all. I shove my full plate slightly in front of me so I can rest my elbows on the table, planting my knuckles under my chin. Humming to myself, I push the food around on my plate with my fork to blend in with my surroundings.

Time goes by in a blur, with shouts and laughs and cheers swirling around me like a tornado. I'm zoned out thinking about what Theo would think of all this when I feel a small tap on my shoulder.

"Are you going to eat that?" Ray points to the bubbling pink pastry sitting on my plate. "It's just… It looks really good, and, uh…all of them were gone before I got the chance to grab one." She sounds hesitant, like this is the first time she has asked anyone for something.

There's fear of rejection glimmering in her eyes that I assume stems from her home life. If I can stoke her with a little more self-assurance by this simple act of kindness, maybe it will grace me with some good karma as well. It's a win-win.

"By all means, it's yours." I throw her a simple smile and shove my plate her way. The smile that spreads across her face could rival the sun, the embodiment of her name.

The innocent encounter is cut short by a calloused hand slamming down on my plate.

What the Empress!

"She needs to eat her own food. There is plenty still left for you to pick on," Hade growls out at Ray, living up to his Cardinal rumors.

Ray gasps in shock and fear, stealing her hand back. "Flowers, sorry," she chokes out. In an instant, all the confidence starting to light up her face disappears. I'm getting really sick and tired of men putting their damn hands where they don't belong.

On instinct, I dig my nails into his hand holding my plate hostage. "If I want to share my food with her, then that is exactly what I'm going to do," I bite out as I feel liquid pooling under my nails. At this point, I don't care who I have to make bleed to get what I want.

"There is plenty of food here to go around. She does not need the food off your plate that is supposed to be in your stomach. Don't think I didn't notice you haven't touched a single thing."

Empress, has he been here watching me this entire time? I guess I shouldn't be shocked, since he is tasked with keeping track of my every move, but I didn't think that meant watching me eat.

"Well, as you see, what Ray here wants can only be found on *my* plate. Since I have no plans to eat it, she's doing me a favor by not letting it go to waste," I seethe.

He scoffs. "Like you're letting your body go to waste by not eating? Look at you; when was the last time you had a proper meal? You need to eat if you want any chance of making it through the Crucible. Food is fuel, and fuel is power."

He almost sounds as if he cares—almost. "I've taken care of myself just fine up until now, and I think I'm doing well enough. Exceedingly, some would even say," I add.

He rolls his eyes, mumbling something under his breath, then signals for a server. He whispers in the server's ear, who nods and strides out of the room. Not even a minute later, the server strides back in with a new tray full of those bubbling pastries.

"I was told you were in need of some cloud cakes, miss?" he questions Ray, holding the tray in front of her face. Her eyes light up when the smoke bursts, and she starts smacking her tongue as the magical smoke floods her taste buds.

Giggling to herself, she grabs one in each hand and plops them down on her plate. Turning, she thanks the server, then Hade before devouring the sweets in front of her. With her attention occupied solely on her food, I turn my gaze back on Hade.

"There, problem solved. Now she has her own to eat, and you can eat yours." He sits there, staring at my plate like he's waiting for me to start eating. Wait...is that what he's doing?

As if reading my mind, he nods. "I will stand here watching you until you eat. I don't care if I have to spoon feed you like a child in front of everyone to get the task done."

Throwing a small tantrum, I stomp my foot and turn towards my plate. "You're insufferable, you know that?"

Twenty minutes later, I've scarfed down over half my plate and even indulged in one glass of "Fire Water", an alcoholic delicacy in Lunaria known to apparently knock you on your ass. Sounds about right, because after downing only one glass, I feel like even brooding Hade couldn't bust my balls from this dizzying haze. The stuff goes down exactly how it sounds: like flames licking the back of your throat. It has zero taste, making it dangerously easy to guzzle.

My dress fits a bit snugger across my tummy after eating more than should be humanly possible. I'm tempted to ask Hade to roll me out of here, and a giggle bubbles up my throat.

Damn, this Fire Water is turning me soft.

"Was that a giggle I just heard coming from you, of all people?" Hade's shocked face comes into view beside me.

Empress, this man keeps popping up out of nowhere like a ghost. "*Was that a giggle I just heard?*" I mock him. I put on my best grumpy Hade impression: scrunching my eyebrows, pouting my lips, and lowering my voice an octave.

"I think you've had enough Fire Water for the night. Let me escort you back to your room before people get the impression you actually have a personality. Wouldn't want to go giving them false hope now, would you, *Nightmare?*"

Ugh, fuck him and that stupid fucking nickname. I hate the way it pisses me off and also makes little tingles erupt over my skin at the same time.

"I think I've had the perfect amount of Fire Water, actually," I grit out. "Your overflowing concern for my wellbeing has been noted, though. I hate to inform you, but the verdict is back, and it rules in favor of me not giving a shit. Shocker, I know," I say dryly, even though on the inside, I'm on the verge of laughter.

Note to self: next time I need a pick-me-up, the perfect medicine is a tall glass of Fire Water. I can't even imagine how Des would act on this stuff, and I don't think I ever want to find out for fear of death by words. What a painful way to go.

Hade disguises what could almost be considered a chuckle with a low grunt. The day I hear that man actually laugh will be the day Lunaria falls out of the sky.

I wonder if his laugh would be deep and gravely, or if it'll be smooth like a melody. My mind conjures up a million different possibilities, and I try to fight the feeling of wanting to know for myself.

Apparently, this Fire Water has gone straight to my head, because I would never in a million years admit that sober, even to myself.

"Now, if you'll excuse me, I can escort myself back to my room. Female empowerment and all that." I wave my hand in his face while sliding my chair back and making a break for the exit.

"Let me walk you," Hade and Aeron say in union as they flank each side of me. When people say they want men throwing themselves at them, I don't think this is what they mean. My head spins, and not from the alcohol. That would be a blessing to this dizzying encounter.

I'd forgotten Aeron was even here, since we didn't talk the entire dinner. He was busy putting on his charm, making sure everyone knew how big of a deal he was. Ever the charmer, that one, except I see right through him and his games. Tomorrow, I need to make a point of training with him. What's the saying? Keep your friends close and enemies closer? Yeah, that.

Hade growls and pins Aeron with a look that, in my normal state, might make my knees buckle, but right now, with the alcohol dancing happily through my veins, he reminds me of a predator protecting its young. *Pfft.*

"You have done enough tonight. Your Vanquisher will escort you back to your room once you're done comparing the size of your manhood to everyone else here. It's not flattering or impressive, but please, carry on," Hade spouts.

Did he…did he just make a joke? No, surely I heard him wrong. There's no way in Fallout Hade could make such a thing. Maybe he indulged in some Fire Water too?

"The mighty Cardinal. Can't wait to see if the rumors floating around Fallout are true. For your sake, I hope they aren't. You can stop by my room later for a measure, and we can set the rumors straight—if you want, that is. You know what they say: everything always has a slice of truth to it," Aeron spews cooly.

"My name is in their mouths, so it sounds like I'm winning." He huffs, then grabs my arm, spinning me abruptly and pulling me towards the door. "Wish I could say the same about the name Gavis, unfortunately for you."

Chapter
Nine

I'M FORCED TO FOLLOW HADE DOWN THE LONG HALLWAY BACK TO MY room. "What was that all about?" I question while trying to keep my feet under me with the brutal pace he's setting.

"Someone needed to set that cocky fucker straight. Today, that man just happened to be me," he grunts.

"Uh huh, sure," I say on a breath. "Because it sounded to me like you guys were having a pissing contest over who got to escort me back to my room."

"I think the Fire Water has gone to that pretty head of yours."

I give him a feline smile. "I think this pretty head of mine has never been clearer. And since when do you compliment me?"

He continues dragging me down the hallway, attempting to look calm and collected. "Since never. When did I compliment me?"

"You just said I had a *pretty head*." I look over at him as the side of my mouth tugs up a smidge.

"That wasn't a compliment, just a statement. Trust me, you would know if I complimented you. It would be far grander than that. I don't take words lightly. I can count the number of times I have complimented someone. It would rival the stars on the clearest night in Lunaria."

"That's a high standard to hold yourself to. I might just make it my life's mission to see it happen. Add it to my long list of things to accomplish." I trail off, thinking of Theo and why I'm here. Before my brain can spiral out of control and get sucked back into the dark corner of my heart that harbors all my pain and heartbreak, I pin Hade with a devious look.

"So, what's up with all the growling?"

"Growling?" He's taken off guard. "What do you mean?"

"You know, that noise you make every time you're annoyed or angry? Which is, like, all the time. You should really try and lighten up, you know. I can see wrinkles starting to take up permanent residence on that pretty face of yours from all the scowling." I can't help but tease him as my drink hums happily through my body.

"I do not." His face turns serious, but I can also see a hint of worry behind his mask of indifference.

Checkmate.

I giggle to myself and then point at him. "That, sir, you absolutely do. You could become a professional growler at this point. I bet you could make a pretty coin too."

Hade growls then huffs at his realization of what he just did yet again, and then he growls in annoyance.

I throw my hands in the air. "Wait, don't tell me. You didn't know you do this...often? You need to lay off some steam. I've heard sex works wonders." My giggle turns into a boisterous laugh, and I feel lighter than I have in months.

"My steam is just fine, thank you very much. Let's get you to bed before you wake up the whole damn castle." The side of his lip inches up the smallest amount, and my breath hitches in my throat. His smirk reminds me all too well of a certain smile that will forever be imprinted on my brain.

"Do that again." The words tumble out of my mouth before I can stop myself.

"Do what, *Nightmare?*" he questions me honestly, no malice behind my nickname for once.

"Smile for me again," I ask, holding my breath in anticipation.

"Only because you asked nicely, and you won't remember this in the morning." He slows his steps and pins me with his beautifully tragic polar eyes, giving me a genuine, unguarded smile that thaws the smallest sliver of the ice around my cold, mangled heart.

Its beauty embodies the first flake of snow, a one of a kind snowflake you want to treasure forever but admire from afar so you don't destroy the moment and ruin it.

"Thank you for that." My voice is barely a whisper.

"Don't go soft on me now, Nyxi."

My name tumbles off his lips like a sonnet and takes me by surprise. He never calls me by my name, and now, I don't want him to call me by anything but. The way he enunciates each letter, as if handling my name with care…he makes it sound special and treasured.

"Never." I grin up at him and shove my shoulder into his side playfully.

"You better shove harder than that tomorrow, or you won't make it past the first round." He's suddenly serious, almost on edge.

"Go eat a bag of oranges." I roll my eyes at him and flip my middle finger up with flare.

"That's the second time you've said that now. Why?"

I gasp. "Don't tell me you're an orange supporter?"

"So what if I am? What do you have against them?" He raises a brow.

"For starters, it takes half a day to peel the blasted things. No one should have to work that hard for a snack. Then, they are covered in those tiny little white strings that taste like butthole and get stuck in your teeth. Once you suck all the juice out of the tiny wedge, you're left with sticky fingers and a wrinkled sack of orange skin that's bitter and chewy. Not worth the time and effort for the tiny bit of euphoria you get from the juice, in my opinion." I huff in annoyance. "They are public enemy one in my book. The Empress would outlaw them if she had any brains." I probably should have kept that last sentence to myself, but it seems my mouth has a mind of its own tonight.

"Interesting." Hade looks at me as he guides me back towards my room. This man is like a walking contradiction with his words and his actions. The way he's looking at me makes me feel like he is truly curious about my silly revolt against oranges, but then I think back to him punching me in the face and not even caring to apologize about it.

Men.

"That's all you have to say on the subject?" I pin him with a fake serious glare. "This is serious business, sir," I grumble.

Hade growls next to me. "I told you not to call me that."

"And I told you, you have a growling problem, but here you are, acting like a wild beast instead of a man." I shrug and take off, skipping down the long, dim hallway away from him. I throw over my shoulder, "You should really take up my idea of letting off some steam."

"Empress, you will be the *death* of me." Hade grumbles under his breath as he starts jogging down the hall after me. "And who do you suggest will help me release some of this so-called steam?"

I gasp dramatically. "Don't tell me you don't have a cattle of women lining up at your door every night?"

Sighing, he continues to chase me down the hallway. "None worthy enough of my time. Now slow down before you hurt yourself."

Peeking over my shoulder, I take in Hade in all his glory. He truly is a masterpiece sculpted by the gods. His shaggy, obsidian hair flops about his forehead as he jogs without breaking a sweat. The man is an anomaly. His one gray eye glows like an orb in the dimly lit hallway. If this scene was a painting, I would call it "beauty masked beneath a beast".

I speed up, giggling over my shoulder. "You're gonna have to catch me for that to happen, *Death Reaper.*" And then, I take off.

I know I shouldn't be poking the beast, but the alcohol running through me has given me the courage to be someone else, if only just for the night. Tonight, I don't want to be Nyxi. I just want to be *free*. Free of the Crucible and my impending death, free of the heart that barely knows how to beat inside my chest now that half of it has been severed forever.

Peeking back over my shoulder, I find Hade is nowhere to be seen, like he has just vanished into thin air. Poof, gone. Maybe the Fire Water is getting to my head?

That can't be right. I swear, he was just a handful of feet behind me. Halting my steps, I look around the eerie hallway, my heart pounding with a mixture of weariness and thrill.

Muscular arms engulf me from behind, blanketing me in shadows. "*Caught you,*" Hade whispers next to the shell of my ear. "What's my prize?"

My heart feels like it might combust from his nearness, and that alone sends a chill up my spine.

"How—what—" I stutter, trying to wrap my brain around what just happened. "How did you disappear and end up behind me?" I'm a jumble of confusion. "I never saw you pass me... That's impossible."

His finger drags down the side of my neck. "Nothing is impossible in Lunaria. Call this your first lesson."

"*Magic,*" I whisper.

"Correct."

My heart skips. "Show me."

He smirks. "Only if you beg nicely."

I shoot him pleading eyes. "You wouldn't."

"Oh, *Nightmare*, I would do a lot worse than that. Now, ask me nicely, and maybe I'll comply."

Closing my eyes, I take a deep breath and grit out, "Will you show me...*please?*"

"No, but I do love to watch you beg." He grabs my arm, dragging me towards my room.

"Hade!" I grunt and press the heels of my feet into the ground, trying to halt us.

"Fine, but only so you'll shut up about it." He rolls his eyes and turns to face me.

I cross my arms, but I can't help the small smile blooming on my face. "Well, I'm getting older by the second, so get on with it."

This alcohol has only emboldened my already-brazen personality, and I can tell by the anger spreading across Hade's face that he's almost to his limit. Well, too bad, because he started this little cat and mouse game, and I've never been known to shy away from a challenge.

To push him a little further towards eruption, I add, "What, does the mighty Cardinal have stage fright? Hopefully, little Cardinal doesn't have the same problem." I flash him a feral grin.

He smirks. "Oh sweetheart, I've never had a single complaint."

"Insufferable," I say under my breath.

Hade takes a step closer, almost pressed against my chest, then disappears completely into nothing. I extend my arm to feel for where he just stood, but my hand connects with a very *large* bulge that drags a loud grunt from Hade.

"Fuuuuuuuckkkkk," he says in a hiss of pain, reappearing again. "A little warning next time."

My cheeks flush, and I pray the hallway is dim enough that Hade won't take notice. "Was that—did I just touch what I think I did?"

"Yes!" he wheezes. "And more like punched, not touched."

I can feel heat spreading up my neck at the realization. "Well, consider us even now. You punched my face, and I punched your…" An embarrassed giggle makes its way up my throat, and I have no choice but to set it free into the world.

"Cock," Hade says bluntly. "Are you foreign to the term, *Nyxi?*" His voice deepens. "Need a lesson on the human body?"

I squirm under his intense, heated gaze and forward demeanor. I should be used to it by now, but this feels…different. Another childish fit of giggles consumes me at the thought of Hade using the word *cock* in front of me. This Fire Water has truly done me in.

"You think this is funny?"

"Very!" I cover my mouth with my hand as another breathy laugh escapes me.

"As you just discovered, I can turn myself invisible, but not fully disappear. I can use my shadow magic to blend into my surroundings and, simply put, reflect them back to you as an illusion."

I shrug. "That's all you got? Invisibility? And here I thought you were one of the most powerful magicals to ever exist."

"*That* is just a party trick, a way for me to spy and collect information for the Empress. My true magic is much *darker* and *deadlier*. You should pray you never experience my true abilities," he says condescendingly.

This man irritates me to my core, but I can't seem to walk away from the wreckage that is this very odd but thrilling thing happening between us. I can't put words to it, but I want to smack the ever living Empress out of him ninety-nine percent of the time. Still, the remaining one percent somehow has an even greater death grip over me.

I feel an unavoidable pull towards this beast that wants to eat me alive. Why does the thought of being slaughtered by this beast make me feel alive again? Like the first breath you take out of water after holding on until the very last second, walking the line of life and death as if it's a challenge. Why do I yearn to know what this beast's fangs would feel like if they ravished my soul?

The question is, will I survive this beast? Or will it devour me whole and drag me into the darkness? Both outcomes seem to call to my stone cold heart—one with the promise of eternal darkness and blissful peace, and the other giving it a reason to beat fully again.

Chapter
Ten

"Wake up, sunshine! Today's the big day."

The mattress around me dips and lifts as I'm drawn to consciousness. My head is slightly groggy from last night's Fire Water incident, and I make a mental note not to touch the stuff again for a while.

My memories come back to me in flashes, parts of the night now clear—including me touching a very unfortunate place on Hade. If I wasn't hyped up on Fire Water at the time, I think I may have died of embarrassment. Alcohol is a wild thing.

A foot connects with my side, and the wind is knocked out of me. "Oww!" I glare up at the culprit.

"Empress, sorry." Des smiles sweetly as she continues to jump on my mattress like a child.

After getting to know Hade more intimately than I would have liked to last night, he walked me the rest of the way to my room and threw me on my bed…literally. The man has zero manners or chivalry—or maybe that only applies to me.

I remember most of last night, but some parts are still fuzzy. One thing I do remember is having the weight of grief lifted off my shoulders just enough to breathe for the night and loosen up. Today, though, that blanket of grief feels as if it's doubled in weight.

"Not again," Des grumbles and plops down next to me. "Did you hear anything I just said?"

"Yes?" My voice raises an octave, giving me away.

She pins me with a devious glare that, for her, is a big deal.

I hold my hands up in surrender. "Okay fine, you caught me." I smile sweetly. "You did tell me you love to talk, though, so no harm no foul, right?"

"I really shouldn't have told you that." She huffs. "But I could never stay mad at you. Dang soft heart of mine," she says to herself while tapping her chest like she's self-scolding.

Des is too good for me and this world, but I am thankful I get the opportunity to know her, even if just for a short time.

"As I was saying, today is very important for you, and we need you looking and feeling your best." She hums. "I'm thinking something you can move around in but that still makes you stand out." She's tapping her head in thought when her eyes spring open, and I can see the wheels turning in her head. That's never a good sign.

"I have just the thing !" she squeals. "Let me work my magic while you freshen up."

She shoves me towards the washroom and slams the door in my face. I slip my silk nightgown down my body and step into the black clawfoot tub, steam radiating off the top of the water. After taking a few minutes to relax and soak my muscles, I scrub every inch of my body clean and wash my tangled mop of hair. Wrapped in a lush robe, I open the door and stride back into my room. The only way to describe the scene unfolding in front of me is a sparkling sea of death.

"Des..." I gasp in awe. "You're a mastermind."

She looks nervous. "You like it?"

"It's one of the most beautiful things I've ever had the pleasure of laying my eyes on." I beam at her.

"Ahhh, okay, so I already knew it was amazing because I made it, duh, but I'm glad you love it too!" She plops her hands on her hips, admiring her work. "I just have a few small finishing touches, and then it will be ready for you. The men are going to have a hard time focusing today. It will be just perfect."

Des continues to poke and prod the material, making sure everything is just so. "I was going for beauty and protection."

I inch closer, bending down to inspect the intricate detail, and it's then I realize what it's made of. "Diamonds!" I squeal. "Holy shit, Des...that's a lot of diamonds."

"One million, two hundred thousand, and six diamond, to be exact." A devious grin spreads across her face as I stare back at her in shock. She shrugs. "What? I'm good with numbers."

A black, skin-tight bodysuit sits wrapped around a makeshift dummy that looks like my exact replica. I don't even want to know how Des made that happen. Every inch of the suit sparkles in the sunlight like an endless sea of glitter.

On closer inspection, the sea of black is actually a million microscopic glittering black diamonds. They are so small, they blend together unless you are pressed up close and know what you're looking for.

"Diamonds are tough to break and make a great outer shell. They are all stitched with spider silk, making it next to impossible to penetrate. The material is breathable and flexible, so it should feel like a second skin. Plus, it's sexy as hell. Simply put, it's genius." She smiles to herself, clearly satisfied. "Another win for Des, boo-yah!"

I slip both arms and legs into the tight sleeves, and it glides on like butter. Pulling the zipper up my front, it squeezes my small cleavage, holding it in place. Des was right—I practically feel naked with how perfect it fits me.

"I also had a Scorch spell the suit, so it's flame resistant. You will be untouchable out there, girl."

"How did you even have time to make all this?"

She draws a ball of magic to her fingertip. "I had some help."

"Right, magic. I'm still getting used to that part."

"Ohh, I almost forgot." She leans forward and points to my hip. "I added a little something extra to the side. There should be a tiny zipper that opens into a pocket." She stares at me. "Go on, open it up."

Sure enough, a tiny zipper is hidden among the little diamonds, blending in perfectly. I give it a small tug, sliding it down the side of my hip. I reach inside, cool metal gliding against my fingertips.

My heart clenches with the realization, and I snatch the chain immediately. "My dagger necklace," I breathe out.

Des nods back at me slowly. "I wanted you to have a safe place for it while you compete. Now, it can always be with you *and* protected."

I close the distance between us, wrapping her in a suffocating hug. This simple gesture has restarted my aching heart and given me the push to make it through the Crucible. In this suit, I feel invincible. "Thank you," I whisper in her ear, giving her another tight squeeze before releasing her.

"Now, let's get this hair braided out of your face and get you on your way, *sparkles*."

"Please no more nicknames, especially *sparkles*," I plead.

Tugging my head straight so she can continue braiding she teases, "Sparkles is it."

"What am I going to do with you?" Des giggles behind me as we fall into comfortable chatting while she braids my hair.

Chapter
Eleven

THREE KNOCKS ECHO FROM THE OTHER SIDE OF MY DOOR, AND MY heart sinks to my ass. I'm not ready to face the brute involved in last night's encounter. I have no choice in the matter, though, so I straighten my spine, quickly puff my breath into my hand to make sure it smells okay, and throw on a face of indifference I'm far from feeling.

Storming over to my door, I fling it open. "How was letting off steam last night? Any complaints?" I drag my eyes up a fluffier body than I expected. My eyes land on a man with short gray hair, brown eyes, and light skin, his face covered in overgrown facial hair, sporting an infectious, warm smile.

Jeez, Nyxi. Can you embarrass yourself any more?

An aged chuckle draws me out of my thoughts, and I know I'm sporting blooming red cheeks…again. "So sorry…sir," I tack on, trying to sound polite. "I thought you were someone else. My apologies." I am seriously flustered right now.

"Now I must know what kind of steam you are referring to? Sounds intriguing," he exclaims.

Empress save me.

"Oh, it's nothing. Just a meaningless saying." I shrug nonchalantly, hoping he gets bored and drops the subject. He winks at me but doesn't push the subject any further. I internally thank him.

"And who might you be?" I ask with more accusation than I intended, already wound up so early in the day.

He shakes my hand. "Name's Winston. I'm your new guard." He splays his hand in the air, swiping it across his body, as if the words are right in front of him. "Protector of 'just Nyxi'."

"New guard?" My mind sputters, but then I remember the 'mighty Cardinal' was just a fill in and has better things to do with his time than, and I quote, 'babysit' me. Why does it still sting, though?

"Vanquisher Winston, at your service, ma'am." He salutes me with a smile, and his round belly jiggles a little from the movement. He is every opposite to Hade. Where Hade is hard and uninviting, Winston is soft and welcoming. Winston is the warmth to drown out Hade's raging storm. He is also much, much older.

"I just didn't know I was getting a new one so soon, is all. Sorry for the confusion."

He smiles down at me. "Little lady, you better stop that nasty habit of apologizing about everything. There's no need."

"Sorry—Empress, sorry—uhhh. My lips are sealed from here on out, promise." This introduction so far is going swimmingly…not.

"Ready to get going? You have a big day ahead of you, little lady. Oh, and I almost forgot. Do you have any idea why this was sitting on the ground outside your door?" He lifts his hand, and clutched inside his palm is none other than a *fucking orange.*

"You've got to be kidding me!" I slap my forehead and let out a long sigh. "Let me have it." I snatch it from Winston.

"Oh, do you love oranges too? I'm a bit of an orange enthusiast myself. We should make a club and name it…" He pauses, scratching his head before his eyes light up. "Citrus Circus—"

"No," I cut him off. "This is just someone playing a cruel joke on me. Actually, here." I shove the orange back in his hand. "You can have it, since you love them so much. It's better off in your stomach than in my waste bin."

When did the little shit even drop that off? Did he spend the night out there, watching over me? Wake up early to drop it off before his shift started? No, that would require him thinking about me and having the time to spare for his schemes. He probably sent someone to drop it off this morning as an afterthought to rile me up…right?

"Thanks, little lady." Winston beams at me. "You're a real peach, you know that?" He starts digging the nail of his thumb into the peel, stripping it of its outer layer. I'm exhausted just watching him do it.

"Well, shall we get going? I'm ready to draw some blood." Winston and Des shoot concerned looks at my morbid statement. "Only kidding. Relax."

I'm not kidding, not in the slightest. I have so much pent-up rage, I wouldn't be surprised if instead of blood running through my veins supporting my life, it solely pumped rage and revenge. They have taken permanent residence in the core of my heart, and unfortunately, they are here to stay.

Winston links his arm in mine, pulling me into the hallway with him. Des yells *good luck* to me from my doorway as we strut down the corridor.

"Just so you know, I'm a Fib. Keep that in mind next time you try to lie to my face." He winks at me with a devious smile.

My pulse kicks up a notch. "So you knew I was lying about the whole steam comment too?" He nods, and I feel my cheeks heat.

"You Vanquishers and your nosy little magic." I shove playfully into his side, and our laughs mingle off the walls of the corridor.

THE RUMORS DON'T EVEN COME CLOSE TO PAINTING AN ACCURATE depiction of Lunaria. The air feels fresher up here compared to the rotting, stuffy scum we breathed down in Vagrant. Everything, and I mean everything, is bright and bold, from the buildings, clothing, food, landscapes, and even people's hair. It looks like a rainbow threw up all over the place, but it also looks oddly cohesive.

Where buildings in Fallout were crumbling with sharp edges, in Lunaria, everything is sophisticated and round, a mixture of big, colorful domed roofs and pointed buildings littered throughout town. Mixed in with houses are shops selling everything from extravagant clothing to mouthwatering treats while street performers showcase their magic for coin. It's magnificent, and I know Theo would be in a chokehold over it.

It's chaotic and full of laughter and smiles. There are people floating through the air in all directions. A gust of wind blows my hair as a dash runs past me so fast, I can't even track them. To my left, a woman uses her magic to revive a dead flower until it grows taller than her. There's magic infused into every square inch of Lunaria, and I love it.

Sitting in the center of Lunaria is where the real show stopper sits: *The Bubble*. That is exactly where we're headed, where my fate will play out.

It's impossible to miss, since it soars into the sky, creating exactly what it's called: a giant bubble. I guess the correct word for it would be *magical force field*.

A translucent dome hovering off the ground emits a blue light, trapping the arena inside. Right now, it sits empty inside, but with the help of magic, it transforms into any nightmare the Empress can conjure in that nasty head of hers.

Residents of Lunaria are able to watch from the outside during the Crucible if they please, or they can watch the giant projection an Illuminist casts in the sky after each round of the game. The Empress also stations an Illuminist in each sector after each round to cast a replay of the games and gore.

Families would gather in the heart of Misery's Crossing with snacks from vendors to feast their eyes on the mayhem project-ed for their entertainment. I never had the urge to watch people toyed with by the devil, so on those nights, Theo and I would slip away to Luna Lake and enjoy its vacancy together.

Harsh sunlight streams down, reflecting off the Bubble, mak-ing it glow. I have to shield my eyes to take in the entirety of the monstrosity in front of me.

Not only does the Crucible take place in the Bubble, but we will also train and have our evaluation there too. Not that training for a single week will do much for our game play, but the Empress likes to consider it a generous offer. I think she just likes to turn up the tension until we are ready to slit each other's throats with just a look.

The Bubble grows as we approach it until I have to crane my neck to take it all in.

"You have any strategies brewing in that pretty head of yours yet, little lady?"

"You think I would spill all my secrets to an orange enthusiast? You're sorely mistaken, Vanquisher."

He winks at me, and it melts my heart a little. "Right answer. Don't trust any of those fools in there, Nyxi. My bet's on you."

"You're just saying that because you're tasked to watch over me."

He smirks at me. "Good thing I'm the Fib and you aren't, so you'll never know."

I know what Winstons' doing. His attempt to get my mind off my looming future helps a bit as I banter playfully with him. I don't miss the way he zones in on my slightly shaking hands clasped behind my back, or the way my steps have slowed a fraction as we approach the Bubble.

He turns to face me and grabs both my shoulders. "I know we just met, kid, but being a Fib means I can read people, and what I see radiating off you is pain. Even more than that, though, is *strength*. Give 'em hell out there and stay true to yourself. You remind me of my late daughter, and I would like to think she sent you to me as a gift to watch over, as a reminder of her."

Yet another person with a void where their heart should sit. It's comforting to know others understand the waring feelings raging inside me.

I nod once. "I won't let you down."

I see the way he's looking at me, like he knows this promise is not only just for him, but for another, someone who is more important to me than *everything*.

Tucking another promise in my back pocket, I flash Winston a feline smile as rage slowly takes over my body again. I'm ready to show the world exactly who Nyxi is. That is the sole thought running through my head as Winston presses his hand to the Bubble, the space in front of us opening, an invitation to the start of my revenge.

Chapter
Twelve

METAL CLANKS AROUND ME AS I TAKE IN THE GIANT ARENA. SOME OF my competitors have already paired off to spar while others are off by themselves, practicing with their chosen weapon.

These first few days are for us to train and get a good look at our competitors. At the end of the week, we will be broadcasted for all of Lunaria and Fallout to watch as we select our chosen weapon and perform in front of the Empress.

The Empress will rank us from one through ten, one being the most impressive and ten being 'good luck not getting killed off round one'. The Empress' scores will be added to the public's votes to provide our official standing for the start of the Crucible.

Our rankings will change throughout the game by votes from the public and will be important during the last couple rounds—if we make it that far. I have never been one to aim for popularity, so this proves to be my first major challenge. I just need to channel my inner Theo and all should go well...I hope.

Approaching the rack along the edge of the Bubble, I look over the weapons in front of me. Weapons in every shape sit like a wall of death calling my name. I approach a single edged sword first, tossing it between my hands. Too heavy and not deadly enough, so I pass. Setting it back on the rack, I eye a bow and arrow next to it, which I consider as an option. I'm comfortable with a bow, but it's not great for close combat. Grazing my fingers past the bow, I notice a collection of throwing knives and stars. My eyes instantly snag on one that looks like the perfect death contraption.

I reach up, snagging a leather grip in the center of the S-shaped double sided blade. Each end spears out with deep serrated blades that look perfect for spilling blood. The center is the perfect fit to grip comfortably while not getting too close to the blades on each side. I can use it as a double sided dagger for dueling multiple people at once in close combat, as well as a boomerang. It's light to hold and easy to strap on my body for traveling.

I glance over the remaining weapons, ranging from spiked clubs and chains to axes and spears. None of them call my name, so I circle back to the double sided S blade and snag it off the wall, tucking it into my boot. Just as I'm about to turn to practice on a target, an arrow wizzes by my head and embeds itself in the rack of weapons.

"Opps, sorry. I'm still trying to get the hang of this thing," a sly female voice coos insincerely behind me.

I grip the arrow and rip it from the rack while plastering on a feral grin. Spinning on my heels, I face the culprit, cocking back my arm and sending the arrow barreling through the air, spearing the tip of Jade's boot.

She screams in rage. "You bitch!" Tank rips the arrow from her boot. There's no blood on the tip of the arrow—pity.

"Unfortunately for you, I have *superb* aim. Just be glad it was your shoe this time and not that pretty face. Would be a shame to add a scar or two to it, don't you think?" I send her a wink for good measure.

"Looks like more than one of us has superb aim. Your ear is making a mess. You better go clean that up before you dirty the place with your filth," she spits back at me.

Sure enough, I feel the trickle of blood seep down my ear and drip onto my shoulder. I don't give her the satisfaction of acknowledging the cut to my ear, tucking the pain away.

This kind of pain, I can deal with easily. It's the pain that makes my heart feel like it's ripped in two that I struggle to breathe through, the type of pain that haunts me not only in my dreams, but also while I'm awake, as constant and abundant as the air around me.

Swiping a glob of blood off my shoulder, I flick it at her. "Good thing I've been told red is my color." I shoot her a venomous smile and strut past without a care in the world, bloody ear and all. Walking to the farthest target on the opposite side of the arena, I prepare myself to practice in peace. I need zero distractions from here on out if I want to win this thing.

Lining up in front of the stagnant target, I angle my body, brace my core, and plant my feet in a sturdy stance. I use my left arm to point at the center of the target and raise the blade above my head with my right arm, drawing it back. Taking one last peek at the target with my left arm still pointed, I close my eyes, draw in a deep breath, and fling the weapon forward, rotating my hips to add more strength.

Before I even get a chance to open my eyes, slow clapping echoes around the quiet corner I'm tucked in. "Impressive." The words are whispered against the shell of my ear, sending chills down my spine.

In one, swift movement, I spin, kicking my leg out and knocking Aeron's feet from under him in seconds. He lands with an umph on his ass, thoroughly caught off guard.

"You should never sneak up on a Vagrant, Gavis." I smirk at him and offer up my hand for help. He snakes his hand in mine and attempts to pull himself up. Just as he starts to lift his body off the ground, I use his arm to spin him around, pinning his arm behind his back and driving my knee into the center of his spine, pressing him harshly to the ground. Straddling his back, I lean down and whisper in his ear. "Lesson number two. Never trust a Vagrant."

"If you wanted to get on top of me, all you had to do was ask," he purrs.

"In your dreams, pretty boy." I push off him and strut to retrieve my blade directly in the center of the bullseye, exactly where I knew it would be. By the time I've pulled the blade from the target, Aeron is back on his feet and annoyingly by my side again.

"I saw that little stunt Jade pulled earlier. That was quite the show. Let me know if you need me to step in next time and be your knight in shining armor." His chest puffs up.

"I can take care of myself just fine, thank you."

He softens his face just a smidge. "Just because you can doesn't mean you should have to, Nyxi."

I turn away from him. "I've been taking care of myself my whole life, and that's not going to change now."

He huffs to himself. "Fine. How about a partner then? Think of it as us having each other's backs out there."

I look him up and down; this is the first time I've seen him look sincere.

"You scratch my back, I scratch yours type of deal?" I raise my brows at him.

He looks at me like I've grown a third eye. "Is that some type of weird saying you guys use in Vagrant?"

Taking the opportunity, I pounce. "Aww, does that pea brain of yours lack in the vocabulary department?" I tease.

"Only while I'm staring at pretty women, it seems," he replies smoothly.

Rolling my eyes, I spit on my hand and hold it up to him. "Shake on it, and you have yourself a deal, *Command*."

"Did you just call me by my sector?"

"It's very fitting, seeing as you like to command everyone around. I'm only sad I didn't think of it sooner." I narrow my eyes at him. "Now, do we have a deal or not?"

"Deal, *Vagrant*." He spits on his hand and shakes mine, officially confirming my first alliance.

This deal better not come back to bite me in the ass, but for now, I need the pretty boy on my side to secure the public's vote. I can already see all the women in Lunaria falling head over heels for prince charming. Having the little devil perched on my shoulder as a pawn is the perfect strategy. Plus, it doesn't hurt to have a strong male on my side.

"Now, get out of my hair so I can get some practice in," I scold.

"I just watched you hit a perfect bullseye with your eyes closed. I don't think you need practice in that department."

I cross my arms over my chest. "I don't need practice in any department, but it doesn't hurt to get the reps in."

"What about shooting a bow?"

"Excellent; just ask Jade's toe."

He thinks to himself. "Endurance?"

I shrug, unbothered. "I could run laps around you."

"Hand-to-hand combat?"

"The best of the best," I coo.

He smirks with an idea. "Prove it."

"W–what?" I stutter.

"Fight me. Right here, right now. Unless you're scared you'll lose, that is?" he challenges.

I narrow my eyes at him. "I've never been scared a day in my life, Command, and that certainly won't start today."

We make our way over to the closest sparring ring in the sand. I line up in the center, spreading my stance, chest to chest with Aeron. He winks at me, spreading his arms wide, and I blow him a kiss in return.

I can't wait to wipe the smug look off his pretty little face.

Aeron's eyes zone in on me, sizing up his prey. The hairs on the back of my neck stand at attention, and I have this strange feeling Aeron's eyes aren't the only ones trained solely on me. Even tucked in the corner of the arena, I have this overwhelming feeling that every single inch of my body is being tracked by another predator. I try my best to ignore it.

It's paralyzing and exhilarating at the same time.

Knocking fists with Aeron to signal the start of the fight, we begin to slowly circle each other, waiting for the other to make the first move. I slowly work towards his right side, pushing him to circle around, giving me a better view of the arena. More importantly, I spy the owner of the eyes that were burning holes into the back of my head.

Hade.

Straying my eyes from Aeron for a split second, I lock eyes with Hade, who leans leisurely against the Bubble's force field on the opposite side of the arena, his arms folded over his chest and his ankles crossed.

The perfect depiction of unbothered.

Looking past his superficial mask, though, it's not lost on me how his jaw is tightly clenched, or how his eyes narrow slightly any time he looks at Aeron.

He's on edge. Interesting.

Aeron takes advantage of my slight distraction and lunges, making the first move. He lands a small blow to my side—or tries to—but my reflexes react at the last second, using my arm as a shield to absorb the blow.

"Lesson number one," Aeron mocks. "Eyes on your competition, Vagrant. You're sloppy and distracted. If you need something pretty to stare at, I'm right here."

I scoff. "Seems to me like I blocked you just fine, distraction and all."

Aeron towers over me, packed with muscle. I know I won't be able to out-strength him, so the only option is to outsmart him. I just need to rile him up a little so he makes a sloppy move, and then I'll pounce. My small size compared to his, paired with my speed, will give me the advantage I need.

Slowly, we begin to circle each other again, and time freezes. I'm focused and locked in on his every move, just as he is with mine. I take a slow, deep breath, which pushes on my cleavage that's on full display in this skin-tight suit.

First plan of attack: distract.

I catch Aeron's eyes trailing from my face down to my chest, where they linger for a fraction too long, and then, as if pained to do so, they trail back up to my face.

"Seems I'm not the only one distracted," I tease.

This sets Aeron off, just as I was hoping. In a rushed frenzy, he lunges at me sloppily out of frustration, but I'm prepared for the move. Setting my trap, I wait until the last second, then side step his attack, grabbing the back of his neck as he flies past me, shoving him down onto the ground. I quickly jump on his back and straddle him with my full weight to keep him pinned.

In one, swift movement, Aeron rolls onto his back, throwing me off him. I fly through the air and land on my back, briefly knocking the wind out of me. I try to regain my bearings, but in those few seconds, Aeron has switched places with me, straddling my body from above.

"I think I like this view better." He smiles down at me, and I clench my fists.

This man is not light by any means, and it's starting to get hard to breathe under his weight. I need to get out from under him so I can level the playing field. Right now, my strength doesn't compare to his, and I need to be able to get back on my feet if I want a fair chance.

With quick but careful movements, I grab sand in each hand, then smile sweetly up at him, batting my lashes. "You know what view I like better?"

"Enlighten me," he purrs.

"You when you can't see." He looks at me confused, and I use that second to throw both handfuls of sand at his face.

I catch him off guard, and he starts coughing, covering his face with his arm to shield his eyes. I use the distraction to slide out from under him and back on my feet.

"No one likes a cheater, Nyxi." His eyes are red and irritated, and he's covered head to toe in dust. It takes everything in me not to laugh at how ridiculous he looks.

"Just admit I outsmarted you, *Command*." My grin turns lethal as we start circling each other again. I know I must look unhinged right now, with blood dripping from my ear and smeared in my hair, sporting a smile from ear to ear, but I've never felt more *alive*.

I live for adrenaline and violence. It's the only thing that drowns out all the noise buzzing around my brain all hours of the day. There's no pain or heartache here, just me and my need to purge my rage. It's empowering, and I know Aeron can feel it too. I hope he sees the way I plead for him to play this game, to let me have this moment to fight my demons.

As if on cue, Aeron nods at me, fastening on his signature shit eating grin. "Show me your worst, *Vagrant.*"

I sigh internally, thankful for his compliance to play along for my sake. I clear my mind of every thought and painstaking memory, ripping out the phantom dagger plunged in my heart. I let it all float away with the wind then focus on Aeron's every move, preparing to release my fury on the devil himself.

I run directly at him, and at the last second, I crouch, sliding on my shin and narrowly missing his punch as I jab him in the back of his thigh. He grunts out a curse but stays standing as I quickly get back to my feet. Now I'm just toying with him, trying to tire him out and force him to get sloppy.

C'mon, Aeron. Make a move.

As if hearing my thoughts, he lunges, and instead of going for my upper body, he takes a card out of my book and kicks out my feet. I land on my back with an umph, and he's on me in an instant. He cocks his arm back to punch me, but I'm faster. I draw my knee up, crashing it against his balls and then his side before rolling out from under him.

He grunts. "Fuuuuuck, Nyxi. Those are precious jewels."

"You should learn to protect them better if they are that important, don't you think?" The corner of my mouth quirks up as I continue to egg him on.

While he's still kneeling, I kick out at him, but he grabs my ankle mid-kick and yanks me forward so I tumble into his lap.

A growl comes from the corner I know Hade watches from as I'm forced to sit in Aeron's lap like I'm his play thing. He secures one arm around my midsection, wedging his chest against my back while he slides his other hand slowly up my throat, latching on. I try to fight his hold, but he only grips tighter the more I struggle.

"If you just calm down, this can be enjoyable for both of us," he whispers against my ear in a playful, seductive tone.

"Too bad for you. I never learned how to play nicely." Throwing my chin down, I slide Aeron's hand choking me into my mouth and bite hard, breaking his skin until blood floods my mouth.

He rips his hand from my mouth, and I take the opportunity to throw my elbow back into his side until he releases me with his other arm. Turning, I pounce on him like a rabid beast, and my fist connects with the side of his face. Blood explodes from his mouth, spraying the both of us.

He looks up at me in a daze, his mouth oozing blood as a bruise starts to form on his swelling cheek. I shove my forearm into his throat, choking him, but not enough to cut his airway off.

"Do you yield, pretty boy?" I purr down to him.

He spits blood. "I think I might be dreaming. I'm pretty sure a beautifully lethal woman just beat me to a pulp, and I've never been more turned on."

I narrow my eyes and press my arm harder into his throat. "Yield, now!" I grit out at him.

He throws his hands up in surrender, that shit-eating grin firmly on his face again. "I yield, viper. Does that mean you have to get off me?"

I scowl and push off him, leaving him in a bloody dirty mess on the ground.

"You're really gonna walk away from a handsome man spread out for you like a feast?"

I scoff at him, but it holds no malice. "Go clean up. Your ego is stinking up the place."

I hear Aeron's pained cries fade behind me as I grab my weapon, shove it in my boot, and make my way back to Winston, who is waiting with a grin on his face to escort me back to my room.

Sweat mixed with our combined blood drips down my face and chest. The force field does nothing to dull the harsh beating sun; if anything, it only intensifies it, making it feel like a hotbox in the Bubble. The fight took more out of me than I would like to admit, only fueling my fire to do better.

I'll have to ask Winston if I'm allowed to go on morning runs around the castle to help with my endurance. That, paired with daily training in the Bubble and eating more food than I'm used to eating in a week, should help my chances at winning the thing.

I have no idea what the Empress has in store for us, so I need to be prepared for anything. It feels like each year, her ideas have only gotten grander and more dangerous.

Yay for me.

Winston's toothy grin comes into view as I approach the invisible door.

"Did you miss me?" I beam up at him.

His belly laugh vibrates over my skin. "Only you could look like you just emerged from hell itself and make a joke like nothing happened."

I shrug, feigning innocence. "So, is that a yes?"

"C'mon, little lady. Let's get you back and cleaned up. You positively stink."

I pout dramatically. "Do not!"

Winston puts his hand against the Bubble to activate the door, and I take that moment to sneak a peek behind me to the corner Hade was tucked into, except he's nowhere to be seen now. He left, and for some reason, that leaves an uneasy feeling nudging my battered heart.

I'm confused; why should I even care? Why does it matter if he stayed and watched me at all? It seems my heart is onto something my brain can't quite comprehend, and I'm scared for the day it catches on. I can't imagine a day Theo isn't the sole reason the pathetic organ in my chest beats.

Chapter
Thirteen

"Here we are, princess." Winston stops in front of my door and hovers his hand over the handle to let me in.

I wince at the nickname, and Winston takes notice, because he stops and turns to face me. Theo would always call me his princess, and the way the endearment rolls off Winston's tongue does not have the same knee wobbling effect.

At first, Theo called me princess to get under my skin, but then one day, it changed from a taunt to a promise. He would forever worship the ground I walked on, and I would always be his princess. His prized possession.

Winston looks over at me with concern on his face. "Did I say something wrong, little lady?"

From what I've learned about Winston, I think he's had enough sorrow in his lifetime, and the last thing I want to do is add to it. Taking a deep breath, I rein in the vortex of emotions floating around my mangled heart and slip on a forced smile I'm all too familiar with.

"It's nothing, really. An old friend used to call me princess, and it brought back some memories. You are no bother at all, Winston. Actually, I quite like your company, which is a strange feeling for me."

He looks at me all knowing, and I guess his Fib ability really means he does most things. I keep forgetting I can't pretend in front of him like I do others. He softens his eyes, radiating a warm aurora, and nods once. He feels no need to dive into details or rehash old feelings. He smiles, but it's not as warm as usual, and gives me a soft squeeze on my shoulder.

"I can feel the strength you harbor around that heart of yours, and it's admirable. I feel honored you consider me good company to keep, Nyxi. Now, this old man will get out of your very bloody hair and let you get clean and rested up."

With that, he's waltzing down the corridor, probably off to snag an orange from the kitchen and scheme about his little club. The thought alone brings a smile to my face.

"Hey, wait!" I call out. "Aren't you supposed to be watching over my every move, Vanquisher?" I yell down the hall to him.

He chuckles, and I feel it nudge up against my heart all the way from the opposite end of the hall. "I trust you won't get into any trouble in my absence."

I cup my hands around my mouth and shout, "And how do you know that? I was quite the rebel down in Vagrant."

"Are you going to cause any disturbances while I'm away, little lady?" he calls over his shoulder.

"Well...not that I know of."

Who knows when it comes to me and getting myself into trouble. It seems to be my specialty, like a moth to a flame. Trouble and I go together like a peanut butter and jelly sandwich. My mouth starts to water, and my stomach lets out a nasty growl.

"No lies detected, so my work here is done for the night. Now, go wash up. I can smell you from here!" He's so far down the hallway, I can barely make out his words as he fades into the shadows.

"Fibs," I scoff to myself. Peeling my door open, I enter my room, ready for a warm soak and some much needed rest.

Slamming my door shut, I rest my head against the back of the door with my eyes closed and release a deep breath. With the weight of the Crucible nearing, Jade's arrow fiasco, Aeron and his dizzying personality, my confusing thoughts toward Hade, *and* Winston dropping the princess bomb on me, I'm not sure I can take much more at the moment.

"That rough of a day, *Nightmare?*"

I practically jump out of my skin at his deep timbre that sucks all the air from the room. I'm gasping like a fish out of water, and I wish I could blame it solely on him taking me by surprise, but the way my heart does a little flutter, I know it might also have to do with the fact that he came to find me…in my room…*alone.*

Why do I let this man have so much power over me? I truly can't wrap my brain around it, but my heart is beating to a rhythm for which I have no roadmap, possessed by this beast in disguise.

"What are you doing here?" I say coolly, though it's the opposite of how I'm feeling. I push off the door with more confidence than I feel, steeling my face in boredom as I approach Hade. He has the audacity to sit perched on the edge of *my* bed like he owns the place.

"I came to check on you."

Those words should hold endearment, but the way he says them makes it sound more a mundane task to check off his list for the day.

"I am none of your concern anymore, Cardinal," I say in a clipped tone, not giving away any of my emotions.

He's up in an instant, but he stops himself at the last second. "You've been my concern since the moment I tore you from that hovel." His chest heaves with deep breaths, like he's trying to control himself.

"That's news to me," I seethe. "I am of no one's concern, least of all yours." I plant my hands on my hips, eyeing him while my pulse hammers in my throat.

He ignores me completely, all too consumed with staring at my hair. His brows pinch. "You're covered in blood."

"No shit, captain obvious." I roll my eyes, which only makes his temper flare.

"I meant you're *bleeding*," he growls. "I never saw Gavis land a blow to you the entire time you were fighting, so please enlighten me why I'm watching fresh blood drip from you? Did it happen before or after the fight?"

He looks positively frightening right now, and for the life of me, I can't figure out why he gives a damn, especially when he disappeared earlier faster than it takes Aeron to get a hard on thinking about himself.

"You were gone by the time I ended the fight with Aeron, so how do you know this isn't from him?" I'm goading him, nosey as always as to why he walked out earlier.

You just can't help yourself can you, Nyxi?

He takes a slow step towards me. "I saw just fine how you blinded him with sand and then jumped on him like the dangerous little creature I've come to know." Another step. "How you were straddling his waist with your chest pressed down on him, arm pressed against his throat, cutting off his air." Taking another step, he comes face to face with me. I can feel his warm breath fan across my lips like both a warning and a caress. "I also saw his blood-smeared, shit eating grin and love sick eyes beaming up at you as you were practically glued to his body."

I draw in a labored breath and blink at him in shock. Did he really watch the whole thing? And why does he sound...angry?

Or is he jealous?

He takes one last step, closing the distance between us. My heart feels like it's about to burst out of my chest and fuse itself to his.

The feeling of having the mighty Cardinal's undivided attention is mind-numbing, like taking the strongest drug Visionary Sector could offer. It's dizzying and all-consuming. It's too much, but at the same time, it's not enough at all. Now that I've gotten the smallest taste, I fear I may become an addict.

He slowly reaches up with gentle fingers and tucks one of my rouge curls that slipped from my braid behind my ear, exposing my bleeding cut. "Now, I won't ask you again." He turns my head to get a better look at the oozing cut and runs the back of his knuckles down the side of my jaw. "Who. Did. This. To. You?" he grits out.

I'm frozen. My heart rate picks up like the closing ballad of a symphony, but at the same time, I can't seem to take a full breath.

This moment is intoxicating.

No, *he's* intoxicating.

"Nyxi," he whispers, but there's an edge to his voice, a warning and a plea.

There he goes, using my full name again, and it's my *undoing*. I'll tell him anything he wants as long as he keeps saying my name like his life depends on it, like I'm the sole reason his heart still beats.

"J-jade," I stutter out. "She shot me with an arrow...or she tried to, but she missed. I think she just wanted to scare me. You know, rile me up before the game begins and all." I take a deep breath, trying to steady my racing heart, but it's a lost cause. "Really, it's nothing. Plus, I kind of stabbed the arrow through her boot in return, so the playing field is even." My breathing picks up again as I drag my eyes back up to meet his intense gaze.

"I can hear the unnatural flutter of your heart all the way from here, Nightmare. It doesn't seem like it was nothing."

I gulp, blinking back at him, reduced to only knowing how to keep my body standing and nothing beyond that. I startle when he tears off the bottom part of his shirt and lifts it to gently dab the blood still angrily pouring from my ear.

A breath escapes me. "My racing heart has nothing to do with Jade."

Empress, did I just say that out loud?

"Is that so?" He slowly backs me up while applying pressure to my ear until the backs of my knees hit the edge of the bed. "Sit. Let me tend to your wound."

I plop down on the bed, and he leans forward to get a better look, wedging my knees between his very large legs. There goes my heart, forgetting how to beat properly again. That doesn't sound healthy.

His overpowering scent of smoke mixed with sandalwood envelops me, giving me a heady high. My mind short-circuits as I take in the mountain of a man in front of me, who's taking care of me with such delicacy, a side I have yet to see from him.

It's confusing in the least and inebriating in the most. I feel drunk off his gentle caress of the side of my face. I get double vision when I take in his ying yang eyes that I can't seem to stray from. There's a story hidden behind those opposite saucers, and I yearn to reach in and dig around for the answers.

My eyes betray me, tracing the jagged scar slashing across his gray eye, and I wince. It looks angry, like it didn't get the opportunity to heal properly, like it's been neglected. It makes me wonder if there's reasoning to his closed off personality? Is it a defense mechanism, protecting his heart?

Does his heart harbor twin wounds with mine? Is he as broken and damaged as I am? A pile of chipped puzzle pieces that will never truly fit back together again?

"It just looks like a flesh wound, a minor tear," he hums to himself. "You should have an aid kit stashed in your washroom. Stay put while I grab it."

"Yes, sir." I can't help the words that rush out of my mouth as I fake salute him. The dense air was starting to shove so far down my throat, it was suffocating me, so I had to change the mood the best way I know how.

Getting under his skin.

Hade growls from the washroom at my remark. The doors rattle around on their hinges as he gathers the supplies he needs.

I hum to myself to pass the time while I kick my legs back and forth like a child. I feel his overwhelming presence before he comes into view, which always seems to happen when he's involved.

He rounds the bed to stand in front of me again, his usual stern face firmly in place. His knee presses against mine, and a spark of electricity zaps through my body.

Get it together, Nyxi.

"May I touch you?" he asks gently.

"Seems like a little too personal of a question to be asking a contestant, Vanquisher," I spew without even thinking. There I go again, making things awkward like it's my damn job. These quiet moments are the ones that make me want to rip the skin from my body. The chaotic events of my life recently have been much easier to immerse myself in to help dull the pile of raging thoughts in my mushy brain.

This feels all too...*intimate.*

"Nightmare," he grumbles under his breath, sighing. "For once, can you not be difficult?"

The loss of my name from his lips threatens to shatter my already-broken heart all over again. There he goes, using that nickname he so graciously gifted me. It helps me, though, helps distance my confused and battered heart from walking the plank to its impending doom.

I push my shoulders back, straightening my spine and slapping on the forced smile I wield so easily now. "Go ahead, get it over with. I'm tired and need to bathe," I huff.

This time, when he slowly reaches forward and wraps one of my curls around his finger like it's a treasure, I keep my eyes focused on the wall in front of me, as far away from his beautifully infuriating face as possible. He doesn't tuck it behind my ear this time, though. He sits there, pondering it like it's one of the sacred wonders of the world.

"It's not black?" he states curiously.

"What, your soul?" I tease.

He tugs the curl at my smart remark, making my head yank to the side with a slight painful jolt to the root. I won't look into the other jolt I feel fluttering up my stomach at the thought of him playfully pulling my hair.

"Your hair. It's not fully black. It's a galaxy of blue and purple hues mixed to create a glittering black vortex," he whispers to himself at the revelation.

I'm still staring at the wall, doing everything in my power to avoid the distraction ogling over my hair color. I feel the gentle caress of a finger hook under my chin, tugging me to look up at him. My eyes stay glued to the wall as long as possible, but they betray me at the last second, flinging to lock with the ones staring into my soul.

He's looking at me with curiosity, like he can't quite figure me out. We stay like that, our breaths labored, the only noise filling our ears for what feels like minutes. He's staring so intently at me, and I don't think he's blinked once.

Finally, he breaks the silence. "These storm cloud eyes remind me of a distant memory I can't quite seem to place," he whispers to himself. He blinks, and his hard exterior slips back in place so easily.

Still gripping my chin, he pushes it to the side to expose my bleeding ear. "I'm just going to clean this up and add some ointment so it doesn't risk infection. I'll wrap some gauze on it to stop the bleeding from getting everywhere."

He's all business now, sticking to the basics and treating me like any other contestant. Am I, though? Does he sneak into other contestants' rooms to check on them? To tend to their wounds? I sure know Aeron has many wounds that could use tending to tonight.

Hade goes to work dabbing my ear with a wet cloth, cleaning the blood away. I let out a hiss when he gets close to the cut, and he lightens his touch. He lays a container on the bed next to me, unscrewing the lid and swiping a glob of ointment out with his finger. He leans in closer, ever so gently applying the ointment all over.

As soon as the cool gel hits my skin, I relax into the bed at the comfort it brings me. It's soothing and must have some type of numbing properties, because the sharp sting lessens to a dull ache.

Hade must sense my change in mood, because he hums to himself, clearly satisfied. My eyelids start to grow heavy from the strain of today's activities and the gentle way I'm being taken care of for the first time in months.

"Does that feel good?" Hade prods. My only response is a soft moan at the fast-acting ointment. The outside world starts to fade as I happily seek out the peace my brain is desperate for the rare occasion on which sleep finds me. I don't fight it right now, though. Right now, I surprisingly feel comfortable in Hade's care. Add it to my long list of things I need to figure out for another day. Right now, all I want to do is sleep and fall into blissful nothingness.

"Are you still with me, Nyxi?" he asks softly.

"Mmmhhhmm," I mumble.

My body feels like it's floating off the bed towards a happier place, a dream. I feel Theo curl me into his chest, but instead of his usual scent of sunshine and fresh air, he smells like sandalwood and smoke. I hear a blanket sliding down the bed as I nuzzle closer into Theo's warm chest, cocooning myself so he can never leave me again. The mattress dips under me as I'm lowered gently to the bed, the blanket sliding over me like a warm hug. Theo's hand, which is normally smooth, now feels calloused as he pushes the hair out of my face and bends down to drop a kiss to my head.

"Sweet dreams, *Nyxi*."

Of course, even in my dreams, this saint of a man takes care of me. I feel his shallow breaths fan over my cheek, warming me from the inside out. "Thank you for loving me, Theo," I mumble before everything fades to black.

Chapter
Fourteen

HOLY SHIT, I DON'T THINK I'VE EVER SLEPT MORE SOUND THAN I DID last night. I don't remember falling asleep, or even getting into bed. The last thing I remember was Hade cleaning up my ear, and then it's all fuzzy. Clearly, exhaustion took over, and I dragged my body up to my pillow and thoroughly knocked out. I do, however, remember a faint dream involving Theo and it leaving a warm fuzzy feeling behind. That is the only time I get to be with Theo now: in my dreams.

Morning sun streams through my window, which means I must have accidentally slept through the rest of yesterday, including bathing and dinner. It looks like someone attempted to bring me dinner—I spot a plate sitting beside my bed. My guess would be on Des, her nurturing personality always shining through.

My stomach growls in protest as I eye the plate and mull over how foul it would be to take a little nibble to satisfy the demon inside me before washing up. I reach to snag something off the plate, which releases a pungent odor from under my armpit, and I physically gag. Forgoing the idea of eating, I decide a bath is a better option.

I feel refreshed and in good spirits after a full night's rest as I hop out of bed. The smell of old blood and sweat hits my nose, putting a halt to said happiness. I positively stink. I'm still wearing the sparkling bodysuit Des made me from yesterday, which surprisingly was very comfy to sleep in.

Gripping the zipper, I slid it down to my navel, exposing more of my cleavage. A knock at my door has my head snapping up as the handle twists and the door slides open. Before I can do anything to cover my body, Aeron waltzes in.

"Just came to see if our little sparring session scared you off, since you failed to show up for dinner last night." He takes a step inside without even asking, and his eyes widen with shock, dilating with unguarded need as he takes in my cleavage almost exploding out of my outfit.

I immediately pull my arms to cover my chest the best I can, but it only shoves my boobs up further, making them appear to double in size.

If there are any gods up there listening, what did I do to deserve this? Haven't I suffered enough in life as it is?

I awkwardly stand there as I track Aeron's eyes moving from my eyes to my exposed cleavage, trying to decide what he's more interested in.

I glare at him. "Ever heard of knocking?"

The side of his lip quirks up. "Technically, I did knock first."

I roll my eyes. "Let me rephrase myself. Ever heard of asking if you can enter someone's *private* room before barging in?" I grit out.

"Hmm, let me think." He taps his chin. "Nope." He smiles and takes a step closer. "I think I much prefer walking in to find you in this tight little number acting all shy in front of me when in reality, I know the girl beneath begs to come out and play."

I bite my lip at his bold accusation. I'm not blind, and I can admit Aeron screams sex appeal, and I'm sure he would be fun to play around with, though his cockiness only pushes me farther away from him. I live to knock men like him off the pedestal they put themselves on. It truly is my favorite pastime.

I take a step closer to him. "Is that so?" I purr. The gleam in his eyes indicates I have him exactly where I want him. I push up on my toes, leaning forward into his face. He leans in to match my pursuit, closing his eyes and licking his lips.

I hover my lips over his and whisper, "Aeron?" His responding yes is immediate, fanning across my lips. "Get the fuck out of my room so I can bathe," I whisper as I drive my knee up, crushing his balls as hard as I can.

He grunts painfully and doubles over in shock. I take a step back and smile sweetly down at him. "Maybe this will teach you not to barge into my room next time. I really should have grown up in Enlightened Sector with all these lessons I've been teaching you." I giggle as I stride to the door, gesturing for Aeron to get the hell out.

Aeron gathers his wits—and balls, checking to make sure they are still attached to his body—then stands to his full height and flashes me that vicious, shit-eating grin he loves to wear so often. Walking over to my door, he grabs my hand and plants a kiss on top. "You know it only turns me on when you're feisty." He winks and strides out the door, calling out over his shoulder, "It's always a pleasure, Nyxi."

I slam my door with extra umph, hoping Aeron hears it all the way down the hallway. Good riddance, if you ask me. I should have pummeled him harder, but my stench was starting to get to me, and even though Aeron annoys the shit out of me, I'd rather not have him smelling the awful odors coming off me. To be fair, part of the blood still splattered on my skin belongs to Aeron, so the stench is partly his fault.

Discarding my suit, I saunter into my washroom and start the tub, turning it as hot as it can go. Vagrant has subpar plumbing, and most days, the best we have is water slightly above room temperature.

Steam billows from the tub as I attempt to run a brush through my unruly hair. The more I tug, the more it seems to tangle. Grunting, I decide to discard the brush, sliding into the now-full bath to attempt to detangle it in the water.

I hiss at the scorching water. After adjusting to the heat, I relax my shoulders as I slide lower into the tub until my chin hits the water.

I sit like this for far too long, my eyes closed and my mind racing like it always does when left in the quiet of my own thoughts. Physically, it's silent, but inside my head, it feels like raging rapids that crash over boulders into giant, angry waves.

Hollow, that's what I am.

A shiver climbs up my spine, and I notice the water has gone cold. That happens a lot these days, getting lost in my own head and losing track of time. Tipping my head back, I fully submerge it in the frigid water, sending a shock to my nervous system, a much needed shock to my brain.

I spend more time than I would like washing and detangling my hair until I can easily comb my fingers through my long, black locks. I double wash my body, making sure every speck of odor, blood, and dirt is banished from my skin.

I opt for simple black pants, peppered with pockets down each side, that I tuck into black combat boots. I pair it with a white cotton shirt tucked into the waistband of my pants. I fasten my dagger necklace around my neck and weave my hair back into a simple braid, pulling my two front curls out so they frame my face.

A knock sounds on my door, and I pray it's not Aeron back for round two. Walking to my door, I cautiously open it. A genuine, easy smile spreads across my face when Winston comes into view—that is, until I see he's holding a fucking orange...again.

This time, though, the culprit has decided to peel the delicate skin, leaving it bare for me.

How kind…not.

Imagining a big, broody Hade delicately peeling an orange this morning brings a giggle vibrating up my throat. I picture him sitting there, attempting to stab his short, stubby nails into the peel, how his giant calloused hands probably engulfed the orange, making it even more difficult for him. But what drifts to the forefront of my mind the most is the idea that Hade was thinking about *me.*

"It was kind of the little rascal to peel it for you this morning at least." Winston strides into my room, his signature rosy round cheeks perched halfway up his face in a giant smile. "Got yourself a secret admirer, do ya?"

I roll my eyes and let out a loud sigh, waving my hand in the air. "Something like that."

He extends his hand out, attempting to give me the expertly peeled orange. I shove it back towards his chest, which only makes him smile wider as he gently rips off a wedge, popping it into his mouth. He chomps down hard, which makes some of the juice squirt out of his mouth to land right on my cheek. He winces a little and swipes his finger across my skin, collecting the runaway juice before he sucks it right off his finger. He sheepishly smiles at me. "Can't let any go to waste. This stuff is like gold to me."

I'm stunned at first but then relax my shoulders and let myself have a normal interaction with another human for once. I shake my head at him. "Never a dull moment with you, Win."

His eyes sparkle with pure happiness, not giving room for any other emotion to crest. "My daughter used to call me Win if I wasn't listening to her or giving her enough attention." He beams at me. "I haven't been called that name in too many years, and it's a damn shame." He freezes for a minute, looking lost in a memory, a happy one.

"How do you do it?" I question in a soft tone.

He looks at me in confusion. "Do what, little lady?"

I nervously chew on my bottom lip, grinding my sweaty palms together, which always seems to happen when I talk about this. "Seem so happy all the time. Go on with your life like you're okay...like nothing has changed."

The room is silent.

"I don't think I will ever be okay," I whisper.

He nods thoughtfully a few times and then turns serious for once, almost in *understanding.*

"I won't lie to you, it never goes away, the pain. It will dull, though, enough that instead of it being a sharp pain constantly digging its claws into you, those pangs of grief turn into good pangs. They show up as happy memories and in people who remind you of them."

He taps my chest right above my heart. I realize then I bring him happy pangs. He said I reminded him of his daughter when we first met, and now, I know what that moment truly meant to him. It means *everything.*

"You need to let go and release the pain into the world, let it bear the weight of it for you. That's when you can start to heal. The wound will only patch itself, though; it will never fully heal. That patch will be what saves you, letting you start living your life again. It will allow you to seek out the *happy pangs.*"

I smile at him in understanding, hoping one day, I will have the strength to let go of it all. The pain. The heartache. The black void growing inside me. Knowing another person is capable of it pushes me to attempt the same.

"Find those happy pangs, little lady." Winston gently squeezes my shoulder, and I give him a soft smile in return.

"I'll try my best, *Win.*"

Chapter
Fifteen

BEADS OF SWEAT CRAWL DOWN MY FOREHEAD AND THE BACK OF MY neck as I pepper the sandbag with a combination of punches and jabs. There's something therapeutic about beating up an inanimate object for two hours straight, purging every emotion from my head out through my fists. My mind has shut off, my body taking over in a therapeutic sense.

I'm alone again in the corner of the Bubble, keeping my focus on myself for the Crucible. No boys. No distractions. Just me and my fists. We are free to train as we please during this week, and I plan to practice a new technique each day so I feel well rounded.

Yesterday, I focused on target practice, and today, I decided to brush up on my hand-to-hand combat. Even though I beat Aeron yesterday, it's not lost on me that I did have to cheat my way through it. Competing against men who are much bigger and stronger than me is going to be a challenge, but if I work on smart moves and quick jabs, I should have a fighting chance.

My knuckles are red and raw, my core aches, and my arms feel like noodles, limp and tired by my sides. I am thoroughly spent.

Looking around the arena, I take in each of my competitors, dotted around the Bubble, working on different things. I catch Jade and Tank sparing on the opposite side, which is comical, seeing as Tank towers over Jade's small frame. She seems to be holding her own, though, as I catch her slide between Tank's legs and jab her elbow into the back of his knee, making him fall to his knees.

I catch Sierra's arrow flying through the air, hitting a perfect bullseye. Looking back at her, I notice her eyes have been closed the whole time. She opens her eyes, flings her long red locks off her shoulder, and nocks another arrow in her bow lighting fast. It shoots off just as fast, barreling through the air. I hear wood splitting as her second arrows rips through the end of the one in the bullseye, perfectly splitting it in half.

Expert with a bow and arrow, great.

Cartwell's bright blue hair snags my attention next as I squint, trying to decipher what he's conjuring up in his corner. He's waving his arms in a sweeping motion, dragging sand back over a pit in the ground next to him. Walking a little closer, I realize he's covering up little wooden sticks he has hand carved into very sharp spikes. There has to be at least fifty of them protruding from the ground, all wedged close together. When the hell did he even have enough time to carve all those?

Master at making death traps, awesome.

As I walk to the edge of the Bubble, my foot catches on something, making me stumble before catching myself on the force field. No, not something—someone. The sand below me starts to wiggle to reveal a youthful boy's face. *Hudson.*

He has to be no older than ten years old, and for the life of me, I haven't figured out why any family would let someone so young enter themself into the Crucible.

Kneeling, I grab his hand and help him up as sand rolls off his body. "Sorry, buddy, I didn't see you there."

He smiles up at me with a goofy grin, his front two teeth missing. "That's the point!" The gap in his teeth gives him an adorable lisp when he talks. His light blond hair is caked with muddy sand, making it look a medium brown. "I've been working on my camouflage skills." A glob of spit flies through his tooth gap, landing on my chest.

He's painted his entire body perfectly to match the multicolored speckled sand around him to the point that I didn't even see him. It truly is impressive. The only dead giveaway is his deep blue ocean eyes that I could spot from the opposite side of the arena.

I let a warm, friendly laugh escape my throat. "I can see that. Looks like you perfected your skills, little man."

He fist pumps in triumph. "You think tomorrow, I will be able to paint myself to blend into the Bubble's wall?"

I ruffle his hair, muddy sand flying everywhere. "I think you can do whatever you put your mind to."

His grin takes over the entirety of his face as he lists off materials he'll need for tomorrow. I actually don't doubt he could blend himself into the wall with how he made himself disappear into the sand. That, and he's from Visionary Sector, which houses some of the most creative people in all of Fallout.

I leave Hudson to his thinking as I round the Bubble in search of Rayah. I spot her bouncing pink curls a little ahead of me, so I lengthen my strides and come up behind her.

"What are you working on?" I question her.

She about jumps out of her skin and whirls around, holding a throwing star in a very shaky hand. "*Flowers*, you scared the poop out of me, Nyxi." She places her other hand over her chest to calm her racing heart.

"What's with the whole flower thing?" I prod.

She lets out a loud huff and rolls her eyes. "Mama always told me proper ladies never curse, and if I ever wanted to be wedded off, I needed to mind my mouth." She giggles to herself. "I guess I started saying flowers instead of the real word as an inside joke with myself, and, well, it just kind of stuck."

I smile at her and wink. "I like it!"

Her face lights up at that and solidifies to me that I'm sure this girl has never had anyone on her side. Maybe becoming friends with Ray will help us both find some happy pangs, or at the least, dull the sharp pains I know we both harbor.

"What were you practicing before I about scared you to an early grave?" I look around her shoulder to find a target with throwing stars littered in the sand around it.

She grunts, growing irritated. "Well, I was trying to work on using these little flower looking blade things, but for the life of me, I can't get them to work." She nods to herself in thought. "I think they are defective. Yup, that definitely has to be the issue." She smiles to herself happily at the conclusion.

"Wrong," I say in a nonchalant voice as I grab her wrist, dragging her arm up to hold the star between us. She sputters in embarrassment and starts to cocoon herself away from me.

I curse under my breath as I soften my face and look at her, proving to her I'm not a threat. "Sorry, I just meant there's nothing wrong with the weapon, just how you're holding it." She offers me a small, shy nod, giving me permission to continue.

"For starters, this is called a throwing star." I point at the blade in her hand, tapping each of the six points. "Your first issue is that you are holding it wrong." I notice little cuts all over her hands from the points.

Prying her palm open, I take the blade to demonstrate the correct form. "You were wrapping your entire palm and fingers around the blades, hence all the cuts and missed throws." I twist the star sideways and pinch one of the points between my thumb and pointer finger. "This is a better way to hold it. Fewer cuts, more accuracy."

Ray smiles at me in thanks and reaches to take the star back, replicating the grip I just showed her. "I guess it does feel better to hold it this way, but I still like calling them flower blades." She giggles to herself and turns to face the target.

I walk up behind, grabbing her shoulders. "Line your elbow up with the target, draw the star—I mean, flower—back to your ear, and then let her fly." I pat her shoulder and take two *very* large steps back so I'm out of her danger zone.

"Okay," she says nervously, "here goes nothing." She draws her hand back to her ear and catapults her arm forward, releasing the star with a grunt. It spins through the air and lands on the outermost section of the target with a centimeter to spare.

"*Flowers*, that was amazing!" She jumps up and down, squealing as she runs to the target to collect all the stars scattered in the sand so she can go again.

I may have just created a monster. She lines back up in front of the target. I smile to myself as I watch her miss the next throw, but then she confidently lands the following two closer to the center of the target. It feels good to know she can now defend herself in the Crucible. She now has power for once in her life, and I think I just experienced a *happy pang* because of it.

I sit and watch Ray practice her throwing for the next hour, giving her tips along the way. Alliances are just as important as training in this game, so I don't mind using my time in the Bubble to strengthen them.

"Helping out our competition, Vagrant?" a deep rumble crawls its way up my neck. Goosebumps follow at the seductive tone, and I squirm under my skin at his closeness. I'm starting to think he's a moth and I'm the light he just can't seem to stop chasing.

"Just evening out the playing field and building alliances is all," I purr over my shoulder to him. I feel him inch a little closer until his chest is pressed against my slick, sweaty back. My heart rate picks up as I feel his warmth seep through my shirt, searing my skin.

A sharp sting zaps my ear. "Such a greedy girl. Was one alliance not enough for you?" His voice has dropped an octave, rumbling from his chest right next to my face.

My brain short circuits as I nervously try to gather my wits. "D-did you just…bite my ear?" I sputter in shock, my voice wobbly. Ray is so wrapped up in her new *flower blade* throwing skills, she hasn't even noticed our duo has now turned into a trio.

"I'm a famished man, Nyxi. You taste absolutely divine, by the way." He smirks down at me, and I think I have fully gone into shock now. "Just making sure everyone knows what's *mine* in this competition." He leans in closer, whispering the words slowly in my ear.

A commotion draws my attention to the other side of the Bubble, where I find a seething, furious Hade staring directly at us.

I was so wrapped up in working with Ray, I had no idea Hade was even in here. He's a glistening, beautiful beast slicked with sweat, the depiction of a life altering deity if they were to live among us. My breath hitches as I greedily drink in his shirtless, chiseled torso. The tattoos on his arm wrap over his shoulder and down the side of his chest, making my mouth dry up. I'm suddenly parched and wouldn't mind drinking a tall glass of Hade to quench my thirst.

Have a little self-control, Nyxi… Maybe just half a glass.

Aeron turns with that shit-eating grin on his face and gives Hade a small, taunting wave. It clicks then, the performance he was putting on. Aeron knew exactly what he was doing and that we had a certain audience watching us. He was making a show of it, of *us*, ruffling feathers like always.

I lean in closer to Aeron, making our bodies flush. "I belong to no one. The dirt under my nails holds more interest to me than the two brain cells rolling around in that head of yours." I tap his shoulder like a mother would to console her child.

A wolfish grin takes over Aeron's face as the ground around us practically trembles. "You know what that fiery little mouth of yours does to me. Don't start something you aren't willing to finish for me...or with me, if you want." He winks, and flames lick at my reddening cheeks.

The ground trembles even closer to us now as heavy breathing floods the air. My focus remains on Aeron as I cock my arm back quickly and slam my fist into the side of his face, his head flying sideways with a loud crack from my knuckles.

Fuck me, that hurt.

Aeron shuffles backwards, his lip now sporting a bloody cut. His face remains smug as he chuckles at me. "A little rougher foreplay than I'm used to, but if you're into that sort of thing, I could oblige."

Narrowing my eyes at him, I cock my arm back in threat, making him raise his hands in surrender. "Maybe next time, you'll learn not to open your mouth so I don't have to shut it for you. If you needed help learning social cues, you just had to ask." Now I'm the one with the smug smile as I track a dribble of blood from his lip down to his shirt.

"Making me bleed twice in one week. One would start to assume you might have a kink." The ground vibrates so hard, I wobble, getting ready to teach Aeron another lesson, but someone beats me to it.

Aeron is violently ripped off his feet by the collar of his shirt, which starts to split down the front. Hade pulls Aeron's face within inches of his, baring his teeth in a fierce scowl. He's seething for Empress knows why this time. He's growling again, except this one actually sounds like an animal foaming at the mouth. I feel it deep in my stomach as little flutters float down my center. All the while, Aeron continues to smile back at Hade, not a single ounce of fear showing.

"Are you blind? It seems to me like you have the wrong culprit here. I'm the one sporting a bloody lip from that spicy little demon over there." Aeron flicks his pointer finger at me, drawing Hade's attention.

"Say the word, and I'll turn him into nothing, Nyxi." Hade's threat spears me right in my ice cold heart, shattering a thin layer.

"Uhhh…" My mind is mush, no words coming out, and I feel like I'm back in school, learning how to form complete sentences. I feel like an owl, my head spinning in a dizzying commotion over these men. Or more accurately, *this* man. What is he getting at here? Why does he care?

What is going on in that pretty little head of yours, Hade?

Aeron crosses his arms, the perfect picture of nonchalant, as he hangs in the air by his shirt, which is still slowly ripping down the front.

"Again, why would you need to do anything to me at all? She's the one who ruined my pretty face." Aeron pathetically pouts now, pointing to his gushing cut.

Hade drops Aeron back on his feet and takes a large step back, acting disgusted to be standing near someone so below him. "I have no doubt it was well deserved. I'm just here to finish the job."

Holy shit.

Aeron scoffs, taking a step forward and breaking into Hade's personal bubble, a single finger on his chest. "I don't see you finishing any other competitors' jobs for them, hmmm?"

This is Hade's tipping point. He takes a step forward, pressing his chest to Aeron's, looking down at him. "My job is to protect *every* competitor here so the Crucible is a fair playing field. She is not *special* to me; she is just a part of my job. If you'd quit eye fucking her and touching her without her permission, then I wouldn't have to waste *my* valuable time putting *you* in your place."

Not special. Ouch.

I let out a long sigh. "Are you two idiots done insulting me yet, or do you need to fight it out?" I say it as a joke, but when both their eyes light up, I groan internally. I see their wheels turning. "That was hypothetical. I wasn't actually suggesting you two fight."

Ray now stands by my side, joining in on the commotion with giant, excited eyes. "Not you too," I whisper to her as I catch the side of her lip tug up in a smirk.

"I wouldn't want to ruin the Cardinal's big, scary reputation by knocking his ass out," Aeron challenges Hade, narrowing his eyes and egging him on.

"Really? Because I wouldn't mind finishing what Nyxi started on that so-called pretty face of yours. Only difference is, Nyxi would only cause temporary damage. What I plan to do would make permanent alterations."

Yup, there's definitely steam coming out of Hade's nose now. So help me Empress, what did I get myself into? The sight of two very attractive men fighting over me might be going straight to my head, because why has my heart rate picked up from a flutter to barreling towards a heart attack? Okay, maybe they aren't actually fighting *over* me, but a girl can dream.

Licking my suddenly dry lips, I nuzzle closer to Ray as I take in both men. Hade's back muscles ripple with energy that blinds me as sun streams down, illuminating the sheen of sweat on his skin, making him sparkle. The things I would do to drag my nails down his…

Where the hell did that come from, Nyxi?

Blaming my delusion on exhaustion and training all day, I clear my thoughts and look over to Aeron. While he is smaller than Hade, he is still all man, packed with muscle, with a jaw that could cut wood. He is attractive in all senses of the word.

The two stare intensely at one another, but they don't exchange another word. Aeron breaks eye contact and drags his eyes over to me. Now, I truly think I'm going delusional, because I imagine black tendrils of smoke swirling around Hade's body. Nope, not delusion…*magic*.

"You're losing control, Cardinal. Do you always leak smoke reeking of death when two competitors look at each other?" Aeron drags his eyes from mine, landing back on Hade's intense ones.

"If you don't want today to be your last alive, Gavis, I suggest you shut the fuck up and walk away now. I won't apologize or feel a single ounce of remorse for the things running through my head. Lucky you, it's my day off, so I have all the time in the world to make sure that *pretty* face of yours is unrecognizable and buried so far in the ground, even the memory of you will be lost for the rest of time." Hade words are harsh, but the calmness overtaking his body makes my skin crawl more than his threats.

On cue, my stomach belts out a loud rumble. Clearing my throat, I attempt to break the tension I can physically taste. "Hate to butt in here, but my stomach is in need of assistance. It's dire, really." I raise my voice. "Life or death type of situation, and would you look at that, Winston isn't here yet to take me back."

It's the last thing I possibly want to ask, but I would do anything to break up this nightmare of a situation. "Umm…I know it's your day off, but would you be able to escort me back to the castle so I can tame the growling demon inside me?"

My nails have magically appeared in my mouth as I nervously nibble on the ends. A bead of sweat collects on my forehead and takes off down the side of my temple, collecting in my eyebrow. Hade tracks it the entire way down my face until his piercing eyes snap to mine. His eyes don't look like opposites right now—they both have taken on an inky black shade portraying a promise of death. He looks lost in a blood thirsty haze, but as his eyes take in my steely gray ones, his soften and return to their original colors.

Interesting.

"Another time then." Aeron pats Hade's shoulder and strolls away like nothing ever happened, the picture of indifference.

I can see the dilemma in Hade's head, the primal need to purge his anger like it's physically hurting him to hold back. To my surprise, he stays put. The swirling black tendrils retreat within him. He blinks a couple times and takes a deep inhale, scenting something that seems to peak his interest...a lot. His eyes narrow on me slightly, looking at me puzzled.

My stomach lets out another aggressive scream, which snaps him out of his spiraling thoughts. "Let's get you fed. *Nightmare,* indeed," he grumbles. With that, he walks past me, expecting me to follow without another word.

This man is so hot and cold. Trying to wrap my brain around what just happened, I stand there for a few seconds. I can't seem to come up with a single reason for what just transpired, though. Turning around, I jog to catch up with Hade, who is already half-way across the Bubble.

"You have some explaining to do, *Death Reaper.*" I throw his ridiculous nickname back at him, just as he had done to me. If he doesn't want to play nice, then neither do I.

I double the length of my strides to keep pace with him and his monstrously long legs. I'm gasping for air by the time I circle in front of him and start to walk backwards. He won't even look at me, though; he just continues to walk, a blaze of fire in his wake.

"Si—"

Hade's eyes snap to mine, cutting me off before I can finish my sentence. "Don't you dare."

I feign innocence. "What, Hadey boy?" I narrow my eyes at him. "Don't dare what? You have no idea what I was about to say."

He knows damn well I was about to call him sir, one of his least favorite things I love to do. Still, I would rather have this side of Hade than the one who looked like he was about to blow the force field right off the top of the Bubble if he thought about Aeron for one more second. This side of Hade, I can deal with.

He grunts and clenches his jaw. "Now is not the time to be pushing my buttons. You have no idea what I'm capable of doing right now."

Now, he has my full attention. I lower my voice so only he can hear me. "And what if I want to find out *exactly* what you're capable of? What then?"

My breaths turn erratic, or maybe his does as heavy breathing rings out around us. Mine is heavy from the jog to catch up to him...at least, that's what I tell myself.

We've both halted our steps, and the world around us fades to the background. The only thing I see and hear is him. His bare chest rises and falls in a harsh cadence. His jaw ticks when I drag my bottom lip between my teeth, letting it out with a slow *pop*.

"Nyxi," he growls in warning, his voice lower than I've ever heard.

"Yes?" I ask on a breath, my heart coming to a full stop.

He takes a deep breath, pinching the bridge of his nose. "Your ride is here." And then, he's gone, just a figment of my imagination left in his wake.

"You ready to head back, little lady?"

Winston.

Chapter
Sixteen

AFTER SCARFING DOWN HALF OF LUNARIA'S FOOD SUPPLY, I'M BACK IN my room, bathed and thoroughly bored out of my mind. Like me, the other contestants have retired to their rooms to rest up for another long day of training tomorrow.

My mind is racing, an untamable beast as I flop like a fish on my bed, trying to seek comfort. I should have known my body would only allow one solid night's rest before it resorted back to its specialty: a fitful sleep.

Huffing, I throw my blanket off and stand to stretch. Maybe moving around will help tire me out. I start by pacing from wall to wall until I've lost count how many laps I've completed. Still, my mind is fully awake and ready to play.

Next, I try some high knees, hoping it will jostle my brain into exhaustion. No such luck. I tackle some lunges next, but then I realize my balance is severely lacking. I turn to face my bed, so when I lunge forward, I can balance my hands on the edge as I lower myself down.

I step into a lunge, disappearing slightly under the bed as I grip the edge with my hands, lowering myself into a deep lunge. As soon as the heel of my foot hits the cold, wooden floorboard, I'm greeted with a loud *creak*.

Not thinking anything of it, I bring my foot back to center and lunge out with my opposite leg in the same motion. This time, the floorboard creaks, but it also slides the smallest amount to the side.

Weird.

Bending down, I use the small amount of light filtering in through the stained glass window to peer under my bed. Blindly feeling around with my hand, I pat and prod the floorboards, snagging a few splinters as I go.

My nail slides into a small groove between two of the boards that would be impossible to notice unless you were looking for it. Wedging my nail under, I pull up, and the floorboard easily moves away to reveal a cavity.

I know I shouldn't be snooping, but I can't help myself as I flatten my body and slide under the narrow bed frame. It's so dark under here, but my eyes eventually adjust to reveal a midnight black, double edged sword with worn black leather wrapped around the handle.

Reaching in, I wrap my hand around the handle, my fingers perfectly fitting into the worn grooves left in the leather. The sword hums to life as soon as my skin makes contact. The hum tickles up my arm and spreads across my body, making me vibrate as I slide back onto my feet.

It feels familiar, like an old friend calling my name, begging me to hold it. My whole body and even the bed starts to shake from the sheer energy it's emitting, growing with intensity. I immediately release it, flinging it across the room, *thunking* as it bounces on the floor.

Shit, Nyxi. Could you make more noise?

I let out a swift curse under my breath, praying no one heard. I'm thankful Winston trusts me enough to leave me alone; I just pray no one else heard the chaos.

I suddenly feel empty with the loss, like a limb has been severed off. I'm clueless as to whose hidden treasure I've found, but I can tell it's very powerful and, most likely, very important. I'm sure it's hidden to insure it doesn't fall into the wrong hands—or maybe it's simply a lost treasure.

An idea pops into my head, and I sway over to my wardrobe to collect one of my spare shirts. Carefully, without touching the sword, I wrap the shirt around the handle and pick it up again. As hoped, no hum takes over my body.

Looking it over, I flip it over, taking in the detail of this beautiful creation. Even though the sword looks as old as time, the blade seems carved to perfection, not a dull section to be found.

Squinting, I focus in on a small carving just above where the leather wraps around the handle. Two circles are etched into the metal, smaller circles carved within them. Taking a closer look, I notice they aren't circles, but instead depict some type of unique black eyes. They look animalistic, maybe even birdlike. The carving is so old, it's faded, making it almost impossible to decipher.

Bending down, I carefully lower the blade into the cavity and expertly replace the floorboard exactly how I found it. I line up the grooves in the wood so you can't tell it's been tampered with.

There's a dull ache in my head now, and I feel drained, exhausted. The pacing and high knees must have finally caught up to me, my limbs heavy and limp. I drag my body up into bed, my head barely hitting the pillow before I'm drifting off into heavy sleep.

Chapter
Seventeen

Judgment day is finally upon us. This week flew by in a blur. My muscles ache from long training days, pushing my body to its limit. None of that matters, though. What matters now is the performance I'm to put on for the Empress and all of Fallout and Lunaria. It's crucial to rank high for the start of the Crucible. Getting the extra help in the last two rounds could mean life or death.

Des woke me up bright and early to prepare for today. Something about looking my best will make me perform my best. She braided my hair back and helped shove all my limbs into the tight bodysuit she made me.

Winston arrived shortly after to escort me to the Bubble. His usual cheery demeanor was a bit sour today as he nervously chewed on each orange wedge he stuffed into his mouth. He forgoes asking me if I want the little abominations that keep magically showing up, now snatching it from in front of my door, devouring it happily. I expected Hade to tire of this little prank, but sure enough, since the night of my confession, a peeled orange has appeared every morning without fail. It's admirable how committed he is to the bit. Neither of us have mentioned it, and I think it might stay that way forever.

Winston was extra quiet on the journey here. He gave me a quick but firm hug, wished me good luck, and slipped away into the shadows as my competitors arrived.

The arena is buzzing with life today, packed full of extra Vanquishers and Magicals setting up for each competitor's performance. We are given the choice of any weapons or materials to use during our performance.

Magicals have worked tirelessly all morning setting up a space specific to each competitor's needs, using objects and magic to make each area unique. I take in the ten specific setups, stretching my body in preparation.

"A double sided blade… That's the best you could come up with? I thought you were smarter than that," a gravelly voice grows from behind me as I bend, touching my hands to my feet, stretching out my hamstrings.

Ignoring the nosey voice, I stand tall and slide into a side lunge, bouncing slowly to deepen the stretch. Hade rounds my body in a flash, his face raging.

He narrows his eyes. "Are you just going to stand there and pretend I don't exist?"

Dragging my body up, I slowly sink into a deep side lunge on my opposite side, the perfect depiction of unbothered. "It appears so. Really great observational skills. Would you like me to ask the Empress to give you an award?" My response is smooth and nonchalant. If he wants to be an ass, I can be one too.

Straightening, I turn around and pull one arm across my chest, looping the other on top, pulling it tight to stretch. Hade grumbles, annoyed, to himself and rounds my body, annoyingly coming into view again.

"You will not impress the Empress, let alone all of Fallout and Lunaria, by simply using a measly, double sided blade. What were you thinking?" he seethes.

A lot of nice things before you arrived.

I decide to keep those words to myself, though. Dropping my arm, I pad forward, shoving my finger harshly into Hade's solid chest. My finger twitches slightly in pain, but I remain stoic. "I was thinking I wanted to use something no other competitor was using." I press my finger harder into his chest. "I was thinking I wanted a weapon with dual purpose, something quick to throw and easy to hit a target." I slam my finger into his chest one last time, inching closer to his pounding heart beneath my finger. "I was thinking this was my best bet at standing apart from my competitors, who, I will remind you, have trained their entire lives for this, unlike me."

I don't mean to let the last part slip, but Hade is so wrapped up in his confusing, overbearing fury, he doesn't take note. He looks at me with fire in his eyes, but I couldn't care less. I'm tired of being talked down to like a child, like I don't stand a chance at winning. Soon, they will all learn just how sharp my claws can be.

"If you'll excuse me, I have a ranking to attend." With that, I turn and strut off, lining up with the rest of my competitors and leaving a blaze of fire behind.

The air turns thick as my nerves zing over my skin with anticipation. We pull sticks to see what order we would perform in, and of course, in typical Nyxi fashion, I pull the shortest stick, meaning I go last. I'll just have to make a grand last impression.

The Empress enters last, dripping in gaudy red silk and jewels. She doesn't bother with theatrics or greeting us. She is not here to play nice; we are simply here to impress her.

No pressure.

The Bubble is dead silent as she walks in front of us, a Vanquisher following close behind, holding her gown so it won't drag across the sandy floor. As previously observed, it seems anywhere the Empress goes, so does her throne. She gracefully plops down in her oversized and exuberantly decorated chair that took multiple Vanquishers to drag inside.

With a nod from the Empress, Aeron steps forward to his dedicated space, commencing the ranking. An Illuminist stands next to him, his eyes cast over Aeron's entire space, committing his performance to memory to be replayed for all of Fallout and Lunaria later. Lining the entire outside perimeter of the Bubble, members of Lunaria peer in with anticipation.

Aeron grabs a giant sword off a table. Squaring his shoulders, he signals he's ready with a small nod, stepping into the center of his area. A second Vanquisher steps up, a young woman with soft features and smooth brown hair. Raising her hands in front of her, a blur of blue magic explodes from her palms, surrounding Aeron in seconds.

The sound of snarls and growls echo off the Bubble's walls as the magic takes shape into massive creatures full of sharp claws and teeth. Aeron spins, catching the first beast through its neck right before it's about to sink its teeth into his shoulder. The beast lets out a scream as Aeron pulls his sword from its limp body before it disintegrates.

Fascinating.

Giving him no time to regroup, another, larger feline beast jumps him from behind, slashing its claws across his back, leaving angry marks behind. He stumbles but pushes through, swinging his sword with immense strength and slicing the head right off the beast.

Two more beasts saunter towards him, and he runs at full speed, aiming for the one on the left. He dives to the side at the last minute, driving his sword across the under belly of the beast, gutting it. Using the dead beast as a step, he takes a running jump, pushing himself off it to land on the back of the other before he plunges his sword straight through its skull.

The crowd surrounding the Bubble claps and chants his name as he effortlessly gets up and bows. He beams, waving and smiling at all the women gushing over him.

If only I had a dick to gain me extra votes. Must be nice.

Hudson performs next, walking up to a table full of colored paste, explaining with his adorable lisp to the Empress that he made them using items found in nature. Swiping globs of paste, he coats his body with a speckled design, blending into the sand below him. After finishing, he lays flat on the sand and closes his eyes, disappearing completely.

The crowd erupts in claps and coos as he stands back up and shines them his toothless, adorable little grin, then trots away happily.

Tank woos the crowd next by slamming his giant fists repeatedly into a thick tree trunk a Vanquisher dragged in. In no time, he has the oversized log snapped in two like it was butter. Jade follows suit, showing off her agility by completing a miniature moving obstacle course blindfolded with perfect precision. Cartwell chooses his brainpower to show off, attaching some type of cord around his body and then touching it to the Bubble's force field. The wire draws the Bubble's magic down to wrap around Cartwell, creating a force field around him. He gestures to the Vanquisher to shoot an arrow at him, which bounces right off the forcefield around him, leaving him unharmed.

The rest of my competitors follow suit, showing off their larger than life skills. Rayah shows off her newly learned throwing star skills. Yazi knocks a Vanquisher's magic made arrow out of the air with a spiked club as they are continuously shot at him. Briar flings her axe through the air, perfectly hitting floating targets, while Sierra stacks three arrows perfectly in the center of one, each splitting the one before it in half.

I have no idea how I'm supposed to follow up any of that, but anger from Hade's comment lights a spark under my ass as I make my way to my dedicated area. The Empress looks bored, beyond ready to wrap this up so she can go do whatever it is she does.

Dragging my fingertips over the multiple S blades sitting on my table, I clutch the wrapped center of one and take a deep breath. A handful of stagnant targets are staggered in my space to aim at.

I hesitantly look around the small crowd left waiting for me to perform. Most have dwindled away to find more exciting things to occupy their time. I catch Hade standing alone to my right against the Bubble's wall, looking thoroughly bored and pissed off. A little closer, I spot a nervous looking Winston, who tries to give me a reassuring smile. My eyes snag on the handkerchief he's absent-mindedly fiddling with, and an idea takes flight in my mind.

Asking the Vanquisher in front of me if I can have a second, he nods, and I jog over to Winston, whispering into his ear. Agreeing, he hands me his handkerchief, adding a quick squeeze to my shoulder before I make my way back.

Committing the targets to memory, I drag the table holding the blades within reaching distance, spacing the blades out to make them easier to grab. I tie the cloth around my face, creating a makeshift blindfold. I have just enough blades as there are targets, with one extra to spare if I miss. I don't intend on missing, though, and have other plans in mind for the spare.

I hear the Empress growing impatient next to me, and my hand starts to tremble with nerves. "Today, *dear*." Her voice carries an edge, and I know it's now or never.

Taking a deep breath, I nod to the Vanquisher, signaling I'm ready to begin. Reaching out, I wrap my fingers around the first blade and visualize each target in front of me. One sits directly to my left, about ten feet away. There's one directly behind it, around twenty feet from me, with two more to my right sitting at the same distances. Lastly, three are placed in front of me about fifteen feet away, but they are stacked on top of each other.

I decide to move from left to right until I've worked my way through all the targets. I angle my body to what I think is the right distance to my left for the first close target. Drawing my wrist back, I fling the blade with medium effort.

The sound of my weapon hitting its mark puts a small, satisfied smile on my face, but it vanishes just as fast as I reach over to grab my next blade and aim it at the target behind. Hearing the clunk of my blade hitting true for the second time, I pluck three more blades from the table. Adjusting my body to face straight forward now, I fire off three blades back to back, making sure each one is aimed a little higher than the last. Three satisfying thuds ring out, confirming I hit each target.

Two targets remain to my right as I turn my body, praying I calculated the right distance. Swiping two more blades from the table, I let the last two fly, both whooshing before hitting their mark.

Now, for the grand finale. Calming my racing heart, I wrap my delicate fingers around the last blade. I hear whispers around me of people confused as to why I'm holding the extra blade.

Angling my body to face the Bubble's wall to my left, I draw my wrist back, flinging my arm forward with as much strength as I can muster. Eagerly ripping my blindfold off, I track the rogue blade through the air, ricocheting harshly off the force field and sailing back through the air in front of me. Dragging my eyes with it, just as I hoped, Hade still stands tucked away to my right in the exact place I last saw him.

To my surprise, he doesn't move an inch as the blade flies through the air. Curving down, it spirals right into the belt holding his sword to his body and rips clean through. His sword falls to the ground in a loud *clunk*. The entire time, Hade doesn't move an inch. His eyes remain intently locked on mine without even bothering to check if I've injured him. I can't tell if he truly fears nothing in life or is lacking brain cells. I don't allow the festering thought that he might fully trust me to sink its roots into my fragile heart. That is not a blow I could survive just yet.

A feral smile takes over my face as I blow him a kiss and saunter off to Winston to take me back to my room. Cheers erupt around the perimeter of the Bubble, and I almost think I hear a chuckle behind me as I skip out and back to the castle.

Chapter
Eighteen

"So...don't hate me, but I sort of ruined Theo's leather jacket." Des nervously paces the length of my room, fiddling with her hands as I lounge on my bed, reading a romance book she smuggled for me.

My heart comes to a complete stand still. "You what? Please tell me this is another one of your silly jokes." I've forgotten all about the love confession scene I was in the middle of reading and now stare intensely at Des, who looks like she's on the verge of fainting.

She takes two deep breaths and carefully contemplates how she wants to phrase her next sentence. "Umm, well, maybe *ruined* was the wrong word. Cut up is maybe a better option." Her voice pitches up at the confession.

There must be steam coming out of my ears now, because her face turns a bright shade of red and her chest heaves. "No, that definitely sounds worse than ruined. Ummm, repurposed... Yeah, that definitely sounds better."

I raise my eyebrows at her in question. "Explain, now!"

She nods to herself, and a bit of her never-ending confidence starts to shine through. "I think it would be better for me to show you rather than explain it." I nod in agreement, and she seems to smile. "So you know how I told you I've been working on a secret project? Said secret project was your outfit for tonight's ball marking the start of the Crucible. I wanted you to stand out, but I also wanted it to be special for you."

"Where does ruining Theo's leather jacket come into play?" I prod.

"The Empress always assigns a theme for the ball. This year, she has chosen Circus Extravaganza. I wanted to make you a custom, one of a kind piece. I was thinking a red and black color palette would be perfect. *Obviously,* I want you to stand out, so a red dress is a must. But then, I was trying to figure out how to incorporate black into it, and I remembered Theo's leather jacket." She nibbles her lip nervously. "Well, next thing you know, scissors appeared in my hand, and then they were chopping away at his jacket before I could stop myself and...ugh, I'll just show you." She turns to grab something from behind the changing screen, muttering under her breath, "Please don't hate me."

I'm up in an instant, running over to her as she pulls the creation out from behind the screen. I gasp. "Des..."

She drops her face into her hands, mumbling through her fingers. "You hate it, I knew it."

"Odessa, look at me right now!" I say sternly.

She slowly drags her face up to meet mine. "I give you full permission to hit me. Just avoid my face, please. It's my money maker." She stands stiff as a board, eyes closed and waiting for impact.

"I have no words," I whisper.

She peels one eye open, anxiously looking at me.

A single tear escapes down my cheek. "I love it. I couldn't think of a more fitting way to carry Theo's memory with me tonight. I confessed to you when we met that I would like to feel beautiful for the first time in my life. This creation, Des, is so much more than that. It's us woven together, something I can cherish forever. I could never repay you for this, even if I traveled through a million lives."

"I knew it!" Des beams under my praise. "I never doubted myself, not even for a second." She winks at me while patting herself on the back, and a small, breathy laugh escapes me. Leave it to Des to turn an anxious, emotional moment into a happy one. No, a happy *pang*.

Taking a step forward, I drag my fingers across the cherry-red silk fabric. It feels like butter between my fingers. The thin shoulder straps are made from dainty black chains connected to red silk triangle cutouts on each side. An intricate black leather corset curves under the breasts, made from Theo's jacket, taking up the middle portion and adorned with vertical bowing and crossed laces to hold its tight shape.

The delicate triangle breast sections are connected to the corset using black metal hoops across the bottom. Sewn into the bottom of the corset is more red silk that tapers tight at the hips and then pools out at the ground. Thigh high slits cut up both sides, making the center panel drape between the legs. Black, glittering feathers dance across the bottom of the hem, making it appear fluffy. The back of the corset has leather straps crisscrossed all the way down to hold it extra tight and push up the cleavage.

"How did you even come up with this design, Des?" She blushes hard now, soaking up every compliment I throw her way. I continue my hand down the dress to swipe against the leather corset, soaking in its familiar feel. Leaning forward, I deeply inhale the worn leather scent mixed with Theo's lingering scent and hum to myself. It smells as though he's standing here with me.

I close my eyes and picture him standing in front of me now, basking in his memory. What would he think of all this? Would he call me crazy? Silly? Maybe brave? Most likely all three, but even more, I know he would call me his princess. He'd make me feel like I was the only woman alive or dead who could hold his attention. My one in a million, my Theo.

"You're doing it again," Des grumbles next to me before continuing with her long speech about how this masterpiece came to fruition. "As I said earlier, every good creation starts with a color palette. I really wanted the piece to speak for itself, so I kept it limited so it wouldn't distract from all the details. I wanted it to be feminine but also sexy, with a little edge to match the circus theme."

She's talking with her hands now, and I bask in her excitement, in awe of the little things that bring her joy.

"Obviously, the only correct answer to portray sexy with a splash of edge is red silk paired with a corset." She points at my chest. "You know, to push your girls up. Then, from there, I just knew I had to involve a chain somewhere to edge it up. Next thing you know, I basically designed a dress to turn you into the goddess of sex. Tah-dah!"

I didn't think she could get any more animated, but now, she's flashing me some sort of jazz hands, slightly out of breath from word vomiting.

"I see." I slowly roll the words off my tongue.

Des smiles from ear to ear. "I just knew you would see my vision. It takes a genius to spot a genius. Oh, wait, there's more. I almost forgot the best part. The *accessories!*" she scream-sings in a wobbly tone that has me covering my ears.

She dashes back behind the screen, filling her arms with glittering items. She plops them onto the vanity with a loud *clink*. "At first, I was thinking long, elegant, silky gloves, but I just know all the other bitches will be wearing those, and we aren't going for tacky here. So, naturally, my brain went to a metal snake arm wrap embedded with black diamonds. This baby is going to be perfect."

Looking down, I slide my fingers over the rough diamonds covering the entirety of the black metal snake's back. It's shaped to look like it's slithering around someone's entire forearm, with its head resting flat just below the middle finger on the back of the hand, the tail ending just below the elbow, ensuring I can still bend my arm.

"This is stunning, Des. I'm surprised there were any diamonds left in Lunaria after you made my bodysuit."

She winks at me. "I'm pretty important around here. If I want something, I get it." She slides the next item into view. "I couldn't let your arm have all the fun, so I sort of made you a crown too."

My eyes pop out of my head when I take in the crown. "Won't the Empress be offended?"

She waves her hand in dismissal. "The Empress loves her themed balls. She would expect nothing less than perfection and class from each of her contestants. I wouldn't be surprised if she still thought this outfit wasn't expensive or on theme enough for her liking. You are now a reflection of her in a way, so the more diamonds the better."

I nod, trying to wrap my brain around it all. Just weeks ago, I was starving and sleeping on a makeshift pillow-bed in a crumbling, mold-infused shack. Now, I'm fed three times a day, sleeping on a huge, lush bed, and wearing a crown worth more coins than I've made in my entire career as a spy.

The crown sitting before me is like nothing I've ever seen. Almost every inch of it is covered in bright red rubies. The halo has a collection of gemstones creating a sea of red. Jutting up from the base are spike-like points, each housing a heart-shaped ruby at the top. It's the most eye-catching piece I've ever laid my eyes on.

Des moves in next to me, pointing at it. "It's not just any regular crown, though. That would be boring, don't you think?" She laughs to herself almost maniacally. "No, this is a magical crown. I had a Float imbue it with their flying magic, so it will hover just above your head, spinning like a carousel all night. Anywhere you walk, it will follow like an obedient pet. I'm a genius, I know." She squeals while she spins; at this point, nothing she does phases me. This is just how Des is, always a character.

"You're right. That is pretty genius." I shove my shoulder into hers playfully. "Honestly, I was getting a headache thinking about that stiff thing being pinned to my head all night. So, really, I should be thanking you."

"You know I love it when you praise me. Goes right to this big noggin of mine." She knocks her fist on the top of her head, and then her cheeks flush a rosy pink.

THREE KNOCKS RING OUT, AND I HEAR DES STRIDE OVER TO MY door, flinging it open. "What do you want?" She spits the words at the stranger who's now striding into my room. It can't be Winston, because those two are thicker than thieves, who also love to gang up on me with their silly little pranks involving oranges most of the time.

Gathering my dress, I step out from behind the changing screen at the same time as two sets of wide eyes land on me. The first is Des, who now looks like she's trying to hold back happy tears at her creation. The second is the thorn I can't seem to rid myself of: Aeron.

"Wow," he says under his breath, and I can't tell if this is another one of his snarky comments, or if he's being genuine for once.

Cautiously, I narrow my eyes at him. "Get all your crude comments out now so we can be done with it before we get to the ball."

"You look… I mean… Just wow. I think I might be speechless for the first time in my life. You look absolutely stunning." Aeron smiles, a genuine, soft smile, one I've never witnessed on his face and doubt I ever will again.

"You're being serious? Did you catch a cold that has turned you delirious? Des, feel his forehead and see if it's warm."

"Ha, ha, real funny. Can I not compliment a pretty lady when I see one?" he counters.

I raise my eyebrows at him. "Not if your name starts with an A and ends with an N."

"Well, then consider yourself lucky, because I'm feeling quite generous today. I came to ask if I could escort you to the ball. After seeing you in this dress, though, I think I would prefer to escort you home instead. That dress looks awfully hard to get off by yourself." He winks.

Rolling my eyes, I add, "And there's the asshole I know and loathe."

He smirks back. "You know you love it when I talk dirty to you."

"I feel like I'm disturbing whatever the heck is happening here. I just need to add Nyxi's finishing touches, and I'll be out of your hair. No ruining said hair or makeup until after she makes an appearance at the ball, though. I'm not trying to lose my job." Des glares at Aeron in her best stern look, but it still comes off cute and non-threatening.

I take in my reflection in the mirror above my vanity. With a heavy suggestion from me, we decided to keep my hair down so my back would be covered. I'm not in the mood to answer anyone's questions tonight. I know Des has seen my mangled back from helping me get dressed, but I appreciate that she hasn't questioned me on it.

My long, thick natural curls bounce down my back, the front two pieces braided back and joined together with a red ruby heart gemstone clip. Des also sprinkled mini red gems throughout my hair, making it glitter like the night sky. The crown now floats just a breath above my head, and I can feel the weight of its magic looming above me.

Using her Luster magic, Des painted a black heart around one of my eyes to match the circus theme. She lined the perimeter of the heart with tiny red gems, making my bright gray eyes pop against the harsh black. The rest of my makeup, she kept mostly simple, wanting the dress to be the center focus. She darkened and lifted my lashes, added a pretty blush to the apples of my cheeks, smoked out my eyes with black, and covered my lips in a bright red to match my dress.

Aeron wasn't wrong about needing help getting undressed tonight. The dress took both Des and I fifteen minutes to slide on and cinch tight to my body. I can hardly breathe, but I keep reminding myself it's like a firm hug from Theo.

Per usual, Des was correct—the corset has indeed pushed my breasts up, creating more cleavage than I thought possible for what I'm working with.

Des slides the jeweled snake up my arm, completing the look. I've never felt more beautiful, and for the most part, I'm comfortable. Besides the corset, the dress is smooth and soft against my skin, a black heeled slipper a cushion below my feet. My lean legs are on full display, sprouting out from each slit cut high into the fabric.

"One last thing," Des coos to me. Opening a drawer in my vanity, she pulls out a small black dagger, its handle covered in tiny red gems. "Beauty and death. The perfect combination." She leans in towards me, aiming the tip of the blade at my chest.

I take a stumbling step backwards. "Woah, where do you think you're putting that death contraption? I'm not in the market for losing a nip tonight."

Des releases a breathy laugh. "Relex, Sparkles. Do you trust me?"

I jab my finger towards her. "Not when you're pointing the tip of that dagger at my goods."

"*Sparkles*?" Aeron chimes in.

"I just like the way her nose scrunches up every time I call her that. Started when I dressed her in the diamond suit, and now, I can't seem to stop. It's just too much fun getting under her skin." A sinister look has taken over Des's face.

"Now *that*, I can get behind. I'd love to get under many things when it comes to her." Aeron's smirk could be seen all the way down in Fallout.

"Enough, you two. Can we get on with the show so I can enjoy what might be my last night alive?" I say it as a joke, but the air suddenly thickens. I smile at them, trying to lighten the mood, and for good measure, I add, "And, if anyone's getting under my skin tonight, it will be myself." I wiggle my fingers at them, which sends both into a howling fit of laughter.

Once Des recovers from her aggressively high pitched laughter and wipes the tears from her cheeks, she summons me with her finger. "Come here so I can finish you off and send you on your way."

A small laugh tries to make its way up Aeron's throat, but he catches it at the last second. "Didn't you hear her? She doesn't need our help finishing anything off tonight. She's got that covered." This makes Des gasp, realizing what it sounded like she was suggesting, giggling again as her cheeks redden with embarrassment.

"You two are no better than children, I swear." I step up to Des, trusting whatever she has planned with the dagger will be safe. Even though I told her I didn't trust her, I do. I know she would never intentionally do something to harm me. Maybe unintentionally with her clumsiness, but that's beside the point. "Go ahead, Des. I trust you."

She takes one step closer and wedges her finger between my cleavage and corset, feeling around. "Ah, there it is."

Peeking down, I notice a small pocket sewn into the underside of the corset, the perfect size to sheath a dagger. She brings the tip of the dagger close, and even though I see the pocket there, I still tense in anticipation. She slides the tip into the pocket, pushing it down until it's sheathed all the way to the red, jeweled handle. It's a statement: an accessory, but also a warning.

I love it.

"Perfect as always, Des." I pull her into a tight hug, which she returns with an even tighter grip.

"Can I have you as a handmaid too?" Aeron chimes in. "I got stuck with someone who has to be older than dirt."

"Hanz?" Des and I question at the same time.

"How did you know?"

I bend over giggling as Des gives me an *I told you so* look. Aeron just shakes his head, confused.

"Well, are you ready, my little circus Vagrant?"

I stride over to him, appreciating his bright red suit for the first time tonight, and link my arm with his. Standing together, we almost look like we planned matching outfits. That is the last thing on my mind, though, as we make our way out of my room and down the long, winding hallways to the first, and probably last, party I will ever attend.

Chapter
Nineteen

THE AIR WHOOSHES OUT OF MY LUNGS AS I TAKE IN THE GRAND BALL-room. There's controlled mayhem in every direction . The vaulted ceiling makes the space feel extra large, even packed with what has to be hundreds of citizens dressed to perfection in a sea of colors.

Where I come from, clothes have a purpose—for staving off the cold, covering skin from the blistering heat, or protection from harsh working conditions. But here in Lunaria, it's a statement of status and power, for entertainment and enjoyment.

Dresses are cut at odd angles and draped over limbs like walking art. It's fascinating to take in, along with their grand masks and accessories. Even the men showcase their style with velvety suits in dizzying patterns and shapes. Some suit coats are extra long, while others are half the length of a normal coat.

The ballroom is dripping in deep reds, accented with white and black. Tall tables are draped with red and white striped cloth, dotting the outer edge of the room. Guests mingle, leaning against them while sipping bubbling drinks.

The center of the room hosts a dance floor with a full sized circus tent blanketing it from above. An orb of light floats at the top of the tent, spinning and flashing lights across the dancefloor.

In the corner, a group of instrumentalists play. Circus themed performers are sprinkled throughout the room. Women with painted faces and scanty outfits float inside giant clear bubbles, performing tricks and spins for the guests below. A long, thin wire connects the walls, where two children balance, holding a Stretch as a jump rope. A third kid stands between them, jumping over the man stretched thin like taffy.

A Scorch makes me trip over my feet when he dashes in front of me, hoisted on stilts while juggling three balls of fire. There's magic manipulation infused in every performer, which makes my heart race. Danger lurks in every corner, but each performer is well practiced and in control. It's chaos in the best way.

I snatch a bubbling drink off a passing tray and take a long swig, downing half the drink in one go. The bubbles down my throat like popping candy, catching me off guard. I should be used to being surrounded by magic by now, but it still surprises me each time. The bubbles immediately send a wave of temporary euphoria through my body, making me burst out in uncontrollable laughter. Nothing is even funny, but my body rocks with laughter, and tears prick the sides of my eyes.

Aeron has already ditched me, off mingling with citizens to help with his standing in the Crucible. That is probably something I should be doing too, but I would much rather spend my night enjoying myself, stuffing my face with any and all magical food I can find. If tonight shall be my last, I want to go out with a full belly and a satiated soul.

I slowly take sips of my drink while standing on the outer edge of the room, attempting to avoid being taken out by wild performers or drunken guests. I spot a few of my competitors among the giant sea of partygoers. A few are grouped together while others stand alone, like me, in awe of the chaos unfolding around them.

I'm searching the crowd for bright pink hair when my eyes connect with the last person I wish to be ensnared by. Hade's eyes bore intensely into mine, even all the way across the room. The chaos melts away, and all the remains is *him*.

He's dressed up for the occasion, forgoing his usual guard uniform. Instead, he's sporting a perfectly tailored suit. It's plain black, paired with a white undershirt and black tie, and somehow, something so ordinary has never looked more enticing. It's tight in all the right places, accentuating his thick arms and legs, but not to the point that it looks too small. On anyone else, this outfit would make them blend into the crowd, but on him, it looks like he is the inventor of plain black suits. It's infuriating how good he looks.

His gray eye swirls with curiosity while his black eye whispers of death. I blatantly glare at him, promising death with my stare in return if he even tries to come near me. I'm still pissed at him for being such a controlling dick, acting as if I'm a child in need of guidance. To be fair, I'm sure he is pissed at me for blindly throwing my last blade at him and ruining his belt, but he can fuck right off for all I care. I won't let him ruin my night.

The corner of his mouth kicks up a miniscule amount at my threatening glare, and my traitorous bitch of a heart thumps loudly in my chest. His lip ticks up another notch, and I swear, the fucker can hear my rapid heart beating from across the room. I can tell it's amusing him. I wouldn't put it past him to have ears lurking in every dark corner of this room. Magic is a limitless avenue for him I envy.

Stomping my foot, I throw back my remaining drink in one gulp, catching sight of Aeron a little to my right. If he wants to play whatever game this is, then I can too. My childish heart knows the perfect way to piss him off.

My feet move of their own accord before my mind has finished hatching my plan. I giggle the entire way from whatever magic swirled in my drink. They deliver me right next to Aeron, who happens to be holding two fresh drinks while he talks to an older gentleman. The drink I just downed has emboldened me, and I reach forward, slipping my arm through Aeron's while grabbing one of the drinks from his hand.

"There you are. I've been looking all over for you. I see you found us some drinks." I plaster on a smile that could win me an award and cozy up next to Aeron, making it seem like we are more than friendly.

The glowing orb in the center of the tent flickers off for just a fraction of a second before regaining its full brightness. I can feel Hade's intense gaze burning a hole in the side of my face, but I pay him no heed.

Just to stir things up even more, I drag my thumb across the soft cushion of Aeron's bottom lip while blushing up at him. "Sorry, you had a little drink left on your lip." I suck my thumb into my mouth, swirling my tongue around it, and then slowly pull it out.

Sucking my bottom lip between my teeth, I give Aeron pleading eyes to go along with the little show I'm putting on. Aeron's eyebrows knit in confusion until he catches the daggers Hade throws our way with his eyes, and then cruel understanding shines on his face.

"Always helping me out, *beautiful*." Aeron smiles down at me and tucks a curl behind my ear. Leaning in, he presses his lips to the shell of my ear. "My little vagrant wants to put on a show tonight. Who am I to stand in her way? I love it when you use me," he whispers against my skin.

Straightening, Aeron looks over to the old man and gives him a small smile. "If you'll excuse us, I believe I promised my girl a dance. It looks like she's come to collect."

I nod goodbye to the gentleman, setting my drink on a nearby table as Aeron drags me to the dance floor, pulling our bodies flush. His hand wraps in mine while the other grips possessively low on my hip.

We get swept into the madness that is the dance floor, blending into the guests around us, who sway to the loud music. Aeron guides my wobbling, unsure legs, keeping us in time with the music.

He smirks down at me. "Have you never danced before?"

Heat rushes to my cheeks, and embarrassment floods me. I hate when people notice weakness within me, even if it is something as silly as proper dancing.

I give him a curious gaze. "And what makes you think that?"

Looking down at me, he mocks, "Hmm, let me think. Oh, maybe from the way my toes are throbbing from the six…" *Crunch.* He winces. "Make that *seven* times you've stomped on my feet already."

Grimacing, I look down at our feet. Sure enough, little scuffs mar the toes of his shoes in every place I've accidentally stomped. "I won't apologize for *your* feet getting in my way."

"I would expect nothing less from you." His wicked smile is illuminated by the glowing orb spinning above us, which makes me swallow the thumps of my heart slowly rising inside me. "Now, are you ready for the real show to begin?"

Before I can question him, Aeron abruptly pushes my body away then yanks me by my arm, spinning me all the way back to him. When my body is flush against him again, he grips the nape of my neck and plunges me in a deep dip. His face comes crashing down above me, closing in on his prey. Time stands still. I now understand exactly what show he intends to put on, and my body freezes in his hold.

Just when his lips are a hair's breadth above mine, the entire ball is plunged in something even darker than the night sky. Small, scared cries ring out around us. My body is alert, ready to fight my way out of whatever threat lies ahead. The room is so dark, even Aeron's face disappears. I straighten as he drops my hands for a moment while a scuffle erupts next to us. A second later, his hands find mine again.

The darkness retreats to wherever it came from, and I take a deep breath, looking around to find no danger lurking. We are safe. It was just a false alarm. Turning my head back to Aeron, I curse under my breath for thinking I was ever safe. It seems like the danger was lurking right in front of me all along.

"*Nightmare*," Hade's deep timbre travels all the way down my spine, turning my insides molten. His large hands engulf my small ones, his broad chest pressing dangerously close to mine. He appears calm and collected, but I catch the way his jaw grinds the smallest amount, giving away the anger brewing inside. He's holding himself back like he always does, ever the tomb of caged emotions.

"What did you do with my date? If you wanted a dance, you could have just asked," I say calmly. My legs are on the verge of giving out completely, and I know he can hear the volcano rumbling inside me, my heart bursting in places, unraveling me from within. Surprisingly, I hide all of that from my voice and face.

"*Date?*" Hade scoffs the world like it's an insult. "He is your competitor, nothing more. You would do well to remember that."

Empress, this man is infuriating, but not in the way most would think. I want to plow my fist right through his perfectly chiseled face, but even I know it would somehow make his beauty just look more lethal. My head knows to stay far, far away from this monster, but my stupid, gullible heart wants the smallest sample. Just a single *taste*. My head tells me this monster's teeth would shred me to pieces, but my heart tells me the thought sounds enticing, enjoyable, even.

My body is at war with itself, a cluster of confusion, anger, lust, and intrigue. I'm burning from the inside out, a never-ending fire lit within me. My body breaks out in a cold sweat, Hade the sickness causing it. I try to fight the way my breaths turn ragged, but it's no use.

"Are you feeling alright?" Hade's knowing smirk shakes me out of my toxic trance, pushing me back to my confident exterior.

"I was having a lovely time, actually, until someone's unsolicited opinions sucked all the fun right out of the air, yet again. I've caught my breath now, and I think I'm ready to get back to my fun." I go to pull away, but Hade grips my hands tighter, refusing to let me go.

His eyebrows hitch up in a surprisingly playful manner. "Who am I to stop you from having a little fun? What did you have in mind?" Hade purrs the words, and my stomach does a summersault.

Traitorous bitch.

I want to say it sounds fun to slam my fist into his perfectly sculpted face, then go find Aeron again, but before I get the words out, a small man shuffles up to his side, whispering something in his ear before striding away.

Grunting to himself, he turns his attention back to me. "I have to go take care of something. Don't let the giggle goop cloud your judgment, *Nyxi.*" With that, he's swept away into the growing crowd, leaving me panting and maybe a touch disappointed.

Giggle goop? He must be referring to the bubbling drink I downed earlier. I know for sure his passive aggressive comment revolves around getting close to Aeron, but why the fuck does he even care? It's my life, not his. He isn't the keeper of me. He means nothing to me—or so I keep trying to convince myself. And that goddamn name. It's like he knows what it does to me, the way it perfectly rolls off his tongue like a taunt and a plea. Each time, it slowly unravels one of the threads wrapped tightly around my heart.

This is not how I wanted my night to go. I planned to get dolled up, have a stress-free night, get nice and buzzed, and dance until my feet grew blisters from one too many spins. Sighing to myself, I decide I can still accomplish some of those things, and go on the hunt for more giggle goop.

The anger rising inside me combined with how tight Des cinched my corset has me searching for fresh air to clear my mind after snatching a new glass of bubbles. Luckily, the ballroom is located on the very edge of the castle, meaning there's a small door in the corner to sneak out while no one is looking.

Dodging a Scorch blowing fire from their mouth, I nearly get my eyebrows burnt to a crisp, but I make it just in time to squeeze by and out the door. Cool air blows my hair off my shoulders, and I let out a deep sigh, taking my first full breath. The night sky twinkles above me, serving me instant contentment.

I've always felt a connection to the night sky. Its endless embrace centers me, a familiar pull towards a reliable friend. It seems to hold all the answers to life. As if agreeing with me, the stars twinkling above me appear to glow a little brighter. I would like to think that's Theo's way of telling me he's okay, that he's watching me.

I look around the grounds of the castle as insects and small animals chirp in the distance. It's peaceful out here. The castle sits at the top of a hill, towering over Lunaria, surrounded mostly by grassy slopes and gardens.

Picking up my dress so I don't trip, I stride happily into the dreamy, dark night, looking for a place to be with my thoughts for a while. Making my way to the garden, I open the small metal gate with a loud, rusty *creek* and then pad inside, closing the gate behind me.

The garden feels intimate and cozy as I walk through the overgrown arch tangled with ivy and wisteria, adding bright purple pops of color. Rows of flowers bloom from the dirt around me, creating an oasis of colors. Little clouds bounce above each flower bush, raining down water on them. I assume they are created by a Soak, popping up each night to keep the garden lush and thriving.

Sitting in the center of the garden is a small wishing well with a single bench next to it. Striding over, I decide this is the perfect spot to clear my mind and enjoy my glass of *giggle goop*.

The night slowly gets darker as the minutes and my drink trickle down. Nothing could ruin the tranquility this garden has blessed me with. Bringing my glass up to my lips, I freeze when I hear the faintest crunch in the distance. The hairs on the back of my neck stand at attention, alerting me I'm not alone anymore.

As I wrap my hand around the dagger strapped to my chest, a faint breath sends a chill down my spine. Whirling around, I fling the dagger out of its pouch, pressing it against the soft flesh of my intruder.

Staring back at me, the perfect depiction of calm, is one storm cloud gray eye and one maliciously dark black eye.

Hade.

"What do you intend to do to me with that sparkly little thing?" The deep cadence of his voice drags talons down my core.

"A blade is a blade," I say nonchalantly. "They all cut and kill the same." I hold my blade steady to the dip of his neck.

"And is that what you intend to do to me, *Nightmare? Cut* and *kill?*" he taunts, his voice a whisper.

I shrug, unbothered. "Give me one good reason why I shouldn't slit your throat right here and be done with it. With *you*." My heart speeds up, and my fingers start to tingle with thrill.

"Is that what you want? To be done with me?" There's madness swirling in his eyes now, a raging vortex of the unknown. He presses in closer, drawing the smallest bead of blood where my blade meets his skin.

I gasp just slightly, giving myself away. My voice wobbles when I add, "I could easily...without a second thought."

"Then do it," he challenges me, calling my bluff. "Slay the villain in *your* story."

I narrow my eyes at him. "Are you saying you aren't the villain in other stories? That you have a *heart?* That the graphic rumors of the ruthless Cardinal aren't true? Hmm?"

Sadness and longing flicker in his eyes for a fraction of a second, but then his walls go back up like armor building around him. He shuts me out and his emotions in. A sadistic smile grows across his face in its place, his mask firmly back in place. It's dizzying, attempting to track all the different sides to him. "I never claimed to have a heart. I never have, or will I ever, *need* anyone in my life. Relying on others makes you *weak*." He spits the words, stoking the fire erupting inside me.

Proving his point, a black tendril of magic appears out of thin air, wrapping tightly around my throat like a tentacle. It swiftly drags me up off my feet, making my shoes slip off. Slowly, as if taunting me, it moves me forward so my neck is now pressed against my own dagger still clutched tightly in my shaky hand, making my face tilt up to bare my throat. Both of us are now pressed against each edge of the blade, noses and lips a breath apart.

I hate him down to his core. Hate the way he's so cold and distant. Hate his harsh words and even bolder actions. Hate the way he toys with me like it's a game. But what I hate the most is the way he makes my body come alive. The way it heats under his gaze. The way my breaths turn labored when he sucks all the air out of my lungs. The way he makes me yearn for the feeling of living again. The way he makes me crave the chaos he dishes out, like he's a drug I'm violently hooked on.

I *hate* Hade, and I think he might hate me too. I'm losing myself to that dark place of rage and heartache at the thought of betraying Theo. I try to calm my chaotic breaths, but the more I try, the harder they seem to take off in a gallop, each time pressing a little more into the sharp blade resting just below my chin.

He zones in where the blade meets my skin. "Careful, or you'll ruin that *perfect*, pretty skin of yours."

Scoffing, I gain my composure. He's baiting me, wanting to see the fire back in my eyes instead of the darkness starting to take over, dragging me back to this game with him—whatever this game even is.

"Trust me, my skin is far from perfect." Pressing myself further into the dagger, I add, "And I like pain. It reminds me I'm alive."

Hunger dances in his eyes. "You know what they say goes perfectly with pain?" He smirks.

I smile back, going along with his little game. "In your dreams."

His eyes are molten lava now. "Oh, but you only visit me in my wicked...dark...nightmares, *Nyxi*." He whispers my name, making me shake with full body tremors.

Words have lost me. A slow gulp is all I can muster while I slowly shake my head. Slowly, he walks towards me, the black tendril still wrapped around my neck, making me float backward until my knees hit something hard behind me.

The black tendril spins me around until I'm bent over a hard surface, staring into a deep, dark hole with water sitting at the bottom. "You know what this is? It's a wishing well." He whispers it next to the shell of my ear, but it still somehow echoes eerily off the walls, all the way to the bottom of the well, like it's haunting me.

"There's an old wise tale behind it. It's said the original owner of this castle built this garden so after they passed away, there would be a place for people to visit for wishes. The spirit would bless those deserving as a way to keep the castle virtuous and honest."

He leans in closer. "You know what I think, though? I think even without this here, you would still be *wishing, begging* for just a single taste of me."

This is a side of Hade I've never experienced, a new door unlocked for reasons unknown.

I'm cracking at my seams, ripped apart piece by piece. Is this what a heart attack feels like? Every part of my body aches, but not with tiredness or pain. It aches to be touched, explored like uncharted land. I feel out of control, a concoction of hesitancy and the feral desire to jump in head first towards the disaster that's undoubtedly to unfold. My mind struggles to fight this unbreakable pull towards him that's only grown since first meeting.

Looking behind me the best I can, I see both of Hade's eyes are now black as night, his white scar glowing like a warning of corruption. He looks like he wants to ruin me, to take and take until I have nothing left except my flayed, broken heart.

Surprisingly, we are both panting, our chests heaving, wild and in sync. Mine tingles each time his presses close to my back.

My words come out choppy. "Mark my words, Hade: I will never beg for a single thing from you, even if I'm dying and you are the only antidote left to save me." I smile sadistically. "I would gladly die with a smile on my face."

The tendril of magic twists me so the side of my face turns towards him. Black smoke appears from behind Hade, the tip slowly dragging up my exposed leg peeking out from the slit of my dress. It scorches me, leaving a path of burning desire where it slithers across my skin, making me squirm in his grip. It continues its exploration of my body, dragging across the delicate dip of skin between my breasts, where my dagger was previously nestled. Painstakingly slow, it drags up the side of my neck, making goosebumps spread across my skin. I gasp when it delicately tucks a rogue curl behind my ear, then curls itself around the shell of my ear.

"Is that a challenge?" It purrs in my ear, and it's my downfall. Hade's mouth remains firmly shut, his seductive voice somehow traveling through the tendril of magic nestled at the edge of my ear.

"No," I whisper pathetically, "it's a promise." I side eye him the best I can with the position this damn magical limb has me in.

"Your traitorous heart is racing, Nyxi."

"I'm thinking about Aeron," I lie on a shaky breath.

He tsks. "I never took you for a liar. Your body betrays you, the way it trembles in my hold. Your breaths are so loud, they're all my damn mind can focus on. Your voice has turned to velvet as you scramble for lies to feed me." A small, traitorous whimper escapes my throat before I can stop it. "I'm a starved man, ravenous, even. So keep feeding me those lies, Nyxi, because you're only fooling one of us here. Maybe one day, you will come to your senses and decide whether you want to play with a *boy* or a *man*."

"I..." My brain fails me. I'm falling apart right in front of him, and by the smile blooming across his face, he knows it. "I—"

"Hade," an annoyed female voice booms behind him. "Aire is requesting your presence. He's waiting to be filled in on the details of tomorrow's Crucible trial."

The Empress comes into view behind him in all her wicked glory. She's wearing a giant poofy dress covered in black and red playing cards bearing her face to fit the theme. Its sweetheart neckline is adorned with straps that droop low off her shoulders. I internally gasp when I notice all the cards are moving, the Empresses smiling and waving.

She takes in the two of us, Hade refusing to release me. She looks thoroughly pissed off that her personal guard is out here, doing whatever the heck he's doing with me. I can't even explain what this is, if I'm being honest. I curse under my breath for letting myself get tangled in this mess, putting a target on my back for *the Empress*, of all people.

She looks me up and down, looking unimpressed. I recede into myself, instantly self-conscious.

"Whoring yourself out will not help you get any further in this competition, *girl*." She doesn't even give me the dignity of using my name. To be honest, she probably doesn't even know it. I stiffen at her insult but keep my hard exterior in place, not giving away any of my emotions. She can't hurt me if I don't play into her game. She wants to get a reaction out of me, but I won't stoop to her level.

Hade tenses, and I pray he didn't notice the little flinch I couldn't control. Knowing him, though, I'm sure he could tell if my heart rate went from one hundred beats per minute to one hundred and one. He grinds his teeth, releasing me as he nods to the Empress. "As you wish. I will head there now." He dips his head in a small bow, and when he looks back up, the Empress is already turned, stomping back to her party.

I let out a loud breath, dragging in a ragged one. Hade goes to leave, but he turns abruptly, striding right back to me. Looking me dead in the eyes with unyielding certainty, he proclaims, "Even the grandest diamond couldn't have drawn my eyes away from you tonight, Nyxi. I fear nothing in the lands below or above could rival your beauty for the rest of eternity, and that is a scary thought."

Then, he's stolen by the night, leaving me lost and confused in my own thoughts yet again, wondering who the heck Aire is.

But more importantly, how I can keep my heart tightly locked away from the thief trying to steal it.

Chapter
Twenty

"CITIZENS OF FALLOUT AND LUNARIA ALIKE, IT IS MY GREAT HONOR to announce the start of my annual Reaper Crucible!" The Empress's voice echoes off the walls of the Bubble, magnified by the Enhancer next to her. Cheers erupt from the hundreds of people gathered around the perimeter, peering in and waiting for the blood bath to begin. Kids sit propped up on shoulders to get a better view over the growing crowd.

My heart hammers in my chest as I look around, seeking any clues as to what today's trial will entail. I come up empty; all that sits in the Bubble are the ten of us spread out in a large circle, the Empress with a handful of her Vanquishers, and, of course, Hade.

He kneels behind her, balanced on one knee, bracing himself on his long, double edged sword stuck in the sand in front of him. His eyes scan our surroundings, looking for any threats to the Empress. I get distracted watching him until his eyes lock on mine, lingering for the briefest second, before they continue his search for danger, like he wasn't just feeding me heart-malfunctioning words last night.

I rein in my confused heart just in time to catch the Empress announce it's time to learn our rankings for the start of the Crucible. I pinch myself, cursing for getting distracted by a pretty man. Today is life or death, and even with zero distractions, my chances of making it out of here alive are not the best.

An Illuminist raises his hands next to the Empress, creating a scoreboard with our names and ranking as she speaks. "As voted on by both Fallout and Lunaria, with additional rankings added by me, here is your official start to this year's Reaper Crucible standings."

Narrowing my eyes, I scan the scoreboard for my name. After last night's run-in with the Empress, I was scared my name would have been listed at ranking ten today, but to my surprise, I find myself smack dab in the middle. I'm more than okay with this ranking, because there are five rounds to work my way up the chart, and this is the safest place for me at the moment. Ranking at the top will only put a target on my back. Ranking at the bottom will show I am weak and an easy target.

Tank sits at the top of the charts, Cartwell following behind him, which I expected—the brawn and the brains. Sitting at the bottom of the chart is sweet Ray, making me dig my nails into the palms of my hands to keep my emotions in check.

The Empress' voice commands the space again, and I slightly jump with surprise. "Do not forget, competitors, your place in this competition can change in a matter of seconds. Don't get complacent, or you may just wind up dead and buried in the dirt."

This is it. My mind races with a million options for today's trial. For all I know, the Empress could make us each fight to the death right here and now until only one of us is left standing. Thinking better of it, I realize she would never do that. She lives for grand, drawn out deaths. It would be over too quickly.

I start to crouch into a fighting stance, bouncing on the balls of my feet as I shove all thoughts from my brain to clear my mind. It's time to fight for my life—literally.

The Empress signals to the Illuminist next to her, and he lets his hands fall to his sides, stopping himself from capturing what she's about to say next. I find this odd, but the Empress loves to add theatrics and suspense to everything she does. She signals to the Enhancer next, who also shuts his magic off, making her voice much quieter.

"There is one part of the Reaper Crucible that has remained a secret for all of time. It creates a fair playing field each year so no one can cheat or try to research prior to the Crucible."

My mind spirals with what this "extra" part of the Crucible could be. I've never heard of anything extra connected to the trials, but of course I haven't; they don't share this part with the public.

"If you can successfully answer this riddle, then the Crucible will immediately be over, and you will be crowned its winner. You have until the last round to figure it out, but you are only allowed one attempt. Choose wisely, and take your time. The riddle has yet to be solved. There is no punishment for getting it wrong, but you will not be allowed a second attempt. You must come to me with your answer when you have one, and you may not talk about this with anyone, or you will be punished. Nod once if you understand all the rules." Her serious tone leaves no room for questions.

We all nod to the Empress in understanding. I'm shocked that, out of all the years of the Crucible, no one has been able to figure it out. Is it a trick question? Is it something simple that people overlook? Does it have to do with the Empress and her history? The options are endless, and it's just one more thing to add to my list of worries.

The Empress clears her throat. "I will only say this one time, so commit it to memory."

She reads from an old leather journal. *"Where three meet, one left behind. A sacrifice greater than mankind. A piercing cry from the one black eye. For that shall reset time before the ultimate crime."*

What in all of Fallout does that even mean? It sounded like she was speaking in a foreign language, gibberish with alternate meanings. No wonder no one has solved this damn thing; it's literally a big mushed up ball of random words. Has the Empress lost her mind? That is the only explanation—how the hell is anyone supposed to figure that out? Committing it to memory, I stash it away in the back of my brain to unscramble later—if I make it out of today alive.

The Empress signals to the Illuminist and Enhancer next to her, and they cast their magic back on her again. She plasters on her larger-than-life smile and continues with her speech. "This year, I've decided on a theme for the Crucible to mix things up. It was getting rather boring, to be honest. Each round this year has been based off one of the many childhood games you have all grown up playing. Except these games will not be all fun, and you will not enjoy playing them on my terms. I, however, will love watching every second of it. Who doesn't love a little danger with their fun?" The crowd erupts in cheers and hollers, egging her on. It's sick.

A shrill screech pierces the air above us, and people outside the Bubble start to panic. I tense; I'd recognize that sound in any lifetime. My legs start to tremble as I'm brought back to the worst day of my life. A huge shadow blankets the Bubble as I spot multiple Necroshrieks circling above.

"Who doesn't love a good game of Hide and Seek? A game as old as time." The Empress spreads her arms wide, gesturing to the crowd outside. "Only this is no regular game of Hide and Seek. No, that would be too simple. Today, you will be playing Hide and Seek with a Necroshriek. Has a nice ring to it, doesn't it?"

The crowd erupts in cheers again, and a loud ringing settles in my ears as the blood rushes to my head. I feel dizzy, like this is some sick personal joke. She can't know why I'm here, right? That one of those rotting beasts killed the one person I had. I feel like I might faint, but I know I need to pull myself together and listen to the rest of the Empress' rules for this round. I catch Hade staring at me, and it almost looks like he's worried for me, but I'm sure it's my scrambled brain getting confused again.

"The rules of this game are simple. Stay alive. Once I leave, one of my lovely Fabricants will create a playing field of their choice. I allowed them creative freedom to design anything their dreams could conjure. Once the field is set, I will release the three Necroshrieks flying above us into the Bubble to hunt you down. You may use the terrain around you to hide or forge weapons. The only rule is that there are no rules. Do whatever you need to stay alive, including killing. The game will finish once two of your competitors have been killed by one of the Necroshrieks—or a fellow competitor—however long that shall take."

My heart sinks with each word out of her wicked mouth. Of course, she would have no rules. She wants a blood bath, and that's exactly what my competitors will give her. I can see them each start to smile at the thought of bloodshed, and my heart hammers in my chest so loud, it's the only thing I can focus on.

I look around, spotting Ray up to my left and Aeron a little to my right. The circle we stand in is so large, they are too far to talk to. My best bet will be teaming up with my allies and then finding a hiding place, one where other competitors won't spot us and none of the Necroshrieks will scent us. They rely on scent, since all they have for eyes are rotting sockets.

The Empress' sinister smile brings me out of my thoughts as she spins in a slow circle, making eye contact with each of my competitors and then landing on me. She holds my gaze as she continues her speech. "Only eight of you will come home to the castle tonight. Time will only tell which ones of you are too weak for this competition and need purged. Only the strongest among you shall prevail. Do not disappoint me; I'm always watching, and my vote has a large sway in the rankings. Good luck!"

With that, she signals to the Fabricant and lifts her dress to stride away to safety, leaving my competitors and I to stare death in the face. I take long, deep breaths, trying to calm myself down, but the adrenaline pumping through my veins has me slightly shaking and on edge. That, paired with the way it felt like the Empress was talking directly to me, holding my gaze when she uttered that the weak will be purged, and there's no doubt in my mind she's not my biggest fan.

The Vanquisher with fabricant magic takes the Empress' place in the center of the Bubble, an equally sinister smile splayed across his face with the promise of mayhem. Hade follows closely behind the Empress, heading out of the Bubble to stand beside her throne propped up high just outside for her viewing pleasure.

The sun beats down on us, the Bubble's force field providing no reprieve from the harsh elements. My body casts a large shadow in the sand as I shield my eyes with my hand from the sun sitting high in the sky. As I turn my head down and away from the sun to rest my eyes, my brain plays tricks on me. I almost thought I imagined my shadow moving from the ground, slithering up my leg.

Shaking my head, I bring my focus back to the Fabricant, who has both his hands held high above his head, his eyes closed with focus. A blinding white light shoots out from his hands, growing bigger by the second. My eyes grow wide as the magic builds and builds, looking like it's about to explode. I reach up to scratch a persistent tickle on the outer shell of my ear as my eyes are torn bouncing back and forth between Hade's retreating back and the Fabricant.

"Don't die on me, Nightmare. I'm not done playing with you quite yet," Hade's raspy voice whispers into my ear as I stare dumbfounded at his back all the way on the opposite side of the Bubble.

A quiet gasp leaves my throat at the shock of his words. Looking down, I do, in fact, see my shadow travel back down to the sand below me again. He controlled my shadow to talk through it to me...all the way from the other side of the Bubble.

I don't have a second to process his words when I'm blinded by a giant white ball of magic exploding around us, knocking me off my feet. I'm launched backwards, flying through the air until my head connects with something hard. When I come to, a dark blanket of stars is in place of the Bubble's force field, surrounded by thick, hilly terrain and giant trees too tall to see over.

There goes my plans of teaming up; there's not a single soul remotely close to me. Looks like I'm in it alone for this trial. I set off in search of shelter.

Trudging through the dense terrain, my feet grow tired from having to pull them out of deep mud with each step. I'm hoping the section I got thrown into is the only place with this mud, or else it's going to be a long, brutal game. I use my hands to part the tall grass around me, batting it away like it wronged me.

I'm in a foul mood, and the fact that the back of my head felt wet when I touched it earlier isn't helping. I have a raging headache from the giant boulder I was flung against, and I'm sure the wetness is blood. It can't be too bad, or I would have passed out by now, but I also know all head injuries, no matter how small, can have huge effects on the body.

The bodysuit Des made me keeps me covered from sharp greenery and branches. I have a few small cuts on my hands and wrists, and I'm sure there are a few scattered on my face as well from my fall.

The fake night sky illusion above makes it dark and hard to see my surroundings. The giant moon above casts faint light down on the tops of the trees. The grass opens up to a dirt path leading into a dark forest with more trees that tower far above me. I decide this is my best bet at survival, using the closely sprouted trees as cover from any Necroshrieks above. I've heard a couple screeches here and there, but for the most part, they have stayed quiet as they stalk their prey.

Gripping the thick base of one of the trees, I wrap my body around it the best I can and start to shimmy my way up the trunk. My nails dig into the bark, making me hiss in pain each time a sliver of wood wedges under my nails. Slowly, I make my way up the tree until I find a branch big enough to hold my weight.

I slowly press my foot on the branch, testing it out. It doesn't move an inch, which makes me feel like it's safe to slide onto and rest my body. I straddle the branch, and my shoulders sag with relief. They were starting to burn from holding myself up for so long. I peek around the remaining branches above me, making a game plan on which ones I can trust to get myself to the very top. If I can make it up there, it will give me the height advantage I need to be able to look over the entire playing field and see where the best place to hide is.

I'm officially out of breath, my hands bleeding from the fifteen branches I managed to drag my body onto, but I successfully make it to the top. I lean my back against the trunk, giving myself a second to catch my breath. If I weren't currently fighting for my life, I would find this peaceful. The starry night twinkling above calms the adrenaline high. The dense forest reminds me of the trees that surround Squatters Village, where I would walk every single day home to Theo. It's quiet, which slightly puts me on edge, because looking around, I don't spot a single Necroshriek.

Necroshrieks are controlled by their bonded Vanquisher and live to please. I wouldn't be surprised if their three bonded Vanquishers are sitting right outside the Bubble, telling them exactly what to do and where to go.

My breathing is back to its normal cadence, and I wiggle myself further down the branch to look over my surroundings. There's a small pond of water up to my right, but the water is an abnormal shade of black, making me think it's poisonous. Every now and then, a ripple glides across the top; some nasty creature lurks inside. I would rather not get anywhere near that and be forced to dive in it if danger presents itself.

Straight ahead, just outside the edge of the trees, is a maze of a garden that looks like it's been possessed. Thorny vines tangle together in big clusters, making it next to impossible to run through. Giant flowers that have to be bigger than me are scattered throughout the vines, and now that I take a closer look, I realize they're moving. Their petals bloom open and shut, baring sharp teeth with thorns inside each time they open. Magic never ceases to amaze me, even after everything I've witnessed.

To my left sits the edge of a rocky cliff. Looks like I was spit out at the highest point of the playing field. At the bottom of the hill sits a shallow-looking cave tucked away in the corner of the Bubble. If I can safely make my way to the bottom of the cliff, I will have cover from above and shelter to my back. That only leaves the cave's mouth to guard from danger.

Looking over my three options, I feel a nudge in the back of my brain to go *left* and pray I don't run into anyone on my way. Then, I just need to safely lower myself down the cliff without injuring myself. In theory, it sounds simple, but I know it will be anything but. I'm still on guard—I haven't seen a single Necroshriek yet, or any of my competitors, for that matter. Hopefully, none of them are hiding out in the cave I intend to make my new home.

My legs shake, and I let out a loud huff when my feet make contact with the ground. I head left in the direction towards the cliff, taking the shortest route to get out of the dense trees. My body grows more tired with each step, but I remain aware of my surroundings, scanning for danger.

I estimate I'm about halfway to the cliff now, my lungs burning and muscles aching from the long, hilly walk. I roll my sleeves all the way up, trying to cool off my overheating limbs. A twig snaps behind me, making me spin and duck low. I search my surroundings for any sounds or movements for a few minutes, but I spot nothing. Standing back up, I decide I'm being paranoid and set back off on my trek.

I take one step forward, but I freeze when I hear a small grunt and the sound of something *whooshing* through the air behind me. Spinning on my heels, something lodges itself deep in my arm that was intended to be a killing blow to my back. I hiss through my teeth, using my other arm to cover my mouth. I would rather not give away my location, no matter how bad my arm is pulsing in pain.

Of course, the spear would hit me in the one place I'm not protected by my suit currently thanks to my overheating limbs.

I spot Tank with Jade propped up on his shoulders a little ways back, holding a handmade spear made out of a long branch, a carved stone arrow head attached to it using a vine. They both see me plain as day, and with the looks on their faces, they easily think they have me beat. Clearly, they haven't learned how much of a stubborn bitch I am. Too stubborn to die by their hands today, that's for certain.

Without hesitating, I rip the arrow from my arm. This time, I do let out an ear shattering scream, noticing they decided to wrap the arrow in a thorny vine, each thorn catching on my skin the entire way out. Blood pours from my arm, making me light headed, but it's the least of my worries. I normally wouldn't rip something from a wound, but I had no choice; it would have been impossible to run with the bulky spear hanging from my arm. It probably would have caught on something anyways and ripped away more skin than I just did.

Holding my hand to the wound to help stop the blood the best I can, I catch Tank and Jade stomping towards me as I spin and take off in a full sprint towards the cliff. Lucky for me, I've already scoped out the land and know exactly where I'm headed, giving me a slight advantage over them. Plus, Tanks huge size will slow them down, even paired against my wounds and aching muscles.

"You're mine, bitch!" I hear Jade scream behind me as I create more distance between us. I'm fading fast and need to get to the cave as soon as possible. It's my only option for survival now, and if I create enough distance, I'm hoping they won't know what direction I went. If they find the cave, then my odds aren't great. With zero weapons and an injured arm, the odds are stacked against me.

Honestly, what's new?

Another spear flies through the air behind me, but it lands in a tree next to me as I weave in and out. *Cut left,* my brain screams at me, and, trusting my instinct, I plant my feet into the dirt and take a sharp left around a tree trunk, beelining sideways out of the forest in hopes of confusing them. Jade's taunting laugh echoes behind me like a threat. After running left for a minute, I feel a pull to go *straight,* and I turn right, going straight again. I'm gasping for air, but hope bubbles in my throat when I spot the trees opening in front of me. Seems my instincts did not lead me astray today.

I make it out of the trees, gasping for air, but I don't slow down. Even though I can't see them, I know they are not too far behind me. The cliff's edge is not too far ahead of me, and now I need to figure out how the hell I'm going to safely get down it. I haven't planned this far ahead, in hopes I could scope out the best route when I got here. I don't have the luxury of time on my side as I barrel ahead full speed.

Screech! A Necroshriek's piercing cry assaults my ears from above. Between Jade's loud taunts and my screams of pain, it seems we've attracted an audience.

I love today!

Whoosh. Whoosh. Thump!

The Necroshriek glides down from the sky and lands hard on the ground in front of me, making four small craters where its talons dig deep into the dirt. I dig my feet into the ground, coming to an immediate halt in front of it, fully blocked off from the cliff's edge now. I know it can't see me, but it can hear me, and it can definitely smell the blood running down my arm. I hold back a whimper when it lets out a puff of rotting breath across my face, blowing my hair back. It's at least twenty feet in front of me, but it's so large, its breath reaches all the way to me, making me gag.

Think, Nyxi; how can I get out of this? Looking back, I still don't spot Jade and Tank, and thank the Empress. I need a plan, fast. Looking around, I seek out anything I can use as a weapon. I come up empty handed when all I spot are fallen branches from nearby trees and rocks scattered about.

The Necroshriek lets out a loud wail again, probably alerting the other's it found dinner. It takes one large step forward but doesn't charge me. It swings its large, horned, bird-like head back and forth, sniffing around for any scent it can lock on. The mud caking my body from earlier must be masking my scent enough from this far away.

Looking back again, I confirm there's still no Tank or Jade and slowly walk backwards as a plan hatches in my brain. As quietly as possible, I gather the materials needed while keeping my eyes alert for my competitors and the Necroshriek now spinning in circles, swinging its spiked tail, trying to find its prey. Apparently, they aren't the smartest things.

That makes two of us, buddy, as I start to second guess myself yet again as to why I entered in this game of death born for entertainment.

I kneel behind a boulder with my supplies in hand and wait. I catch the smallest rustle of brush to my left that the Necroshriek hasn't picked up on yet. Holding a stick in my hand, I draw back the band wrapped around it I pulled from my hair and release, the rock wedged in it flying across the clearing, hitting the center of the tree just in front of where I heard movement.

The Necroshriek lets out another ear-shattering scream, running towards the sound I made where I know Tank and Jade are camped out. I watch as black smoky acid pours from its beak, disintegrating the tree to nothing in seconds. I fling into action, taking the opportunity to run for the cliff now that the Necroshriek is distracted and out of my way. I hear screams behind me, but I don't turn around as I push my body to its limits.

I approach the cliff's edge, and my brain scrambles for a plan I know it won't be able to come up with this fast. There's no good options here, but I pray there's at least one that keeps me alive. A faint sensation makes me *duck*, and, listening to my instincts again, I catch more of that black acid fly over my head, almost turning me to nothing. It must have heard me running and turned around. I trip over my ankle as I scramble, catching my foot on a rock. My body flies forward, and then I'm falling, down, down, down, over the edge of the cliff to a certain death.

My body bounces like a rag doll the entire way down the hill, knocking the breath out of my lungs. I tuck myself into a tight ball the best I can, attempting to limit my injuries. Rocks dig into my body each time I hit the hard, unforgiving ground.

This is it. This is how I die. What a pathetic way to go. My first encounter with danger, and I fold like a blade of grass to an unforgiving wind storm. Theo would be disappointed in me. I'm disappointed in myself. After all this, to go out in the first round? I feel like I'm falling for hours, a never-ending cycle of floating through the air, bouncing harshly off the jagged ground, and then launching into the air once again. At least being melted by the Necroshriek would have been fast.

Brace yourself! my failing mind shouts at me, but my brain and body are no longer in sync. I'm tired and hurt, and I just want it to be over. *Make the pain stop, please*, I beg in my head. *You are going to be okay*, it seems to say back to me, and I smile, knowing this is where it all ends. I embrace it happily. Relaxing my body, I connect with the ground, and everything goes black.

TAP. TAP. TAP.

Even in death, my body still screams at me in pain.

Tap. Tap. Tap.

Apparently, I'm also not allowed peace in the afterlife, because my body is being poked and prodded in an annoying, consistent tapping pattern.

"Can a girl not have some peace after falling to her death?" I groan.

"Death?" a soft voice calls next to me. "Who died?"

`I sit quietly, hoping the annoyance will get bored and go pester some other dead soul, leaving me to wallow in my pain.

Tap. Tap. Tap.

"For fuck's sake!" Painfully slow, I peel one of my eyes open, ready to give hell to whoever won't leave me alone. I hope they have Fire Water in the afterlife, because I need something stiff.

I blink a few times, and my vision clears. Staring down at me is the cutest little boy whose face I could never forget—*Hudson*, his small body expertly painted to blend in with his surroundings like a pro.

"Mommy always said never to say the word *fuck*." His lisp makes his words slur adorably.

Sitting up, I drag my hand down my face and sigh. "Fuck, sorry." Hudson's eyes turn to giant saucers, and I grunt, realizing my mistake. "Well, if you're a big enough boy for her to let you enter the Crucible, I think you should be allowed to hear the word fuck too." I add, "And *fuck* it, you should be able to say it too, because who cares at this point?" I throw my hands up, shrugging, and gesture for him to let his mouth run wild.

He nervously licks his lips and then, at the top of his lungs, he screams, "FUCKKKKKKK!" Giggling to myself, I quickly slap my hand over his mouth, realizing my little escapade could backfire on us and bring danger our way. He takes the hint and stops screaming into my hand, and when I pull it away, it's covered in spit.

"That feel good, little buddy?" He nods back to me with a giant smile on his face. "Next time, how about we do it a little quieter so we don't draw any danger to us?" His smile drops from his face, but he nods back to me in understanding. "I'm all about sticking one to your mother, but I also don't want us to die." I still can't wrap my brain around how his parents ever let him enter the Crucible. Did they force him?

As if reading my mind, he states, "You can't stick anything on my mommy because she's dead. Same with Papa."

Well, *fuck* me. That was honestly the last thing I had on my mind when conjuring up his evil parents in my head. And of course, in typical Nyxi fashion, I've corrupted this poor parentless child in seconds. *Go me!*

Grabbing his hands, I look at him with soft eyes and try to do some damage control. "I'm sorry to hear that, buddy. I also don't have any parents, so I know how hard that can be." His eyes grow a little bigger at my admission. "You know what I think, though?" He nods, intently waiting to hear what I have to say. "I think that sometimes, the strongest people are chosen to receive the greatest challenges in life, like you and me. It's our superpower because we are tough enough to make it through the challenge when others would crumble. We haven't crumbled, though, have we?" I ask him. He slowly shakes his head, and a small smile creeps back onto his face.

"How do you make sure you don't crumble?" he asks me.

Smiling back at him, I'm brought back to a recent conversation I had with Winston, when I asked the same thing. "Someone else who has our same superpower once told me we must seek out happy pangs, and life will be okay. Do you know what a happy pang is?" I question him. He slowly shakes his head again, looking confused as ever.

I reach out, tapping my finger over his heart softly. "It's when it feels fuzzy and warm right here. When something makes you happy, even if it's just for a brief moment. If you collect all those happy pangs in your heart, then you won't ever crumble. I promise."

His face lights up, and he dives forward, pulling me into a tight hug that makes every inch of my body scream, but I happily squeeze him back just as hard. "I'm happy we share the same superpower," he whispers into my ear.

I still need to assess my body for fatal injuries, and I grunt when Hudson pulls away. He winces, and then his eyes light up with an idea. "I used to collect flowers for Mommy every time she was sick. She would always smile at me and tell me they healed her, and it would make my heart feel warm and fuzzy."

He turns on his heels, skipping away with a smile on his face while looking back over his shoulder at me. "I want to feel a happy pang." His smile is the most precious thing I've ever witnessed, and I hope it never leaves his face again. I capture this raw, honest moment to live on endlessly, creating an untouched capsule within my head.

Just as I'm about to tell him there's no need to pick flowers for me, his tiny body disintegrates to nothing right before my eyes. Smoky acid devours him whole, only to leave behind the memory he once was. A parentless child, sent to see his family too soon. One moment, he was skipping happily, and the next, gone. The giant smile on his face will be permanently ingrained in my memory, the same as how permanent his death is. Another name on my list, right next to Theo's. All that's left is a pile of dust where his happy, healthy body was just skipping, seeking a happy pang... and I *scream*.

I'm hyperventilating as a loud sob rips from my throat, but a firm hand slaps over my mouth from behind, and my body is dragged backwards. I thrash in their hold, but my body is so tired, my mind so weak, it's useless.

"Shh, it's me, Vagrant. I've got you," Aeron whispers into my ear as he lifts my body effortlessly to cradle me in his arms. I nuzzle my head into his chest as my body shakes uncontrollably, and he slowly drags his hand over my hair in a soothing manner. I don't know where he's taking me, and at this point, I don't care. I'm the reason Hudson is dead. He wanted to help me. He wanted to feel a happy pang, and instead, he ended up dead.

I didn't see or hear the Necroshriek approaching because I was too busy trying to keep my lungs working while attempting to cheer up Hudson. I wanted him to feel special in a world turned against him, but instead, I got him killed. I feel like I'm having a seizure, my body flailing as I lose total control of my sanity. I see Hudson's crooked smile on repeat in my head, and then he vanishes before my eyes. Then, I see Theo's lifeless, torn up body in our house, and it's an endless cycle back and forth that hurts too much. I just want it to stop, the sadness, the guilt, all of it.

"Make it stop! Make it stop!" I chant like a broken record into Aeron's chest. I fist his shirt, all the pain once in my body blown away with the wind. Now, the only thing that remains hurt and aching is my heart.

"I need you to calm down, Nyxi." I let out another loud sob. "Please, I'm begging you. I'm going to get us to safety, but I need you to try and stay quiet for me. Can you do that, sweetheart?" Aeron pleads.

I'm numb at this point. My brain and heart are no longer working organs inside me. Slowly, I calm my breathing and nod the smallest amount into his chest. "That's it. You're doing so well. We're almost there. Just stay calm for me."

He walks with me tightly in his arms for what seems like hours, but it was probably only a couple minutes. The air turns musty, and the sounds of our breathing echo. My body is slowly lowered to the ground, and I open my eyes. We are in the cave I was searching for. By the looks of it, he has been camped out here since the start. He has a small fire going that casts shadows on the jagged cave's walls. Looking behind me, the cave continues deep into the pitch black.

"Are you hurt?" Aeron drops into a crouch, his hands on both sides of my face, looking me over. I lick my chapped lips but say nothing, staring with lifeless eyes back at him. He drags his hands down my body, feeling around for injuries. Each time he finds one, I wince but say nothing. "You have cuts everywhere, and your arm is pouring blood. What kind of trouble did you get yourself into?" He stares at me, waiting for an answer, and I think he would wait all night.

I open my mouth, but nothing comes out. He nods, encouraging me to try again. I take a deep breath. "I…" My lungs burn, and I break out into a coughing fit. Aeron crawls over and slowly rubs up and down my back to soothe me.

Collecting myself, I try again. "I climbed one of the trees above the cliff to scope things out. I saw the cave at the bottom of the cliff and decided it would be my best chance at survival. I was making my way here when I ran into a little trouble."

He stiffens next to me. "What kind of trouble?"

I take a deep breath. "Tank and Jade snuck up from behind me, and that's how I ended up with a spear in my arm. I ripped it out and took off through the trees to the cliff's edge, but that's where I ran into even more trouble. I accidentally screamed when I ripped out the arrow, and I caught the attention of a Necroshriek. It dropped down right in front of me at the cliff's edge.

I tried to draw its attention to Jade and Tank behind me, which worked for a second as I ran for the cliff's edge, but it heard me. Then I tripped over a rock, and, um…"

"Out with it," Aeron gently pushes.

"I fell and sort of tumbled all the way over the cliff's edge. When I landed, it knocked me out. When I woke, Hudson was standing over me and the Necroshriek was gone. You saw what happened next." A small sob escapes my throat. "He was going to pick flowers for me, to make me feel better. He is *dead* because of me."

Aeron leans into me, drawing me into his chest again. "It's not your fault. He's a child who wouldn't have been able to protect himself, let alone compete in the Crucible. This is no place for a little boy. It was bound to happen, and sadly, this was probably the most peaceful death he could have been dealt. He was just lucky to have you by his side until the very end."

I quietly cry into Aeron's shirt as he rubs my back, attempting to soothe me. He doesn't know how broken I am, though. The pieces of my heart are warped forever and will never fit back together the same way again.

He pulls away from me, looking into my eyes. "I'm going to take care of you now. Can you let me do that for you?" he asks, and I nod in agreement. He rips the bottom part of his shirt off, wrapping it tightly around my oozing arm to stop the bleeding. It hurts like hell as I see the once-white fabric turn a dark crimson. "There; that should at least make sure you don't bleed to death. As for the cuts, there's nothing I can really do. By some miracle, it doesn't feel like you had any broken bones. Maybe a few badly bruised ribs and a concussion, but it seems the mud absorbed most of the impact when you hit the ground. You're lucky you didn't snap your neck on the way down."

I let out a sad laugh. I don't feel lucky. I think my neck snapping would have been a mercy at this point. The Empress' wicked voice snaps me out of my morbid thoughts.

"One down, one to go." Her voice is enhanced, traveling over the Bubble's playing field. She's taunting us, reminding us that she's watching. It's sickening, and my stomach threatens to spill at the thought of her having zero emotion announcing the death of an innocent little boy.

I turn to Aeron. "I'm so tired." It's barely a whisper, but he sees the exhaustion written across my face. I need to rest my mind, let it escape to that happy place I can only visit while asleep. A place where Theo is laughing by my side, where a little boy gets to experience all the happy pangs his heart desires, with the biggest toothless smile on his face. I need that place right now, so I lean back, settling my head into Aeron's soft lap and dozing off into a reality I'll never experience again.

Then comes a scream.

I jolt up, looking for threats as my pulse thumps harshly in my neck. I hear the screech of a Necroshriek on the other side of the Bubble, and then another loud scream follows. It sounds like death, slowly dragging on until it tapers off, eerie silence following.

I blink, and when my eyes open again, everything is gone. Aeron and I sit next to each other, now in sand instead of the harsh cave floor, the Bubble's force field arching above us once again. There's no cave or cliff, no trees or Necroshrieks. All that remains are my seven surviving competitors, Hudson and Briar now just a memory.

It's over.

I survived another day, but at what *cost*?

Chapter
Twenty-One

My new favorite activity to clear my mind is running. I spend my mornings running around the castle grounds until my feet ache and my mind is blissfully empty. We get one week off before round two of the Crucible. A healer was sent to fix me up after the first round, and my body is as good as new. If only they could heal my heart still painfully aching for Hudson.

I felt a slight reprieve when I found a metal chain bracelet with a tiny paintbrush charm dangling from it in my room. A note was next to it that read, *Made from the magic of the best Fabricant in Lunaria so Hudson may never be forgotten.* I didn't recognize the handwriting, but it helped me all the same.

I start my day the same as the previous four: throwing on joggers and a t-shirt Des gave me before the sun is up. The castle is always quiet and peaceful this early in the morning, and I soak it in. There's something about walking down the dark, silent corridors alone before the castle hums to life that calms my racing thoughts.

Rounding the last corner, I approach a dark wooden door. Grazing my knuckles against it, I place three soft knocks, alerting Winston. We've created a system of trust. As long as I knock three times on his door each morning, he lets me travel out of the castle alone to run. He knows how much I need it, and I'm thankful for this bond of trust. When I return, I knock three more times, letting him know I'm back.

It's risky on his end. If I were to run away, he would be brutally killed by the Empress without trial. I would never do that to him, though, and he knows it. It feels good to have a little control over my life, even if it's the smallest amount.

Turning on my heels, I make my way through the castle and sneak into the grand ballroom, like always. Striding through the now-empty room, I cut diagonally through the open space to slip out the back door.

The familiar garden comes into view, the sun slowly rising behind it, casting a golden glow around the flowers. It's a sight I commit to memory each morning, bringing me a tiny sliver of happiness to start my day.

I enter through the small gate, heading straight for the wishing well in the center. I sit here each morning, perched on the edge, waiting. Twirling a curl around my finger, I draw my knees up to my chest, wrapping my arms around them.

As I look over Lunaria, the sun slowly makes its way up the sky until it finally peaks over the tall buildings below. The sky turns a warm pink, mixed with soft blue hues, and no matter how many mornings I've spent here, it still takes my breath away.

It's become a ritual for me now, to start my mornings watching the sun rise above the sleeping city below—not a care in the world, just a simple girl enjoying the nature around her, pretending her life isn't a crumbling mess. Once the sun rises to its full height, I bend over, whispering the same wish into the well, and then take off to run my brain into exhaustion.

After my fifth lap around the outer edge of the castle, my lungs heave and my brain has calmed enough to think straight. I snatch the fabric scarf I have hidden behind a rock, wrapping it around my head and shoulders before I slip into the bustling city below thriving to life.

It's packed full of magicals now, working together to create a flowing system. It's impressive to watch, and I take in each part and its impact on making Lunaria so magical. There are Soaks watering gardens, Scorches burning away dirt and grime littering the streets, and a man who shifts into a bird right before my eyes, scouring above for a lost toy for a crying child.

I take the familiar cobblestone road weaving through the heart of the city, leading to the small wooden bridge arching over a small stream below. Bending over the railing of the bridge, I drop a few worms I snagged from the garden and watch the fish flop out of the water, snatching them up.

Trudging on, I duck down a back alley, trying to avoid the main paths packed full of people. Everyone knows what I look like now, and I shouldn't be wandering the streets of Lunaria alone. The scarf keeps me hidden for the most part, and with the busy lives the magicals live, most are too wrapped up in their own worlds to pay me any heed.

Hoisting myself up over a brick wall, I drop down the other side, landing softly on my feet. The smell hits my nose before I spot the cozy little bakery nestled in the corner of town. I stumbled upon it my first day wandering the city trying to clear my mind of the Crucible, and it's now become one of my favorite places. A familiar pull akin to home draws me back each time.

The sparkling dome comes into view as my hurried feet stumble through the flowing crowd. I shade my face with the back of my hand from the sunlight that bounces off the stained glass windows that cover the exterior of the domed shop. It looks like a glowing orb with a single deep brown door in the center. A wooden sign hangs above, the word 'Knead It' burned into it in. A square wooden planter rests next to the door, sprouting bright yellow and pink flowers.

As I open the door, a copper bell rings, alerting the staff of my presence. There's a few rustic wooden tables scattered about the small space. Sunlight pours in through the glass windows from every angle, making the space glow in warm orange light. It's a welcoming environment, and by the group of people lounging in chairs, eating and reading, I can tell I'm not the only one who thinks so.

"Hey, sugar!" a woman's deep raspy drawl brings a smile to my face. Her dark chocolate skin peeks out from the apron tightly wrapped around her, covered in flour. Her round face is rosy from working all morning, and she shines me the warmest smile, her bright white teeth on full display. Deep set smile lines pepper her face around her plump lips and next to her kind, rich brown eyes. They're the type of lines created from a life full of laughs and fond memories. Her dark curly hair is thrown up in a bun that has slowly started to slide off her head from a hard day's work.

Moji.

"Mo!" I reply warmly as I approach the woman standing behind the counter stocked with fresh pastries. I've made it a habit to come here each morning to snag two strawbana bread slices for me and Des.

Mo is the owner of Knead It and wakes up before the sun rises to bake the most delicious and unique pastries I've ever tasted. From spiced breads to herbal teas, she has it all. My favorite, though, is her strawbana bread, a unique, spongy take on banana bread. She sneaks in fresh strawberries among the mix, adding to its sweet flavor. It reminds me of the strawberry and cream cookies Theo would make me, and I smile at the memory.

"The usual?" she asks as she makes her way to the counter.

"That would be amazing, Mo. Thank you!" I reply while drumming my fingers on the counter.

She packages my order, and in typical Mo fashion, I see her sneak in a third slice while she thinks I'm not looking. She slides it onto the counter between us, and when I reach into my pocket to pay her, she just shakes her head, closing my hand around the coins.

"Save those for something special, sugar."

I chuckle. "You're too good to me, you know that?"

Patting her round stomach, she smiles back at me. "If you don't take those, I would have eaten them all. So really, you're doing me a favor. Plus, this world needs some more good in it."

I nod in agreement. She's not wrong, and I know firsthand just how cruel this place can be. Cradling the goods to my chest, I thank her and turn on my heels. It's time to make my way back to the castle before I'm caught.

"See you tomorrow morning?" she calls from behind me.

"Wouldn't miss it," I shout over my shoulder.

ROUNDING THE LAST CORNER, THE LOOMING GOTHIC CASTLE TOWERS high above me, sticking out among the rainbow the rest of the city produces. It's just as dark and haunting as the inside, with its high, pointed arches, black gargoyles, and steeply pitched roof. It's here to make a statement of power against the warm, colorful hues of the city.

Making my way to the back, I pass the garden, but I freeze when I see two Vanquishers having a conversation right in front of the door into the ballroom.

Shit.

Turning, I rush away before they can spot me and decide to walk to the other side in hopes of finding another door to slip through. Crouching behind a long, rectangle trimmed shrub, I scan this side of the castle, and to my luck, pressed back in the corner of the courtyard is a small door.

I'm not sure what this door opens into, but at this point, it's my only option, so I break into a sprint. Placing my hand on the handle, I twist, thanking the Empress when it moves smoothly. It creaks open as I swing it wide open.

It's dark when I step in, my eyes slowly adjusting to the dimly lit, abandoned hallway. Quietly, I close the door behind me and look around. I don't recognize this hallway; with all the cobwebs draped from the ceiling, it looks to be a place not often frequented.

The walls are plastered with dark gothic wallpaper like the rest of the castle. Three vintage Victorian paintings are hung on the wall. The left depicts a woman with red hair who almost looks like a younger version of the Empress, her hand held up, holding a ball of flame. The one in the center shows a young girl, maybe aged six, in a beautiful black glittering gown. The last one on the right shows a man with slicked back black hair and strong features, black mist swirling around him.

They are covered in dust, as is everything else stashed here. A few odd trinkets wedged here and there look aged and well loved. I make my way down the hallway towards the light flowing in from the other end, assuming this is the way back to my room.

Peeking out from the end of the hallway, I notice it opens into the main entryway of the castle where I spotted the piano on my first day here.

Footsteps click on the floor, approaching me, so I roll my body, blending into the shadows. Something hard jabs me in the back, and I hiss between my teeth. Turning around, I notice a handle to a door I missed the first time I scanned the dark hallway.

A small window sits high in its center, and, being the snoop I am, I press up on the tips of my toes and peer in through the window. I let out a small gasp when I take in the room. It's a library with shelves stocked full of books, probably hundreds stacked on the shelves in all shapes and sizes.

Surprisingly, this room looks well-kept and cozy. Two velvet lounge chairs sit across from each other in the center of the room, separated by a short wooden table. One is smooth, but the other shows a round indent in its seat, like someone sits in it regularly.

The wheels start spinning in my head with all the things these books could contain. Stories for entertainment. The history of Lunaria, maybe. Potentially the background of the Empress. Thinking about the riddle, I decide this could be a great place to start my search for the answer. Just maybe, there will be something in here that could give me a push in the right direction. Making a plan to come back when I have time, I rush back to my room, knocking three times on Winston's door on my way to get ready for training with Ray.

Chapter
Twenty-Two

"You should have seen Winston's face when I told him there was an orange shortage in Lunaria," Des wheezes next to me, snuggled under the covers of my bed, same as me.

Each night, she shows up with a blanket wrapped around her shoulders and two books tucked under her arm. We read in my bed, shoulder to shoulder like inseparable sisters while giggling over the books. I don't know where she finds them, but at this point, I'm so invested, I don't care. Anything to take my mind off this cruel world is welcome. Each night with her heals me the smallest amount. We nibble on the strawbana bread I bring from Knead It and plot new ways to annoy Winston.

"I wish I was there to see it. I'm sure he acted like the world was ending." I laugh softly while knocking my shoulder into hers, sending her into another fit of hysteric giggles.

Holding her palm to her chest, she tries to calm herself. "You would have thought the pants he was wearing were on fire. I eventually had to tell him I was kidding because he started to have a panic attack. Can someone say *dramatic*!" She sings out the last word at the top of her lungs, and I have to cover my ears before she ruptures my ear drums.

She winces. "Sorry. Sometimes, I forget how to use my inside voice. I'm just a girl with a big personality." She pulls me into a tight hug that constricts my breathing and plants a big sloppy kiss on my cheek. Pulling away, I drag my hand down my face, wiping the spit away.

"Too much?" she asks.

"Too much," I respond with a laugh.

"But you still love me?" she pleads with big pouty eyes.

I playfully roll my eyes. "Yes, I still love you."

She beams back at me, and I can't help but get swept up in her positive orbit. She's everything I wish to be one day: strong, independent, loyal. She loves fiercely and is unapologetically herself. She's my hero.

She lets out a loud yawn next to me, stretching her arms above her head. "I think it's about time this rollie pollie rolls on back to her own bed. I have a date with the rest of this book…and maybe my hand." She wiggles her fingers, and I groan as I shove her out of my bed.

She skips to my door, laughing the whole way, and then turns serious. "Always and tomorrow?" she questions me.

I nod back with a genuine smile. "Always and tomorrow, Des."

She strides out my door, humming to herself, which echoes all the way down the corridor. We started promising each other 'always and tomorrow' each night because this friendship is eternal, but each day is not guaranteed. It's a reminder that there is no end to us; there's always a tomorrow, whether it's in this life or the next.

Pushing my covers off, I slide my boots on and throw a cloak over my shoulders, pulling the hood over my head. Slowly, I open my door, looking left and right for any Vanquishers. Luckily, this end only houses me and Aeron, and, as hoped, his Vanquisher must be using the bathroom. The hallway is left empty.

I sneak out into the hall, quiet on my feet as I make my way to the library I spotted earlier. I guide myself by memory, since I don't have a light to lead the way, rushing through the multiple hallways to the entrance of the castle. Crossing the piano, I tuck myself into the shadows when I hear feet approaching. Once they pass, I leap into action, traveling the small distance to the abandoned hallway and out of sight.

I wrap my hand around the weathered handle of the library door and let out a *yelp* when it burns my hand. What the...? Trying again, I reach forward, hoping it was just my imagination.

"I wouldn't," a deep, gravelly voice threatens behind me.

I feel the sharp blade of a dagger pressed against my neck, even with the fabric of my cloak between me and it. I would recognize that voice even in death, plaguing me for eternity.

Hade.

He's like my shadow, inescapable no matter how hard I try. If I didn't know any better, I would think he was stalking me.

I freeze, trying to come up with a way out of this mess. I know I shouldn't be out unattended, especially trying to sneak into a place not meant for me, but this was my only chance to solve the riddle.

Gripping my shoulder, he spins me around, shoving my back against the door, and presses his dagger harshly to the dip of my neck. "I should have known it was you, *Nightmare*. Always getting into trouble instead of minding your own business." His face is serious. "What are you doing here?"

Every time he's in my personal space, my brain forgets how to work, and so instead of answering him, my logical response is to spit on his boot. It was obviously not the correct response, though, and I know it—not that I would ever admit that to him.

A wicked smile blooms across Hade's face, which makes me equally excited and wanting to piss my pants at the same time. I am well and truly *fucked*.

He tsks. "You're looking for answers to the riddle, aren't you?" he questions, but there's no uncertainty about it. He knows exactly why I'm here, and he wants me to know it.

Prick.

My lips thin, and I narrow my eyes at him, but I don't answer.

A velvety chuckle escapes deep from his chest, making my legs quiver. "Haven't we already gone over this? I always get what I want. So, are we going to do this the easy way or the hard way?"

My heartrate kicks up to a roar as the blood rushes to my ears. The ground is starting to spin, or maybe it's me—I can't tell the difference anymore. My stubbornness holds true, though, as I remain silent. A small part of me wants to find out what exactly the hard way would entail.

Grunting, he takes a step back from me, and for some reason, I feel slightly disappointed. "Hard way it is," he states, which has my heart fluttering back to life.

"You're looking for answers to the riddle because you're hoping it can help your odds at winning the Crucible. You're a scared little girl who's in over her head, and you're freaking out, looking for the easy way out, like always. You're hoping you can find your answers in the library behind you." He lays out the facts with certainty.

My cheeks heat with embarrassment. I hate that he's right, the way he can always read me like an open book. "You know nothing about me, so don't act like you do," I grit out.

"I beg to differ, but you know what I do know for sure? That you need information. That it's potentially life or death for you. I also know that door you tried to open is sealed with *my* magic. I'm the only person in the entire castle who can unlock it for you. So, what I do know is that you *need* me." His wicked smile could make even the strongest of men cower in fear.

It's worse than I thought. Of course, this would be sealed by the Empress' right hand. Why wouldn't it be? Nothing in my life has ever been easy, and it's not going to start today. I'm willing to do just about anything to get inside this room, though I still plan to play my cards close to my chest. Slowly, I shake my head, denying his very accurate description of my desperation.

His sinister smile grows larger, taunting my thoughts and out of control heart. "Beg me." His whispered words suck all the air out of the room.

"Please?" I say between gritted teeth, feeling it burn all the way out.

He cups his hand to his ear pretending he didn't hear me. "Couldn't hear ya. What was that?" he asks, feigning innocence.

Rolling my eyes, I say it a little louder and with a little less attitude. *"Please*, Hade."

He ponders for a second, and then the playfulness drops from his face. "Kneel," he commands in his Cardinal voice, leaving no room for questions. My mind sputters, not sure I heard him right.

"On your knees, Nyxi. You'll do as I say, and I'll grant you chaperoned access to the library."

I hesitantly shake my head, but the look he gives me makes my shaking, traitorous legs slowly lower to the unforgiving floor. I'm kneeling in front of him, fully at his mercy. Adrenaline pumps through my veins, making me break out in full body sweats.

His sinister but seductive voice cascades down from above. "Clean your spit from my boot," he says casually.

Is he serious? Reluctantly, I reach a shaky hand forward to wipe my spit away, but I stop when I hear him tsk.

"With your tongue, *Nightmare.*" He smirks down at me, and fuck me, if I'm not turned on and pissed off at the same time. I hate giving up control and feeling beneath someone, but I also feel powerful knelt before him, as if I'm just as in control. I can tell by the way his chest heaves in time with mine that he's holding on by a thread, and I'm the one doing it to him.

Knowing this is my only option, I lean forward and ever so slowly lick the tip of his boot all the way to the laces. It's gritty and dirty, but surprisingly, my stomach also flips with excitement that I nervously stash away to ponder another time.

I look up and watch as he quickly unclenches his fists. "Again, you missed a spot. Eyes on me this time," he commands, though his words have turned breathless.

Narrowing my eyes, I lean down, holding firm eye contact as I swipe my tongue across his boot while simultaneously flipping him off. His eyes close briefly, and a low growl escapes his throat. He's crumbling before me, and all I've done is lick his shoe.

Leaning back up, I cross my arms over my chest and glare at him, making my mood known. I may be feeling things I'm currently confused about, but that doesn't overpower the feeling of being thoroughly done with his little game. He towers over me from down here, and I wonder what it would be like to curl up in bed with him. Would he take up the entire bed? Would it feel like I was drowning in his embrace? Would he be firm from his muscles, or would I melt into his body like a dream?

It's like he knows I'm thinking about him, because he wears the smuggest smile now, looking proud of himself. The last thing I needed was make him think he can control me, but I keep reminding myself I had good cause for bending to his will—though I'm not sure what my excuse will be the next time I crumble at his demands.

"I hate you!" I seethe up at him.

He chuckles again as his eyes turn heated, both obsidian in the dim hallway. He takes a step forward, his feet touching my knees now, and lifts my chin up with his thumb and pointer finger. "I don't think you hate me at all, Nyxi." I let out a small whimper but keep my face masked in anger.

I shake my head no, but he doesn't buy it. Looking back and forth between my eyes, he speaks straight into my soul. "I think you hate that you *don't* hate me at all. I think you might even *like* me."

I go to spit on his shoe again, but he shakes his head at me in warning. I dig my nails into my palms to stop myself from punching him straight in the dick. I stand, fed up at this point, but he steps closer, backing me against the wall. I'm trapped, our chests brushing with each deep breath. I can't think straight when his towering presence makes it hard to form complete sentences.

"I'm not a liar, and I promise, I would never waste a single precious second of my life thinking about *you*." I'm not convinced with the words coming out of my mouth at this point, but I hope they come across strong enough to land the jab.

He has the audacity to laugh at my response, like he knows I'm pulling shit out of my ass. He leans forward and scoops up one of my curls, slowly tucking it behind my ear as he whispers, "Should I go get Winston then and settle this once and for all? Because even without his Fib abilities, I can smell your lie for the shit it is."

He's so close, I can smell his overpowering smoke and sandalwood scent wrapping around me. Fuck him and his giant ego that has me questioning my sanity and morals. Just a couple inches separate our lips, and if I wanted to, I could easily find out exactly how his full lips would taste on mine. Instead, I draw my knee up, slamming it into his balls, giving him a personal relationship with my signature move.

He doubles over but chuckles, knowing he's won this round. "Open the fucking door, Hade." I growl the words, leaving no room for question. "I held up my end of the bargain, and now, it's your turn."

He nods while holding his balls protectively and shuffles past me, wrapping his hand around the handle as shadows slither down his arm to push the door open. The damn thing doesn't burn his hand off like it did mine, though I secretly wish it did.

He strides in, gesturing me inside with his arm, and then plops down into a weathered chair sitting in the center. I guess the permanent indent must be from him, meaning he spends a decent amount of time here. He leans back in the chair, crossing his legs and propping them up on the coffee table. He pulls a book up that was wedged between the side of the chair and settles in to read.

I stand frozen just inside the door, not sure what to do now. Looking over the top of his book, he gestures with his arm. "Browse away, little hellion."

Looking around, I take in the tall shelves packed with all types of books. It doesn't look like they are organized in any particular order, which only makes it harder. I'm inside, though, and that's a small win for today.

The thick odor of aged paper permeates the air, making me relax. There's something about the scent of bound paper that comforts me. Each of the bookshelves differ in size, height, and color, creating a collage that oddly makes sense. I can tell which shelves are used more often, while others carry a thick coat of dust on them. I assume the untouched shelves might be the best start to my investigation.

Walking to the back left corner of the room, I approach the first dusty shelf and crouch down, starting at the bottom. The spines hold different titles ranging from agriculture to health remedies. I make my way up to the top shelf, but nothing seems to peak my interest.

I move to the next shelf over, bending down to start my search again. There must be thousands of books in here, so I don't get my hopes up; I can at least make a dent today. I continue down the line, finding books about different recorded sicknesses, species of poisonous plants, and how to forge weapons.

Every so often, I catch Hade watching me from over the top of his book, but I try not to acknowledge him. I can feel his eyes burning into the back of my head without even looking at him. His overbearing presence is thick and palpable.

He catches me staring and winks at me over his book just as something bumps into the back of my head. *Ow!* Before I can turn to see what hit me, my eyes snag on a book floating through the air and into Hade's waiting hand.

"Really, is your aim so bad, you couldn't avoid hitting the *one* person inside this giant room?" I massage the back of my head to dull the tingling. It didn't hurt that bad, but he doesn't need to know that. "And how did you even do that?"

"Trust me, my aim is superb in *everything* I do. I never miss." He smirks. "You were looking a little tired, so I thought I would help you out. You're welcome. As for the floating book, I feel like that is self-explanatory. *Magic.*"

He starts reading his new book, dismissing me, but I scoff in frustration. "Use your words, Nyxi," he snarks without looking up at me.

Planting my hand on my hip, I glare at him. "No shit it's magic. I want to know *how* it works. If you could please be so kind as to explain, *sir!*" I grit out, pushing his buttons to their max. This game of push and pull is like an addiction, even with how hard I try to stop myself from playing.

I have his attention now. Closing his book, he plants his feet back on the ground and sits straight. "Each book in here has been spelled. If you know the title of the book and think it in your head, it will come to you. It's as simple as that."

"And if you don't know the exact title of the book, then what?" I ask.

He ponders my question for a moment. "I have every title memorized, so I'm not quite sure. I would assume if you were to think about a specific topic, maybe it could call to you. But you have to factor in that there are many similar books in here, and that could turn into chaos quickly, so I wouldn't advise." He leans back in his chair, bored of this topic, and dives into his new book.

Thinking this over, I return to my hunt for answers. I snag a few books along the way that may be promising, books about the history of Lunaria and the limits of magic. They are all factual and to the point, but it couldn't hurt to flip through them later. There could be a detail in one of them that can lead me in the right direction.

I let out a big yawn, about ready to retire to my room, but I decide to try something first. Closing my eyes, I call to the books around me and recite the riddle in my head. I wait and wait, but nothing happens. No books fly through the air or spark my attention. Trying again, I decide to change tactics. Calling to the books again, I simply ask them for answers.

Nothing happens at first, but when I go to leave, my feet won't let me move. It's like my body is pulling me away from the door. Closing my eyes, I reach inside myself, feeling around for that pull again. Like an invisible rope, I latch on to the feeling, and my body takes over, dragging my feet across the room until I'm standing in front of a bookshelf hidden in the corner.

My eyes search the shelf and catch on a row of brown, leather bound books with no titles on their spines nestled at the bottom. They're uniform in size; there has to be at least twenty of them pressed together.

Looking over at Hade, I make sure he isn't watching me as I snag the first one off the shelf. Peeling it open, I realize it's a journal. There's a name carved into the front, but it's so weathered, it's impossible to read.

I briefly flip through the pages, noticing handwritten entries each dated by age. I'm not sure whose journal it is, but I know there must be something inside to help me. I slide it under my cloak to hide it away. I know Hade is okay with me taking a few history books to read, but I don't think that applies to someone's journal collection that is obviously important and hidden for a reason. I'll start with one and slowly trade them out so he won't notice.

Walking back over to Hade, I tap his shoulder. "Thank you, *Death Reaper*. It's always a pleasure." I fake bow, mocking him with as much sarcasm as I can infuse into my tone. "Now, if you'll excuse me, I'll get out of your hair and leave more room for your giant ego."

I go to walk away, but his hand darts out, tightly gripping my wrist. "I'll walk you back."

"I'd rather you didn't," I grunt, trying to pull my arm from his hand.

"You make it sound like I was giving you a choice."

I go to say something snarky, but I decide better. Schooling my features, I nod to him once. He can't possibly know I stole one of the journals, but it's not smart of me to push his buttons right now and possibly out myself—or even worse, drop the journal in front of him. My body loves to turn to mush when Hade's involved, and I'd rather not have to explain myself out of that one. *Oops, sorry, sir, I didn't notice there was a journal stashed under my arm. How silly of me.* Yeah, no thank you.

I rip my arm away, making him chuckle as he strides in front of me to open the door. I sarcastically curtsy to him, and I swear, I notice the slight curve of his lip in a genuine half-smile. I commit it to memory, loving the ease at which it bloomed across his face. My little heart pounds like a drum from the simplest things this man does, force feeding me little parts of himself I want to stash away like a hibernating animal. It's confusing and infuriating.

I try to put as much distance between us as possible, hoping I can blend into the shadows and sneak back to my room. In three large strides, though, he has caught back up to me with ease. Grunting, I keep my face forward and pretend he's not there.

He lets out a breathy, soft laugh. "Brat," he says in an amused tone.

Spinning on my heels, I turn to face him, which only makes him run right into my chest. "I only agreed to let you walk me back to my room, I never agreed to acknowledge you while doing it." I have to crane my neck to look into his eyes.

He takes a step forward, making me take a step back to match him. "Forgive me for being a gentleman, *Nyxi*."

My stomach erupts in a cascade of butterflies, light as a feather, floating through the wind. No matter how many times this man says my full name, it always seems to catch me off guard. He makes it sound like a prayer rolling off his tongue, like I'm his salvation, the answer to all his problems. Even though he's fed up with me, no matter what, he always says it in the softest tone, handling it with care.

Nyxi, the girl made of glass.

He's still staring down at me, and I realize I've zoned out thinking about this man calling me by my damn name. Nothing is ever all sunshine with Hade, though, and it's something I've grown accustomed to.

"Would you have liked me to treat you like the brat you are? Throw you over my shoulder like old times and march you back to your room? Parade you around the hallways for everyone to see? Showing them you're my little play thing? Or, more accurately, my personal *nightmare*."

Yes! my brain shouts without thought, and I'm stunned. This man is not nice; he's not even good, and he's certainly not *Theo*. I shouldn't get excited over his threats, but my mind also takes note of the fact that I'm *feeling* emotions again, something I thought would never return to me. Unfortunately, Hade happens to be the one drawing me out of that very dark place I've expected to rot in for the rest of my existence. It's too confusing for me to understand, and so all I can do is continue in ignorant bliss.

I turn around and continue to walk again before my traitorous body does something dumb, like kiss enemy number one. If I stayed there one moment longer, I'm not sure how my body would have reacted. I'm not sure my heart is ready for the consequences. I slow my pace this time, looking over at him every few steps to show I'm not entirely ignoring him anymore.

He just chuckles and keeps pace with me, halving his strides. "I thought so," he says, making me roll my eyes. I can play nice and not ignore him, but I also don't have to be sunshine and rainbows.

Instead, I decide to ask him something that's been sitting at the back of my mind since the ball, attempting to change the mood. "Who is Aire?" I question. He looks confused as to why I'm bringing this person up and how I even know who they are. "The Empress, when she walked out on us in the garden, she said you were to inform Aire of the details of the first round of the Crucible."

He nods in understanding. "He lives in the castle and runs Lunaria for the Empress while she is in Fallout. She spends a lot of her time down there, keeping the peace, and so when she's gone, Aire steps in and acts as interim Emperor, basically."

That was not what I was expecting. "Why have I never heard of him then, if he's that important?"

"The Empress likes to be the face so they don't get confused on who's in charge or try to rebel. Aire likes to stay in the shadows and control things in the background. He likes to remain a secret so he can move about Lunaria without drawing attention. He is a powerful player in the Empress' pocket and has more sway than you would think."

Now, I'm just plain confused. "Why tell me this, then, if he's to remain a secret?"

He licks his lips, looking more exhausted than I've ever seen him. "I honestly don't know. I guess I'm tired of holding everyone's secrets, and this one seems harmless enough. For some odd reason, I trust you, Nyxi. Trust does not come easy to me, so don't prove me wrong. Since the day I met you, I've felt this weird pull, like I've known you in a different life. It sounds silly, but I have always listened to the greater call in life. It has yet to fail me."

I nervously swallow and catch him watching the dip of my neck. Nodding back, I try to unravel this bomb of a confession. I find it weirdly comforting knowing he has felt this same indescribable pull that I've been failing to push aside. I'm not sure I believe in destiny, but since day one, there's been something nagging under my skin when it comes to Hade. It's unfamiliar, as if my body is telling me I can trust him before my mind has caught up. I usually try to scramble away from others, but my body seems to notice his presence before my eyes have even spotted him, like it knows something I'm not privy to yet. Just what that is, I'm not so sure of.

"Your secret is safe with me, Hade. I promise." I shoot him a soft smile to try and draw the stiffness from his body, the torment from his face.

He relaxes, letting his shoulders drop and his strides soften. "Thank you," he replies softly.

We walk a comfortable silence this time. Approaching my door, he turns and abruptly grips my face in both hands. He searches my eyes for answers I'm not sure I could give me, trying to pluck the meaning of this pull we feel straight from my very soul. My heart pounds in my ears as I look up at him with wide, vulnerable eyes, willing him to find the answers he wants. He looks like he can taste it on the very tip of his tongue before he sighs, frustrated. Slowly, he plants a soft kiss on my temple. "Sweet dreams, Nyxi." And then he disappears to nothing right before my eyes.

Chapter
Twenty-Three

Journal Entry

Age 12

I noticed a small, intricate marking on Mama today and asked her what it was. She sat me down and explained to me what an Eternal is. She told me her and Papa are Eternals, so they share identical markings that signify their bond. They share a bond stronger than what the word <u>love</u> covers, and this marking signifies it. It was destiny that brought them together, a greater power drawing them to one another since the day they were born. I asked her how she knew she and Papa were Eternals, and she looked me straight in the eyes and said the world changes the day you find your Eternal, like an awakening. Your lungs intertwine with theirs, so if they breathe, you breathe, and if they don't, oxygen ceases to exist to you. Once you find your Eternal, your fate is set, and you are connected for life, however long that may be. She explained some Eternal bonds are so strong, if one dies, the other to passes away from a broken heart shortly after. I asked her how strong her and Papa's bond was, and all she did was smile down at me with watery eyes and kiss my forehead. She pulled me into a hug and whispered that she prays every night I will be lucky enough one day to find my Eternal, that I will have someone I can trust to watch over me, to love me when she and Papa can no longer. This made me cry, and I asked Mama why she would ever leave me. She just brushed away the wet strands of hair sticking to my face and told me the world isn't always a kind place. I don't want Mama and Papa to ever leave me.

Chapter
Twenty-Four

"Congratulations, contestants, on making it to the second round of the Reaper Crucible." The Empress stands before us, wearing one of her signature red silk gowns. Her hair is pulled back into a high slicked ponytail, and rings adorn each of her fingers like pieces of art. Her voice is amplified, her face smug.

"Your hard work has paid off for now, but do not get too comfortable. You have fared better than two of your competitors, but today is a new day. Keep your wits and never underestimate any player. Each round is designed to test a different skill to find the most well rounded among you. The first round tested your stamina, speed, and agility. Today's round will test not only your brain, but your strength. You cannot excel in one without the other." She looks down the line of us.

I'm not the smartest here, seeing as Cartwell is a certified genius, but I'll bet on myself any day over those like Tank. He's all muscle with nothing going on up top. I'm also confident enough in my strength and light enough to hold myself up if need be.

Hade stands next to the Empress once again, but this time, he avoids eye contact with me, which sets me on edge. I miss the way his gaze feels like a warm presence, like a piece of him is with me, watching over me. It's embarrassing to admit, but his lack of attention has soured my mood. I shouldn't be upset over this, though, because every time he tries to get close to me, my instinct is to be a bitch and push him away. It's my default setting, a visceral reaction to being backstabbed and left to rot one too many times. At this point, I don't know any other way to live life.

Drawing my eyes away from the man who seems to attract all my attention, I focus back on the Empress. "I will now announce this week's rankings before explaining this round."

The Empress motions above her as an Illuminist projects the rankings. I squint against the harsh sunlight pouring in and look for my name. Tank and Jade sit at the top of the leaderboard, and I'm angered that their names are even on there. Scanning down, I see my name with Aeron's in the middle again. Yazi and Ray sit at the bottom, which makes my heart break a little for my friend. My intentions were to ally with Ray and help her out, but the circumstances didn't allow such opportunities.

"For one to be deserving of the power magic holds, they must be sharp, strong, inquisitive, adaptable, and a leader. Today's game will test some of these traits to weed out the weak." The Empress snaps her fingers, and two towers of wooden blocks are unveiled. The crowd outside scoots closer to get a better look, chattering loudly.

I try to search my mind for any clues. Growing up in an orphanage, I wasn't allowed the opportunity to play many games as a child, but that doesn't mean I didn't hear others talk about the most popular ones and how fun they were.

"I'm sure none of you are unfamiliar with the classic game of Tumbling Towers, but you may be confused. In classic form, this game is much smaller and involves zero strength or danger. Where's the fun in that, though?" She gestures to the crowd outside the Bubble. "So, I decided to turn up the heat. We have increased the size of the blocks, making them large and awkward to carry. Now, they tower high above even your biggest competitor, Tank." She points over to him, his cheeks turning a rosy red.

She walks forward to stand next to the closest stack of blocks, gesturing to it. "You will be randomly split into two groups of four, going head to head with three of your competitors. You must choose wisely as to which block you select to slide from the tower using your hands. You may climb up the tower to pull any block. If you knock the tower down at any time, the game is over, and you lose."

With the help of a Float, the Empress waves her hand at a block sitting in the center of the stack, and it slides out, floating over to her. "Once you have successfully chosen a block, you will notice a trivia question burned into its face. You must read it out loud and guess the correct answer. If you guess correctly, you will then have to climb up the stack of blocks holding your chosen piece and stack it back at the top without making it tumble. *But*, if you fail to answer correctly, you must pull another block until you get one right. You then must stack all the blocks you've pulled at the top. You will take turns until one person on each team knocks down their tower. Be precise, thoughtful, and keep your wits about you, because if you fail this task, then you are sentenced to death at the hands of the Cardinal. Once both towers have been knocked over, the game will be finished."

After finishing her speech, she quietly asks each of us if we have come up with an answer to her riddle. Of course, we all shake our heads in defeat. Her eyes seem to snag extra long on mine, and I catch the faintest clench of her jaw in disappointment. I brush it off and focus back on the game.

I've definitely never played this game before, but it seems simple enough. The tricky part will be trying to balance the oversized block on my shoulder while simultaneously climbing up the tower to stack it. I have scaled many buildings while on spying missions, so I feel confident in my light feet and grippy fingers. My small frame will fare better over some of the men, who can easily topple the tower over with just their body weight.

Making a game plan, I decide most of my competitors will probably start at the bottom of the stack, pulling the easier blocks in hopes it won't make it back to them again. My plan of attack is to lean on my climbing abilities to scale the tower and pull a block towards the top of the stack. As long as I can answer the question correctly, I will only have a small section to scale while holding the block before stacking it. My competitors will have to scale a majority of the tower holding their block if they pull from the bottom. My only challenge is the trivia question. Knowing the Empress, she has not made them simple by any means.

The Empress calls out our names, dividing our group. As I line up in front of the right tower, my mind wanders back to what the Empress said. While this round will be less dangerous than the first, two people will still die today. Not only will they die, but they will sit there knowing their fate after the game has ended and can do nothing about it.

Hade, the mighty Cardinal, oversees sentencing the two losers to death in any way he chooses. My heart races at the thought of him taking my life like it's nothing. Will he do it right away in front of everyone, or in private later? Will he make it fast and painless, or brutal and painful, slowly dragging it out over hours or days? Will he feel guilty, or will he carry on like it's just another task to check off his list? Would he look me in the eyes as he drains the life out of me? For some reason, I feel at peace knowing if I were to lose my life today, *Hade* would be my demise. The truth is, I think Hade has been my demise long before today.

Looking around, I spot Sierra, Rayah, and Tank lined up next to me, leaving Aeron, Yazi, Cartwell, and Jade standing in front of the left tower. A Vanquisher approaches us, holding his palm out, four stones nestled in the center. We each grab one and flip it over to reveal a number on the backside, giving us our playing order.

Looking down, I see the number one etched into my rock. I'm more than okay going first; the tower will be at its peak sturdiness for me to climb. Looking up at the tower in front of me, I look around for any blocks that look less wedged in than others. I feel a pull towards the top left of the tower, my body turning me on its own to look. *This one*, it seems to tell me, and I notice a block three rows down from the top that, if you look at just the right angle, is slightly hanging off the edge.

"Those who have selected rock one please step forward now." The Empress stands between the two towers, her face the personification of evil. She enjoys this too much. Stepping forward, I line up in front of the tower, craning my neck to look up to the top.

"May the brightest and strongest competitors come out on top." With that, she claps twice and gracefully strides out of the Bubble, Hade and the other Vanquishers in tow. The citizens outside scream, chanting for their favorite competitors.

The sun makes my palms slick with sweat, so I drag them down my legs, attempting to dry them off. The last thing I need is for one of my hands to slip off the side of the tower, bringing it tumbling down, my life with it.

I bounce back and forth on the balls of my feet, warming my body up. My adrenaline is at its peak, fueling my body. I feel like I could take on a beast right now with the way my body hums to life. Looking over, I see the Empress settle into her throne chair, nodding to the Illuminist standing between the two towers to capture all the drama up close for all of Lunaria and Fallout's viewing pleasure.

Of course, Aeron has also chosen rock one, standing in front of the tower next to me. He shoots me a heated wink; I roll my eyes at him, laughing softly. Leave it to Aeron to lighten the mood, even when faced with potential death.

"You may begin." The Illuminist gestures to the two of us, and everything fades to the back of my mind as I zero in on the one block between me and my safety.

Racing forward, I wedge my foot into the crevice where two blocks meet and hoist myself up. Flinging my hands up, I latch on to a block in the center of the stack that seems the sturdiest. Thankfully, the tower holds, and I continue my pursuit. I make quick work maneuvering around the blocks, avoiding ones that look off centered or wobbly.

I'm halfway up the tower when suddenly, my left hand slips on a simple side shuffle from sweat coating my palm. I squeal as pains pulses in my right shoulder from holding my dangling body. From this height, I wouldn't die, but it still would hurt like hell.

My fingers slowly slide closer to the edge of the block as my feet aimlessly try and find purchase. I feel a bead of sweat roll over my forehead and down my nose, landing on the top of my lip, forcing me to taste its saltiness. I close my eyes and take a deep, calming breath. Looking down, I see the perfect crevice to wedge my flailing feet in and secure them under my body again, drawing my chest close to the tower.

Looking up, I count eight more rows until I can reach the block I want. Slowly, one hand at a time, I drag them each down to my leg to wipe them dry again, before I continue with my climb. Reaching the last row, I look over to see Aeron has already successfully pulled his block and is reading his question. I can't hear what he's saying over the loud screams from outside the Bubble ringing in my ears.

Twisting to lean against the tower, I slowly prod the block with my fingers, finding the best angle to dislodge it. At first attempt, it doesn't move an inch. When I go at it from the opposite side, it slowly wiggles free enough for me to wrap my hand around it and slide it out.

I draw it close to my chest, catching my breath before going any further. Flipping it around, I read the words burned into its surface. I read it three times through in my head, just as confused as the first time reading it over.

"Out loud, contestant!" the Illuminist screams from below over the raging crowd.

Cursing to myself, I hold out the block and read it aloud, "What is so fragile that saying its name breaks it?"

What kind of trickery is this? I should have known the Empress wouldn't have given us easy questions…but this? This is just nonsense. How does solving a silly riddle like this prove I'm intelligent? If anything, I thought the questions would be on the history of magic, the lands we live in, and our *perfect* Empress. Maybe some of them do contain questions like that, which, honestly, I wouldn't know the closest answer to either, so maybe this is my best bet.

I assume there is no time limit to this, but I'm sure my competitors are not far off from scaling this tower just to throw me off at this point. My mind races a million miles a second, trying to latch on to anything. There's too much noise around me, making my brain foggy and confused. Citizens scream while beating their chests and stomping their feet to a loud rhythm. It's too much for me to focus. I just need silence.

Silence! What is so fragile that saying its name breaks it… The answer is silence. A huge smile takes over my face as I confidently shout my answer, earning a nod from the Illuminist.

I silently praise myself for somehow pulling that answer out of my ass. Who knew I had it in me? Chuckling to myself, I look up to the top of the tower and scout my path while figuring out how to carry the block up with me.

It's only a short way to the top, so I decide to wedge the block long ways between my thighs and use my upper body strength to pull myself up another row. My feet dangle in the air, my legs gripping the block for dear life. Once my hands are both wedged in tight a row up, I reach one hand down and grab the block so I can wedge my feet in again for stability, relieving my one arm holding me up. With only two rows between me and the top of the tower, I decide I'm close enough to carefully hoist the block high above my head and slowly stack it at the top.

Grabbing the top of the block, I shimmy it up between my body and the tower, making sure if I accidentally drop it, I can still throw my body into it to stop its descent. Once the tip reaches the top of my shoulder, I pull it up and balance it on the top of my shoulder, making the very tip of the block go slightly higher than the top of the tower, leaning against it. Grabbing the bottom resting on my shoulder, I slowly push up, the top tip cresting over the upper row and sliding into place.

Not thinking, I look down and realize just how high I've climbed, making me dizzy. Shaking my head out, I realize climbing down is going to be a bit more difficult than the ascent, but not impossible, seeing as I've scaled down more buildings than I can count.

I make quick work of my travel back to the ground, looking down every now and then to scan over my competitors. Aeron is already safely back on the ground, and Jade is now scaling the tower next to me, making quick time with her tiny frame. Jumping the last few feet, my shoes hit the ground, and the tower remains stacked high above me. I look over to the Illuminist, who nods his head to Rayah for her turn to start.

Getting back in line with my opponents, I watch as Rayah follows my lead, climbing a decent way up the tower before deciding which block to pull. Reaching for one of the blocks, she goes to tug it free, but the block holds steady, making her arm fling back and knocking her unsteady. Her other hand slips, and she topples backwards, freefalling to the ground.

Letting out a loud gasp, my heart lodges itself in my throat as I go to lunge forward, attempting to lessen her fall. My feet stay planted where they are, though, no matter how hard I tug at them. Shocked, I look down and notice two shadowy black rings binding my legs together, rendering them immobile. A loud thud draws my eyes up as I see Ray's small frame encased in a cloud of dust from harshly hitting the sand.

The dust clears, but she remains still for a few seconds before her body starts to wiggle the smallest amount. She lets out a loud gasp, drawing in her first full breath. She slowly sits up and tries to regulate her breathing. Looking down, I notice the small, barely noticeable black rings are gone, and I run over to my friend to check on her.

"Are you hurt? Can you move your arms and legs? Talk to me, Ray," I beg.

"Flowers, that was both exhilarating and just plain painful," she huffs out in a breath. "Remind me never to do that again, Nyxi. Do you think everyone saw that? My family is going to be so embarrassed."

Grabbing her face in both my hands, I look intensely into her eyes. "Listen to me very carefully when I say this. Who gives a fuck what anyone thinks? You're here and you're doing the damn thing, and that's a hell of a lot more than any of these people will do with the entire remainder of their pathetic lives, your family included. Now, what I care about is if you're hurt or not." I give her no room to object.

I couldn't care less what anyone says about her, as long as she makes it through this round alive. This woman is sweeter than sugar and deserves the chance to finally have a life worth living. She pokes around her body, wincing at a few places, but she shakes her head at me that she's okay, making her vibrant pink hair bounce.

Helping her up, I brush the dust off her back and give her words of encouragement and tips on a few places I saw some easy blocks to pull. Returning to the line, I watch in awe as Ray makes quick work of scaling the tower once again, like she didn't just almost fall to her death.

I notice Jade has pulled her block, and she must have answered correctly, because she is now placing it securely at the top of the tower. The back of my neck suddenly tingles, and I squirm uncomfortably. I drag my eyes back to Ray, and they snag on two piercing eyes that are undeniably solely focused on me.

Hade.

I should have known the second I saw the black bands holding me that it was his doing. He lives to control me in any way he can, which apparently extends to when and where my body can go. I don't believe for a second he did it out of the kindness of his heart to protect me. He must have some ulterior motive behind the move, one I can't name.

Flipping him off, I choose to ignore the beast and settle my focus back on my friend, shouting her words of encouragement along the way. She makes it back to her original spot but decides to pull the block to its left, which was one of the loose ones I pointed out to her. She then reads the question out loud for all to hear.

"What is the species of flower that resembles a white feathered bird taking flight?" Ray giggles to herself, making it seem like everyone should know the answer to this question. If I got this question, I would be shit out of luck, but seeing the sweet smile bloom on Ray's face makes me confident she is certain of the answer.

"White Egret Orchid," she calls down, and the Illuminist nods in agreement. She stacks the block on her shoulder, following my example, and slowly climbs to the top, placing the block next to mine. She takes her time making her way back to the ground and successfully makes it back without toppling the tower.

She skips over to me with a huge smile on her face, looking damn proud of herself. Ruffling her hair, I pull her into a side hug as we turn to watch Sierra take her turn next.

"That was something else!" Ray squeals next to me, coming off her adrenaline high like an addict. She's literally bouncing next to me like a kid hyped up on candy. I grab one of her shoulders, slowing her down.

"You need to preserve your energy. There is still a chance you may have to go again. I don't want you to be exhausted from all this shaking before you even step a foot back on the tower," I say to her, but I add a side smirk so she doesn't think I'm scolding her.

"She's not wrong. It would be wise of you to reserve your energy." Aeron's smooth voice slithers over my shoulder. Turning my head, I come face to face with his icy blue eyes and tan skin. "That was a nasty slip up you had there, but I'm impressed with your determination," he coos to Ray, making her blush.

Knocking my shoulder into his, I say, "Shouldn't you be over there studying your opponents and keeping your head focused instead of being a shameless flirt to anything that moves?"

"I would have to feel ashamed for that to be true, Vagrant, and that's just not the case, I'm afraid." He gives me a flirty wink and goes to step closer when I catch the faintest black floating line in the corner of my eye. Aeron's foot snags on it, making it look like he tripped over himself, and he lands face first, snagging a mouth full of sand in the process. Most people would be embarrassed, but leave it to Aeron to gracefully stand back up and beam down at me. "You literally have me weak in the knees every time I lay my eyes on you."

I shove him, but he just chuckles to himself, getting ready for the possibility of climbing for a second time. Quickly, I shoot my eyes back to the troublemaker I know was at fault for Aeron's little misstep, but Hade remains scanning for any danger around the Empress. This time, though, he's flaunting a shit eating grin on his face, looking proud of himself.

Empress save me.

Suddenly, a piercing scream makes me throw my hands up to cover my ears, looking up just in time to see Sierra's bright red hair tumbling towards the ground. Blocks litter the space above me, raining down alongside her.

Grabbing Ray's wrist, I drag her back with me, just narrowly missing a large wooden block that hits the ground right where we were standing. *BOOM!* The sounds of block after block assault the ground, creating a giant dust cloud. I've lost where Sierra landed, her small frame now piled with a tall stack of fallen blocks.

The dust clears, and half of the tower now resides on the floor, ending our portion of the game before Tank even had a chance to go, which doesn't seem fair. The other contestants are still competing for their lives next to us. I spot a couple blocks being shoved, and a bruised and bloody, but very much alive, Sierra emerges from the rubble. She looks devastated, and even though I know it's her or me, I still feel sick to my stomach at the thought of her losing her life.

A Vanquisher walks over, dragging her away to stand on the side to wait for the second game to finish. She thrashes in his hold, but she's too weak to put up a fight. I focus my attention back on the other tower, noticing Cartwell has just successfully pulled a block.

"State the five sectors of Fallout in ranking order and their specialties," he reads out loud, rolling his eyes at how simple his question is. Leave it to the genius to be upset at getting an easy question.

"Command Sector who makes and enforces our laws. Enlightened Sector are our scholars who pass down knowledge through each generation. Visionary Sector houses our creatives and healers. Sweat Sector provides physical labor, building our lands and tending to our food supply. And that leaves Vagrant Sector... They, uh, they just are, I guess." He shrugs. The Vanquisher gives him the go ahead, and he makes his way to stack his block at the top.

I try to focus on Cartwell and his vibrant blue hair, but I fail because my mind keeps thinking about another man. A man whose rough hands have delicately caressed my face. Hands that have slipped between my curls and gently tucked them behind my ear. Hands that have made my body come alive under them, and now, they are about to take another's life.

How many lives have these hands claimed? How many times have they blindly obeyed an unjust ruler in the name of duty? These revelations should bother me, but I can't seem to push aside this growing ache within me. Embarrassingly, though, what does bother me is thinking about how many other women those hands have explored before me that I am not privy to. My body is not unique in knowing the effects this man can pull out of it without even trying.

The hands of a *killer* have brought me back to *life*.

Cartwell successfully makes it back down, and Yazi takes his place. Yazi is an older man, probably in his late fifties, his hair having long turned gray. After talking with him during training, I've learned he has a kind soul. After tragically losing his late wife, he vowed he would enter the Crucible in hopes of earning magic and never having to feel powerless again. It's way to take control over his life, and I find it honorable. He is in great shape for his age, but it will still be a challenge for him to climb to the top of the tower. He opts to pull a block from the bottom, where it's still sturdy. Reading it off, he hesitantly answers and fails to guess correctly. He slides to the other side of the tower one row up and slides another block free. Reading his second question, he confidently answers it correctly and stacks both blocks on his left shoulder, attempting to carry both to the top at the same time.

Slowly, he takes his time dragging his body up. Leaning, he attempts to wedge his foot in a small crack as one of the blocks on his shoulder slips and topples backwards. He quickly lunges for it, attempting to catch it before it's out of reach, but his momentum drags the tower along with him, and they all come crashing back down to the ground. Just like that, another life has been sentenced to death in a matter of seconds.

Yazi shoots up from the rubble, frantically looking around for an escape route. He lunges, sprinting for his life right past me, knocking me down in his pursuit. I crash to the ground next to Ray, who looks at me wide eyed.

"I'm okay," I promise her, dragging my body up off the ground. I can tell this part of the trials is too much for her, the reality of people losing their lives settling deep within her. Her breaths turn a fraction deeper, and a younger-looking Vanquisher, who I assume is her guard, drags her to the side, whispering who knows what in her ear. Whatever he said seems to have calmed her, which I find intriguing. He whisks her away with a hand on the small of her back, heading back towards the castle.

Hearing a loud grunt, I swivel on my feet, catching two Vanquishers tackling Yazi, taking him to the ground. He swings his arms furiously to no avail as they slowly choke him into unconsciousness, his body going slack.

"Now, now, children, you all knew what you were signing up for when you entered this greedy game for magic," the Empress purrs out from in front of us, suddenly appearing back in the Bubble. "Now, it is time to pay up. Two lives in payment for the opportunity of a lifetime. Hopefully, you have better luck in the afterlife. Maybe you can strike a better deal with the gods while you're there."

Hade rounds her body, kneeling on one knee with a mask of indifference. Right now, he is not Hade, the man who bent me over a wishing well and whispered filthy things in my ear, who delicately cleaned and patched my wound. This is the Cardinal, the brute in charge of the Empress' bidding…her killing machine.

"My dear Cardinal," her seductive voice makes me squirm in disgust, "as my trusted right hand, I leave the choice of their deaths to you. Your wish is my command. My only rule is that it must be now, for all to see."

Hade's indifference slips the smallest amount, almost looking thrown off guard at her request. He recovers quickly before anyone can notice. He nods once to the Empress, and I see him conjuring up a plan in his head. He looks off to me, his jaw clenched a fraction tighter than normal, his face a shade slightly paler, but I doubt anyone else can see the difference that's as clear as day to me. I realize I may know Hade better than anyone here. I may be in too deep with this beast.

He gets up, walking to stand in front of Yazi, who is now awake and being held between two Vanquishers. Sierra is being held in place by one Vanquisher next to him. Donning a mask of boredom, Hade speaks with a monotone voice.

"I'm quite tired and hungry, to be honest, and your lives hold zero value to me. So, I will make this quick." With a simple flick of his wrist, two black shadows swirl around both of their necks, squeezing tight, turning their faces bright red. He's choking them to death with his magic. Their wide, scared eyes slowly start to droop shut as they fight, failing to take a single breath. Their shaking bodies flail less and less until they both fall limp, sucked of life.

Two more souls sacrificed in the name of entertainment.

"Not the theatrics I was looking for, but death is death, I suppose. I'm quite famished as well," the Empress pouts.

My stomach threatens to unleash itself, a panic attack looming over me. I turn to look away, bending at the waist to put my head between my knees. I take long, deep breaths, trying to regulate my breathing before it takes off in an untamable beast I've grown too familiar with. I feel a warm hand drag up and down my back and realize it's Aeron standing next to me.

Calming myself, I manage to keep my breakfast down as Aeron pulls me back to my feet. Linking arms with him, the Empress dismisses us back to our rooms for the remainder of the day, and Aeron pulls me towards the exit. We pass the two lifeless bodies on the ground, and I force my eyes to look away, shaking slightly.

Just as we reach the edge of the Bubble, I feel the soft, familiar tickle at the edge of my ear. "Do you trust me?" a faint, desperate whisper speaks into my ear.

I could recognize that magic in my sleep at this point. The voice sends a shiver down my spine like a caress. I hesitate for only a second, but my answer shocks me. I do, without a doubt, trust this man. I can't explain it, but something in my body tells me that not everything is as it seems.

I nod at something Aeron spouts next to me, but this nod is not meant for him. It's for the man across the other side of the Bubble who I know is watching as I leave. "That is all I could hope for," he whispers, and then I feel the small shadow nestled on the edge of my ear slither away, taking a sliver of me with it.

Chapter
Twenty-Five

Hade has been ignoring me. How pathetic am I to be bothered by a man who literally killed two innocent people right before my eyes? Apparently, this girl.

He meets me at the library each night as promised to let me in. He doesn't say a single word; he just sits in his chair, reading about Empress knows what. I tried to make small talk at first, uncomfortable sitting in silence, but I gave up after he so clearly did not want to speak to me.

He's been different, off. No snarky or sassy comments. No taunts or threats. Just eerie silence. I'm honestly fed up with it. All this time, I've pushed him away, but as soon as he stopped talking to me, it felt wrong, and I yearn to have his attention back.

For the third night in a row, I search the shelves for answers as Hade reads quietly while slouched in his chair. I peek over, finding him lost in his book. It's like the world around him is dead. I take this rare opportunity to study him.

His unruly curls are disheveled from running his hands thoroughly through his hair. It looks perfectly imperfect, like everything else about him. His two beautiful opposite eyes that should scare me off have the opposite effect, captivating me in the dimly lit room. They bring a side of mystery, making me want to know how they came to be. I'm realizing I don't know much about Hade, but I want to, and that is a scary thought.

While he's distracted, I quickly switch out the journal I smuggled for a new one, sliding the old one in its place. I haven't found any leads to the answer for the riddle, but I've still learned some interesting information. I just know the answer has to be somewhere in one of these journals, so I'll keep reading them until I find it.

I'm still clueless as to whose journals these are, but I'm hoping eventually, a name will be dropped in one of the entries. Looking back over at Hade, I decide to ask him a question that's been nagging me.

Nonchalantly, I ask, "Do you believe in love?"

He looks up from his book, and I'm shocked he's even paying me an ounce of attention. His face is blank when he responds, "I think love is fickle and demanding. I think the word can mean a million things, or it can mean nothing at all. I think love likes to take and take until it can leave a person hollow. One can believe in love but not endorse it. I stand in the middle. Love can change a person, and not always for the best."

I nod in understanding—who am I to disagree? Love has gotten me nothing but a scrap of memories to float inside my aching heart for the rest of eternity. It has left me fractured and alone. Love made me give a part of my heart away to another who was then ripped from my grasp. Love can be kind and warm, but it can also feel like a knife to the heart, a killing blow. Love is a gamble on all ends, a game of risk and vulnerability. But if risked on the right person, no matter how short lived, love can be worth it.

"Do you think there is something stronger than love?" I try to sound unbothered, like it's just a random thought. I slowly walk over to his chair, holding eye contact with him. He looks like he isn't going to answer, so I continue past him, accepting this small win of having at least one conversation with him again.

"Why are you asking?" I feel my arm tugged back, and I jump in surprise with a soft gasp.

His face turns down, looking disappointed as his jaw ticks. I realize then he must think I'm scared of him after what I saw him do for the Empress. That must be why he's kept his distance. He's trying not to scare me off. The silly thing is, I'm not scared of him at all. I was just shocked by his bold touch after days of distance.

"Sorry," he mutters, quickly pulling his hand back.

I shine him a soft smile, attempting to show he doesn't scare me. "It's fine. You just surprised me." He nods back, but it's devoid of any emotion, as if he doesn't believe me.

"Just forget I asked," I rush out, not wanting him to implore further about why I'm asking.

"Nyxi," he says in a strained voice, but I'm already halfway across the room.

"I'm quite tired, Hade. I think it's time for me to retire to my room. Will you escort me?"

He nods and approaches my side, leaving his book sitting on his chair. Sliding my arm in his, we walk in silence back to my room. I reach for my door, exhausted and ready to slip into bed, when Hade stops me.

He searches my eyes again. For what, I have no idea, but I feel laid bare before him with the intensity his gaze holds. A million emotions run across his taut features, looking confused and frustrated. Unsatisfied and out of words, he lets out a deep, long breath.

"I would like to hope there is something out there stronger than love, but not all of us are deserving of it." He rushes away without another word, leaving me confused and out of breath, standing alone with nothing but my jumbled thoughts.

Chapter
Twenty-Six

Tired from a long day, I'm ready to slip into bed and peacefully drift off into thoughtless bliss. My entire body aches from pushing it to its limits. I slip off my shoes and make my way over to my bed.

Suddenly, my window shatters, glass spraying everywhere, and I jump back in surprise. A loud shriek draws blood from my ears as I attempt to cover them. The giant, rotting corpse that flies in through my window stares me down from the center of my room, wailing at the top of its lungs. Its pungent smell fills the room, making me gag.

Necroshriek.

I stagger backwards, slipping the covers down the bed to reach for *him*. I scream at the top of my lungs when I discover Theo's tattered, blood-soaked body lying dead in our bed. A loud sob escapes me, hysterically crying while trying to shake his body back to life like there's any hope of resurrecting him.

There's not. He's gone, taken from me too soon.

His skin has long gone pale. His eyes are open but lifeless. He's unrecognizable from the deep gashes that mar almost every inch of his body. His beautiful, torn up face that will never smile at me again looks haunting now.

I'm choking, gasping for air that is no longer there. His arm lurches up, the skin dangling in slabs of torn flesh as he tightly grips my throat, cutting off my air. I try to pull away, but he has a death grip on me.

"You let it kill me," he growls in a demonic tone. "You failed me, left me to die alone. No wonder nobody loves you. You have no one in your life because you're not deserving. You didn't deserve my love. Your family realized that the day they abandoned you at the orphanage as a baby. It got me killed instead." His red rimmed, lifeless eyes hurt to look at.

"No!" I let out a sob as I furiously claw at his hand, trying to remove it from my neck.

Gripping one of his boney fingers, I rip his hand from my neck, falling backwards and taking my first deep inhale. I turn to run out of the room but immediately stop in my tracks.

"Everything you touch dies." The little boy standing in front of me is barely recognizable. Hudson is motionless, his skin burnt to a crisp, his eyes red and unseeing. "You are the reason I'm dead, Nyxi!" He takes a step towards me, and I scream at the top of my lungs.

They chant out truth after truth around me, riddling me with guilt that drives me to insanity. Dropping into a ball on the floor, I cover my ears and rock back and forth in hysterics.

I can't stop screaming. "Make it stop! Make it stop! MAKE IT STOP! *Please.*" The plea comes out weak, in a whisper.

"Nyxi, wake up!"

I lurch up in bed, gasping for air as I aimlessly flail my arms. A panic attack sinks its claws in me, the *nightmare* bringing back every raw emotion I've pushed to the back of my brain.

"Shhh, you're okay," a deep voice soothes next to me. "It was just a nightmare. Take deep breaths for me. I'm right here. I won't let anything happen to you."

The voice sounds far away, unrecognizable in my frantic state. I'm lost in a haze, trying to decipher dream from reality. My body trembles, hyped up on adrenaline. Sweat coats my skin, my hair slicked to my face. I feel and look like a mess, my disregarded emotions finally catching up to me. I've had nightmares of Theo's death on and off since he was taken from me, but never were they this dark and cruel. It felt so real, the guilt of it all laid on thick for me to face.

I feel a hand start to slowly rub up and down my back. After a few minutes, when my breathing has calmed, I slowly lift my head and look into a set of concerned, deep blue eyes.

Aeron.

"What are you doing here?" I whisper, my voice hoarse and scratchy.

He gives me a soft smile, one full of pity. "I heard you screaming from my room. I ran over as fast as I could." I give him a small nod. "Turns out, it was just a nasty nightmare. I tried to wake you, but you were thrashing around so hard. I screamed your name, and it finally broke you out of the chaos."

I nervously twist my hands together, not sure how to respond. I'm past the point of exhaustion, and my heart sits heavy in my chest. Aeron seems to take note of my reluctance to talk about it, so he doesn't push.

"I have nightmares sometimes too, you know. I have a specific one when I'm stressed. I will wake up in full body sweats, confused as to where I am. I've learned to cope with them, though. Now, each time when I wake up and can't seem to shake the nightmare, I make myself think of one good memory to distract my brain."

He grips my hand and nods, and I give him a small nod back in understanding. He's trying to help calm down in the best way he knows how without pushing me to tell him the deepest darkest parts of myself.

I close my eyes, still gripping his hand as I think about my favorite place. *I'm sitting at the edge of Luna Lake, the sun slowly setting in front of me, casting a warm pink hue across the flat water's surface. The sky above me is starting to twinkle, breaking out in glittering stars. I'm chewing on a wedge of bread as I watch the beautiful man in front of me keep himself afloat in the smooth water while trying to convince me to join. I giggle at something ridiculous he says, making me choke on a chunk of bread. He launches out of the water and tackles me, drenching my clothes in the process. He pretends to do chest compressions on me, bending down dramatically to give me mouth to mouth. I playfully shove off his sloppy wet lips, making him tumble in the grass while letting out a deep chuckle. His smooth, rich laughter makes my heart flip in my chest, content on living off the sound of his laugh for the rest of my life. The heart beating inside me belongs entirely to the gorgeous man staring at me like I am the entity who breathes life into him.*

Opening my eyes, I take note of my body now fully relaxed and mostly back to normal. My heart beats steadily in my chest, the clouds fogging my brain washed away. All that remains is a happy memory sitting at the forefront of my mind and a kind man sitting on the edge of my bed, looking at me with pride in his eyes.

"Thank you," I rasp, giving his hand a soft squeeze. He smiles back and pats my pillow for me to rest back on. Sinking back into the lush pillow, Aeron drags the covers over my body, tucking me in.

I panic for a fraction of a second, scared to be sucked back into that hell the second I close my eyes. Aeron must take notice, because he slides his body next to mine, pulling me tightly between his chest and shoulder. He slowly drags his hand down my hair, calming me.

He whispers down to me, "Sweet dreams, Nyxi. I'll be right here to slay your nightmares for you."

I close my eyes, my head rising and falling with the cadence of his chest below me. My breaths start to even out as I ride the edge of consciousness, the world around me growing fuzzy after minutes of blissful silence.

"I'm sorry," he whispers next to me, and then a blinding pain explodes from my side.

I start convulsing on the bed, my vision blurring around the edges. I can't breathe from the intense pain radiating from my side. Springing my eyes open, I look down and spot the handle of a dagger protruding from my side, his hand still wrapped tightly around it.

He reaches down, tucking a stray curl behind my ear while looking at me with a stone cold face I've never seen on him before. Gone is the playfully cocky man I've come to know. Placing a finger to my lips, he shushes me. "It's nothing personal, Vagrant. I actually came to like you, but the opportunity arose, and I would be a fool to pass it up."

I can feel sticky, warm blood seeping from my side, drenching the sheets beneath me while I try to choke out words. "W-why... why did you sa–save me in the first round? Why n–not take me out then?"

His wicked smile comes out to play, showing me his true colors as he drags his finger down the side of my face. "You're too smart for your own good, you know that?" He chuckles to himself. "I had to let the public and the Empress see me as the hero, the nice guy who saves the damsel in distress. I had to make them fall in love with us to raise my rankings. You were just a pawn in my game, but you've served your purpose. I'm afraid you pose a greater risk as a fierce competitor now, and that just won't do."

He tsks at me while tapping his finger on my nose. "So, when I heard your pathetic screams from down the hall, I knew the opportunity was too good to pass up. All I had to do was run in here like a white knight, coming to your rescue yet again, and make up a couple stories about suffering from nightmares to get you to let down your walls. I will admit, it was easier than I thought to get inside. Just had to flash you a couple smiles and pretend to care, and you melted in my palm like butter. For someone so closed off, you really are too trusting and desperate for any sort of attention."

I'm half-conscious at this point, my head spinning while I slowly fade in and out. This is how it ends: a knife in the back for all the pain I've caused others. A fitting end. At least now, I can be reunited with Theo.

"No one will be able to pin this back on me, just another broken soul lost to the wind and forgotten about for the rest of eternity. I can play up the sad lover role for some sympathy points. I'm sorry it had to be this way, but you were a means to an end. It was either you or me, and I will always choose myself." He thinks for a moment. "I will actually miss your spit fire attitude, though. What a shame," he sighs, as if he's truly worked up about it.

I weakly ball my hands into fists. "F-fuck you, you coward," I seethe.

His eyes dance with mischief as he flashes me his bright white teeth and then quickly rips the blade from my side. The pain is unlike anything I've ever felt before as I shake uncontrollably, blood pouring from my wound. I let out a scream that makes the furniture in my room rattle, knocking items to the floor.

I hear the splintering of wood and a feral snarl from somewhere in the distance, but I'm fading too fast. The room is suddenly plunged in pure night, my skin erupting in goose bumps from the deadly presence hovering in my doorway. Death stands before us, seething like the reaper himself coming to collect. I can't see him, but I can feel him like always, and I know exactly who it is, even in my dying haze.

"Who's there?" Aeron whispers on a shaky breath.

"The monster in your nightmares," his deep, gravelly voice echoes around us, ensnaring us like prey. "Remove your hands from her before I remove them from your body."

"I'm not scared of you," Areon shouts breathily, but the way his body trembles next to me says otherwise. He knows it, I know it, and the embodiment of death in front of us revels in knowing it.

A deep, rich chuckle vibrates the walls with each step he takes towards us. "Wrong." *Stomp!* "Fucking." *Stomp!* "Answer." *Stomp!*

Aeron is ripped away from me in a flash of fury. I'm fading fast, barely able to keep my eyes open or follow what's going on. Aeron's limp body dangles in the air, held up by Hade's hand gripped tightly around his throat. I notice his face growing redder between each blink.

"It's no use," Aeron chokes out. "You're too late. She won't survive it."

Hade lets out a vicious growl. "She is the strongest person I know, she can survive anything."

Aeron slowly shakes his head the best he can with Hade's death grip on his throat while flashing an evil grin. "My dagger was laced with poison. See the way her body shakes, the way her skin is now deathly pale? How her chest is barely rising? She will be gone within minutes; seconds, maybe. The damage is done, and there's nothing you can do to stop it."

"Dagger?" Hade breathes the word shakily. Roaring, he throws Aeron across the room, his body slamming into the mirror above my vanity, shattering it into a million pieces. His body drops to the floor like a doll, shards of glass piercing his skin while raining over the floor.

I take a shallow, rattling breath, desperate for any air I can find. It sends me into a coughing fit, and blood sprays from my side all over the bed. I let out a small whimper from the pain, and the room goes eerily quiet. My head spins, my vision completely blurred at this point, but I can barely make out a tall, dark figure frozen from my cry, as if breaking him out of his haze of destruction.

He lets out a low grunt, picking Aeron up by his neck again, slamming him against the wall. Glittering black tendrils of magic seep up from between the floorboards, making the room shake. The tendrils tornado around Aeron's body, encasing him in magic that keeps him afloat. Hade releases his hand from Aeron's throat while his body thrashes in the air.

Hade turns swiftly, stomping over to my bed with a face only found in nightmares. Just when I'm about to give in and fade away, Aeron lets out a scream of death unlike anything I've ever heard. He cries at the top of his lungs, screaming like he's being torn limb from limb, slowly and delicately. It's haunting.

Hade kneels next to my bed, coming into my blurry vision. I try to give him a soft smile, but I'm paralyzed. My body is giving out, and my mind is slowly approaching death's door behind it. He pushes the hair back from my sweat-soaked forehead, smiling back at me.

"You're gonna be okay," he chokes out, and I'm not sure if he's saying it to convince me or himself. "I'm going to fix it." He repeats the words to himself twice over, seeming lost in his own head.

I just give him a watery smile, knowing my seconds are numbered but not wanting to give in just yet, guarding this last moment with him like a lost treasure. I'm exhausted, but I would be lying if I said I wasn't selfish enough to take one last moment of this unguarded Hade.

"What are you doing to him?" I choke out.

He growls next to me, his body vibrating, trying to refrain from finishing the job. He scoops me up like I weigh nothing, and I let out a soft whimper of pain, making him curse under his breath. My limp body melts into his giant, warm chest as he nuzzles me into his embrace.

"I'm making him live out his future death on repeat in his head until I can make it a reality. My magic gives me control over everything involving death and the dead, a variation of Necromancy magic. I can talk to the dead, control the dead, or in this case, show someone how they die until it drives them to insanity."

He's rushing me down the long hallway to who knows where. My body is freezing, and I know I won't last long enough to make it there. I push my face farther into his chest and take in these last moments of my life, surrounded by his intoxicating scent of smoke and sandalwood. It's a heady last memory.

"My death magic is just an extension of myself, letting me pick things up with it, talk or listen through it, and even encase my body with it, turning myself invisible. What you just saw is the true extent of my magic. I am no saint, Nyxi. I am *death*."

My body trembles, but it's not from his admission. It fascinates and intrigues me, and I only wish I could have had more time to see him in all his glory. I close my eyes, just needing some rest as my body turns heavy and numb. I take a shallow breath, and then I lay my heart bare before him, knowing I won't have to face the aftermath of my words.

"It was a p-privilege to have known you, Hade. Thank you for letting me see the d-darkest parts of you that helped me face the darkest parts within me. You are no dark to my l-light. You are *the* dark that sparked a light within me. I l-look forward to being on the other end of your magic in the afterlife." I give him one last, weak smile as my lungs deflate. "Have an orange waiting for me there, would you?"

Chapter
Twenty-Seven

My body shakes, the edges of my sanity slowly fading in and out. My body bounces as I hear feet pounding below me. My body shivers in the arms wrapped tightly around me. I hear panting above my head, someone screaming out orders, but my mind is too weak to follow.

My body is gently lowered onto something soft. I'm left for a moment, the sound of water starts quietly in the distance. Two warm hands grip each side of my face, turning my head to look up at them. Two soft thumbs swoop under my eyes, attempting to wake me, to drag me away from the warm, inviting place just beyond my reach.

"Nyxi, please stay with me. I'm going to heal you. I just need time," they plead, their voice laced with pain.

Hade?

"Tired," is all I manage to whisper back.

"Sleep is friends with death, and I'm not letting you have an intimate relationship with either of them. I never did learn how to share." The words tumble from his lips, broken and defeated.

All I can manage is a soft, breathy laugh in response. His thumb gently strokes over my cheek, and I nuzzle into it.

"You're freezing. We need to get you in the bath. Healers are on their way, but I need you to hold on until then. Can you do that for me?" He tries to sound unaffected, but I can hear the slight strain in his voice. I nod my head slowly in answer, but it's weak.

"Good girl," he whispers, kissing my forehead before he scoops me up again and walks us into the connecting room.

Setting me down on the counter, his hands bracket me, holding me up. I let out a small whimper of pain, which makes him curse under his breath. My eyes remain closed as I sit limp in his hold.

He speaks to me softly, like one would a child. "We need to get your top layer of clothes off. Is that okay?" I nod softly, trying to breathe through the pain while opening my eyes to stare into his piercing gaze. I try to lift my arm to help, but it's no use; it ends up lying limp by my side. "Here, let me help you."

He gently strips my clothes off, leaving only my undergarments on. I sit there helpless, my vision blurring more by the second. I whimper as he lifts me, walking me over to the full tub before he slowly lowers me into the warm water. Heat surrounds me like a warm hug, lulling my eyes to close.

I could die peacefully wrapped in this warm water, surrounded by his intoxicating scent. *What a way to go.*

I struggle to peel my eyes open when I feel his hands retreat from my body. The water around me is slowly turning a soft red from the blood still pouring from my side, except I notice a thin wrap over my wound attempting to stifle the blood flow that he must have put on me while in my haze.

Hade takes a step back, and my heart crumbles. Reality seeps its way to the forefront of my brain, taking hold of me, paralyzing me in its grip. It's a selfish request that wasn't afforded to the one I loved most, but I don't want to die alone.

"Please don't leave me," I beg on a cry. "I d-don't want to die alone." The words are barely a whisper, and I'm ashamed by how weak I sound.

His face crumples. "Shhh, you're okay, sweet girl. I'm not going anywhere, and neither are you," he assures me.

He must notice me losing my battle to stay awake, because panic flashes across his face, unsure on what to do. In a blur, he steps up to the edge of the tub, sliding his boots off, and then he submerges his fully clothed body, making the water slosh over the edges. He wedges his body behind me, gently placing me between his large legs and dragging my back up against his chest. My long, curly hair makes a barrier between us.

It feels instinctive to rest against him like this, as if my body was made to mold into his. I'm shocked at how natural it feels, like an extension of home, a comfort I've only been afforded one other time.

I can feel my life seeping out of me, reaching its end, so I take these last few moments to ask him the question that's been burning my tongue.

"How?" I ask weakly.

His hand reaches forward, absentmindedly playing with one of my curls. "How did I know that piece of worthless shit stabbed you?" he says gruffly behind me.

"Yes, h-how?"

"I was coming to drop an orange at your door. Normally, I would do it early in the morning, but I felt this strange sensation to do it tonight instead. I followed my instincts by luck... *Luck*," he chokes out in a laugh devoid of any humor. "I heard your heart shattering scream and busted through your door without another thought. I didn't care what monster was sitting on the other side of your door, as long as it turned its attention on me instead of you.

I knew something was deeply wrong, and there was nothing that was going to stop me from getting into your room. *Nothing*, Nyxi."

A breathy laugh escapes my throat, making me cough. "So you're telling me an orange saved my life?"

He lets out the most beautiful laugh behind me that takes all my pain away for the briefest second. Medicine could be made from its healing properties. He subtly reaches forward, gripping my wrist, I assume keeping tabs on my pulse's slow descent toward my impending death sentence. I let out a soft sigh and melt into him, more than content with this being my last moment.

A soft knock rings out in the distance, drawing my fading attention. Hade grunts for them to come in, but he doesn't move an inch, intent on staying put right behind me. Two women shuffle into the bathroom, wearing red robes, their hoods drawn up. Hade's tone turns hauntingly serious when he speaks to them.

"Spare no expense. There is no room for failure here, or it will be your lives on the line. Do you understand?" he demands.

They both nod and roll out their cloths full of the supplies they need.

"We will need to assess her wounds first, and then we can get started on treating her. Can you carry her to the bed?" one of the women says.

"There is no time," he grunts out. "You can heal her right here in the bath. She's been stabbed with a poisoned dagger in her left side. I tried to stop the bleeding the best I could, but she had already lost a lot by the time I got to her. The poison is fast-acting and has already taken hold of her body."

The two healers listen intently, taking note of everything he tells them. They get to work fast, one mixing a few things, the other hovering over me, removing the wrap from my wound. It sits just above the low waterline. She prods my side, making me hiss. Their faces looks like blurry blobs now as I struggle to draw air into my lungs.

"Looks like the dagger narrowly missed her spleen. This is good news. Her symptoms are mostly due to her blood loss and the poison. I can heal her wound with my magic, but her life depends on if the antidote works faster than her failing body. She is already so far gone, it will take a miracle to bring her back."

Luck, I internally laugh. My life has been one big game of chance for as long as I can remember.

"Then it's a good thing you are the two best healers in Lunaria. Get it done!" His temper flares to life, his concern laced with anger.

"Hold her down. This is going to hurt," one of the women says.

I feel Hade's arms wrap around my chest, holding me tightly to his body without cutting off my weak air supply. "Do it," he demands.

She reaches down, placing her two hands on top of my wound. Bright white light erupts from her palms, searing my skin. I scream, my throat going hoarse from the sob that escapes me. It feels like I'm being stabbed all over again, my side a living fire.

"I've got you," Hade whispers from behind me as he tries to hold down my flailing body. It feels like every mistake I've made in life is coming back to torture me, making me pay for my sins with this ungodly pain.

"Make it stop," I whisper weakly. I feel a hand stroke the hair back from my slick forehead as stars dance behind my eyelids until I give in to the call beckoning me to sleep. The pain fades to the background, and then everything goes black.

See you soon, Theo.

A DEEP RUMBLE VIBRATES MY BACK, DRAWING MY ATTENTION AND waking my senses. The smell of smoke and sandalwood swirl around me, a scent all too familiar. My body feels light like a cloud.

There are voices arguing around me, but I'm still too foggy in the head to understand.

Slowly, I blink my eyes open, my surroundings coming into focus. I'm still weak, but the blinding pain that was too much to handle has lessened to a bearable ache. My skin now feels warm and cozy as I take my first full, deep breath without choking on pain.

"You're okay?" a hopeful, gravelly voice breathes behind me.

I feel a heavy presence wiggle at my back. Water sloshes around, and I realize I'm still sitting in the tub, wedged between Hade's giant thighs. Now that I'm more coherent, it's comical seeing Hade's giant body smashed in the small tub with me while fully dressed.

"I must have passed out." My words come out thick, my throat raw and scratchy.

"How are you feeling, miss?" one of the healers asks.

Taking note of my body, I feel mostly in good spirits. "Okay, I think. Mostly just tired, and I'm a little sore when I breathe, but it's not unbearable," I say honestly.

She nods happily with my statement. "I was able to close your wound with my magic. It should fully heal over the next few days. I had to use almost my entire reserve to close it up, so please rest and don't push yourself. My magic is strong, so you should be back to full strength by the next trial, but you will be left with a slight scar down your side. The antidote appears to be working so far, but I would still like Trina to check on you daily to make sure you don't regress." She leans forward, giving my hand a soft squeeze. "You're one tough cookie. I wasn't sure if you would come out the other end, but Hade here never doubted you."

"Thank you," I say softly, giving her a grateful smile. "I'm forever indebted to you two. Name the favor, and it's yours."

She gives me a genuine smile in return, one between two people who have known each other their whole lives. "Live a long, happy life, dear. That is the favor I ask of you."

She grabs her belongings and walks out of the small washroom, taking the other healer, who I assume is Trina, along with her, leaving Hade and I pressed together in the tub. The water is surprisingly still warm, which makes me think he refilled it to keep it warm for me while I was passed out.

The silence is deafening, and even though I feel like I could sleep for a week straight, I am very aware of how little clothes I currently wear and how close our bodies are pressed together. I awkwardly wiggle, unsure of what to do now, but all the worry washes away when he gently places his palm on my thigh, rubbing soft circles with his thumb.

"I thought I was going to lose you," he whispers behind me. "I should have known you're too stubborn to die."

"You know me so well, Death Reaper," I tease, attempting to lighten the mood.

I look down at my body, noticing the blood smeared across my skin. I look and feel like a mess. "I should probably clean myself up. I'm definitely not the most beautiful woman you've ever shared a bath with, that's for sure. Maybe the most memorable, though," I say with a laugh.

He grunts from behind me as I go to scoot away, but I wince when pain shoots through my side from the movement.

He reaches out, gripping my shoulder, stopping me. "Let me help you," he insists. "It's the least I can do. You should be resting anyways. Healer's orders."

I turn to look over my shoulder at him, and hollow eyes stare back at me. I've never seen such unguarded emotion, like his walls have fallen, and he's not sure how to put them back up. He gives me pleading eyes, acting as if his life depends on helping me in this moment, and because of that, I give him a small nod. I can let him have control over something. His need to provide and regain control over the situation shines like a star, and it makes me want to provide the sky for him to shine for everyone to see.

A light sparks behind his eyes, the fire inside him gaining a flicker of fuel. Unsure of himself, he slowly grabs a wash rag hanging next to the tub and submerges it under the water. Bringing it up, he pauses while holding my gaze, waiting for me to tell him to continue. I give him a soft smile and turn face forward again, giving him full control.

I hear the trickle of water, feel the warm cloth touch my shoulder, and a shiver travels down my spine. He squeezes the rag, a stream of water cascading down my side, leaving goosebumps all over my skin. I let out a small hum of pleasure, the warm water soothing me. A low, satisfied growl escapes his throat, and my heart flutters in my chest.

He meticulously drags the rag across my shoulder, then down my arm, adding a dollop of soap to scrub me clean. He continues his pursuit across my chest, squeezing the rag again and letting the sudsy water drip down. The cold air makes my nipples pebble, chafing against the lacy fabric separating me from the cloth. I let out a soft moan, content on spending the rest of my day being bathed by the gentle brute behind me.

The noise lights a fire in him, his hand becoming more sure of itself, perusing every inch of my body. He moves the cloth slowly under my lacy strap before pausing. "Is this okay?" I hum happily, nodding my head before he continues dragging it down until the cloth slightly dips under the thin fabric covering my breast. "And this?"

"Yes," I sigh.

He makes sure his skin never touches mine, using the cloth as a barrier to wash the sweat and blood away. The rag gently drags across my left nipple, my body pushing back against him without thought. My head tips up on its own accord, bearing my neck to him.

He reaches out with his other hand, gently wrapping his fingers around the base of my throat. Leaning down, he whispers against the shell of my ear in rasp, "If you keep doing that, I won't be able to focus on getting you clean."

"Sorry," I whisper, then swallow deeply, feeling his hand twitch around my neck. He peels his hand from my throat and brings the rag back to my front, dragging it down my stomach, making sure to avoid my wound. The rag cleans away each swipe of blood across my stomach and then down my thighs. He avoids getting too close to my center, trying to be a gentleman. I melt back into his chest, happily letting him take care of me.

He finishes with my front, then grips my shoulder, gently pushing me forward. I'm so lost in my relaxed haze, I don't register what he's doing until it's too late. He collects my hair in his fist, slowly dragging it up and over my shoulder. I go to stop him, but it's too late.

I try to turn away from him, but he plants his hand on my shoulder, holding me in place. I look forward, too embarrassed to face him. He's deadly silent, and I can feel his heavy gaze searing my back that I've successfully kept hidden until now. He's not saying anything, which is setting me more on edge. Seconds go by until I'm brave enough to swivel my neck and look back at him. What I see makes my heart lurch in my chest.

He sits frozen, his face ghostly pale. He's staring at my back in shock, his eyes never blinking. I expected him to be mad or concerned, but not this. He looks like he's seen a ghost, lost inside his beautiful head, trying to come to terms with whatever has him so shaken.

"Hade?" I say softly, getting his attention.

He blinks, snapping out of whatever world he was lost in, and lets out a low growl that makes little waves vibrate over the water.

Now, he looks furious, fire dancing behind his eyes, promising ret-ribution. If only he knew I learned to slay my own demons a long time ago.

"Who fucking did this to you?" he seethes behind me. "I need names."

I try to shake my head for him to drop it, but he gives me a look full of pain, needing to fix me once again. If only it were that easy to erase the past.

"It doesn't matter. It was a long time ago," I whisper, trying to sound sure of myself.

"That's where you're wrong. Everything relating to you is the only thing that matters to *me*," he says with unyielding certainty. "So, I won't ask you again, Nyxi. Who hurt you?"

I shake my head, but he shoots me a pleading look that pulls at my heartstrings, making me want to spill all my deepest secrets for him to harbor with me.

I sigh, defeated. "The headmaster of the orphanage I was raised in was an older gentleman. If we acted out of line or did something he didn't like, we would get sent for private lessons with him. Sometimes, we were sent just because he was having a bad day and needed to let off some steam, but he would never admit that. We would get sent for lessons if our shoes weren't tied cor-rectly, or if we didn't sit straight enough at the dinner table. The lessons were supposed to teach us how to be better children so our chances of being adopted would go up."

My body shakes a little as the nightmares of my past are dragged to the surface for me to face. Hade starts to trace each mark with his finger to soothe me, but for some reason, it feels like he is tracing a different pattern, the feeling abstract and for-eign to me.

"He took a particular liking to me, so I was sent for more lessons than the other orphans. He had a thing for fire, something about burning away our sins to cleanse us. The marks on my back are supposed to be a reminder of each of my lessons so I may never forget."

My chest feels lighter after digging up the pain from the past. The only other person who knew was Theo. He would help me when he could, taking care of me and cleaning my wounds after each lesson. He was the reason I made it out of there alive and with my sanity.

"Are each one of these burns across your back a lesson?" he asks softly, almost choking on his words, and I tentatively nod in answer.

His face grows red, the embodiment of rage. He stops his finger from tracing whatever mysterious pattern across my back, and his voice cracks the smallest amount.

"Nyxi, there are dozens of burn marks across your back."

I don't know what to say to that. I avoid looking at my back at all costs, not ready to face the memories. I lost count of each lesson long before they stopped.

"It's in the past. There is nothing to do to change it now. Life goes on, whether you are ready to ride the wave with it or not. So, I did too," I plainly say, willing him to understand I can't change this, all the stuff that came before him.

"Life may go on, but that doesn't mean *his* should. I would gladly burn him to a crisp in the name of your retribution. Let me be the match to your flame, the sword to your deadly blow, the magic to your pursuit to claim every last breath from his lungs." His voice turns deathly low. "Use me as a weapon, and I will gladly deliver your demons to your feet for you to slay. I would love nothing more than to watch you take back your life by setting fire to *his*."

I've never felt such blind loyalty. This man would serve me my wildest demand on a silver platter without a single ounce of a second thought. It's madness in theory, but this little thread growing between my soul and his makes me irrational. The way this man is laying his life before me makes me want to worship him.

My voice comes out soft and unaffected, but my heart rate tells a different story. "As riveting as that sounds, I have already slayed my demons. I'm not sure even your best Vanquisher could unearth what is left of him now. I'm no saint to worship, and I'm okay with that."

His chest vibrates behind me as he grips my chin to look at him. "You can cover a saint in the blood of his enemies, but that does not taint who he is underneath all the gore. The same person remains hidden below; it just takes someone who's fought the same battles to spot the holiness that lies beneath." He looks between my eyes, peering so far inside me, I'm scared of what he'll find. "Merit is in the eye of the beholder, and it is up to you whose eyes you value to truly see your worth. Don't let the trials you've faced define how bright your light shines, Nyxi, because that would be devastating."

I'm shocked, speechless, not accustomed to such depth and emotion coming from the hard man sitting at my back, who is handling me with such pristine care, like I'm his greatest treasure. I'm used to his playful banter, a man who's rough around the edges with a mind and heart more heavily guarded than the Empress' private chambers. That man, I know how to handle, but this man is uncharted territory. I think he feels the same way, but his bravery makes me want to hand him a raw piece of myself in return as a peace offering, a way of saying we are in this together, whatever that journey may be.

I hold his unblinking gaze and whisper softly between us, "And what do your eyes see when they look at me laid bare before you?"

He smiles, pride and yearning shining through like a bolt of lightning striking me right in my chest. "I see a raging fire that has weathered an entire life's worth of storms but refuses to go out. I see the brightest rainbow that peeks out of a flurry of rain clouds, demanding to be seen. I see a soul screaming for a break from this unjust world, desperately wanting to find something to lay over its deep wound to pacify it. But above all, I see a darkness that calls to mine, something that stirs so deeply inside me, it has uprooted my destiny for the rest of eternity. I see *you*, Nyxi. The real, raw you, and it's my favorite version."

I heave a deep breath, caught in a trace of his admission, and it isn't from just being almost stabbed to death. My skin is over-heating, going flush right before his eyes. I've never felt so stripped bare, like he dove under my skin and rearranged everything I've ever known true.

"You see me?" is all I'm able to get out, my mind melting into a puddle.

He smiles deeply and unashamed, and it's my *undoing*, a zap straight to my dying heart, bringing it to life once again. He sees me for who I am, and he's not afraid. Instead, he welcomes my darkness with open arms.

"I *see* you," he responds in a breath, and I swear, I can hear his heartbeat over the ringing of my ears, his chest dipping with each deep breath. "And I also *see* your hair's current state is a rat's nest, so come here so I can wash it for you." An unguarded laugh escapes me, and I go to refuse, but before I can get the words out, he cuts me off. "I won't take no for an answer."

Rolling my eyes, I slowly lower myself back until my head rests above his lap. He looks down at me, satisfied, and then reaches over the side of the tub, grabbing something. He dips it below the water now growing cold, and then brings it up to my hairline, slowly pouring water from the cup in his hand down the back of my head, soaking my hair.

We fall into peaceful silence as he gently washes every stand of my long, unruly hair, laughing every now and then when his giant fingers get stuck in one of the knots. He's patient, though, massag-ing my scalp with a feather light touch. It's heaven and hell at the same time, a peace uncommon to me, making my skin burn from the inside out. Because never in a million years would I predict this godly man would be sharing a bath with me, washing my hair and looking at me like I'm the air that sustains him.

Finishing with my hair, he scoots me forward and then drags his wet body from the tub, dripping water everywhere in the process. He turns to me, staring me straight in my soul, and I'm captivated.

"Stay right there," he says sternly and then disappears into the conjoining room.

A few moments later, he returns wearing a fresh outfit that isn't sopping wet. Gray cotton pants stretch over his massive thighs, pulling them tight. He's paired them with a simple white cotton shirt that hugs his biceps. I spot a thick vein traveling down from the center, drawing my attention. He's dressed casually for once, and I think this might be the most delicious I've ever seen him. I blame the dizzying thought on the lingering effects of the poison, for my own sanity.

Before I can even register what he's doing, he wedges his arms under my body like I weigh nothing and lifts me from the tub, and I let out a small yelp in surprise. He chuckles in response, with a small, satisfied grunt he's unable to control.

Smacking his arm, I playfully chastise him, "You treat me as if I'm broken. I can get myself out of a bath, you brute."

He plops me softly on my feet and then wraps a warm, fuzzy towel around my shivering body. Wrapping one arm around my center, he draws me to his chest for support as he uses his other hand to carefully wring the excess water from my hair.

This man.

"Just because you are capable doesn't mean you should. I could kill every person who resides inside the castle in the blink of an eye, but it doesn't mean I should. So, in the kindest way possible, shut your mouth for once and let me take care of you."

Rolling my eyes, I let him win just this once, too tired to put up a fight, reveling in the feeling of being taken care of.

Once he's satisfied, he picks me up again, cradling me to his body and walking into the conjoining room. I look around, my breath hitching. Similar to the rest of the cattle, the room is bathed in black accents and furniture, but where everything else feels cold and lifeless, this room has character and exudes liveliness.

A bed fit for a king sits in the very center, the focus. It floats above the ground, being elevated by black fluffy clouds made of magic. The bed itself is bathed in black, but the headboard is regal, a golden vintage aesthetic. Placed right above the bed, secured to the ceiling, sits a gold, round-edged, rectangular Victorian mirror. A circular, oversized lounge chair sits in the corner next to a giant window that takes up a majority of the wall to its left. A painted canvas of an owl hangs on the adjoining wall just above the chair, bringing a smile to my face. Across from the chair on the other side of the bed sits a vintage cart storing bottles of liquor and two crystal glasses. Sitting next to it stands a golden bookshelf full of books that look weathered with love, spines cracked and pages wrinkled. It feels like home, and in my soul, I know it's him encased in a room.

"We're in your room," I say, more a statement than a question.

He nods and plops me down on his bed that floats above the ground, making it bounce a tad from the force.

I quirk a brow at him. "I assume this is floating because of your magic?"

He smiles, looking proud of himself. "I can't remember why, but one day, I wanted to test the limits of my magic, and it's stayed this way ever since. It brings me peace, surrounded by my magic while I sleep."

I smile, trying to imagine what it must feel like to have so much magic within my grasp at any moment. Is it all-consuming and painful, or does it feel like a second skin?

"I love it," I say with a giggle as I cross my legs under me and test its bounciness, shoving all my weight down into my legs, feeling it dip slightly then float back up.

Hade walks over to an armoire I didn't notice at first and pulls out what he wants. He sets down an oversized t-shirt on the bed next to me.

"You can wear this for tonight." He sees the confusion in my eyes, so he answers before I can respond. "You will be sleeping in my bed so I can watch over you. I will take the chair in the corner, seeing as I don't usually sleep much anyways."

I go to open my mouth in protest, but he shoots me a warning glare, leaving no room for argument. Crossing my arms over my chest, I glare back, but even I know, with the exhaustion trying to claim my body, it doesn't hold a strong punch. He must notice this too, because he laughs at me as if I'm a child throwing a pathetic tantrum.

"Well, are you just going to stand there gawking at me all night, or are you going to give me some privacy to change?" I say with a sassy edge.

He smirks at me, and I can already see the words forming on the tip of his tongue.

"That wasn't an invitation to watch me change, you pervert," I shout while picking up one of the giant pillows and launching it at him. It makes a slight pain shoot through my side, but I hold in my wince.

He chuckles, catching the pillow before it hits him in the face. He turns around where he's standing. Apparently, that's the extent of the privacy he's planning on granting me.

Letting out a huff, I unwrap the towel from around my body and drop it to the floor, the wet fabric making a slapping noise when it hits the ground in front of the bed. The sound draws a low groan from Hade, knowing I now sit mostly naked in *his* room on *his* bed, but he stays firmly rooted in his place like a gentleman.

I peel off my wet lacey undergarments next, dropping them to the floor slowly, making a soft slapping noise against the hard floor.

Hade's deep, strained voice breaks the silence. "Nyxi," he growls.

Feigning innocence, I respond, "What? Would you like me to *soak* your bed?"

He chokes, knocking his fist into his chest before a deep rumble leaves him, making the room vibrate. He clenches his fists, his knuckles going white with restraint.

Silently giggling to myself, I grab the large shirt he left on the bed next to me and slip it over my head. It's oversized, and my body drowns in it, looking more like a nightgown instead. It smells of him, and I take in a deep breath, letting his smokey sandalwood scent flood my senses. It's heady in the best way.

"Are you finished?" he asks in a deathly low tone.

"Yes, sir," I croon sweetly, trying to hold in the laugh the threatens to spill at the name I know he hates so much.

Grunting, he turns around, and pride flashes across his eyes seeing me all wrapped up like a present in his clothes, until his eyes travel down and catch the slight swell of my breast pushing against the soft fabric of his shirt, my nipples peeking through.

In an instant, his dark magic shoots out, picking up the blanket thrown across the bottom of his bed and draping it around my shoulders to cover me from view. A longing, pained look flashes across his face.

"You looked cold," he says, practically choking on the words.

I raise my eyebrows as his magic slips beneath me, picking me up and spinning me around so I'm facing away from him, making me squeal in surprise.

Looking over my shoulder, I see him take two large strides until his knees collide with the edge of the bed behind me.

"Face forward," he demands, and being the good, obedient girl I am tonight, I turn forward without putting up a fight, more intrigued than wanting to push his buttons.

I feel a light pull at the back of my head and realize the familiar tug of a brush dragging through my curls. He starts at the tips of my hair, slowly making his way up so as not to tug my head harshly. It's heaven until he opens his mouth.

"What was the name of the headmaster at your orphanage?" he prods, trying to feign nonchalance.

"Why?" I ask wearily.

"Just curious," he quickly responds, taking on a bored tone.

Playing into his little game, I respond, "Azul."

"Last name?" he asks immediately.

Looking over my shoulder, I give him a questioning look. He gently tugs my hair, making me face forward again.

"Calix," I slowly state, not wanting him to rip the hair from my head if I keep ignoring him.

He grunts to himself, satisfied with my answers, and then I feel him start to twist and pull my hair, braiding it down the center of my back.

"Are you braiding my hair?" I ask, surprised he knows how.

Ignoring me, he ties off the end of my braid with a piece of ribbon and gives it a firm tug, letting me know he's finished. Walking to the head of the bed, he pulls down the top sheet and gestures for me to climb under. I tuck my small body inside, sinking into the giant mass of pillows plopped against the headboard. I swear it feels like there's a perfect Nyxi-shaped indent carved into the bed for me to melt into. I let out a deep sigh, all the pain and exhaustion of the night settling deep into my bones, making me feel like I've lived a thousand lives.

"I will be taking over as your guard," he states firmly, looking over my body, seemingly satisfied I'm tucked safely away in his bed.

"Why?" I protest, not liking the idea. "I like Winston, and didn't you once tell me you were too busy to babysit me?" I huff.

"Why?" he says with an edge to his tone. "Because he *failed* you. His only job was to keep eyes on you, and he failed miserably, almost resulting in your *death*. You should know by now that I'm never too busy when it comes to you." He sighs, the pain from today's events lingering under his eyes. "Now rest for me please."

I nod softly, words feeling foreign to me after what he just admitted. He bends down, brushing his soft lips against my forehead, then saunters over to the chair nestled in the corner. He lets out a deep sigh as he plops down and opens a book hidden under the cushion.

"Thank you, Hade," I whisper as sleep takes hold of my body, dragging me under.

Chapter
Twenty-Eight

Journal Entry

Age 13

Mama took me on a walk to the edge of Lunaria today. I've never traveled that far away from the castle before, and it was fascinating. She took me through the heart of the city, and we stopped by one of my favorite bakeries for a sweet treat on the way. We traveled on until there was no more land to travel. She gripped my hand, leading me up to the edge of the giant rock we call home, and let out a deep sigh. She told me this was her favorite part of Lunaria to visit when she was feeling like the walls of the castle were closing in on her. Through the clouds in the distance, I spotted buildings far below, circling what looked to be a giant lake in the center. Confused, I asked Mama who lived down there. She told me sometimes in life, we come across bad people who want to hurt others. She said the place below was created a long time ago for the bad people to live because they have fallen out with the good people who live up here. She said it's like being put in timeout—permanently. She said it's an old practice that doesn't happen anymore, but the people decided to stay down there and start families and grow communities. I snuggled into Mama's side and prayed I never got sent down there to timeout with the bad people.

Chapter
Twenty-Nine

LIFE HAS BEEN POSITIVELY BORING RECENTLY. HADE LET ME RETURN to my room, but he hasn't graced me with the ability to leave my bed yet, besides using the bathroom. He says it's "healer's orders", but not once has Trina told me I couldn't get out of bed. She is actually impressed with how fast I'm recovering and assured me I should be almost fully back to normal by the next trial.

Hade has been weird and distant since the accident. He checks on me each morning, bringing me breakfast, but he doesn't stay to chat. He's been avoiding me like the plague, looking pained to be around me. As promised, he has taken over as my guard, but he spends most of the time on the other side of my door, as if I carry some deadly contagion.

After arguing with him about Winston, he decided to give back some of his guard duties. Winston apologized with big, tear filled eyes, swearing he would lay his life down before anyone came close to touching me again. I gave him a big hug and assured him it wasn't his fault. He gifted me a citrus candle to try and make things right, which made me laugh until tears ran down my face.

Not being able to train or run has been making me want to pull my hair out. In the interim, I've grown fond of reading entries in Theo's journal and thumbing through the one I stole from the hidden library, switching back and forth to fill my time.

Today, I reached reason 1,724 why Theo loved me. It read, *"Those damn eyes. She is like a siren, calling me beyond my free will. Those eyes make me want to do good, make me want to dive in and get lost in them. I would be content drowning in their stormy gray depths for the rest of my life. She is my religion, who I devote my life to each night. Her stormy eyes are the clouds that call to my sunshine."*

Des has made it her life's mission to spend any second she isn't working being glued to my side. After she found out I was hurt, she swore she was never leaving my side again. She even went as far as sharing my pillow so she could "be closer to me". If death by cuddles was a thing, I would be long gone by now.

Nuzzling down into the pillow fortress Des built around our heads for "protection from intruders", I slide Theo's journal out from under the pillow we share, content on spending the rest of my night peacefully reading. Des is reading some fluffy romance book next to me, but she keeps trying to sneak peeks at Theo's journal, thinking I won't notice. Digging my elbow into her side, she lets out a deep huff and pretends to be severely wounded.

"Snooping again?" I question.

Rolling her eyes, she responds, "Why should I be interested in a book about made up love when I can read about a beautifully raw and *real* love story in front of me?"

I'm about to make fun of her for being a hopeless romantic when two solid knocks echo from the other side of my door. Quickly stashing the journal under my pillow, I yell for them to come in. The door swings open, and a very serious looking Hade stomps in, fully dedicated to his Cardinal title.

Clearing his throat, he looks between me and Des until his eyes finally settle on me.

"How are you feeling?" he asks in a monotone voice.

"Same as the last time you so dutifully checked on me, *sir*," I respond snidely.

He grunts in response, but honestly, I couldn't care less. If he wants to be cold and distant, two can play that game. I'm not sure what crawled up his ass, but if it isn't swiftly removed, I'm not against removing it myself. I'm not a woman afraid to get her hands dirty if it comes to it.

He turns to walk out, leaving just as fast as he swooped in. He reaches for the handle of my door, but something inside me yearns for just a drink longer of his presence, so I falter in a moment of weakness, my pride nowhere to be seen.

"That all?" I mutter on a soft breath, full of hope.

He lets out a deep sigh, sounding as if he's at war with himself. He turns to face me, and he looks downright tormented, his jaw locked tight. He goes to say something, but then he shakes his head, thinking better of it, and his knuckles turn white from gripping my door handle. His eyes look pained, deep crescents swooping under them, letting me know just how little sleep he's been getting.

I wish he would let me in, let me dive under his skin to see the darkest parts of him, so I may come to understand them like he has mine. I thought we got past this barrier between us, but it seems the wall has been fortified twice as thick and tall.

He gathers himself, building his walls back up so instead of Hade standing before me, it's the Cardinal, devoid of any emotion. "That is all," he says sternly before spinning on his heels and storming out my door.

I relax back into my pillow, letting out a deep breath I didn't realize I was holding, my mind left more scrambled than the eggs I ate this morning.

"What was that all about?" Des questions with a raised eyebrow.

"How should I know?" I say with a scoff, trying to look unaffected and clueless. Des smirks at me, her face all-knowing and her smile growing by the second.

"Seems to me you know something I don't. Care to share, Sparkles?"

"He's being an ass, per usual," I say defensively. "I'd hardly call that something to write home about."

Des raises her hands in surrender. "Woah. No need to get your biscuit in a buttery mess. It just seemed tense between you is all." She plays with her hands in her lap, pretending to let it go, but I can see the wheels spinning in her head.

I let out a deep, resigned huff. "Out with it."

Her face lights up with a huge smile, having been given the okay to pry into my life like one of her juicy drama books she loves to read. "So…no hate sex then?"

My jaw drops, shocked from her blunt words. I rip the pillow out from under her head, making her let out a yelp when her head hits the bed. Raising it above my head, I playfully launch it at her face, making her erupt in a fit of giggles.

"No," I say abruptly. "There *hasn't* been, *nor* will there ever be, any hate sex happening between me and that brute as long as the heart in my chest continues to beat."

Des peaks out from under the pillow I shoved down on her with a slight smirk. "Woah, woah, woah, Sparkles. Never say never to something like *that* until you've taken it out for a nice spin first. Learned that lesson the hard way."

I raise my eyebrows at her in question, wanting her to divulge further. She shrugs her shoulders in response, trying to look unfazed. "I might have had one too many ales and told a man—no, a very *large* man—that his ego may be large, but I was sure his penis was small." Thinking, she adds, "No, I think the word I used was miniscule." Shrugging, she carries on, "Anyways, we bet on a game of Jezzle, and if I lost, I had to spend one night with him so he could show me just how *small* his…you know what was." She swats her hand back and forth in the air. "Next thing I knew, I woke up in a random man's bed above a tavern downtown after the best night of my life, and for the next month, the little trai-torous bitch wouldn't get excited for anyone, me included. The longest dry spell of my life. I tried to go back for seconds when I was fed up with it, but he just looked me in the eyes and told me he would be taking his *small* penis elsewhere," she huffs defeatedly. She turns to me very seriously. "Don't make the same mistake as me." Pointing down she adds, "I swear she starts purring every time I walk by that tavern now."

Patting her shoulder, I let out a small laugh I'm unable to keep down. "I'll keep that in mind."

Grunting, she grabs her book and rolls over to read. Sliding my hand under my pillow, I slip Theo's journal out and dive back into a time when it was just me and him against the world.

BENDING DOWN, I FINISH LACING UP MY LAST BOOT THEN BRAID MY hair down my back so it's out of my face. I slip my dagger into my left boot; I would sooner be trapped alone in a room with a brood-ing Hade than go anywhere without being able to defend myself. Checking myself over in the mirror once, I turn to leave my room.

I push my door open, but I falter when I run into a hard mass. Dragging my head up until my neck is painfully pulled tight, I stare into a pair of stone cold eyes that promise death.

"Where do you think you're going?" the deep voice that haunts me vibrates over my skin.

I go to step around his large form, but he grips my wrist, halt-ing me. Seething, I turn around, ready to lay into him. "I'm going to train, and you cannot stop me."

Hade tenses for a moment, fisting his hands. "I don't like the idea of that."

I could punch this man in the throat right now if I didn't think it would result in breaking all my fingers in the process. "What, and you think I'm going to magically be healed by tomorrow for the next round of the Crucible? Going in after almost a week of resting is more harmful, Hade. I *need* to train."

I step around him dramatically storming down the corridor right past Winston, who dutifully keeps his mouth shut. I hear harsh footsteps catching up to me in seconds, making me whirl around, pinning him with an angry glare.

"What the fuck are you doing?" I yell, getting more worked up than I should be. At this point, I'm not even sure what all I'm angry about, just that I need to let off some steam, and Hade is the perfect target to aim it at.

"I never said you couldn't train, but if you want to fight, you can fight me. I don't trust the others when it comes to you, and I'm not sending you into the lion's den alone," he states.

"I don't need your help. I've been taking care of myself for a very long time," I mutter.

Grunting to himself, he responds, "Good thing I'm not giving you a choice then."

I turn, ignoring him, and continue my pursuit down the hallway towards the Bubble. Hade keeps in stride with me, both of us silent but sending death threats with our eyes every few moments. I can feel the pent up emotions of the past few days vibrating inside me, needing to be released. Seeing how tense Hade is beside me, I think he is in need of the same reprieve.

We enter the Bubble side by side, drawing all the eyes of my competitors. I ignore them all, striding to the far end where it's empty and spacious. I stretch out my stiff limbs that haven't been used in days and groan at how tight they are, which draws Hade's wide eyes my way. I flip him my middle finger as I dip into a front stretch, folding my body in half until it feels like my hamstrings are going to snap.

Feeling much looser, I step into the small ring drawn into the sand, where Hade is patiently waiting for me. He drags his eyes lazily from my toes all the way up to my face, checking me over one more time before he deems me fit to fight.

"Give me hell," he says with a smirk, and before he can even finish his sentence, I lunge at him, trying to take him by surprise.

He's much bigger than me, so I have to rely on my speed and smart moves. I'm too worked up to dance around with him aimlessly until one of us makes a move. I came here to draw blood, and I don't mind shedding some of my own in the process.

Spinning, I kick my foot out, aiming for his side, but before my eyes can even register the movement, he catches me by my ankle and yanks me forward so I tumble awkwardly into his chest. He moves at an unnatural speed for me to even keep up with as he pins me to him, looking down with piercing eyes.

"You need to work on making calculated moves with a plan instead of rushing into combat. Never underestimate your opponent, and always look for their weaknesses so you can exploit them," he states while looking back and forth between my eyes.

My body heats at every place our bodies meet, but I push those thoughts aside as I shove him away and plant my feet in a fighting stance once again. This time, I assess my opponent instead of making moves fueled by rage.

We circle each other slowly as I look over his huge frame for weaknesses. Of course, there's none to be found, since he is quite literally perfect at everything he does. He wouldn't be called the Cardinal or tasked to protect the Empress if he was anything short of perfection.

I can tell he is exhausted mentally and physically, even with his muscular body and godly speed moving a fraction slower than normal. If I can tire him out and play with his mind a bit, it may give me a slight advantage, since I'm well rested. His lighter eye that glows like a lightning bolt lags slightly behind his dark one, making his left side an easier target.

We continue to circle each other, both waiting on the other to make the first move. I never knew death could be so beautiful.

"You've been avoiding me," I say calmly, knowing he can't run away from my question for once.

"Hardly," he responds, never missing a beat or moving his eyes from mine.

Slowly inching my way closer to him, I continue to berate him with questions, attempting to distract him but also falling into my own selfish urges of needing to know why he's been so distant. "What, are you afraid you might break me?" I question, raising a brow at him.

He grunts, looking slightly pained, but he remains composed when he responds, "Quite the opposite, actually."

"Are you *fragile*, Hade?" I purr, dragging the words out.

He looks back and forth between my eyes, thinking of a response, and I take the opportunity to pounce. I aim for his left side, where his reaction is a fraction slower, and jab out my elbow, but he side-steps me at the last minute. I was planning on that, though, and I instantly spin from behind him, kicking my leg out to knock him off balance. My foot catches the back of his knees and, to my surprise, he doesn't block it, but it also barely makes a dent in his steely composure, like he's physically rooted to the ground.

I wince, and Hade turns to face me again with a smirk. "Do you think I'm fragile? If anything, I might break you without even trying," he says in a low, raspy voice.

We start to circle each other again as I feel a small blush creep up my chest. "I have yet to break, and I doubt you of all people will be the cause of my ruining." I try to sound sure of myself, but I'm starting to crumble right in front of him, and the little prick knows it.

"Oh, *Nightmare*, after I'm through with you, you would be reduced to nothing." I bite my lip at his vivid words. "The havoc I would wreak on your body would level entire cities." He stops circling me to take a step forward. "You would *never* stand a chance at surviving me, Nyxi. Body and soul included." His eyes turn molten, darkening before me, zoning in on his prey.

Fuck me.

A chill runs up my spine, making the hairs on the back of my neck spring up, lighting my body on fire. I'm overheating, my body and mind warring. My brain tells me this man is a danger zone, but my body wants to dive head first into that black abyss, hoping I catch fire in the process.

I go to respond but choke on my words, worked up from his admission. He chuckles under his breath and flashes me a feral grin, which makes my blood boil. He may be my demise, but that doesn't mean I won't drag him with me to the pits of hell so we may burn in ruin together.

"All talk," I taunt as I round his body again, slowly watching his every move. "That's a pretty big declaration to live up to, *sir*. I only feel *pity* for the poor girl who will have her head filled with pretty promises, only to *undoubtedly* be disappointed in the end."

A tickle of dark magic runs up my body until it settles on the edge of my ear like a snake slithering across my skin. "I don't break my promises, *Nyxi*. Would you like to find out firsthand?" he whisper growls into my ear through his shadow, setting my body ablaze.

I am well and truly *fucked*. I slap his magic away with the back of my hand and lunge at him, yelling as I throw my body at him. I punch out with my right arm, aiming for the side of his face, but he catches my fist midair and throws my arm to the side as he yawns.

"You can do better than that," he taunts as I strike out my left elbow, aiming for his side. He deflects it easily without even looking down, and I let out a growl of frustration at the smirk on his face. "You're out of practice. Pity." He finds this amusing, but it only stokes the fire of rage building inside me.

It's not lost on me that he's only playing defense, never taking any opportunities to lash out at me when I'm distracted by my rage. He's letting me take my anger out on him, but he won't hit me back, and it's only making me more pissed off. He's treating me like I'm fragile instead of something worth his time, someone beneath him instead of his equal.

"Why aren't you fighting me?" I demand in a snarl.

Shrugging, he responds, "I don't know what you're talking about."

I huff, frustrated. "You weren't scared of hitting a girl when you punched me in the nose the first time we met," I taunt, trying to get under his skin, attempting to push him to lash out at me and play this game.

"That was an accident," he replies softly as we start to circle each other again.

"One you still haven't apologized for," I seethe in response. Apparently, I'm still not over it.

"Nevertheless, I wouldn't want to ruin your pretty face again." He smirks, looking like the devil incarnate.

"That's rather unfortunate, because I would love nothing more than to turn your face black and blue for the rest of eternity. At least then, it would match your soul," I sneer.

He shrugs indifferently, and I fist my hands with anger. I'm starting to believe this man lied about his magic and instead has the ability to slide directly under my skin with just a look. Words are proving to be a faulty method, so I change my approach and try to rile him up by violence. Surely, he won't let me draw blood without drawing some of mine in return.

Screaming, I run at his right side, but at the last second, I draw my right shoulder back, spinning so my back is to him, and jab my right elbow down into his side. I land the blow, but he wraps his arm around my neck, my exposed back to him.

He harshly drags my body back until my back is flush to his chest. I let out a loud breath, the force almost knocking me out cold. "Never leave yourself vulnerable to an opponent," he whispers into my ear.

"Prick," I say under my breath, making that infuriating but toe curling chuckle leave his damning lips. I take the opportunity to stomp my foot on his boot, making him grunt in return. He tightens his arm around my neck, restricting my movements but not cutting my air supply off.

"How will you ever get out of this mess?" he taunts from behind me, making me dig my nails into the palms of my hand out of frustration.

I swing my elbow towards his side again, but he catches it with his free hand and pins it down by my side, rendering it immobile. I huff in frustration, my temper a living, breathing thing at the moment.

"Think," he says from behind me, but it's not mocking. He's pushing me, wanting me to be able to defend myself and make calculated moves.

I gather my wits and do the only thing my brain can think of to get out of this sticky situation, holding true to my promise of drawing blood: I sink my teeth into his flesh. I draw blood from the arm strangling my neck. He lets out a grunt and softens his grip enough for me to slip out of his hold, ripping my arm from his grasp.

I drop low, spinning on my heels as I kick out my foot aimed for his ankles. It doesn't knock him over, but it gets him just enough off center for me to pounce at his chest, wrapping my whole body around him as we crash to the ground in a tangle of limbs.

When the dust we kicked up settles, I find myself on top of Hade, straddling his oversized body, my legs barely big enough to wrap around his chiseled torso. He looks up at me with a soft smile on his face, looking lost in a haze of…of lust, maybe? Except his gaze isn't heated or suggestive. No, it's full of awe, maybe pride. The thought makes me wonder if it's not lust at all that I'm interpreting in his lethal eyes locked on mine.

I grow soft under his praiseful gaze, as if he's melting me with his unwavering devotion of just looking at me. My cheeks heat, and the man I see under me is the man who carried me gently in his arms. Who woke up healers in the middle of the night to save me. Who washed my body and cleaned and braided my hair. I see the man who made my heart beat again.

In a blink of an eye, he spins us, wedging my body under his so I'm the one now pinned under his hard, and I mean *very* hard, body. He squeezes his thick thighs on each of my sides, holding me in place. My chest rises harshly, pressing up against his body where it sits above me, drawing a soft, uncontrollable whimper from me. He grabs each of my wrists and pins them above my head, making sure I have no way of fighting him back. I have to blow my hair out of my face so I can see him clearly. When he's looking at me like he sees me instead of some broken object, the thought of fighting him off becomes so foreign, I forget its meaning.

He shoves my wrists together, his giant hand wrapping around both now, engulfing them in his grip so he can use his other hand to play with his prey. He smirks down at me, and in that exact moment, every hair on my body stands at attention with excitement and a pinch of fear. My breathing picks up, the only sound, like a soft melody on repeat.

He bends in until his lips are barely pressed against the shell of my ear. "Looks like you got yourself in a terrible predicament, *Nightmare*," he whispers, making my body sing to life. "How ever will you get yourself out of this one?" he taunts, and I can feel his smirk as his cheek brushes against mine, his stubble undoubtedly leaving red marks across my flesh as he drags his face in front of mine again.

Batting my eyelashes, I lower my voice in a sultry tone. "Who said I'm not enjoying the predicament I've found myself in, *Hade*?"

Hunger flashes across his eyes, his eyes darker than I've ever seen them. He's a starved man, and I'm his prey pinned helpless beneath him. A deep rumble vibrates through his chest; I wiggle nervously beneath him. He's one moment away from snapping, and I'm not sure either of us would survive the fallout if that were to happen.

The way he's looking at me is making it terribly difficult to resist the wicked things running through my head. He's staring at me with an intensity I have no doubt could level entire cities, but it's also laced with slight hesitation, like he's doing everything in his power to hold himself back. Something is hurting him, and I want to know what it is, why, ever since that night, he looks like he can't take a full breath around me.

I can tell he's slipping away, worry riddling his gaze. He's building his walls back up right before my eyes, so I do the first thing that comes to mind to try and drag him back to me.

I suck my bottom lip between my teeth, sinking my teeth into it like a pillow. Slowly, I drag teeth across it seductively, and I watch his eyes zone in on my lip, tracking it intently the entire way. He closes his eyes, letting out a deep, throaty growl while squeezing my wrists in his calloused palm he still has pinned above my head. I yelp in surprise, sinking my teeth harder into my lip, drawing blood.

His eyes flash open and trail the single bead of blood slithering across my lip. Letting go of my wrists, he drags his thumb slowly across it, wiping the blood away. He goes to move, but I lean forward, sucking the tip of his thumb into my mouth until my cheeks hollow.

He lets out a choked breath and goes to lean down a fraction of an inch, but he halts when he feels the cold edge of my dagger pressed against the delicate flesh of his neck.

"What was that you said again?" I say sweetly, smiling up at him, leaning in until our faces are mere inches apart. "Never underestimate your opponent. Oh, and my personal favorite: find their weaknesses so you can exploit them." I lick my lips methodically, the tip of my tongue barely lashing against his bottom lip from how close we are. He lets out a strangled, breathy moan, his eyes following my tongue. "Thanks for the tips, *sir*."

I'm trying to keep my composure on the outside, but I'm one second away from losing it, saying to hell with this little game. I can see the way Hade is looking at me right now, and it's the same look I know he sees within me.

Our breaths turn ragged, beating to the same drum as my hand turns pliant around the handle of my dagger pressed to his neck. Neither of us have blinked, both scared to make a single movement and shatter whatever is happening between us. I catch him staring at my lips like they are a temptation he's no longer strong enough to fight. He inches slightly closer, his neck digging into my blade.

"Hade," I whisper against his lips.

He looks defeated, like he's okay with losing this war and throwing in his sword. There's so much pain in his gaze, calling to mine in likeness. Growling to himself, he flies backwards through the air, propelled by his magic, until he's a hefty distance away from me, leaving me in a panting mess of lust and confusion.

He strides over to Winston, who I notice has been here all along, standing on the edge of the Bubble, probably watching this entire catastrophe unfold. He whispers something in his ear, and Winston nods back in understanding. Then, Hade disappears altogether, like he was never just pressed on top of my body, about to do Empress knows what to me.

I squeeze my eyes shut, fisting my hands until I wince. So much for training. If anything, all I got out of today was an even more messed up head and some cardio with how fast my heart was beating. I guess if I were him, I wouldn't want the responsibility of trying to wrap two hands around a crumbling heart, too difficult to grasp and keep whole.

The task was *doomed* from the start.

Chapter
Thirty

MY NERVES ARE SHOT, THE NUMBER OF US LEFT IN THE CRUCIBLE dwindling to a staggering five. One would think making it this far should reassure me, but with only two more rounds, the chances of myself being the last one standing seems daunting.

I'm standing back in the Bubble next to Rayah and our remaining competitors while we wait for the Empress to announce the next game. I got next to no sleep last night, too hyped up on adrenaline and nerves while trying to think about what today's trial might entail or skills it will test. A million possibilities ran through my mind as I pondered previous Crucibles. I know, at some point, alliances will be tested, so maybe today's game will play into that. I'm not exactly sure how that will work, since we are down an extra competitor than we should be, but I wouldn't put it past the Empress to carry on as if nothing changed.

I'm not blind to the whispers of my competitors asking where Aeron is, gossiping things like, "I bet he's warming the Empress' bed and slept in," or "Maybe his big mouth finally got the best of him." I, too, wonder where Aeron is, but for a very different reason.

A commotion draws my attention to the entrance of the Bubble, the tension palpable as the air shifts around us. The Empress strides in wearing a glimmering, black, floor-length dress with a sweetheart neckline, mimicking the mood around us.

She gracefully saunters through the sand to stand before us, a stoic look plastered on her face. She turns to look back at the entrance, waving her arm. "Bring him in."

My stomach drops like an anchor, souring on the spot. My palms turn sticky, and I feel slightly light headed all the sudden. If the "him" she's referring to is the person I was hoping to never see again, then I think my breakfast might make a reappearance. My body starts to tremble, and Ray must notice, because she slides her hand into mine without looking over at me, making sure not to create a scene. It instantly calms my nerves, centering me. I'm not alone, and he *can't* hurt me anymore.

I hear stomping in the sand to my right and slowly drag my eyes over until they land on *death* himself. The Cardinal marches in like he's taking off to the front lines for battle, his face set with deep lines from scowling so hard. Floating behind him like a shadow is… No that can't be right. Can it?

A black mass of wispy magic tornadoes around a body hovering above the ground behind Hade. He pulls it along by a rope of black magic like an animal on a leash. As they near, my heart stops, the scene sharpening.

Aeron floats behind Hade, wearing the same outfit I last saw him in. It's dirty and tattered and smells of piss. Looking down, I notice a wet path down the front of his pants, where it looks like he's repeatedly soiled himself. His eyes are wide open and unblinking, like he's frozen in shock and fearful for his life. His mouth is so agape, his jaw almost looks broken, as if he's screaming, but his voice is long gone.

He looks exactly how he did the last time I saw him, minus the eerie screams, and that was…days ago. A chill runs up my spine. If my insights are correct, then Hade has kept him in this loop of seeing his impending death play out in his head for multiple days now, to the point that he's lost his voice and pissed himself.

Death Reaper indeed.

Hade stands in front of us and clears his throat, Aeron floating behind him. I hold my breath for whatever chaos is about to unfold, something deep in my gut telling me it won't be pretty.

"Be this a *reminder* and a *warning.*" His deep voice rings out clear as day, demanding to be heard. "If you so much as lay a single unwanted finger on another competitor outside of the confines of this game, it will be seen as a direct act of disrespect against the Empress and will be dealt with accordingly." He looks down the line to each of my competitors, making direct eye contact. "I do not tire of teaching lessons, so let it be known here and now what the consequences of stepping out of line will entail."

He turns to face a silently screaming Aeron, and his voice turns lethally low. "It seems your competitor…" He pauses for a moment, pretending to forget his name. "Allen—no, that's not right. Ah, Aeron here decided to volunteer as a demonstration to what happens if you don't follow the rules your Empress has given you."

He slides his hand through the swirling magic and pats Aeron's shoulder. Aeron's expression remains the same, like he isn't even aware of what's happening.

"So, shall we proceed?" Hade taunts with a wicked gleam in his eyes and a devious smirk tipping his lips. "Aeron here put his grimy fingers where they don't belong. He touched something that was not his to touch, and he's been paying the price ever since."

With a flick of his wrist, the black magic swirling around Aeron's body dissipates from his face. He remains floating above the ground, but the trance-like state he was in vanishes. He starts to shake, looking around aimlessly for help. He starts to hyperventilate, thrashing in the air as his pants grow wet again. He shakes his head back and forth, pleading for mercy, trying to speak, but no sound comes out.

Smiling, Hade takes a step closer and hooks his finger under Aeron's trembling chin, drawing it up to look at him. "I think you know exactly what comes next."

I have yet to see this side of Hade. He's honed like a weapon, harsh at every curve and dangerously dead inside. He bears no morals in this moment, emotions carried away by the wind, never to be seen again. He is death itself and will stop at nothing, sacrificing his soul included, to show everybody exactly what he was created to do.

Reaching forward, he grips Aeron's hand and pulls it in front of him. Reaching into his belt, he plucks out a sharp dagger and flips it in his hand. He's playing with his prey, and it's working—Aeron looks like he's on the verge of dying, seeming to know exactly what comes next.

"What do you think is a fair price?" Hade asks, flipping Aeron's hand back and forth. "A digit for each minute you had your hands where they didn't belong?" After a moment, he adds, "Seems fair to me."

Bringing the dagger down, he grips Aeron's thumb, holding it steady as he slowly draws the dagger back and forth over his skin, fileting him like a piece of meat. He saws through the bone, taking his time as Aeron chokes on his sobs with breathy screams. I hear a final crunch, and I try to hold the contents of my stomach down as Hade drops the detached thumb to the sand. "One."

He grabs the next finger and repeats the process as Aeron grows pale, on the verge of passing out. Sweat coats his skin, and his head starts to bob. Hade's magic reaches out of its own accord and holds Aeron's head up, making sure he stays awake for his punishment. "Two," he states plainly, dropping the finger next to the thumb in the red-stained sand.

He continues cutting off each finger of his left hand and then reaches for his right. Aeron lets out a loud sob, trying to pull away, but Hade has a death grip. "What, you thought we were done? Oh, but the fun is just getting started, my friend." He peers down with a questioning look. "I seem to have forgotten what number we were on. I never really was good with numbers, so I guess I will just have to take them all."

I turn my head as Hade methodically cuts each finger from Aeron's hand, my stomach not strong enough to handle the gore.

"There. Much better," I hear Hade state, and I turn back around to face the chaos again. Blood drips from both Aeron and Hade's hands, the sand a deep crimson. I almost see a look of defeat in Aeron's eyes, but it morphs into something seeming like relief, which seems odd. He closes his eyes with a soft smile on his face, prepared for whatever comes next.

"Let this be a lesson you may never forget," Hade threatens each of us, avoiding my gaze. Looking back at a smiling Aeron, he adds, "Your participation in this lesson has seemed to run its course, and you are no longer of use to me." Hade reaches out, and black tendrils stream from his palm, snaking into Aeron's ears, mouth, and nose. I catch Aeron take one last deep breath of submission as Hade turns his head, making direct eye contact with me. Holding my gaze with his arm outstretched, he forcefully closes his fist, and Aeron's head explodes, shattering into a million pieces and coating the side of Hade's face in blood. Aeron's headless body falls to the sand with a loud thump, and Hade steps over his lifeless body to trot out of the Bubble, a few of the other Vanquishers moving to clean up his mess.

I should be a wreck, fearing for my life, disgusted even. I will admit, I'm definitely more than shaken up, but the only thing truly running through my mind is if the same gory blood bath would have played out if Aeron had touched someone else. My head is telling me yes, but my heart is telling me I might just be something special. I'm not sure how to process that, but I don't think I'm as opposed to the idea as much as I should be. I think his darkness has slithered beneath my skin and dug its claws in so deep, I can't tell where his ends and mine begins.

Chapter
Thirty-One

"Now that we've gotten that taken care of, let the real fun begin," the Empress belts out to the growing crowd outside the Bubble. "Today's game will test your ability to make strong alliances. Hopefully, you haven't sided with someone who will stab you in the back."

I hear Jade and Tank snicker next to me, and heat licks at my cheeks. I won't let them get to me, not today. I tune them out the best I can as I focus back on the Empress.

"Ignore them," Ray whispers next to me, and I give her a small smile in return that isn't very convincing. I just need to get through another round, and then I can rot in bed for the rest of eternity.

"Before I explain the rules of today's game, you must split into two teams. Since our dear friend Aeron won't be joining us, there will be a team of three and a team of two." Gesturing to her side, she adds, "Before choosing your teams, I will announce the rankings from last week's game. I will give you no hints, so choose your partners wisely."

A bright flash of light appears next to her, our names flashing into existence mid-air.

Tank sits at the top, somehow earning a perfect score last week, even though he didn't even get to participate, which seems unfair. Moving down, his evil twin and Satan's spawn herself, Jade, sits in the number two spot. After seeing the way she climbed up the blocks like it was second nature, her score makes sense, even if I don't want to admit it. I find my name next, sitting in third with Cartwell right behind me. Even though he is basically a brain mounted on legs, his agility is what cost him in the last round. My heart hurts a little bit as I spot my sunshine, Ray, sitting in last place.

None of this knowledge will change the alliances I plan to make, but it's still good information to have. I spot Jade and Tank fist bumping next to me, giant smirks on their faces, and it makes me want to slit both their throats. I think Hade might be rubbing off on me.

I spot worry in Ray's eyes, like she fears no one will want to partner with her, but that's the farthest thing from the truth. If there's one person I would trust with my life, it would be her. She's perfect in her own quirky way; I just wish she could see it for herself. She's fiercely determined, and when faced with trouble, she got right back up and tried again until she got the task done. She's an inspiration, and who doesn't love pink hair?

"You may now split off into two teams," the Empress' elevated voice beckons us.

Without thought, I grab Ray's hand and drag her to my side, staking my claim. On cue, Tank and Jade saunter over to the opposite side, thick as thieves as always. I would expect nothing less. That leaves Cartwell standing in the center between our two groups, looking back and forth in deep thought.

I won't lie, Cartwell could be an amazing ally if this challenge has anything to do with knowledge, but I also know Tank is the strongest among us. It just depends if he trusts those two, or if he wants to side with someone he would get along with. I could see them using Cartwell and then discarding him when they are through. That thought must cross his mind too, because he peaks over at us, and I give him a small, encouraging smile back. He turns on his heels and slowly walks over until he's standing right beside us, which puts the biggest smile on Ray's face. Jade sends threats across the sand with her eyes, and I smile and wave at her innocently, rubbing it in.

The Empress once again discretely asks each of us if we've solved her impossible riddle. We all fail to come up with responses, making her move to the game. "Right. Now that that's settled, are you ready to learn about today's game?" She gestures in a sweeping motion to us and the crowd outside, and they erupt in loud cheers and screams. "Today's game is all about strategy. Strategy to pick the right team, strategy to make the right moves. Since we are already a player down, only one contestant will lose today. Pray it is not you."

The Empress snaps her fingers, and the Illuminist beside her raises their hands. Blue magic erupts from their palms, creating a miniature three dimensional diagram.

"A game of strategy and luck, just like life. Who doesn't love a good game of Submerge?" She pulls at the edge of the diagram, stretching it for us to see. It depicts two sides, divided by a tall wall down the center. Each side moves fluidly, like flowing water.

"For those of you not familiar with this game, I will lay the rules out." She plucks a small, glowing boat made of magic and places it in the water on the right side of the wall.

"Each team will have two boats to place on their side of the wall anywhere they would like. There are corresponding squares under the shallow water, laying out the playing field. The number of seats in each boat determines how many squares the boat will take up. Once a boat is placed, it will be locked in place in the water, marking your board."

She turns to speak to Jade and Tank. "Since your team is short a person, you will both be placed in a boat." She then turns to face our team. "Seeing as you have three players, you will decide amongst yourselves which two will be placed in a boat and which player you would like to elect as your game master. The game master will oversee placing your boats, as well as casting your shots against the opposing team. Keep in mind, the game master will be safe from elimination, but they could also win you the game if they are strategic enough."

Shit.

I look over to Ray and Cartwell, trying to make a game plan in my head. I'm not selfish enough to vote myself as the game master to save my own ass, especially if it might be at the expense of Ray, but I also don't want to die. Logically, Cartwell would be our best bet, but that also means putting our lives on the line.

"Tank, Jade," the Empress gestures between them. "You will also need to select a game master for your team, but since you will both be placed in a boat, your game master will *not* be exempt from elimination. You may make your selections now."

Ray and Cartwell scoot close so we stand shoulder to shoulder in a tight circle, creating a rainbow of blue, pink, and black hair. We all sit there silently for a few moments, unsure how to start the conversation. Taking initiative, I decide we need to think logically and talk through our options.

"Okay, why don't we go over pros and cons for each person to narrow it down?" They both nod in agreement, and I go to speak, but Rayah beats me to it.

"Flowers, I won't even lie, I have never had good luck in this game. I used to play it with the neighbor kids all the time growing up with rocks in the dirt, and I have won a whopping *zero* times.

Whew, that felt good to get off my chest." Clapping, she adds, "Who's next?"

Shaking my head, I stifle back a laugh—leave it to Rayah to give cons about herself and no pros when fighting for her life. This woman is a different breed entirely. I decide to follow in her footsteps, because at this point, if she's not volunteering herself, then neither am I.

"Alright, I guess I'll go next." I shrug. "Honestly, I've never played this game before, growing up in an orphanage and all, so my vote is for Cartwell, since he seems like the most logical answer."

Cartwell looks between the two of us, his mouth slightly agape from shock. Smiling, he gives us a small nod, accepting the position.

"Thank you for trusting in my abilities," he says eagerly, like he's never been picked first for anything in his life. "I played this game extensively when I was a child and know it well. It's a game of strategy, but I won't lie—there is a good chunk of luck involved as well. I will try my best to keep you both alive." He wrings his hands together, looking suddenly nervous.

"Well, that's good enough for me," Ray shouts, patting him on the shoulder.

The Empress clears her throat, gathering our attention once more. "Have you made your decisions?" We all nod as Carwell and Jade both raise their hands as the nominees.

"Wonderful! Moving on then," the Empress says in an excited manner. "Once your game master has placed their two boats in position, we will flip a copper to see which team will start. On each side of the dividing wall will be a replica of your opponent's playing field for you to use as reference. Each game master will take turns calling out a square to attack, hoping it will hit one of their competitors' ships. Using the catapult provided, your game master will state the dedicated space they would like to target and pull the lever, which will fling a ball of magic over the wall. The goal of the game is to sink one of your opponent's ships. You must hit each square the boat covers to sink the ship. Whichever player is sitting in the first ship that sinks will be eliminated from the Crucible. Each shot taken will show as a circle for a hit or an x for a miss on the dividing wall in front of you to use as a guide."

The Empress smooths her hands down her shiny dress, taking a long breath after word vomiting the rules to us. "Do you all understand?"

We all nod, and the nerves start to creep in as my reality sets in. I have zero say in if I survive this game or not. I just have to pray Cartwell can sink one of their ships before Ray's or mine does, and I can't do a damn thing about it.

"Right then. Fabricants, you may begin." She gestures to two Vanquishers standing at the edge of the Bubble, and they saunter over to us.

I take two very large steps back, learning my lesson from the last time one of them conjured up mayhem. They cup their hands in front of them as small orbs of magic glow between their palms. Slowly, they drag their hands outwards, making the ball of magic grow until it explodes out of them and a giant towering playing field appears in front of us, a perfect duplication of the tiny one the Empress used as an example.

The wall towers too many feet above my head to count, and two large bodies of water adorn each side. A checkered grid appears on each side of the wall with numbers across the top and letters down the left side, marking the spaces. Two boats are placed at the edge of the water on each side of the wall, one with five seats in it and the other with three.

I share a glace with Ray, both of us realizing one of us will have a better chance at survival depending on what boat we choose. Leave it to the Empress to test us any chance she gets. This truly is a game to test our alliances and relationships.

"Competitors, you may now choose your boats. Game master, please make your selections and communicate them to the Vanquisher dedicated to your side."

Something in my gut is telling me to choose the *smaller boat*, even though it will lessen my odds of making it out alive. I can't stomach the thought of either me or Ray not walking away from today, but I'm also not naive to my reality.

Pointing to the boat with three seats, I tell Ray, "I'll take this once." She scrunches her nose, looking confused, but I shoot her a look that says don't even bother trying to change my mind. Huffing, she struts over to the larger boat and hops inside after the Vanquisher lowers it into the water.

I may be dooming myself, but my intuitions haven't led me astray so far, so I won't start ignoring them today. My gut tells me I've *made the right choice*, and content sinks into my bones.

Cartwell makes his choices, and the Vanquisher uses his magic to guide each of our boats to their respective places. I take two deep, steadying breaths and peak over at Ray on the other side of the water from me. I give her a small, reassuring smile and wave before facing forward to look at the wall.

"Jade has won the coin toss, so she will make the first selection. Since she is also placed in a boat, she will relay her choice to the Vanquisher, who will pull the catapult lever." A wicked smile takes over the Empress' face as she looks to both sides of the wall, staring us down.

"Good luck to you all, and pray to the gods you aren't *submerged*." She trots off but stays inside the Bubble for today's game, her throne now inside so she can have up close viewing pleasures.

I falter when I spot Hade standing next to her, freshly washed and in new clothes, not a single drop of blood to be seen. I didn't expect him to return, and now, my nerves are shot. I rush to look away, praying he didn't catch me, but it's like he can feel my gaze, turning immediately to lock eyes with me, and my heart stops dead.

I turn into a living ball of nerves, not sure what to do with my-self or how to act. He just brutally murdered the man who tried to kill me. Not only that, he meticulously tortured him for *days* first, and I'm about to start a game that could very likely get me killed before the sun has even set tonight.

I nervously turn away, breaking the electric eye contact we shared that was quite literally sucking the life out of me, making it difficult to breathe. My hands start to shake a bit, so I wedge them under my butt, praying no one notices.

A phantom breeze blows across my face, pushing back the curls spilling over my face. A gentle caress glides across my cheek, so soft, I barely notice it. A tiny black shadow pushes up against my cheek like a caress, and my anxiety melts away in an instant.

It's *him.* I could never forget the way his magic feels against my skin, as essential as needing food each day, a familiar comfort that always seems to show up when I need it most. I smile to my-self, softly pushing into the shadow, and it seems to purr back in response.

Everything is going to be okay. I can feel it in my bones.

"Hit!" the Empress squeals from her chair, making my smile falter and my stomach plummet. Lost in my own thoughts, I hadn't even noticed the game started.

Swiveling, I see a giant orb of red magic in the seat directly be-hind Ray. Somehow, Jade has landed her first attempt, and I don't like the idea of that. She sees me wearily staring and gives me a soft smile, waving me off like she will be fine. I pray for her sake she is, because her odds aren't looking great if Cartwell doesn't hit a ship soon.

"C three," Cartwell calls out and pulls the lever. A *whoosh* sounds above me as I watch a giant orb of magic catapult over the tall wall and make a splash when it hits the other side. My stom-ach sinks for a second time—the sound of it hitting water doesn't make me very hopeful.

"Miss!" the Empress shouts excitedly.

I drop my face into my hands, collecting myself before sitting back up again. Everything is going to be okay...I hope. Squaring my shoulders, I see a giant x marked on the wall where Cartwell's move landed.

I hear the whoosh of the catapult on the other side and brace for impact just in case. It barrels over the wall aiming for the back left corner where Ray is perched. The orb hits the water to her left one square back, splashing her in the process.

Thank the Empress.

"Another miss!" the Empress belts.

"F Seven," Cartwell states as he pulls the lever and lets another orb fly. It wizzes by in a flash, making contact on the other side.

"That's a hit!" the Empress squeals as a giant circle appears on the wall in front of me, marking the start of a ship. I pray it's the smaller boat for Ray's sake.

Whoosh! Sploosh!

The orb narrowly misses Ray again, landing to her right and one space back this time. They are closing in on her, and my heart starts to pound with anticipation. I place my trust back in Cartwell, knowing he is our best bet at survival.

"E Seven," Cartwell calls out, launching another orb.

Splash!

"Oh bummer, another miss!" Sarcasm oozes from her voice.

Shit on a brick, this is not going well. The playing field is big, so tell me why both the game masters have latched on to boats faster than it takes Winston to start listing facts about oranges. I won't let them take Ray from me. She deserves to breathe more than the two devils sitting on the opposite side of this wall. She deserves the world.

Woosh!

My eyes track the orb through the air above me, aiming at the back corner again, right at Ray. I hold my breath, praying they miss for a third time as my heart sinks. It barrels through the air, dropping until it plops into Ray's lap, making her let out a small yelp.

"I'm okay," she shouts over to me, looking more embarrassed than hurt. I don't spot any blood, so I assume the orb absorbed most of the impact, leaving her unharmed. Two orbs now sit in her boat, one behind her and one in her lap, leaving three seats open.

"Another hit!" the Empress screams, jumping into the air like this is entertaining to her.

Holding eye contact, I give Ray a soft smile, trying to ease the anxiety I know is rising in both of us. It seems to work, because she relaxes her shoulders and puts on a brave face.

"G Seven," Cartwell yells, pulling the lever and sending the magical orb flying into this abyss. I close my eyes and cross my fingers, praying this is a hit. My heart can't take another miss.

"Would you look at that, another miss!"

If I have to hear the she devil say the word 'miss' one more time, I might not be able to control my rage.

I turn, glaring at the Empress, rage overtaking my control for once. Big mistake, though, because I lock onto an endless black hole and a pot of melted silver staring me down. I gulp, trying to look away, but it's like his eyes are a magnet, holding me in place and devouring me whole.

His shaggy wet hair flops over his forehead as I spot tiny beads of water dripping from the ends. His simple cotton tunic clings to his arms and chiseled torso, accentuating every hard line. He's mouthwateringly handsome, and it *pisses* me off.

A dimple appears on his left cheek as a smirk takes over his face, clearly noticing the way I'm ogling over the man when I should be focused on not dying. Chastising myself, I pinch my arm to snap me from my trance and discreetly wipe the corners of my mouth to make sure I wasn't accidently drooling. Spinning forward again, I spot another x appearing on the wall in front of me as a deep chuckle rings out in the distance.

I need to mark him with an x for trouble.

Already knowing what's coming, I brace as another orb floats over the wall, plopping into the seat directly in front of Ray with a soft *thunk*. Cursing under my breath, I drag my eyes up to peek at Ray, who oddly seems very calm. She better not be throwing the towel in already, or I'll have Hade use his death magic to haunt her for eternity.

"Marvelous, another hit!" The Empress squeals.

Groaning to myself, I think about sending death threats with my eyes to Cartwell, but when I peek back at him, I notice a thin sheen of sweat coating him from nerves. The poor man has the life of a sweet, innocent woman in his hands, and he's crumbling under the pressure.

Cartwell yells out, "F Eight," and another orb blasts off into space, heading towards what I pray is a hit.

"Pity. Miss!" the Empress says in a soft tone, sounding bored.

It's going to be tragic when my fist accidently connects with her fragile face. Apparently, rage is taking over the fear and anxiety thundering inside me.

Call me a coward, but I can't even look back at Ray, too scared to acknowledge the very possible near end in her future. Why has life come to this? Playing a game to the death for the mere entertainment of a tyrant Empress and her obedient followers. Why can't we simply get along?

Life is just one big sick joke that I am clearly missing the punch line to.

The sound of an incoming orb from above aims once again at my pink haired friend. It plops down two seats in front of Ray, marking the fourth seat in her boat.

I hear Cartwell grunt behind me and then shout out, "F Six," which is the only direction left for him to make, seeing as he has guessed every other side surrounding his first hit. On cue, I hear a loud *thunk* from the opposite side of the wall.

"Hit!" the Empress shouts to the stars, and for once, I'm not mad at the bitch.

Dread slams into my heart like a sword puncturing my lungs, making it hard to breathe. This is it, the deciding move of the game. There is one space remaining in Ray's boat, except Jade won't know if the spot left is in the front of the boat or the rear of the boat. It's a fifty-fifty chance of her guessing correctly.

If luck has ever been on my side, I pray it's now. If she guesses wrong, that could leave the game open for Cartwell to secure the win. There's only one direction he can guess, so his next move will be a sure hit. It just depends if he is shooting at the boat with three seats or five.

A glowing orb crests over the wall, and time moves in slow motion as it dips lower, lower, aiming for Ray. I look away, too scared for the outcome. A loud *thunk* shatters my heart into a million pieces.

It can't be; I won't accept it. But fate is a fickle thing and doesn't always make sense. It's tricky and disguised in ways to make you lose salience in its holiness. Fate left me with no parents. Fate took away the man I loved, and now, fate is claiming another innocent life from my grasp. Everything I seem to touch dies right before my eyes, like a sick game on loop, and now, the word fate seems more like a punishment than a destiny.

Slowly, I turn my head to lock eyes with the beautiful ray of sunshine behind me who deserved better, just like Hudson. She gives me a soft watery smile, trying to hide her shaking hands as the Empress screams, "Seize her!"

"Nooooooooo!" I scream at the top of my lungs, ripping my throat to shreds, ready to jump off my boat and swim to her if it comes to it. I can protect her, I *will* protect her. Giant arms envelop me, holding me in place right as I'm about to launch myself into the water.

"Let me go!" I seethe through a sob as tremors rack my body.

The arms squeeze me tighter, drawing me into their chest as the smell of sandalwood and smoke floods my senses. "Shhh, it's me, I'm here. I need you to calm down for me, love," Hade whispers into my hair as I try but fail to fight the restraints holding me back, slowly battering my weak fists against his arms until they fall defeatedly to my sides.

"You have to save her!" I weep on choppy breaths. I don't care how pathetically weak and desperate I sound. I *need* this. "*Please*, Hade. Save her for me," I whisper defeatedly. This could be the final thing that sends me to the point of no return, the final push off the ledge I've been teetering on for far too long, free falling to a fate full of destruction and lost humanity.

He grabs my face, tilting my chin until I'm staring into his soft eyes pleading with me to understand him. "I need you to trust me. Can you do that?" he literally *begs* me.

Those are the only words he offers. My body locks up for a second, drawn back to the last time a man told me to calm down and trust them. They pretended to take care of me and show me love, only to turn around and stab me in the back. I look between his perfect, opposite eyes, and my gut tells me I can *trust him and everything will be okay.*

I hesitantly nod, which sets his body at ease. His shoulders relax, and the worry lines on his forehead wash away. He plops a soft kiss to my temple, and I fight the mixed emotions of grief, betrayal, longing, and death taking over my mind.

"Ladies and gentlemen, we have ourselves a winning team!" the Empress shouts as Jade and Tank appear at her sides, their fists raised, waving to the Illuminists who have been watching the game to later broadcast.

Hade guides our boat back to shore with his shadows and helps me out, gently placing me back on solid ground. I take a glance over my shoulder to see the Vanquisher tasked as Ray's guard guiding her boat to the opposite side of the water's edge, plopping her back on solid ground and marching her out of the Bubble to Empress knows where.

I yearn to run after her, needing one last moment, a proper goodbye. I'm not ready to let go of another soft spot that wedged its way into my dead soul. I attempt to take a step in her direction, a list of parting words and praises on the tip of my tongue, but I halt when she turns to look at me right at the edge of the Bubble. She gives me an easy smile of farewell while mouthing the word 'flowers'. I stand frozen as I watch her walk away, and my heart gains another fissure next to the others littering its surface.

Just as her body is about to slip out of the Bubble, she gives me one final glance, and I shoot her a small smile in return, mouthing the word 'flowers' back. It draws a beautiful giggle out of her, even while striding towards death's door. Deep in my heart, I know we will meet again in the next life, and the one after that, for the rest of eternity.

The Empress clears her throat and then gestures to the chanting crowd outside the Bubble. "I think we've had enough gore for today, and I'm quite famished, so my Vanquishers will dispose of today's loser in the dungeons. Rest up, because there are still two rounds standing between you and being crowned this year's Reaper Crucible champion."

The need to rip her throat out returns full force as I contemplate getting the job done right now. Who complains about being famished when the life of an innocent is about to be brutally taken?

My body vibrates with rage, the calm Hade washed over me disappearing as fast as it came. I want to scream and cry and plead with the gods for a different fate. I want to kill and maim and become the embodiment of destruction, but the loss of another friend mostly makes me want to curl into a ball and never emerge again. Death is becoming all too familiar.

Death is just a five-letter word, yet it consumes my entire existence, driving me to the brink of becoming the word itself. And the day that happens, I pray for all those who stand in my way.

Chapter
Thirty-Two

I HURL MY BODY THROUGH MY DOOR, HADE FOLLOWING CLOSE BE-hind. Today's events slam into me like a fist, and I finally break. It's all too much, leaving no more room in my head to fit another devastating blow. Everything I've ignored finally comes crashing in like a tidal wave. Theo, Hudson, and now Ray. When is it enough? When will people stop being ripped from my grasp too soon? When will my heart beat without it being excruciatingly painful?

My chest heaves, unable to draw air into my lungs as I suffo-cate on all the pain. Broken breaths rip from my mouth as a panic attack grips me. I bend over, trying to catch my breath, bracing my hand on the edge of my bed.

I feel like my skin is suffocating me, trapping me beneath a wall of black as a haze starts to dance in my eyes. The pain is drawing me under, and I feel content to let it swallow me whole so I may never have to feel anything ever again.

A warm hand lands on my back, slowly dragging up and down my spine. "Breathe for me, Nyxi," he says in a strong yet defeated tone. "How can I help? What do you need?"

I go to open my mouth, but my breath lodges in my throat, making me gasp for air as the tears finally break through. The crack in my wall turns into a full blown break as tears flood through, finally set free. I'm hysterical and inconsolable, a pit of darkness with no light on the horizon.

"It's too much," I choke out through the tears. "It's not fair," I say on another sob, scrambling to catch my breath.

"Shhh, beautiful, I know." He strokes my hair and draws me into his warm chest. "Right now, though, all I care about is you," he whispers into my hair. "What normally calms you down?"

"The lake," I heave between breaths. "Being under the night sky has always been calming," I admit easily.

Memories of spending warm summer nights with Theo at the lake under the stars assaults me. It always seemed to call to me, to draw away the darkness that liked to sweep in at times. Theo always saw when the walls started to cave in on me. He would whisk me away to the lake until the darkness turned into belly laughs and memories that are ingrained in my brain forever.

Thinking back to some of my favorite memories, my breathing evens out the slightest so I'm able to catch my breath. Emboldened by my emotions, I decided to share a little chunk of myself with the man who seems to have taken over the role of my anchor.

"I used to visit there with someone special to me, and all my favorite memories reside there," I admit as warmth envelops my heart.

"Theo?" Hade asks softy.

My heart lurches. I drag my face up, my red rimmed eyes meeting his soft ying yang ones. He looks at peace but also curious.

"How do you know that?" I ask—how does he know Theo? I certainly have never talked about it with him.

He gives me a casual smile and brushes the wet hair slicked to my face by tears off my cheeks. "The night I fixed up your ear," he begins. "You passed out on me, and when I went to tuck you in, you called me Theo." There's no venom or anger in his tone. If anything, he seems content, like he's getting to know a piece of me that came before him.

I nod—there's no point in denying what he already knows. "Theo would take me to the lake so we could sit under the stars and feel free, alive."

"Do you love him?" he questions while looking between my eyes with a softness I didn't know the Cardinal could possess. He seems to surprise me at every turn when it comes to me and me only.

"I did. Very much," I whisper. "Now, there's a wall of stars between our love."

"I'm so sorry to hear that," Hade says against my temple, and I lean into his embrace, soaking in his words. "There is no void deeper than the crater love leaves behind in someone's heart."

He speaks as if he knows firsthand the catastrophic damage the absence of love can wreak on a soul. It brings up a slew of questions in me, but I shove them down, not wanting to add more fuel to the fire. Maybe another time, we can dig up our pasts. Right now, all I want to do is let go and not feel a thing.

I manage a nod as the last tear slowly falls down my cheek, my reserves all dried up. Hade scoops the lone tear with his finger, dragging it up and off my face. His thumb returns to my cheek in a sweeping motion, back and forth, as he smiles down at me. I could die happy in this moment, his smile a siren calling me home.

"C'mon, let's go," he whispers. Striding over to my armoire, he snags a fresh shirt and pants to replace my bodysuit then scoops me up, drawing me close so I'm nuzzled into his chest. I look up at him with confusion, and he lets out a soft, content sigh. "Let's go feel alive and free."

His magic wraps around us like a warm blanket, and its familiarity is a welcome comfort tonight. A phantom gust of wind swings the stained glass window in my bedroom open, letting in fresh air. Hade's magic floats us out the window into the open sky.

The sun is slowly making its descent, getting ready to dip behind the towering buildings in the heart of the city. Warm hues of pinks and oranges take over the once-clear blue sky, making a halo over the city. It's breathtaking, and I picture it's Theo's way of saying hello, his contagious personality personified through cotton candy clouds and golden rays.

"It's stunning," I say, more to myself than to Hade.

"I couldn't agree more," he breathes. I turn back to face him, only to find him staring intently at my face, and my body instantly breaks out in chills.

His magic carries us over the busy city, Magicals milling about with their families and friends, heading to taverns for the night's festivities. It's amazing to see the way the citizens all move like one body of flowing water. Children run about the streets, laughing and playing, while their parents shop the vendors lining the cobblestone. It's peaceful and unlike anything I've ever witnessed.

The thrum of magic can be felt from every corner, even from above. It's the heartbeat of the city, keeping it alive and running. We near the edge of Lunaria, and I spot where the ground turns to nothing, a giant drop off just beyond my view. Hade looks down, shooting me a playful smirk.

"Ready?" he says excitedly.

Fisting his shirt, I respond, "I'm ready to feel alive."

Hade lets out a deep, satisfied growl then tightens his arms protectively around me. "Try not to shatter my eardrums," is the only warning I get before he releases his magic from around us and we start to free fall over the edge of Lunaria.

I let out a loud shriek, caught off guard by this man once again. I should have known this was in my future, seeing as I asked him to make me feel alive. This wasn't exactly what I had in mind, but what I do know, with certain clarity in this moment, is that I wholeheartedly trust this man with my life.

We freefall, wrapped in each other's embrace, and the world melts away. My stomach flips, and adrenaline fills my veins as we fall through the sky without a care in the world. Life stops around us, the sky a blur, my eyes only focusing on one thing.

Hade's eyes are locked on mine, and my ability to breathe vanishes again. He's looking at me in awe, like I'm the only thing to exist in this world besides himself. I feel the click of the metal lock around my heart come apart at the same time I do.

Hade is death and life all the same. He is as deadly as the creatures that plague my nightmares and a lifeline to hold onto at the same time. He is my *remedy* to surviving life. He is the *air* that fills my lungs. He is the *reason* I want my heart to never stop beating.

He is the *fate* to the rest of my existence.

The rope tethering me to him pulls taught, finally at its limit since the first time I laid eyes on him. There was no avoiding this, avoiding *him*. His very being is etched into my skin like a prophecy from the gods. He chipped my darkness away until I was left in my rawest form in front of him, and he *reveled* in it.

This moment feels like a change of tides, destiny rearranging the stars to paint a portrait of us. It rewires my brain until all I can see is the light shining through the storm that has plagued my life.

The loudest laugh bubbles up my throat, vibrating from deep in my chest. It's raw and real and everything I have not been for a very long time. It's my way of letting life in and rising above it on the other side. It's freeing and tastes like taking control instead of letting it suffocate me.

I throw my arms out wide and tip my head back, letting out a loud whoop of joy, like a child experiencing a core memory for the first time. I laugh and scream as the crippling emotions slither from the depths of my soul, purging them to the abyss.

Hade's deep, warm chuckle washes over my skin, urging me on. I can feel his gaze burning my skin like a brand, and I bask in it. My back tingles right between my shoulder blades as a warm rush of energy skitters over my body, zapping me to life.

The world rushes by, but all I see is *him*.

We are locked in a stand still, eyes unblinking and smiles taking up the entirety of our faces. His magic lashes out, wrapping us in darkness right at the last second, dragging us to an abrupt halt right before we touch the ground.

"That was extraordinary," I say, trying to catch my breath.

He looks at me with the most intense stare. "Yeah, extraordinary, Nyxi," he whispers, looking back and forth between my eyes.

My breathing picks up and my heart skitters a beat. He gently sets me back on my feet as an idea slams into my head.

"We need to make one stop before we head to the lake," I tell Hade, and he agrees immediately, ready to grant me anything I desire.

I ask Hade to float us over to Visionary Sector, and he gets us there in minutes. He plops us down in the center of Harmony Hills, surrounded by a tall field of wildflowers in every color. Each flower glows in the golden light of the dying sun. It's one of the most majestic sights I've ever seen.

Hade watches me as I start to spin, my arms stretched out wide, letting the warm sun dance over my skin. I take off in a gallop, letting the tops of flowers drag over my fingertips as I weave in and out of rows. I hear Hade let out a satisfied groan, then the sound of his feet pounding the ground behind me.

He catches up to me quickly, and I can't stop the childish giggle that takes over my body. I feel large arms wrap around me from behind as he picks me up and spins us in circles. His foot catches on a rock and sends us toppling backwards. He cradles me to his chest as he takes the impact of the harsh ground. I laugh hysterically, twisting in his arms until my chest is pressed against his, with him sprawled on the ground below me.

He shines me a toothy grin as flowers make a crown of colors around him. I reach forward and flick his nose playfully.

"Help me pick some flowers," I say sweetly and then peel my body from his. We spend the next ten minutes picking until our hands are too full to hold another.

I inform Hade we will be walking back to the lake instead of floating there, and he easily hums in agreement. We spend the entire walk to the lake, leaving behind a trail of flowers, painting the city a rainbow of colors. Everywhere I look, I see a piece of Ray, and it brings a smile to my face. There's not an inch left untouched by color and life.

I see her bright pink hair in the astilbes, her glowing yellow eyes in the daffodils, her warm freckles in the pansies, and her rosy cheeks in the cherry blossoms we leave behind. I force the world to see her in all her glory so they may never forget the beautiful soul she was.

The memory of her takes over my body, and my heart speaks freely, the song forming without thought. My voice carries a soft warmth as I let the memory of Rayah free into the world, dropping flowers along the way.

"There once was a little girl born from the sun,
Her hair so bright, it could rival anyone.
She sang to her own tune, unafraid to stand out.
Her soul a living drum, vivid and stout.

A beautiful soul, a beautiful child.
A field of flowers grown in divinity.

She weathered the toughest battles alone.
Emerging a warrior, standing tall she rose.
She taught the world being different is okay,

A rainbow destined for breaking through the fray.

A beautiful soul, a beautiful child.
A field of flowers grown in divinity."

Hade's hand finds mine as my voice carries with the wind, emotion spilling from me. My voice is the only thing to be heard around us, the citizens all stopping their activities, ensnared by the story of a girl named Ray.

I belt the last line as we near the lake's edge, dragging it out until my lungs have nothing left to give. A haunting silence takes its place as the first drop of water falls from the sky, as if it's weeping in response. A downpour erupts, drenching us in seconds, the warmth of summer still clinging to our skin.

Hade takes my face in his hands, tipping it up to look at him. I see the faintest watery glaze over his eyes, but it's most likely from the rain. He smiles at me, his dimple making an appearance, and my heart flutters.

"Dance with me?" he breathes, and I let out a loud laugh as he draws me close. We dance to the melody of the rain falling around us like there will be no tomorrow.

For now, there's only *us* and this moment.

Chapter
Thirty-Three

Journal Entry

Age 15

Mama's prayers worked! I found my Eternal.
Mama said I'm special—most people don't find
theirs this young, or even at all. She said our
bond is so strong, the stars rearranged so we had
a direct path to collide. The look of pride on her
face made my tummy warm with love. Mama's
words didn't make sense to me until my eyes
landed on <u>him</u>. My whole existence rewired from
my very core. A piece of me has always resided
with him, and now, it's come home and clicked
into place, making me whole. The bond does not
feel like love; it's deeper than that. It feels like

a lifeline, a fire burning beneath my skin to protect him, and he, me, from anything that could ever keep us apart. It's devotion in its rawest form. I do not remember my life before him, only the life that lies ahead. He arrived from another land to personally invite us to his coming of age celebration for his sixteenth birthday. As soon as our eyes locked, my back lit with flames, searing my skin for eternity. What rose from its ashes was an intricate black swirl marking wrapped around a ball of fire in the center of my back, between my shoulder blades. A matching twin marking appeared on his back at the same time. He dropped to his knees in front of me, unable to breathe. He gifted me his personal sword to protect me in his absence—it was beautifully crafted, all black, with two owl eyes etched into the blade, just above the handle. He said it was imbued with his magic so only he can wield it, and since I was his Eternal, it would recognize me as part of him. Mama forgot to mention all the other things that come with being Eternals. Connected by our souls and fused as one, any emotions I felt, he would feel as well. The same with communication. We can tap into our bond and talk to each other over long distances. He had to return to his kingdom, but in his absence, we've used the bond like a lifeline to get to know each other. It feels like I've known him my whole life, and a piece of me feels hollow in his absence. Every time I close my eyes, I see his two midnight black ones watching me like a god above. I found my Eternal, and now, life as I know it will never be the same.

Chapter
Thirty-Four

THE RAIN FINALLY CEASED, LEAVING AN CLEAR BLACK SKY GLITTERING with a million stars. The air is still warm, even with the sun long leaving us. Insects chirp as the cities slumber along the border of the lake. Hade and I are the only people in sight, and it feels right.

We sit at the edge of the lake in the grass, taking everything in. There is something about sitting with someone to whom you don't have to say anything, both of you just content sitting in the moment of peace.

I feel Hade's eyes on the side of my face, so I turn to face him. I can tell he is thinking about something but is unsure if he should break the silence. I raise my eyebrow in question, which makes him chuckle.

"What was he like?"

I smile, thinking back to the many happy memories I shared with Theo. "He was everything. He was the best person I've ever known. He was warm like the sun in the morning. He was laughter, joy. Selfless, caring. He was my favorite part of each day. He is the reason I'm still alive," I admit in a whisper. "He was the best of the best, and he was too good for this world. I like to think he was destined for more than what life dealt him here, so destiny called him home early."

"He sounds like a good man," he states in a gentle, loving voice. "I'm happy you got to experience his love for however long the fates allowed."

I nod in agreement, because I would live through all the pain again to have more days with him. There is not a day that goes by, nor will there ever be, when Theo is not on my mind. One day, we will align again on the same side of the stars. Until then, I will hold him in my heart.

"Can I ask you something personal?" I question while turning so our knees are pressed together.

"Only seems fair," he states.

I lick my lips nervously and catch his eyes wavering, tracking my tongue before reluctantly gliding back to my eyes.

"What happened to your eye?" I say softly, intrigue lacing my voice. Ever since meeting him, his one eye has always drawn my attention, and I have yearned to learn how it came about.

I see him retreat into his head like an old memory plays out for him. He subtly nibbles his lower lip, trying to decide exactly what he wants to say. It's almost like his eye knows we are talking about it, because it seems to glow for a brief moment.

"I was struck by magic trying to protect someone. It lashed out across my eye and pulled some of my magic out with it, leaving this scar. When it drew out my magic, it took part of the coloring as well."

I open my mouth to ask another question, but he rushes ahead of me, halting the conversation.

"I don't remember much," he states firmly. "The magic messed with my head and left me with gaps. All that remains is a faint memory and this scar."

His tone leaves no room for further discussion. He wasn't rude or harsh, but he clearly drew a line in the sand, and I do not intend push him.

I lean forward and drag my thumb softly over his scar, which makes him shudder under my touch. "I'm sorry that happened to you, but I'm glad you're okay," I say softly.

With an idea to change the mood, a mischievous smile blooms over my lips as I stand. His eyes drag up my body until they land on my face.

I giggle loudly as I make my way to the water, Hade grunting behind me as I strip my shirt off, then my pants, stepping out of them right before my feet touch the start of the water. I dive head-first into the lake, fully submerging my body and reveling in the way the cold makes my body hum to life. It's calming below the water, and I take a minute to soak it in.

When my lungs can't last another second without air, I kick my legs, pushing myself back towards the surface. My face breaks through, and I draw in a loud, deep breath.

"Christ, Nyxi. You scared the shit out of me." Hade huffs from the very edge of the water, concern etched on his face.

I keep my body submerged so my mouth barely hovers above the water. "Did I rile the mighty Cardinal?" I tease, dropping my voice an octave.

"Never," he growls while narrowing his eyes on me. My skin somehow heats in the cool water. "I just didn't want to have to explain to the Empress why she is down another contestant outside the confines of the Crucible."

I swim backwards until I'm floating in the center of the large lake. "Seems like a better way to go, honestly," I shout across the water and then submerge my body again. I swim around for a few seconds, feeling the water glide between my fingers. When I finally emerge again, Hade is bent over the water's edge, looking intently where I went under.

"Over here, big guy," I yell, making his jaw tick.

"Stop that," he grunts in frustration.

"Or what?" I taunt, trying to get him to play with me. "Is the big Cardinal scared of a little water?"

He growls in response, and the hairs on the back of my neck rise. I may be poking the bear, but it's too fun to stop now. I'll suffer the consequences when they come, and who knows, I may even like them.

"Well, are you just gonna stand there all day, or are you going to join me? You aren't getting any younger, you know. I actually think I might see a gray hair from here!" I shout.

He reaches for his hair before he can think better of it, then grunts in frustration, making me giggle. "*Fuck it*," he mumbles under his breath, slipping his shirt and pants off in record time.

He dives headfirst into the water and disappears deep below the surface. A few seconds go by, and I look around, trying to spot him. I yelp in surprise when I feel a hand land on my ankle, yanking me under. I collide with a giant, warm body that wraps around me then shoots us back to the surface. I feel Hade's magic wrap around us, keeping us afloat.

My hair falls over my face, blocking my vision as I catch my breath. I get my breathing under control, and then my heart decides to take off when I realize how our bodies are still flush, his big arms trapping me against him. Every place our bodies touch leaves a trail of heat blazing like a wildfire. The contrast of the cold water and his warm, bare chest pressed against me is dizzying.

His eyes lock on mine as we float in the center of the lake for what feels like minutes. Not a single word passes between us, but I don't need to hear a single thing out of his mouth when his eyes are telling me everything I need to know. Like a window to his soul, his eyes tell me a million things about him. He lets me in for once, and I bask in the feeling of reaching in and finding something real just for me.

His eyes glimmer under the night sky, and water drips in a steady beat from the tips of his inky curls. If I were a painter, he would be my muse, and this would be my picture-perfect setting. He has always made my heart dance wildly, but in this moment, he looks like a god, and those soul devouring eyes are planted right on *me*.

He peels one arm from around me and slowly drags away the wild curls stuck messily to my face, clearing my vision. I heat under his touch as his soft fingers glide against my skin. It sparks an inferno in me, ready to jump at his every command so long as it involves his skin keeping contact with mine.

I try not to squirm under his intense gaze as he drags the last of my hair out of my face. I let out a loud, slow breath, entranced by the beautiful beast in front of me. I nervously nibble my bottom lip, unsure what to do with myself. Whenever I'm nervous, I resort to humor, which is exactly what my brain tells me to do right now.

"You've never seen anything prettier, have ya?" I tease, knowing full well I undoubtedly look like a mess. I can feel my curls sitting in a knot on the top of my head like a bird's nest.

"Never," he says in a low, husky voice that sends shivers up my spine. His eyes remain fixed on me, and not an ounce of playful banter shows across his face. His eyes somehow darken, the black one turning into a bottomless pit of madness and his gray one swirling with the promise of ruin.

I still under his gaze, and air seems to be a faraway thought I'm no longer capable of grasping. It's like I'm a child again, learning how to walk, but instead of walking, it's my will to keep air in my lungs under his unyielding eyes ripping me apart right down to my core.

Is this what it feels like the moment death finally takes your soul? The warmth of eternal peace taking over your body and setting you free? I feel like I'm dying every time this man made from death looks at me, but my body also roars to life in a way it never has before.

His eyes slowly sweep across my face, taking time to soak in each part like they are equally important to him. He studies one of my eyes then drags his gaze across to my other one. His pupils dilate the slightest amount when he deepens his study, and it makes me curious as to what exactly he is seeing. I feel his stare slide down the slope of my narrow nose and land on my plump lips. I lick them, feeling self-conscious, and the taste of lake water slips over my tongue.

Hade lets out a deep, rumbling moan as his eyes remain transfixed on my lips. His grip tightens around me the slightest, and I'm not even sure he noticed his action. Instead, it comes across as a reflex. He continues his thorough study of me by dragging his eyes lower until they land on my narrow neck, leaving tingles in their perusal.

If his exploration of my body lasts a single second longer, I think I might combust. I've never been studied so intently, like the answers to the world's continued existence lie within me.

His free arm reaches forward on its own accord and grips the back of my neck. His thick fingers slide into my hair at the nape of my neck like they belong there. His thumb lashes out, rubbing the front of my neck, making my throat bob. Water trickles from his thumb, sliding down the front of my throat to my cleavage, leaving a cold chill across my body.

Hade tracks the droplet the whole way, turning eerily still as it drips until it rolls over the curve of my breast. He swallows harshly, his eyes fixed on where the bead disappeared. He looks at me in awe, and I can tell he's slowly unraveling, on the verge of losing control.

He leans forward slowly, and I hold my breath in anticipation. He draws the lobe of my ear into his mouth and nips at it playfully. "Do you know the torture you bring me, woman?" Hade whispers against my throat, his lips dragging across my delicate skin, making it pebble. Fluttering takes over in my chest, and my body heats deep in my core.

"No," I manage to whisper back, but it's barely loud enough to hear even in the silence.

"No?" he mumbles against my skin.

"Enlighten me," I huff, barely able to get the words out when his lips are pressed into the perfect spot on the side of my neck. The urge to push into his touch takes over my body, consuming my every thought.

He purrs against my flesh, making my skin vibrate, shooting straight to my center. I'm fully at his mercy, my body moving to his every demand. I let out a soft whimper, unable to keep the effect he has over me hidden a moment longer.

The sounds spurs him into a frenzy, making him push his lips harder into my neck, drawing out a gasp. His warm, lush lips kiss my skin with expert precision, like kissing me is his life's purpose. He swipes his tongue across my neck mid-kiss, making my head spin and legs clench. This man will be the death of me, and the thought of that only heats my core more.

He releases my skin, and I'm sure if I could see my neck right now, there would be a soft pink circle blooming where his lips damned me to hell. He hovers just above my skin, and his warm breath fans across my neck. He leans forward more, but this time, his lips make contact with the center of my neck right where it dips.

I think my eyes might have rolled to the back of my head from the way he is giving my body the attention it's been craving for so long, but my brain seems to be of no use. I let out a soft moan, his lips drawing out a song of pleasure without a care about him hearing.

He kisses me with such care, applying just the right amount of pressure. I unravel my legs and wrap them around his thick body, crossing my ankles to hold him in place. They can barely lock around his huge frame, and the thought makes my head swim. I swallow deeply, my mouth watering.

My throat bobs when I do, and he lets out a growl of pleasure as he feels my neck dip. His lips release my neck, and a pang of sadness hits me in his absence. It doesn't last long, though, as he stretches his neck to reach the opposite side of my neck begging for attention too and presses his lips there, making sure each part is worshiped equally.

He laps at my skin, making me dig my heels in, drawing him closer even though there is no more space between us. I'm sure my heart is beating at its full capacity, a heart attack on the horizon if he keeps this up. He pulls away, dragging in a harsh breath, gathering himself with crazed eyes.

He brings his face right in front of me, his nose a centimeter from touching mine. Reaching up, he tucks one of my wet curls delicately behind my ear as want and need radiate off him. His face turns darkly serious as he pins me with his gaze illuminated by the glowing moon.

"That is how you make me feel every second of every fucking day that I have to spend in your presence without being able to lay claim to your body," he whispers against my lips, gritty and full of desire. I can see the war raging in his eyes, swirling with restraint and the need to take me right here and now, damn the consequences.

"I cannot think straight when we share the same air. My body begs to be let loose to claim the life of any person who even dares to look at you the wrong way. My lungs refuse to work when your eyes strip me bare like they are doing right now," he admits, making my knees go slack. "You make me want to do very bad, dark, and deprived things, Nyxi, and I'm not sure I have the strength left in me to stop."

A beat of silence echoes between us, the only sound my labored breaths I can't seem to tame any longer. I'm wrapped around this lethal man like he might vanish right before my eyes. I can feel my pulse pounding on the side of my neck so hard, I can hear it in my ears. I'm lost in his endless midnight gaze, and I have no plans on being found. His darkness nudges up against mine, urging me to let go. If I do so, I know it will create an addiction I won't have the will to squash, but right now, I welcome it with open arms.

"Then don't," I whisper, but before I can get the words fully out, he tightens his grip at the nape of my neck, drawing me forward. He crashes his lips to mine with a punishing force. It's not gentle or timid, but rather feverish and desperate, like he couldn't waste a single extra second without tasting me, devouring me.

I melt into his embrace, letting him take the lead and enjoying the ride. My center flares to life, a warmth growing inside me as my pulse kicks up. His mouth tastes like mint and sin swirled together that would for sure make my knees buckle if we were standing.

He plays with the hair between his fingers at the base of my neck as he draws my mouth into him. He's like a starved beast let out of its cage for the first time, getting to devour its prey. There's no time for exploring or sweet nothings, only a need to reach further inside each other and draw out the pleasure we've both been deprived of for too long.

He plants his other hand on the side of my face, sliding his fingers into the hair threatening to spill. He moans into my mouth and uses his hand to tilt my face so he can kiss me deeper. I'm lost as I press my almost fully bare body against his warm chest. My nipples pebble against the lacy white undergarment that leaves little to the imagination.

Hade's tongue darts out, swiping across my lips, asking for an invitation. I open for him eagerly, and his tongue happily slides against mine, drawing a deep groan from him that I echo back. His lips mold to mine perfectly, lighting fire to every inch of my body. He sucks my bottom lip into his mouth, nipping at it playfully until it pops free from his teeth.

"*Fuck*," he breathes against my mouth as he tries to catch his breath. "Fucking perfect." I dig my nails into his back, unable to hold myself back. I dig my heels into his back, drawing him impossibly closer, and let out a strangled moan when I feel just how much he is enjoying the taste of my lips.

"Nyxi," he warns, looking at me with utter despair, trying to hold himself back.

"What?" I whisper against him, impatiently drawing his lips to mine again in a claiming kiss. He moves his hand from my face so it rests on the small of my back, keeping me flush to him. He kisses me back with burning desire, like he's breathing the promise of devotion into me with each swipe of his tongue.

I can't help the way my body moves against him, my lace underwear softly gliding across his skin, making it shift a little each time. Hade lets out a strangled moan as his hand starts to dance along my spine, making me squirm with need.

It's nothing I could have ever dreamed up. Not a single inch of my body feels neglected as he worships me with his mouth and hands until I'm overheating. Surprisingly, Hade doesn't replace or overshadow my relationship with Theo but rather helps fill the gaping hole he left behind.

He presses his lips against mine one last time, memorizing my taste before he slowly pulls away. My lips feel swollen and puffy, and I can't help the smile that takes over my face as I'm lost to the haze Hade's presence always seems to bring.

I notice his lips are slightly battered too, and a pang of pride flutters up my core as I see the remnants of my actions left on him for all to see. He looks lost to the moment, his cheeks slightly rosy. His eyes zone in on my authentic smile, and he lets out a sigh of content.

"Lie back," he states softly, and my body obeys immediately. I unwrap my legs from around him and slowly lower myself back until my head connects with the cool water. My legs follow suit, floating up until they bob above the water.

Hade moves in, placing one hand under my neck to support my head as the other softly presses against my lower back, keeping me afloat. The twinkling night sky takes over my entire view, and a calmness washes over my body. This is exactly what I told him helps calm me down, and of course, he made it a reality. He put my peace ahead of the million other things I'm sure demand his attention right now, and it doesn't go unappreciated.

The dark sky calls to me, making my body relax. The stars take over the sky like an ambush, impossible to count. I let my arms float freely out to my sides as Hade slowly swims us in a circle, my view ever changing.

"What is your favorite time of day?" I question while attempting to count the stars lighting up the sky above me.

I get distracted when I feel Hade's hand behind my neck playing with one of my curls between his fingers. I turn my neck until his face comes into view, and I find him staring at my inky curl twirling between his fingers.

"Night," he admits confidently as his gaze remains glued to my hair. "It's the most ethereal thing to be in the presence of. It's all consuming, because if you stare at it for too long, you will get lost in it for eternity. Darkness has always called to my soul," he whispers as he drags his eyes away from my hair until they land harshly on mine.

A chill racks my body, and I'm not sure if it's from the cold air now dancing across my bare skin or from his words that glided across every inch of my body. His black magic emerges from beneath the water and slithers over my skin like a blanket. If only it could protect my body from the effects of his words too.

I let out a soft, satisfied moan as a thin blanket of his magic drapes over my body like a soft wind. It feels like an extension of him, wrapping itself around me. It leaves fluttering tingles along my skin as it washes over me like a wave. I stroke a portion of the magic wrapped around my center, and it purrs back, twisting around my finger, making me giggle.

With the lust driven from my body for the time being, I take the time to properly study the parts of Hade's body I can see above the water in the glow of the moon. My eyes trail up his arm, gliding over the smattering of tattoos that all blend together, covering every inch of his tanned skin. My eyes draw up to his shoulder and then snag on a tattoo hidden under his arm on his side—the outline of an abstract owl stares back at me.

"What does your owl tattoo mean?" I ask before I can stop myself.

"I have always loved owls," he admits. "They have always felt like home to me. I've been drawn to them from a young age. They are deep thinkers and lovers of the night, and I see myself in them. Most live in solitude, content leading a calm life."

This man is nothing like what I expected. The more time I spend around him, the more layers he sheds, letting me get to the core of him. Each new thing I learn draws me a little bit closer. He feels like a familiar soul I used to know but lost contact with while traveling through many worlds, living out different lives.

"That is beautiful and very fitting," I say with a small giggle as my eyes trace the delicate lines across the side of his ribs. "And what about the rest of your tattoos?" I resist the urge to dedicate my night to tracing each one of them with my fingers.

"Some are purely decorative, others have meanings, and some are reminders of past battles." He looks over his arm, and I notice his eyes linger on a few in particular. I hope one day, I may learn the meaning of each and every one of them, but I'm not sure how much longer my life will last.

I must not mask the hint of sadness that takes over my face, because Hade drags me until my body is pressed against his, cradled in his arms. "Let's get out of here before you turn into a giant ice cube," he murmurs before placing a soft kiss on my temple.

His magic pushes us through the water until we arrive at the shore. Hade wades out of the water with me still clutched against his body. I would normally swat his hand away and tell him I'm capable of walking myself, but that is the furthest thing from my mind right now.

He plops me down on my feet, and I gather my clothes, shrugging them back on my body. They cling to my wet skin, making me shake with chills. Hade finishes pulling his pants up his thick legs, and I can't help the way my eyes roam over his muscular body before he covers up again.

"It's too dark for me to comfortably guide us back up to Lunaria, so I would feel better if we stayed down here for the night, if that's okay with you?" he asks while slipping on his last shoe.

I nod, and his eyes narrow at my body shaking slightly from the cold.

"First, we need to find you some warm clothes, and then, we can figure out a place to stay," he states, leaving no room for argument.

"I know where we can get clothes," I say softly as Hade steps up next to me and gently grips my hand.

"Lead the way, *beautiful*."

Chapter
Thirty-Five

THE FAMILIARNESS OF BEING BACK IN FALLOUT WASHES OVER ME AS I effortlessly guide us through the thick wall of darkness. I have no clue what time it is, but judging by the pure black surrounding us, I assume it's late into the night.

Dragging Hade by the hand, I round the last turn and approach the central stable. I hear soft neighs in the distance, and a smile takes over my face. I pray the sliding wooden door is unlocked as I reach out and wrap my hand around the metal handle. Hade gives me a questioning look as I tug the door. To my luck, it easily slides open, and I shoot a snide smirk at him. We slip in silently, and the smell of hay and horseshit assaults my nose, making me silently gag. Clearly, someone has been neglecting cleaning up.

I stride to the closest stall, greeted by a playful gray mare whose head stretches out over the stall door. I drag my knuckles down her muzzle, giving her a scratch. She burrows into my touch, letting out a high pitched neigh, whipping her tail back and forth in greeting.

"How's my beautiful girl?" I ask her, and she neighs louder in response, telling me just how much she's missed me. I feel Hade saddle up to my side; he seems content watching the interaction from a small distance.

"Hade, meet Willow." Dragging my eyes back to the mare, I gesture to Hade. "Willow, meet Hade." She lets out a questioning chuff, and I laugh. "I know he looks scary, but I promise, he's a big softy under all that hardness," I whisper to her while rubbing my palms up and down her muzzle.

She looks at him curiously and extends her neck out to sniff him wearily. He slowly raises his hand for her to smell, and she eagerly presses into it, sniffing deeply. She seems satisfied with her findings, playfully nipping at his hand.

"Phew, that went better than I expected," I say under my breath, slowly letting all the air out of my lungs. "She tends to be picky with who she deems fit to be in her presence." Hade raises his brows like I'm some crazy horse whisperer, and I casually shrug. "She can be a little stubborn at times," I admit.

A knowing smirk shoots across his face. "I can see why you two get along so well." He chuckles, and I shove my shoulder into his side. Willow lets out a grunt in protest. He gives her a deep scratch with his knuckles, and she immediately melts into his embrace, forgetting any ill thoughts towards him.

"He has that effect on me too, friend," I whisper into her ear, low enough so Hade won't hear me.

He grunts beside me, and I turn to his perfectly chiseled face, briefly brought back to the way his lips felt against mine. Shaking my head, I clear my thoughts and respond, "Yes?"

"What was your plan going to be if my new bestie over here decided she didn't like me?" I roll my eyes dramatically—they are so not best friends—but I stand corrected as I spot Willow practically falling over the stall door so she can drape her neck over his shoulder and rub her head into the side of his neck.

Traitorous bitch.

"There are only two horses here that I know wouldn't be noticed if they were missing come morning," I state happily. "Willow girl here, who happens to strongly dislike the stable hand with a burning passion…" I trail off, dragging my eyes to the far end of the stable until they land on the very last stall. "Hank," I say with a soft chuckle. "Better known as my Plan B."

I can't help the giggles that rack my body that's probably fueled further by the exhaustion taking hold of me. I bid Willow farewell with a kiss to her nose and a promise to return before I turn to walk down the long hall. I stop in front of the last stall. Hade follows willingly and slides up right next to me, looking inside with wide eyes.

"Meet Plan B," I say with a laugh as my eyes rake over the old gelding laying against the side of his stall. Hank is the oldest horse stabled here and is slower than molasses. It would undoubtedly be faster to walk somewhere rather than ride on his back. Tufts of hair are missing from his palomino coat due to his old age, and he barely pays us any attention as he lounges happily. The only way I can ever get him motivated enough to do anything is if I bribe him with fresh carrots. Even then, it's still a fifty-fifty chance he listens.

"Are you sure he's even alive?" Hade asks, squinting to get a closer look.

"Hank, you want a carrot, buddy?" I yell over the stall door loudly so his old man ears can hear me, which makes his ears perk up in response. "See? Perfectly alive, just old as dirt and very *lazy.*" I say the last word with extra umph, making him neigh in disagreement. "I knew you could hear, you little hellion," I playfully scold him. Turning to Hade, I add, "Someone seems to have selective hearing, apparently."

Hade's rich chuckle floats over my body, and time stops for a brief second. I could die happy in the sound of his unguarded emotions. They make me want to keep shoving parts of myself into his hand to hold forever.

I reach into a bucket hanging on the stall door and grab one large, bright orange carrot. Leaning over the stall door, I toss the carrot over to him so it lands right in front of the lazy beast. He stretches his neck out and swipes the carrot off the ground, munching happily.

I grab Hade's hand, dragging him along behind me. "C'mon, let's grab Willow and get out of here. I'm freezing." He leans in, wrapping his arm around me and dragging me into his side, attempting to warm me up. I can't hold in the slight blush that takes over my face.

We lead Willow out of the stable into the sparkling night. She obeys happily, eager to stretch her limbs and be free of the confines trapping her wild soul. If I were a horse, I think I would be Willow.

She nibbles on the grass below her as I approach her side. Saving time, I decided to skip strapping her down with a saddle and prepare to hoist myself up on her bare back. Hade plants his hands on each side of my waist, halting me. I look over my shoulder at him in confusion, and a sly smirk kicks up at the side of his mouth.

"Allow me," he says against the side of my face and then lifts my body effortlessly, making me squeal as he plops me down softly onto Willow's back. There goes that dramatic blush rushing up my chest and cheeks I can't seem to contain tonight.

"Thank you," I say shyly as he kicks his leg over her in one swift move, planting himself directly behind me. I can feel the heat radiate off him, and it warms my back while simultaneously making a chill run up my spine.

He reaches around me, trapping myself between his two very large arms and grabbing the reins. I'm thoroughly caged in by a dangerous beast with no way of escaping.

Poor Nyxi.

He gives Willow a soft tap with his foot, spurring her to start walking. She jolts forward, making me slide back into Hade's chest and wedging my ass tightly between his large thighs.

I wiggle, trying to recenter myself on her back, but all it seems to do is make my ass grind against him harder. He lets out a low growl behind me, and I manage to swallow the whimper threatening to spill from my lips. This man knows how to draw every emotion and feeling out of my body. I feel his harden behind me, and I can't help the satisfied smile that stretches across my face knowing he's just as affected by me as I am by him.

I decide to see just how far I can push him, pretending to adjust myself more as if I'm uncomfortable. I plant my hands in front of me and shuffle my ass back and forth slightly, pushing back as I wiggle into him, trying to get comfortable.

"Stop that," he grunts from behind me, and I'm sure if I looked over my shoulder, I would see steam pouring from his nostrils.

"I'm simply trying to get comfortable," I respond innocently.

"And Aeron was the most handsome man in Lunaria," he quips back, lightning fast. I throw my elbow back, attempting to jab him in his side. He catches my elbow before I can make contact, because of course the man has the reaction time of a god. It makes me wonder what other godly traits he may possess, the thought making me twitchy.

Hade leans forward, pushing his wet chest into my back at the same time he wraps his right arm around my waist, pulling me taunt against him. "I thought we were taking turns spouting lies?" he whispers against the shell of my ear, and I know he doesn't miss the chill crawling up my spine, making me squirm within his grip.

"I don't know what you're talking about," I say under my breath, and the words shake with nerves as they leave my lips.

"Quit being a brat, Nyxi." His deep, gravelly voice washes over my body like a wave, drawing me under. "You know exactly what that body of yours is doing to me right now. Unless you intend to finish this fun little game you started, I suggest you stop your little charade before I halt this damn horse and take you right now against the ground. Would you like me to shred your clothes to scraps and fuck you senseless until your voice goes raw? Make you scream my name for every single fucking sector in Fallout to hear as you come on my cock? Because that's exactly the lesson I'll teach you if you don't stop grinding this *fucking* ass into me." The words tumble from his lips in a seductive threat, and my legs try to clamp together but end up tightening around Willow's back instead.

Well, that certainly wasn't what I expected, but I won't lie— I'm not complaining in the least. Flames lick at my cheeks, but I pay them no mind.

"Pretty promises, as always, Hade darling," I purr back to him, but even I can hear the way my voice wavers, betraying my true feelings. I'm panting in my head, begging him to just make the choice for me so I don't have to think about what it means if we cross that line.

"Do not push me, Nyxi. My body holds fewer morals than fucks," he growls.

Oh fuck.

I disregard the consequences and attempt to shove my ass back again, but before I can move one more delicious inch, black tendrils of magic whip out from beneath Willow and wrap around me. I let out a yelp as they drag my body suddenly into the air and spin me around so I'm facing Hade. They plop me back down so I'm straddling Willow backwards, conveniently away from being able to grind my ass into Hade's crotch. My legs drape over his large thighs as I stare into the eyes of the man who looks like he's about one more second away from losing total control.

A girl can dream.

His breaths are choppy, his eyes dark as sin. I wouldn't mind being the reason behind his sinning tonight if it meant he would keep staring at me like he can't go on without knowing exactly what every inch of my body feels like.

I'm on a suicide mission tonight as I open my mouth to shove him fully past the point of no return, but once again, before I can attempt my plan, a single black tendril wraps around my face, covering my mouth.

The fucker silenced me with his magic. I hate that even though I'm pissed, I'm also slightly turned on. I'm not sure what that says about me, but it's a subject for future Nyxi.

"There, much better," he says with a shit eating smirk, kicking his heels into Willow, making her take off in a fast gallop. Apparently, someone is impatient and wants to get to our destination *immediately*.

I glare at him the entire ride, throwing a temper tantrum in pure Nyxi fashion. He fixes his eyes on mine the entire silent ride, making me point anytime we need to take a turn.

I shift uncomfortably the entire time, because even though I'm pissed at him, I also feel like I'm burning alive under his sensual gaze. The man is pure sex appeal and infuriating all the same.

We take the last turn, and a shocked look comes over his face. He knows exactly where I'm taking him. We slowly approach the crumbling shack as Hade brings Willow to a halt.

Hade jumps off and reaches up to slide me off Willow's back. His magic vanishes as he plops me to the ground next to him. I look over the crumbling home, smaller than I remember.

Home.

I think back to the first time I met Hade, when his impatient ass accidentally punched me in the nose. I laugh internally and make a mental note to plan something sinister to get him back for that—I can't let him get off that easily.

Approaching wearily, I yank open the rusty door. It's dark and dusty and smells of must and rotting walls. I take in my surroundings, and a pang of guilt and sadness racks my body.

"You lived here with him?" Hade questions softly as he follows behind me through the door.

"I did," I respond under my breath. "He hasn't lived here for quite some time, though."

Everything is exactly where I left it, but I can tell a few wild animals have taken residence in my absence. I spot crumbs of food and poop scattered about the floor and counters. It's just four walls and a crumbling roof, I remind myself. While this is where I would spend most of my time with Theo, everything of importance to me resides in my head, and I'm at peace leaving this shack behind.

"C'mon." I gesture to Hade. We enter the bedroom, and I focus on finding clothes instead of staring at the bed we shared in the corner of the room. I pull out a shirt, pants, and dry undergarments for myself and then sift through the pile of Theo's clothes, looking for something large enough to fit Hade.

I gather the items and turn to find Hade looking over the room, taking it all in. Not an ounce of jealousy or malice shows on his face—only curiosity and a need to know more.

"Here." I shove a dry shirt and trousers into his hands, and he looks down at them in shock. "They might be a little snug and short on you since you're bigger than Theo, but they should work well enough for tonight."

He shoves them back towards me in protest. "I'll be fine in my clothes."

Huffing, I shove them back into his chest. "Don't be ridiculous. You are soaked to your bones, and I can tell your thighs are chafing by the way you keep shuffling uncomfortably on your feet. Theo would want you to have them anyways. Trust me, he was the most giving person I knew. Plus, he never even wore these. I bought them for him, but I liked them so much, I stole them before he even got to wear them. So technically, they are mine."

I give him a look that says *don't fuck with me*, and he rolls his eyes in return, grabbing the clothes from my hands and politely thanking me. We each turn and change into our dry clothes, which feels incredibly better.

We turn back to face each other, and a beat of silence passes between us. "I can't sleep here," I weakly admit, which he understands instantly, giving me an easy nod.

"I know a place in town that should have available rooms."

I cock a brow at him, confused as to why he would know of a place down here.

"I've spent my fair share of time down here on missions for the Empress," he admits.

I shake my head because that sounds about right with the people who live in my sector. Gather up a bunch of rowdy dangerous misfits, and trouble usually follows. I pick up my wet clothes and snag the extra shirt I pulled from Theo's pile to bring back with me to Lunaria before following Hade out the front door. I take one last look at the shack I used to call our home and feel at peace with leaving it behind. Now, it just feels like four walls and a crumbling roof, nothing more.

Life keeps moving regardless of your circumstances, and it's time I hop on the horse and keep riding along. Instead of Theo by my side, I'll carry him in my heart.

Chapter
Thirty-Six

"BE A GOOD GIRL, AND I'LL LET YOU EAT ALL THE CARROTS YOUR WILD heart desires," I whisper into Willow's ear, giving her a parting kiss on the muzzle. I give her a little wave as a nervous stableboy attempts to walk her away to the small stable around back. She gives him hell the entire way, and I chuckle under my breath at her stubbornness.

Hade takes the lead, walking in front of me to open the door of an old, weathered inn. Its red brick exterior is crumbling in places, bleached by the sun. One window sits next to the door, but the curtains are drawn shut. A rotting sign dangles from above the door, the words 'Rusty Copper Inn' splayed in gold across it.

It's a good thing I'm not a princess, or else I would be running for the hills. Growing up in Vagrant has made me appreciate the finer things the castle has provided, but I will never forget my roots or be ashamed of them.

I duck through the door, avoiding the cobwebs hanging from the corners as Hade gestures for me to go in first. It's dark inside, and a thick, musty smell assaults my nose as I approach the small desk nestled just inside the door, where an older woman lies face down, snoring loudly.

I reach forward tentatively and give her a gentle poke, attempting to wake her. She whips her head up, swinging her arms wildly as she yells threats about having a knife. Her glasses are crooked, resting half way down her nose, not a single tooth in her mouth. Her gray wiry hair lays in a wild pile atop her head, and wrinkles mar every inch of her tanned face.

"We mean no harm, ma'am'. We're just hoping to get a couple rooms for the night. I'll even throw in a few extra coppers for the trouble." Hade's firm voice carries through the small room, bouncing off the walls with authority, but it also comes off non-threatening, which makes the old lady's shoulders relax a bit.

She eyes Hade up and down for longer than appropriate and smiles at him with her toothless, rotting gums. "Well, why didn't you say so, sunshine?" She beams up at him as her old, withered voice drags uncomfortably over my skin.

Her neck is practically snapped backwards from her height in comparison to his. She stands from her chair, but her height stays the same, her face barely reaching over the top of the short desk while she reaches for something hooked under it. "Though I only have one available room tonight, I'm afraid." She narrows her eyes, trying to look seductive as she adds, "There's extra room in my bed if you need a place to sleep tonight, big fella," she purrs.

"One room will work just fine," I respond quickly, snagging the key out of her boney fingers before she can pounce. She pouts, giving Hade wounded eyes, and he looks so uncomfortable, I have to put my hand over my mouth to stop myself from bursting laughing.

"Well, in that case, you'll be in room four, right up those stairs." She points to the crumbling stairs on her left, opening her mouth to say Empress knows what next. I'm pulling Hade up the stairs as he quickly tosses her a few coppers over his shoulder.

"Why the hurry?" he grunts behind me as I race us up the stairs before she changes her mind. He suddenly gasps dramatically. "Nyxi, are you jealous of a toothless old woman?" he teases me, and I roll my eyes at him over my shoulder.

"Hardly," I spit defensively. Now that I think about it, I did just agree to sharing a room with this man without asking him first. I chalk it up to wanting to get out of there as fast as possible instead of laying claim to the man like a circling vulture. That would be *insane*.

His deep chuckle crawls up my spine, and I tighten my grip on his hand without thinking. This man makes me act irrationally, and I can't even stop it if I tried. We shuffle down the dim hallway, and dust kicks up from the floor, making me sneeze. I approach the door with a four etched into it and slide the key in. I twist a few times, and it doesn't budge. With one final twist, I slam my shoulder into the door, and it gives way, flying open and bouncing on its rusty hinges.

I stride in like I own the place, acting as if I didn't just have to win a fight with the door to get inside. I can tell Hade is holding back a laugh, but I ignore the hellion as I rake my eyes over the small room. The small room with the even smaller solo bed, which barely looks big enough to fit Hade.

This is just...perfect.

"Well, it's...something," I say under my breath, inching around the small bed sitting in the center of the room. There's a tiny ensuite that houses a small toilet and surprisingly a tub. Even with its old age, it surprisingly looks decently clean, and I thank the Empress for that.

"It's definitely no castle," he jokes beside me lightheartedly, but he doesn't actually seem put off.

I curtsey low and respond, "Welcome to Vagrant Sector, Your Majesty. We are arguably the best sector, but if you ask anyone else, they might not agree. I call bullshit, though." I send him a wink, and he chuckles, making my insides turn gooey. This man has too much power over my body.

I think about plopping down on the bed, but I decide better when I notice the dirt and lake water riddling my body and hair. My stomach lets out a scream in protest, making Hade cock a knowing brow at me and my protesting stomach that always seems to need food.

"Why don't you wash up, and I'll go next door and grab us some food?" he suggests. I nod in agreement, because food right now sounds amazing, but I also know I'm in need of a major washing. I most definitely shouldn't be seen in public like this.

"Are you telling me I stink, Hade?" I say incredulously, gasping dramatically. "I'm insulted, sir."

He rolls his eyes and pushes me towards the ensuite. "Make sure to wash away your attitude while you're at it," he shouts over his shoulder and slips out the door before I can spew a response.

Wasting no time, I strip my clothes off, leaving them in a pile in front of the door as I switch the water on and drag my cold body under the blistering hot stream.

I tip my head back, letting the water soak my knotted hair. Luckily, I spot a bottle of liquid sitting on the edge of the tub, and I squeeze a dollop into my hand, massaging it thoroughly into my curls.

My head starts to wonder as my hands rove over my body. I'm taken back to how it felt to have Hade's lips pressed against mine, the way his mouth laid claim to mine like a promise of devotion. My hand drags across my neck, and I remember the way his lips felt pressed against my pulse point. My hand travels south, and I'm forced to remember the way his hard body felt pressed up against mine. I drag my hand lower, running my sudsy fingers over my thighs, remembering the way he felt squeezed between my legs like an anchor.

I wash away all the suds along with the lasting memories, but the ache between my legs remains steady no matter how hard I try to push Hade and his big...personality out of my head.

My pulse is racing, and my body heats from more than the hot water streaming across my skin. Before I know it, my hand has traveled to the inside of my thigh, slowly dragging up as my mind falls back to the one constant in my life I haven't been able to escape.

I let out a soft whimper as my fingers continue their exploration until they land right on the sensitive spot between my legs. Biting my bottom lip to keep quiet, I slowly start to circle my fingers, applying slight pressure, imagining it's someone else's thick, rough fingers learning exactly what my body craves. I pretend it's his fingers slowly sliding back, dragging through the growing slickness between my thighs. I picture his blown pupils as those fingers slip inside me seamlessly like they were made for that very reason.

My back bows, and soft pants leave my lips as my fingers pump in and out in a painstakingly slow rhythm. I picture him taking his time, dragging out the pleasure from deep inside me. I quicken my pace as water rushes over my body, making every inch of my body tingle.

A swirling current of warmth flutters low in my stomach, building with each pump. I close my eyes when my vision starts to get hazy around the edges and lean against the wall for support as my legs start to tremble. The ache builds until it's too much to handle, making me spill over the edge with Hade's name flying from my lips. I see stars, vibrating everywhere as I dig my nails into my palms to calm myself.

The ensuite door flies open, crashing against the wall, and I squeal in surprise. Hade is panting, concern laced on his face.

"Are you okay?" he asks frantically, assessing the room for any danger.

I stand frozen before him, as if my dream just conjured the man in real life. "I…" I trail off, sputtering for words.

"I was calling your name, but you weren't responding," he rushes out worriedly. "Then I heard you whimper and yell my name. Are you hurt?"

He rakes his eyes over my body, and it's then I come to the sobering realization I stand fully naked before him, on display for his viewing pleasure. I should feel embarrassed, but my body only thrums to life under his fierce gaze, ready to play again.

His eyes widen in shock, and he spins around lightning fast, coming to the same realization. "Fuck," he hisses.

"Hade," I breathe. He grunts for an answer, not turning back around to face me. "I'm okay," I push, trying to figure out exactly how to explain why his name was sinfully leaving my lips. It doesn't take a genius to put the pieces together, and I'm sure it's written across my flushed face.

"Good," he says in a flat tone. His muscles tense, like he's unsure exactly what to do with himself now, so I decide to offer the poor, flustered man an olive branch.

"Join me?" I ask boldly. "I could use help washing my back." I am desperately giving him any excuse at this point.

He shifts, unsure what to do, and the floorboards creak under his weight. I see him fighting an internal battle, his fists opening and closing with confliction.

"Or you can wash up, and I can go eat," I rush out, second guessing myself from his hesitancy. Maybe this is all too much for him. Maybe it's all too much for me too, and I'm just as confused, but I can't help the way my body feels around him. It's like a magnet drawing us closer any time we are near each other, and I'm done questioning or fighting it. It's otherworldly, and I can't even begin to decipher it, so for once, I let it guide my actions. My body begs to be touched by him and to touch him in return, but my mind is clouded with my past. A small part of me knows it always will be, but I'm working on opening myself up again, one day at a time.

He turns abruptly, reaching me in two strides. He grips my chin between his fingers, dragging my face to look at him. "You will do no such thing," he grumbles in a low tone, leaving no room for argument.

His eyes are deep pools of ink blown by lust. I can hear his labored breaths he's trying his best to contain. It's taking everything inside him to hold himself back, and all I want to do is make it so he loses that precious control he prides himself on and see what forges in its wake when he inevitably breaks.

His face is right in front of mine as we share the air between us. The room turns charged with need as he slowly reaches out and drags his knuckles down my cheek, and I close my eyes and lean into his touch. He lets out a tortured moan that goes straight to my core.

"Hade," I whisper, my eyes pleading.

"Yes, beautiful?" he questions with a softened gaze.

I grab his shirt, tugging him against me. "Kiss me," I pant, and he wastes no time as he finally breaks and devours my mouth. I fall limp, the sheer force of his devotion making my knees buckle.

He kisses me with burning fever, cupping my face, holding me hostage as water runs between our mouths. He plants kisses across my jaw, slipping out of his shirt between each kiss he brands me with. His pants follow, falling to the floor in a woosh.

An excited giggle leaves my lips between kisses as he rips me off my feet, crashing my body into his. I eagerly wrap my legs around his torso, gluing myself to him.

My back collides with the cool wall behind me. The water lines up directly above his head, cascading down him, and if he weren't holding me up right now, I think I would fall to his feet and pray. The water runs over his golden skin, making him practically glisten.

This man will be the end of me.

I squirm when I feel his magic lash out, traveling over my body, lighting a fire in its path. It deliciously tingles over my skin, so slow that a chill wracks my spine, and I let out a small moan. A tendril snakes over my stomach, traveling over the peak of my breast, making me gasp. It continues its exploration, slithering under my armpit and wrapping back around the top of my shoulder. I suck in deeply when it glides over the dip of my narrow neck and disappears under my arm to wrap back up around my shoulder, creating a harness across my upper body.

My eyes roll back in my head as the tip of the tendril stops at the top of my shoulder and presses into the pulse at my throat, which is beating faster than should be possible. Hade must feel it through his magic, because he lets out a shattering growl as he releases me, standing straight. He looks over my body and his magical creation holding me to the wall while my legs still pathetically cling to him.

I shake and crumble under his gaze as he slowly scrutinizes every single inch of bare flesh. The air evaporates from my lungs as I look into the eyes of death himself. His eyes are deep, dark chasms full of the promise of destruction, and I'm the only thing standing in his path.

I pant loudly as I feel his eyes blaze over my hardened nipples while he plucks one between his fingers, massaging it tenderly. My body reacts to his touch, my back arching and shoving my breast further into his large palm.

"*Fuck!*" He hisses between his teeth as his last shred of restraint finally vanishes.

He snaps his hand out, wrapping it fully around my neck and applying just the right amount of pressure without taking my breath away. His thumb strokes softly back and forth over the dip of my neck, making me swallow harshly against it.

I gasp as his mesmerizing eyes finally lay claim to mine, my heart lurching to a halt. They promise ruining, and every time I'm ensnared by them, my body begs to give in to his every command, even at the mercy of corrupting my soul.

"You. Are. Perfection," he growls, and it echoes off the walls around us.

He's breaking right before me, and it's the most beautiful thing I've ever seen. I want to dig my nails under his skin until all that's left is the feeling of me etched deep within his soul. It's intoxicating and addictive. There are no words to describe the string tethering us together.

Our breaths heave in time with each other as a million emotions crash through his eyes, painting a vivid story. I can physically taste his lust against my tongue, but there's also questioning. There's plea and restraint. He's not quite sure what this is between us, or if it's okay. I know this because I feel all those emotions pushing against my heart as well.

I wash my thoughts away and lean into his touch. A low rumble trembles from his throat, making me drag my bottom lip between my teeth while a soft breath leaves my throat. I stare the beast down in front of me as my body hums with anticipation.

"You make me want to do very *bad* things, Nyxi," he says in a strained tone.

I reach out and drag my nail up his chiseled torso until it lands at the base of his neck. "What happened to flowers first? Chivalry is dead," I say in a teasingly seductive purr.

He flicks his wrist, and a thorny rose appears in the air, made from his black shadow magic. It floats between us, bobbing softly as it spins slowly. My eyes widen in surprise, and I can't help my smile.

He plucks the rose with a dark gleam in his eyes. I pout as he grips the rose instead of handing it over to me. The magic seems to purr in his grasp, recognizing him as its maker.

"How am I supposed to admire the pretty offering if you won't hand it over?" I pout dramatically.

A shit-eating grin makes the side of his lips kick up, and my pulse rises with it. "Who said flowers were only good for looking pretty?"

Leaning forward, he brings the rose between us so it sits just below my nose. I inhale deeply, making some of the magic flow into my nose. My head floats and my body hums like a drug is racing through my veins. I'm nothing and everything at the same time as I feel his magic work through my body, carving out a chasm deep within me.

"*Hade*," I moan, my eyes closed as his magic settles deep in my core. I could combust just from the feel of his magic coiling through my body like a claiming.

My eyes spring open when I feel a soft caress of something dragging across my chest. I tremble as he runs the top of the black rose across my skin like a feather, leaving electricity behind where it connects with my heated skin. It feels familiar but also a little denser than his usual magic, as if real rose petals were made from fluffy clouds.

One of the thorns drags across my hardened nipple, and I gasp—not in pain, but pleasure. The thorn pushes against my skin but doesn't cut me, leaving behind a delicious sting that turns heated.

He continues his pursuit of my body, dragging the head of the rose down my stomach, feather light, coating my body in chills. It's a delicious, heady feeling, and I never want it to stop. I would happily love to receive flowers from Hade every day if this is the outcome.

I flinch as I feel the rose press right above the sensitive nerves between my thighs. He teases me, dragging it in circles across my lower stomach but never lower, driving me to insanity as I thrash in the grip of the tendril of magic around my upper body.

"Tell me to stop," he breathes, tortured.

"Don't....stop," I chant the words.

The feral moan that leaves his lips makes me feel things that shouldn't be possible, and I'm wound into a tight ball of need and wanting from his teasing, addicting touch.

"I..." I pant, trying to make my brain work through the fog.

"What, *beautiful?*" he taunts as he continues his torture on my body.

"*Need,*" I drag out in a breath, the only word my tongue is capable of making.

"Tell me what you need, Nyxi." His voice drops dangerously low. "Use your words and tell me exactly what that pretty head of yours is thinking."

"*You,*" I sputter as he swipes the rose dangerously close to my center. I freeze for a second as the realization of my words come crashing in. I can see the hesitancy in his eyes as he tracks my movements.

Hade is my *inevitable* and always has been. I feel it deep in my bones, to my very soul, that our paths were always meant to cross. This chaos between us is bigger than the two of us, and there is no escaping it, only forging through the madness. I can't walk away any more than he can right now.

The fates do not care about our pasts, only our futures and fulfilling our destinies. In this exact moment, I finally realize Hade is my *destiny.* He is the answer to it all, no matter how complicated our pasts may be, and I'm learning to give myself grace. There can be a then, and there can be a now. Both are equally important without replacing each other.

Hade drags his thumb across my bottom lip slowly, pulling my mind back to him and out of this endless cycle of self-criticism. I look up at him with big, emotional pits for eyes as he drags his thumb down, making my lip bounce.

"You're so tense, Nyxi," he says softly. "Stressed, tired, and emotionally drained from the past few weeks." He drags his thumb across my cheek, making me sigh and lean into it. He's pulling me from my head once again, like he knows every self-deprecating thought. My body relaxes as his touch brings a calmness without him even trying, like it recognizes him as part of itself.

He leans forward, bringing his lips to the shell of my ear. "Let me help you relax," he whispers, sending toe curling chills down my spine. "Just *release*. Let go of some stress," he promises. "You make the rules here, Nyxi."

He's giving me an out to settle my brain. He reads me like a book and can tell I want this badly, but my brain is having a hard time letting go. Deep down, I know this is okay, but it doesn't mean my brain will allow it easily. He's giving my brain a reason to justify this, but he's also not pushing me.

"Just release," I say under my breath while my body turns uncomfortably hot under his gaze. My breathing is slow and deep as time freezes. I'm ready to dive headfirst until I crash at the bottom, emerging something wholly different in the aftermath.

He nods animalistically slowly. "Just release," he promises. "Nothing more." He pauses as the air slowly turns electric. He waits and waits, looking at me with respect and patience in his eyes.

"*Yes*," I breathe desperately, falling to the beautiful spell Hade has had on me since the moment I laid eyes on him. He looks between my eyes, making sure this is exactly what I want, and it is, wholeheartedly. I want and need this.

He sees exactly that reflected in my eyes, and a strangled moan escapes his lips before they crash to mine. This time, they don't feel rushed or desperate—they feel like a call home. They feel undoubtedly right. They feel like a claim that cannot be broken or overturned.

They feel like *mine*.

I feel his magic fall away as Hade draws me against his chest, wrapping one arm around my waist, the other resting at the nape of my neck as he digs his fingers into my hair.

A tingling explodes where our lips meet, and I moan into his mouth and dig my heels into his back, trying to make every inch of our bodies touch. I grind against him, and I can feel his hard length pressed against my core, butterflies erupting in the pit of my stomach.

He grips my hair and tugs my head back so he can attack my neck with his soothing lips. His stubble drags across my skin, lighting my body on fire and setting me on edge as the soft contrast of his lips create a trail of need across my throat.

I moan loudly, the word dignity so far from my brain, it holds no meaning. I score my nails down his back as the hot water makes the air steam. At this moment, I never want to be found. Being lost to this man for eternity sounds like a dream.

I grind against his length again, and he lets out a groan of desperation. His tongue slides into my mouth, lapping against mine as the taste of him floods me. He tastes like sin and devastation, my favorite flavor.

The water shuts off abruptly as Hade walks us out of the ensuite into the dimly lit room. I let out a loud gasp as he drops me onto the bed below me, my wet back colliding with the soft cotton sheets. The room is so dim, making Hade look like a haunting shadow above me. The soft glow of the moon barely trickles into the room, illuminating every hard cut of his body.

Biting my lip, I stare up at him, charged with an aching need that feels like it will be the death of me if it isn't satiated soon. I go to sit up, the need to touch him overpowering, but he tsks at the same time four tendrils of dark magic lash out, wrapping around both my ankles and wrists, tethering me to the four posts of the bed. I tug on them, but they give no budge as they hold me in place.

"Exquisite," he breathes as he looks over my body laid out before him like an offering.

I'm burning from the inside out, every nerve standing at attention. It's painfully blissful, and I'm so close to begging for him to touch me. He continues standing between my legs, tearing me apart with his eyes.

"What are you doing?" I question him eagerly, squirming in my restraints.

A dark gleam takes over his eyes as his face turns predatory. "Looking over my meal and trying to decide how it will taste."

I let out a soft gasp of pleasure. "But you've already tasted me," I sputter.

"Not yet where I want to, *Nyxi*." Two black pits of hunger stare down at me greedily. "I'm a starved man, and I've been dying to learn how divine you taste upon my tongue," he growls.

"Oh," I gasp, my pulse racing like a drum.

He leans forward so he's towering over my body. His muscles and tattoos on full display. "Tell me you want this," he demands. I nod back, words lost to the wind with my body wound so tight. "Words, Nyxi. I need to hear you say it."

"I want this," I rush out desperately. "Please, Hade," I beg like a crazed woman.

My begging is his undoing as he slams his lips to mine, nipping and kissing me desperately. I pant louder as sparks ignite from his hot skin.

A moan escapes my throat as he moves down and captures one of my nipples into his mouth, his fingers working my other one with a mouthwatering rhythm. He sucks and bites, dragging my nipple out, making me arch my back, chasing his touch. I whimper when he sets my nipple free with a pop.

My eyes roll to the back of my head as his hand takes over for his mouth, both his hands massaging each of my breasts thoroughly as he slowly plants hot kisses down the center of my stomach. I push eagerly into each kiss and squirm in my restraints, needing to touch him.

"Mmmmm." His hot breath fans over my center as he looks up at me from between my thighs, and it's officially the most beautiful sight I've ever witnessed. "Mine!" he growls before diving into my core like he's famished and I'm the only meal in sight.

"Hade," I cry as I fall to the pleasure he's dealing. His wet tongue slides up my entrance slowly as he holds eye contact with me, and I forget my name for a brief second.

"Fucking delicious, just like I thought." His voice is lower than Hell itself, and I shudder under his damning eyes. A wicked gleam takes over his face as he eagerly drops to me again and sucks my clit into his mouth, drawing it between his teeth.

"Oh my…" I choke out as he devotes all his attention to my center. He swirls his warm tongue in small circles, drawing electricity to the tip of each nerve.

I arch into him, my toes curling as I fist the sheets, so hard, I hear a slight tearing noise, but it's the farthest thing from my mind. I lift my hips on instinct, begging for more friction, and he chuckles against me.

"So needy," he teases. "Does your pussy always weep this much? You've already thoroughly soaked the sheets and my face, and I've barely just begun."

True to his words, I notice his face glistening with my wetness. I should be embarrassed, but it only turns me on more, seeing myself all over him. It makes my ego thrum to life.

A whimper is the only answer I manage, and his dark laugh fans across my center. My mind goes blank when his tongue lashes out like a whip, swiping inside me and dragging all the way to my clit, paying it extra attention before lapping against my core again.

Every inch of my body is humming and overheated as I moan so loud, I'm sure the crazy old lady downstairs can hear it. I grind against his face, begging for more, yearning to sink my fingers into his messy hair. Anything he gives me, I take eagerly as a ball of butterflies grows and grows in the pit of my stomach.

"More," I pant, making Hade growl excitedly as he grips my hips, digging his fingers deep into my flesh.

Hade comes up for air to look me dead in the eyes. "I thought you'd never ask." His pupils dilate as he raises his fingers to his lips before drawing them into his mouth and coating them with his spit. He pops them out and shines me a smirk straight from the devil himself. Quirking a brow at me with his dripping fingers right above my center, he asks, "You want more?"

I suck my bottom lip between my teeth, nodding while swallowing down the ball of need rising in my throat. Just when I think I can't wait any longer, he plunges his fingers into my pussy, making me cry out.

He pays me no mercy as he expertly pumps them in and out of me, growing that ball of scorching heat with each delicious slam of his thick fingers. Just when I think I can't take any more, his hot lips latch onto my clit, switching between sucking and licking.

"*Fuck*, I can't take anymore," I whimper. I let out a breathy moan when he nips my clit at the same time his fingers hit deep, rubbing against the perfect spot, making my stomach flutter in a wave of heat.

"So let go for me," he demands. "I want to hear you scream my name as I force every drop of ecstasy from your body." A crazed man stares back at me while I choke on my breaths. "Sing for me, *beautiful*," he growls right before driving back in with a force that throws me off the cliff.

"Hade!" I scream as my body convulses under his sinful touch while the strongest orgasm of my life racks my body. Stars dance behind my eyelids as a pulse explodes against his lips drawing me towards death's door. He rides out my orgasm with his mouth and fingers as I fight to stay conscious. A million tiny sparks dance though my center while my mind floats in the clouds, lost to a memory of who I was before this demon got his claws in me.

My body jolts every time his stubble drags across my sensitive center as he watches me try to come back to reality, and I fight to calm my breathing. I feel his magic evaporate from around my limbs, my body collapsing limp on the bed.

I peel my eyes open to find Hade standing to his full height above me. He drags the back of his hand across his lips, smearing my wetness coating his face. His tongue lashes out, dragging across his lips to lick away every drop. He looks absolutely delicious as the biggest smile I've ever witnessed spreads across his face.

"I can die happily now." His gravelly voice goes straight to my center, making it roar to life again like the greedy bitch she is. His inky eyes twinkle under the light, the moon casting into the room.

"What about you?" I breathe.

He smirks back at me. "I can promise you, that brought me more pleasure than it did you. Tonight was all about *you*," he says with so much certainty and devotion, and my heart perks up at his words.

"If only you could see yourself through my eyes right now," he says softly. "You have ruined everything for me. I will never be able to experience anything more exceptional than the privilege of laying eyes on you, Nyxi."

I think I may be dreaming—my heart is beating at a happy pace it hasn't been capable of for a very long time. A man made of steel and death is looking at me like I mean something in this world. Life feels bearable again under his praise. It feels right.

I lie there with a dopey smile across my face, lost in his words and a cloud of lust. "Lie with me?" I plead softly, hoping this bubble won't burst at any moment.

"Anything you want, it's yours." He smiles back at me as my body grows heavy for darkness to claim. He scoops me up and draws me in to his warm chest as his magic lashes out, closing the cloth blinds, plunging the room in darkness. He slides us into the center of the bed, drawing the covers up so we're wrapped in a ball of warmth.

I let out a sigh of contentment as I wrap myself around his warm body. Snuggling in, I rest my head on top of his bare chest, listening to his steady heartbeat. He shifts below me, raising his arms to rest behind his head.

My eyes snag on the dark ink etched into his skin, and my hand reaches out without thought. I slowly trace the dark lines on his side with my finger, unable to resist touching it. The owl seems to stare back at me like an old friend, and I smile at the comfort it brings.

A deep rumble comes from Hade, vibrating my face pressed against his chest as he revels in the feeling of my touch. I lean forward and press my lips to the tattoo, which draws a deep sigh from him.

"It's mesmerizing," I say under my breath. "I think one day, I would like to have one of my own to wear the pain my heart bears."

"I'll make it happen," he says lovingly as he presses his lips to my skin in a feather light kiss. He strokes his hand down the back of my head while my eyes grow heavy, his beautiful owl the last thing I see as my eyes finally draw shut.

Right now, I feel safe and cared for, and I let my mind pretend this is my reality for the time being, even though I know it can never be. For now, though, I pretend to live in this warm bubble where people don't die and happiness can exist.

"Thank you for tonight," I mumble, sleep almost taking full control of my body.

I feel his body press closer to mine, making sure I won't vanish right before his eyes. "I would do anything for you, Nyxi. My heart only beats for *you*," he whispers as sleep finally drags me under, making me wonder if I'm dreaming again.

Chapter
Thirty-Seven

My body thrums with life as I round my last lap, the sun finally perched high in the sky. Beads of sweat slip down my temple as I slow my feet to a soft walk. It feels good to get back to my routine after being away for so long.

Hade flew us back to Lunaria early this morning, as duty called his attention. I about doubled over when I saw a dainty flower and radiant sun charms sitting on my bed with a note that read, *To add to your bracelet of love*. A placeholder for Rayah and Theo to have with me forever, right next to Hudson's paintbrush charm. I have no idea when he had time to have them made, but it's one of the most thoughtful things I've ever been given, right next to Theo's dagger necklace guarding my heart.

It was exhilarating getting a real look under Hade's skin, unraveling the story etched beneath it, even if it was only bits and pieces. These charms are another look into his heart.

Forced to leave our cushy little bubble this morning was harder than I thought, and it makes me wonder what lies ahead. Will we go back to stolen looks and lust buried beneath a façade of hate and loathing? Will he continue to keep his distance like it's painful to be near me? Will he think of me when he's alone in his room? Or was yesterday just a blip in time, never to surface again? Time will only tell, and for now, I need to keep relying on myself and only myself to make it through another day up here in hell.

My morning run has seeped through every inch of my body, grounding me again. I live for the quiet, peaceful mornings when the city still sleeps before it explodes to life. Now, with the sun fully risen, the city is thrumming as I slip down a back alley, weaving through the chaotic crowd. Magic pushes at me from every angle, brushing up against my skin like I can reach out and grasp it.

I finally spot the glowing orb radiating under the warm sun, and I silently rush through the crowd to slip through the door, the soft bell chiming above me, announcing my arrival.

A calmness flows through me, same as it does every time I step foot in here. It's extra calm in here today, only a few patrons lounging in chairs in the corner, reading and basking in the sun streaming through the stained glass.

A giant gasp draws my attention, and I can't help but smile. "Well, c'mon, sugar. Get over here so I can give you a proper greeting."

A small laugh leaves my lips as I stride over to Mo, the owner of Knead It. She encases me in her arms, squeezing me to her chest until my face is pressed snugly in her cleavage. Her sweet smell of cinnamon sugar floods my nose, and I relax in her hold like a child would in a mother's embrace.

"Where have you been, sugar?" she scolds me like a child. "It's been ages since you've paid me a visit."

She unwraps her arms from me, planting her hands on each of my shoulders as she looks me over for injuries. "You look just fine… Maybe even more than fine." She shoots me a little smirk that cracks my walls. "What's got your skin glowing and cheeks rosier than ever?"

My cheeks flush under her scrutiny, and I try to turn away, but she holds me steady.

Busted.

"I know you enjoy those cute little romance novels, but you've never radiated this bright before," she states knowingly.

I bat her hand away and try to sound unaffected, like my heart isn't plastered right on my sleeve for her to see. "It's nothing," I say under my breath, walking to the pastry counter. Mo follows, rounding the counter with raised eyebrows.

She points to my chest with a gleam in her eyes. "That blush creepin' up your chest is not nothing." She draws out her words with a rich accent that feels like a warm hug. "That blush tells a story of stolen kisses and passion words could never convey," she purrs. She pins me with a stare, waiting for me to crack like I always do for her and only her.

"There may have been a kiss involved," I admit sheepishly.

"I knew it!" she gushes, a giant smile taking over her face. "I need all the details. Just one kiss, or a night full?" she questions, right before her eyes light up. "Wait, was it on the lips?" Her eyes narrow on me expectedly, and I let out a loud, dramatic gasp.

"That's all the details you're getting!" I throw her a scolding look, but she knows it's all show as she waves her hands at me in defeat.

"Fine," she huffs. "Then you're gonna tell me why you've been gone for so long. The strawbana bread has piled up in your absence."

I chew my lip nervously as I'm brought back to the night that flipped me on my axis, slightly more than I already was. I feel a phantom ache in my side and grab it instinctually. Mo tracks the movement, and her eyes darken uncharacteristically.

"What happened, sugar?" she presses, deadly serious, concern etched across her brows.

I think carefully, deciding how I want to phrase my next words. "I was injured and had to take some days to rest," I say carefully.

"Exactly how did this injury come about?" she presses.

"It was really nothing," I say under my breath, downplaying the events. "Look, I'm totally fine." I do a spin, showing off my good health.

"Nothing?" She scoffs. "I haven't seen you in around a week. You're more addicted to my bread than you are to those silly little romance novels, so I know you wouldn't have missed getting them for just 'nothing'."

Double busted.

I let out a loud sigh as she plants her hands on her hips, waiting for my response. This woman is more persistent than Winston searching the castle for oranges. She raises her eyebrows at me in question, and I crumble beneath her hard gaze.

"I may have gotten a small cut on my side that required some down time," I mumble under my breath quickly, hoping she takes the information I've given as satisfactory.

"What created this so-called 'small cut'?" She makes air quotes, looking totally unimpressed with my explanation.

I bring my hands up to my face, trying to hide from her. Peeking out between my fingers, I squeak, "A dagger."

Her face grows red with anger, and I shrink back a step. "A DAGGER!" she bellows loudly, making the hairs on the back of my neck rise.

I nod back but offer no other words. I don't know why I'm withholding information from her; it's not like I care about spilling the shady side of Aeron to the world. He deserved what came to him, and I believe in a balance of actions. What hurts more is how used I felt, and I'm embarrassed for letting my walls down again just for them to be smashed to smithereens.

Mo's features soften, and that motherly side comes back out, ensnaring me in her caring gaze. She grips one of my hands, gently stroking her thumb over the back of my hand.

"What really happened? Are you okay?" she says softly, seeing the way this conversation is affecting me.

"I was stabbed in my sleep," I say defeatedly. Her hand tightens on mine, but her eyes never stray. "The dagger was laced with poison, but one of the Vanquishers saved me. I'm okay now."

I think back to the raw anger that radiated off Hade when he walked into my room to find Aeron standing over my body, a dagger in my side. I've never seen something so lethal bottled up inside someone. He's saved me in more than one way since that night.

"I presume the culprit was dealt with accordingly?" Mo says protectively.

A tremor racks my body as I nod back to her, remembering exactly how Aeron was dealt with. I can still smell and vividly see the state of his body the last time I laid eyes on him.

"Well, good! I'm glad that piece of shit was taken out with the trash then." She says it harshly, which is the opposite of how I know her to be. A piece of my heart warms knowing I have people in my corner who exude such fierce protectiveness.

I smile. "Me too."

Mo drops my hand and reaches into the pastry window, grabbing a handful of strawbana bread slices out and shoving them into a box. She slides the box across the counter to me with a toothy grin.

"To make up for all the slices you missed while you were away," she says softly.

I reach into my pocket for some coppers, but she smacks my hand with a tsk. "I don't need your money, sugar. Just your company will do."

"Thank you," I respond earnestly. She flashes me a wink, and I decide to stay awhile longer, making my way to one of the velvet chairs in the corner.

Sliding deep into the large chair, I prop my feet up on the matching ottoman, snatching out one of the slices. The vivid flavor of strawberry and buttery banana explodes on my taste buds, and I let out a quiet moan of pleasure.

The loud ring of the bell draws my attention away from my sweet treat as a tall, slender man struts through the door. He walks up to the counter confidently, slamming his hands down, alerting Mo to his presence.

"What can I do for you today, sir?" She looks impatient with the man, which is off character for her, but I would be too with the way he charged in here like he owns the place.

"I'll take everything you have in the pastry window," he says sternly. "And you will give it to me for free." The air turns thick, as if magic is sweeping over the room, and I find it odd.

"I will do no such thing," Mo retorts with a scowl and a mocking laugh. The man looks at her, stunned, caught off guard by her noncompliance.

"You will, and you will do it with a smile on your face, *darlin'*." His voice is monotone but strong as he breathes the words, trying again.

"The only thing that will put a smile on my face is when my foot kicks your ass out of my shop." The man takes a step back, stunned by her response, like he's never been told no before. She leans forward, mumbling under her breath, "Your coercion magic won't work on me, *darling*. So I suggest you take it someplace else."

He swears under his breath, something my ears can't pick up. He turns on his heels swiftly and storms out the door, looking beyond embarrassed and angry. Apparently, there's bad people everywhere, whether you live in the dump I grew up in or on a magical floating rock. You learn something new every day, I guess.

I shoot Mo questioning eyes, and she shrugs like it's just another day on the job. "He's a Manipulant. Their magic allows them to control people, but it doesn't work on me. Perks of my own magic." I take in her words, wondering exactly how she is immune. I'm about to push her further on the matter when my eyes snag on the clock above her head. It's then I realize how late it's gotten.

"Shoot!" I rush out, jumping to my feet as a few crumbs of bread fall from my shirt. "I didn't realize it was so late." I trot over to the counter, snatching Mo into a tight embrace. "Thank you for the bread and caring enough to notice my absence."

She rubs my back with a serious expression that hits me straight in my heart. "I have always and will always care for you and notice your absence, sugar. I'm just glad you're finally back." She sighs happily into my hair, seeming more sentimental than just missing me.

She plants a warm kiss on my forehead just before I slip from her arms and out the door, a giant smile on my face. I race back to the castle with a box full of sweets and an even sweeter heart.

Chapter
Thirty-Eight

Blowing out a loud breath, I slam the book back on its shelf and grab the one directly next to it. I drag my thumb across the beveled lettering on the cover spelling out 'The Origins of Magic - A guide to harnessing its full potential'.

Crossing my legs, I lean back against the shelf behind me and open to the first page, looking over the guide in the front. It breaks down each basic elemental magic and where they stem from. I'm sure this book will be another dead end in my search for an answer to the riddle, but I will tear apart each one in this room before I give up.

I skim through the book, growing more bored by the second, until I'm sure it will be of no use. I slam it shut more aggressively than I should and toss it aside while dragging my hands down my face.

"Stupid fucking book," I mumble under my breath.

I feel a tingle drag up my bare leg, where I spot a small shadow making its way over my skin. It crawls up my leg and slithers over the silky nightgown I'm wearing until it grips the side of my chin and turns my head to face the center of the room. My heart stops when I find Hade's intense eyes pinned on me from the chair he's lounging in casually.

After training with him in the Bubble earlier, I crashed for a few hours before I joined the other contestants for dinner. My midday nap made me restless and resulted in me tossing and turning as I tried to pick apart the riddle. I eventually dragged myself out of bed and asked Hade if he would take me to the library.

"No luck?" he questions with a smirk, like me being riled is amusing to him.

"What gave it away?" I tease, the tension slowly falling away the longer his eyes roam my body.

"I know it's never good when you start talking to books. We really need to find you some friends."

I throw him a scowl and flip him my middle finger. I swear he knows exactly how to push every single one of my buttons. His deep chuckle draws flutters in my stomach, and I silently curse him for affecting me so heavily, even when I'm mad at him.

"You're tense, Nyxi," he says, an edge to his tone.

"According to who?" I respond innocently.

He sets his book to the side and leans forward in his chair, resting his elbows on his knees. "Your shoulders are taut and your fingers are digging into your delicate palms. Your legs are crossed so harshly, your thin excuse for an outfit is drifting up your thighs, and if you tense even the slightest amount, I'll have better entertainment to look at than the book I'm reading." His gaze turns heated as he draws out his next words. "So yes, it appears you are very, very *tense*."

A shiver travels up my spine, making me jerk slightly. I feel the cold silk of my nightgown slide another inch up my thigh, and

Hade's eyes snap to it instantly. My skin heats every place his eyes drag over, and my breathing hitches the slightest amount.

I slide my hands down to the hem of my dress and rest them there, forgoing dragging it back to its proper length. Looking up at him through my lashes, I purr, "Maybe I am, *Hade*." I raise an eyebrow at him. "What are you going to do about it?"

I trail my finger across my upper thigh, absentmindedly drawing a pattern, which makes my finger graze the hem of my dress, dragging it up another delicious inch. I spot Hade's jaw tick in response, gripping his armrests, turning his knuckles white.

A deep growl is drawn from the depths of his chest, and there is no mistake who it's aimed at. His eyes lazily trail from my face to the hem of my dress, down my legs, then back up to my face.

A wicked grin takes over his face as he leans forward again, and my heart picks up with adrenaline. I can see every dark, depraved thing running through his beautiful head, and I'm both scared and exhilarated.

"Lean back and spread your legs for me," he commands.

All the air from my lungs leaves me, and a dark chuckle leaves Hade's lips, looking fully amused. I shoot him a questioning look, and his mouth kicks up to one side.

"I've never been one to shy away from a challenge." His deep voice bounces around my insides, igniting me until I'm flooded with an overbearing heat all the way to my toes. "Now, be a *good girl* and do as you're told, Nyxi."

There's a dark challenge in his voice, one that, no matter how defiant I want to be, it's impossible to ignore. He holds the reins to my body now, and I think he has for some time. Being the good girl I am, I slide my back further against the wall and uncross my legs so they are spread in front of me.

"And how exactly do you intend on doing anything while sitting on the other side of the room?" I challenge.

A darkness takes over his eyes until they are two chasms of death. "I don't have to lay a single finger on your body to make it come alive for me, beautiful."

He licks his lips, making wetness pool at my center. Slowly, he slides back in his chair and spreads his legs wide, dominating the space like a god. He rests his hands softly on his legs as he drags his heated eyes lazily to my center. Black flames burn from within his eyes with such intensity, my throat goes dry, and I resist the urge to clench my legs together.

I gulp loudly as a bead of sweat trickles down my forehead from the charged air between us. "Now what?" I breathe seductively.

"Now, *Nyxi*, you're going to touch yourself for me until every ounce of tension is forcefully rung from that sinful body of yours," he commands.

"Oh," I gasp, words leaving me in a puddle of writhing need. "And you?" I question, but it's barely a whisper.

The devil stares back at me, and I almost faint on impact. "Me?" His deep voice makes my legs tremble. "I'm going to enjoy tonight's *entertainment*."

I stare down the devil and wet my chapped lips. I've never backed away from a challenge, and today will not be a first. I draw each shaky knee up, letting my knees flop out. The action makes my nightgown draw up past my hips, laying me bare to Hade's hungry eyes.

A breath escapes me when I feel his eyes connect with my center, but I remain rooted, refusing to cower. I watch his throat bob as he slowly swallows and curses under his breath. I'm glad I'm not the only one at the edge of sanity.

Biting my lip, I scrape up the courage to slowly drag my palms up my bare thighs to my hips. Looking up, I drag my hand ever so slowly, hovering it directly over my center, teasing him.

"And here I thought you would be the one drawing the tension from my body," I taunt, my voice breathless.

"Who said I wasn't participating in the fun too?" His voice is so low, it feels like talons dragging across my skin. Before I can even register his words, a tendril of black magic lashes out, slithering across the floor, aimed directly at me. It takes its time crawling along the floor like a predator cornering its prey until I feel the tip of it crawl across my foot.

Cold air drags across my heated skin, making my head spin. It leaves chills across my skin as it makes its way up my upper thigh. My eyes track the magic the entire way, anticipating its next move as my heart lashes aggressively against my chest.

The tip latches on to my arm, wrapping tightly around my pointer and middle finger, resting a breath above my aching clit. My body shudders, realizing exactly what he has in store for me, and a thrill dances up my spine.

When I look up, my eyes connect with soulless black pits as Hade sits lazily back in his chair, a look of ruin across his face. I've never felt more alive than I do in this moment. His eyes twinkle with mischief, and it's my final undoing.

"Come alive for me, *Nyxi*," he growls.

I feel the influence of Hade's magic take control of my fingers, pushing them forward with a tingling pressure, right where I'm dying to be touched. I gasp loudly as they press further until my body vibrates in pleasure.

A breathy moan trembles from my lips as his magic takes control of my fingers, expertly swirling them around my clit. Hade remains composed across the room, staring at me without blinking, but I can see the beast beneath begging to be uncaged. I choke for air when my fingers pick up in pace, spreading my wetness around until I'm a panting mess.

"Hade," I pant, unable to form a coherent sentence.

"Yes, beautiful?" he smirks, looking thoroughly pleased with himself.

"More…" I choke, desperate for more friction as I ride the edge of pleasure and sin.

In an instant, everything goes pitch dark, and I gasp in shock and excitement. I suck my bottom lip between my teeth as the familiar sensation of Hade's magic wraps snuggly around my eyes like a mask. My senses heighten with the loss of my sight, and I let my head roll back as my body melts into the floor.

My fingers fall under the spell of his magic wrapped tightly around them. They continue to take and take until I'm trembling, on the verge of coming fully undone right before his eyes. Butter-flies erupt low in my stomach as a fire starts, growing until it's a giant ball of mind-numbing ecstasy.

Even without sight, there's no denying the feeling of Hade's eyes dragging across my tight skin, a weight sitting on my chest. A low, satisfied rumble erupts from deep within his chest, and my back arches, whimpering and on the edge of crashing over the dam of pleasure, falling to his desires.

I hear rustling and then steady steps stomping across the floor, growing louder by each step. My breaths fill the silent room, my skin growing slick from overheating. Stars begin to dance behind my eyelids as I feel an orgasm barreling towards me.

A breath fans across my neck, and I moan in response. Hade strides to my side in an instant, swiftly squatting beside me. His overbearing presence is something I've grown fond of.

His tongue lashes out, scorching a trail of fire up the side of my neck, and I angle my head in response, begging him to take more. I would give him anything in this moment, as long as the feeling of heaven he's raining down on me never ends.

His lips graze the shell of my ear, and my eyes roll to the back of my head. "It's a shame, really," he purrs against my neck, bare-ly above a whisper. All I manage is a loud moan, my brain working on overdrive to keep my body upright with the pleasure he's ripping from me. His dark chuckle makes the hairs on the back of my neck stand, the rope going taut in my core with another flick of my fingers. There's no denying I'm seconds from exploding.

His magic drags my fingers down until they rest right above my entrance. My breath stalls when his next words leave his punishing lips. "That not a single soul gets to experience the madness of watching you come undone like a goddess of sin. I could not possess a single copper to my name and still consider myself the richest man in the world, as long as I get the pleasure of laying my eyes upon *you*," he grumbles possessively.

The second the last word leaves his damning lips, his magic thrusts my fingers deep inside myself, and I cry out as I finally topple over the edge.

"Hade!" I scream, loud enough to wake the whole castle.

He crashes his lips to mine with a whimpering moan, greedily devouring my orgasm as he demands more and more. Everything goes black, and stars dance happily behind my eyes as magic akin to pleasure seeps through my entire body. It feels like a rebirth as I float in the unknown, no longer possessing a name or purpose but rather caught up in the moment of feeling nothing and everything at once.

I convulse below him while his lips absorb the sounds of havoc lashing against my body. He kisses me like his soul would rip in two if his lips were to leave mine. He's all predator above me, taking command over my body and drawing out every last drop of my orgasm until I'm nothing more than a pile of broken, limp limbs below him.

I feel his thumb press to the pulse point of my throat, tracking the beats like they're his lifeline. I'm barely coherent, the orgasm he tore from me making me feel like I ran for hours. He softly brushes his lips against mine one last time, leaving the faintest taste of himself, and it's my new favorite flavor.

"*Perfection*," he breaths against my lips, scooping me up to cradle against his chest. I relax into him as he carries me all the way back to my room, where I pass out with the blissful feeling of his lips branding something that feels like no return.

Chapter
Thirty-Nine

I COULD *DIE* TODAY.

The mantra has been a never ending cycle, running through my head from the moment my eyes opened this morning. Another round of the Crucible is here, which means two of us will die today. The harsh reality crashes into me like a tidal wave. Will I be one of the lucky ones, surviving another day? Or, will I succumb to the fate licking at the back of my heels for years now and finally retire to an eternity among the stars?

The thought of making it to the fifth and final round of the Crucible sends a jolt of electricity straight to my heart. In past events, the fourth and fifth rounds have had significant sway in difficulty, depending on your public popularity ranking. Seeing as I am not the most likable, I have no hope of any extra help this round.

Hade is on extra edge today for some reason. I haven't seen him this worked up, and it's making me curious. Does he know today's events? Is he worried for me? Will he show his concern once we step out in front of the masses?

I took my time getting ready this morning, basking in Des' company and praying it won't be our last time, cherishing it wholly if it was. Only the stars know my fate, and I'm putting my trust in them.

Des was her usual chipper self this morning, rambling about making me look perfect for today, but I could see the slight dull behind her eyes that normally isn't there, hinting at the worry within her. My bubby friend lost her shine today, and I tried to not let it dampen the mood. Still, seeing her worry over me both warmed my heart and chipped away at it all the same. We are kindred souls, both with pasts, who, through it all, have come out the other side again and again. I don't wish to be another weight added to her back.

No, today, I will fight for my life. I will fight to keep the sparkle in Odessa's eyes. I will fight to keep the memory of Theo alive. I will fight to prevent the darkness from overtaking Hade. And I will fight for myself, in spite of fate and all that has stood in my way. I will fight for a better tomorrow.

Grief is like an ocean. It comes in waves, ebbs and flows, calm and content at times and all-consuming in others. You just have to learn to weather the storm, and that is what I will be doing today: using it as the fire that licks my back until there is no other option but survival. Grief may be debilitating, but today, I will be wielding it as my weapon.

A knock sounds on my door, pulling me from my thoughts. I rush over, throwing it open and expecting it to be Hade collecting me, but I'm pleasantly surprised to see big, rosy cheeks shining me the biggest smile as Winston comes into view.

"I'm here to whisk you away, little lady," he beams down to me. I spot a tiny bit of dried orange juice on the side of his mouth, and I can't help the laugh that bubbles up my throat. He notices my eyes on his mouth and bashfully reaches up, wiping away the evidence.

"Saving a little for seconds, I see." I tease, shooting him a wink.

"Tastes even better the second time," he jokes with a cheeky smirk, and I can't help but smile at this big teddy bear of a man. "Are you ready?" he asks with a hint of worry he masks behind a big smile.

I nervously nibble my lip and nod in answer. "As ready as I'll ever be."

As I follow him out into the corridor, we easily fall into step next to each other. I hook my left arm though his elbow, habitually rubbing the dagger necklace hanging from my neck.

"No Hade today?"

Ever since Hade took back over for Winston, I have seen less and less of him. I'm starting to think Hade has a bit of a controlling problem when it comes to me—not that I'm complaining, but it means I have seen less of Winston than I would like. He has been a rock to lean on while here and has helped me more than he will ever know.

"Daddy Death was summoned to inform Aire of today's events, but don't you fret—he will be joining us later." Winston says it so casually, I choke on my breath, caught off guard. He shoots me a concerned look as I clutch my chest, trying to collect myself.

"Did you..." I sputter, trying to hold in my impending laughter the best I can. "Did you just call Hade *Daddy Death?*"

Winson looks at me out of the corner of his eye, sporting a slight smirk. "Is he not?"

I lose my small sliver of composure and howl with laughter, bending over at the waist. After collecting myself, I reply, "I suppose you're right, though I would love to see you call him that to his face."

"Whose face?" A deep voice crawls up my spine just as I crash into a hard body. Strong arms wrap around me before I go crashing to the ground. I drag my eyes up, colliding with two swirling, opposite-colored saucers. A blush creeps up my chest just from his nearness and the memories of his magic wrapped around my fingers in the library.

Shaking my head, I clear my thoughts and shoot a side glance at Winston in question. Hade slips his hands into his pockets casually, staring between the two of us. Silence carries on until it's painfully awkward. Being the troublemaker I am, I nudge my shoulder into Winston's, making him stumble a bit until he lets out a loud sigh in defeat.

"Yours, sir," Winson says in a professional tone, making me giggle under my breath.

Suck up.

Hade lets out a short grunt, looking at the end of his extra short fuse. "And what exactly are you saying to my face?"

Winston turns beet red, looking like he can't decide if he's embarrassed or about to piss his pants. If I didn't know Hade was a secret softy underneath all his hard exterior, I would be fearing for my friend right now, but I would never let Hade do anything to Winston. I know he wouldn't lay a finger on him anyways. I keep my lips sealed, though, enjoying the sight of Winston flushed and squirming uncomfortably under Hade's deadly stare.

Daddy Death, indeed.

"It's nothing really, *sir*," he rushes out. "Just a silly little nickname *we* came up with."

Did he just say we?

"Out with it," Hade barks.

"Daddy Death!" I shout before losing all my composure again, slapping my hand over my mouth to muffle my laugh.

Winson freezes, looking like a mouse trapped by a predator. Silent giggles rack my body, my chest shaking uncontrollably.

Shock flashes across Hade's face for the briefest moment before he schools his features again, back to the mighty Cardinal. Then, the strangest thing happens. The side of his lips betrays him, lifting ever so slightly as the smallest chuckle sneaks its way up his throat.

"*Daddy Death?*" Hade repeats in an amused tone. Leave it to Hade to be impressed—as if he needed another thing to fuel his overflowing ego. Winston gulps loudly before letting out a long breath, relaxing again.

"Well, if you two are done ogling me and my magic, I'm going to take this one off your hands." He points to me, and my damn heart does a little somersault in my chest.

"It's no bother," Winston says with a smile. "I do not mind escorting her to the Bubble."

"I wasn't asking," he states. "She's going with me."

"Hade," I scold, narrowing my eyes. "You can be nice, you know."

"This is my nice," he shoots back.

Rolling my eyes, I pinch the bridge of my nose, letting out a dramatic sigh. I go to respond, but Winston beats me to it.

"She's all yours, sir." He turns to look at me, a slight sheen glazing his eyes. Pulling me into a tight hug, he whispers into my ear, "Good luck out there, little lady. I believe in you; you just have to believe in yourself. Give them hell so we can make some more happy pangs together."

I squeeze him back, holding in the emotions threatening to rise to the surface. I step back from his embrace, and he leans down to plop a wet, citrus-smelling kiss on my forehead.

"I'll be watching from the sidelines," he says softly before spinning on his heels and disappearing down the long corridor. I spot the slightest round bulge in his pocket and let out a breathy laugh, realizing he has another orange stashed away for later.

"We need to talk!" Hade rushes, a slight nervous tick to his tone. Before I can respond, he grabs my wrist and pulls me into the nearest room so fast, I stumble over my feet. He slams the door behind us, pushing me against the wall as my eyes adjust to the dark closet.

"Does this conversation need to happen right this moment?" I hiss. "I kind of have somewhere to be, and I would rather not be late and piss off the Empress more than I already have."

Hade presses forward, trapping my body between his and the wall at my back. I lift my chin defiantly, looking up at him with narrowed eyes. I attempt to ignore my racing heart and glare at him, waiting for whatever important thing he couldn't wait any longer to tell me.

"Yes, this conversation is important, and yes, it's happening *right now*. Whether you want it to or not is irrelevant to me," he grits out before softening his eyes, looking slightly pained.

I try to stay angry at him, but it all melts away the second I see the emotions swirling in his entrancing eyes. I used to think his light eye looked haunting, but now, I recognize it for what it is.

Strength and resilience.

"Okay," I say softly. "Speak."

His chest rises with a deep breath, desperation taking over his face. He looks on the verge of dropping to his knees and begging me for something, but instead, grunts flow from under his breath.

"You need to fight harder than you ever have today. I cannot help you. Today is permanent," he pleads, his voice strained. "I cannot save you from today's events, Nyxi."

His voice almost quivers, but he keeps himself together, and I can tell he's panicking. I wish he would give me the real him all the time—every ounce of him, the light, and more importantly, the dark. The strong *and* the weak. I would take it all with open arms. Nothing he could ever do or say would scare me away or be too dark for my battered soul to handle.

"Every trial is permanent, Hade," I remind him. "I will fight today as I have for the last twenty years of my life. I will do everything in my power to stay on this side of the stars. You don't need to start worrying about me now, big guy," I tease, giving him a soft, reassuring smile, but he still looks so desperate, it sets me on edge.

What did he know that I didn't?

His arms lash out, crashing onto the wall on both sides of my head, caging me in. He looks at me, and all I see is a broken man staring back. Leaning down, he presses his forehead to mine, letting out a long, defeated breath.

I relish in the feeling of his warm skin on mine, fortifying the tether running from my soul to his. My hands move instantly, reaching up to rest softly on each of his muscular shoulders.

"You don't understand," he says under his breath, more to himself than me. "I cannot help you, and I've never felt so helpless in my life."

Giant, warm hands grasp each side of my face as he drags my head up to look at him. I've never seen him this worked up, and it's starting to scare me. He looks like he has seen a ghost. His brows plunge low, a crease forming between them as he fights to keep himself under control.

"Promise me," he whimpers. "Promise me you will fight for your life today and come back to me." His voice cracks, and a part of my heart crumbles along with it.

"I promise you, I will do everything in my power to fight to stay alive." Leaning forward, I press my lips softly to his, sealing that promise. "I will not make a promise to you I cannot keep, so that is all I can promise you for now, Hade."

A deep sigh leaves his lips before he leans forward, pressing one last desperate kiss to my lips. He holds my face close, showering me with his desperation to be close to me, and I melt into him. He tastes like heaven and a second chance at life.

Our lips part, but his hands remain on my face, his gentle thumbs stroking my cheeks. He nods, accepting my promise for what it is. Tucking a loose strand of hair behind my ear, he whispers, "I'll always bet on you, Nyxi."

"Welcome to the fourth round of the *Reaper Crucible!*" The Empress' voice is amplified by an Enhancer, ringing out to the citizens of Lunaria watching excitedly from the sidelines.

"Before the fun begins, I must have a private word with my competitors. Fear not, though, for today's events will be full of enough excitement and gore to satisfy your needs for a lifetime."

The Enhancer next to her cuts his magic, making her voice dull to its normal volume. Tsking sternly, she slowly eyes Tank, Jade, Carwell, and me standing in front of her. "I'm truly wounded by your lack of brains," she says dramatically. "And here I thought this would be the year one of my competitors would finally complete my riddle."

She acts as if the damn thing is common knowledge, not some foreign language I'm sure she made up in one of her drunken stupors.

Her words strike home, though, as disappointment in myself seeps through my body. No matter how many times I've searched the library, or how many journal entries I've flipped through, nothing seems even remotely close. If I gave up every time life was tough, I would have died a long time ago, though, so I won't stop my search, because I know the answer lies within that library. I just have to find it. My gut tells me to *seek out the journals.*

"If any of you think you have the answer, then speak now, or else you will be left fighting for your life today." She looks down the line of us with a face that could cut glass. Everyone remains silent. "Very well then." She claps. "May today have mercy on you…or not."

She nods to the Enhancer next to her, who releases his magic again, amplifying her voice for the masses. "Now that's out of the way, shall we check the rankings?"

The crowd erupts in cheers and chants for their favorite competitor. Surprisingly, I hear a couple people scream my name, and it throws me for a loop. Light shines in front of us, each of my competitors' names typed through the air, ranking us one through four.

"Sitting at the top of the rankings, we have none other than Tank from Sweat Sector." The Empress' giant, wicked smile gleams while Tank's name is chanted in the background. "Coming in second, it's no surprise we have Jade the Vagrant from our winning team of Submerge."

The crowd roars as Jade smiles and waves her hand like a princess, but I can still see the rotten heart beating in her chest. Apparently, I'm the only one who can, as the Empress has a hard time collecting the audience's attention again, going crazy for Jade.

"In the third place ranking, we surprisingly have another Vagrant, Nyxi." The crowd cheers, but nowhere near as loud as they did for Jade and Tank. I could honestly give two shits about what random people think of me, so I pay them no mind...for the most part. Instead, I focus on readying myself for today's events as the Empress announces Cartwell in the fourth and final spot.

Movement catches my eye, Hade stomping into the Bubble with another Vanquisher I don't recognize. He looks every bit the killer, with his black uniform, weapons strapped on every inch of him, and a fierce scowl slapped on his face.

My eyes can't stop drinking him in, no matter how hard I try to pry my eyes away. He ignores me, focusing on the job at hand, his hand casually on the hilt of his sword. I know he can't show me any attention, and honestly, he doesn't even owe me that. I'm not quite sure what this thing happening between us is, or what it means. All I know is it feels right, and I don't want it to stop anytime soon. I want to permanently plant myself beneath his skin until he cannot tell where he ends and I begin.

I want to know all of him.

I sigh happily when I feel the familiar essence of his magic, his scent carried on the wind, wrapping around me. It settles itself in the crook of my ear like always. I used to think it tickled, but now, it kind of feels like *home*.

"You're staring," Hade whispers into my ear through his shadow magic. I nibble my lip, but my eyes stay planted on him. I wish so badly I could talk back to him, but I don't need my competitors and the entirety of Lunaria thinking I've gone crazy by talking to myself, so I stay silent.

"Stop that," he hisses, his tone hushed. "Those fucking lips of yours are distracting me—and don't even get me started on your eyes."

I gasp quietly, swallowing hard to force my emotions back down. I know I should be paying attention to the Empress, and I know I promised Hade I would do everything in my power to stay alive, but I learned a long time ago there is no going against the pull my body has to Hade. It's out of my hands now.

"Who's ready to hear what today's game entails?" The Empress' voice finally pulls my eyes away from Hade, and they go reluctantly. I swallow, readying myself for the worst.

It's time to fight for my life.

"*Promise*," Hade desperately whispers one last time into my ear, and this time, I do answer with a small nod.

"No matter how poor or wealthy, there is always one childhood game that has been constant for all time, the one thing children excel at over adults." The Empress gestures her hand out to us and the growing crowd outside. "Any guesses?"

Small murmurs chatter around us, but no answers are given. The Empress' smile grows until it takes up the entirety of her face, making my skin crawl. "Imagination," she shouts. "The ability to play pretend. I'm afraid, though, there will be no pretending with today's game."

My mind whirls with all the possibilities, but her vagueness leaves my mind empty. One thing I do know is my ability to play pretend. I've been pretending to be whatever I need to be to stay alive my entire life, and that won't stop today. I will forge myself into anything needed to survive this.

"Little girls can be found playing pretend princesses or unicorns. Little boys, dragons and princes," she drawls. "But what, my lovelies, is the greatest play pretend game of all?"

The crowd goes silent with anticipation. I look left and right to my three competitors, taking in their expressions. Tank looks disgustingly excited. Jade wears a small smirk, and Cartwell looks petrified but doing his best to mask his fear. And me? I have no idea how I feel right now, but I guess I'm about to find out.

"Pretend fighting," she says excitedly. "Little boys and girls dueling in the streets like knights with wooden swords is a game as old as time." She shifts her gaze back to us, and I can physically see the malice swirling behind her eyes.

"Today there will be no pretending, though, and no wooden swords. You will each face one of your competitors in a fight to the death. The game will only finish when one of you drops dead, slain by the other," she says dramatically.

Chants and screams sting my ears as citizens stomp their feet and chant. My face falls for a brief second, realizing I have no idea which of my competitors I will be paired with. I'm avoiding the part about me having to kill someone altogether. Now I understand why Hade was so frantic today.

"Per tradition, your ranking in the competition holds importance for the fourth and fifth rounds of the Crucible, and this year is no different."

It dawns on me now exactly how we will be paired up for our duels right before the Empress speaks. "Rankings one and four will compete against each other, leaving rankings two and three to face off. Being in the first spot ranking gives that competitor an advantage by getting to face off with our weakest."

Cartwell curses under his breath next to me, and my heart sinks. Each round is to test us in different ways, but this round doesn't seem as fair to some as others. I guess that's the point of the rankings and public vote aspect of the game.

"This means Tank will be facing off against Cartwell, and Jade will be taking on Nyxi. Paired by gender, how funny." She laughs to herself.

Jade sniggers next to me, acting like she has already won. I know she won't be an easy competitor, but she's smaller than me, so I have a slight advantage. I would much rather take her on than Tank, and I silently thank Theo for having my back.

"You are each allowed to pick one weapon of your choosing. Tank and Cartwell will go first, since Tank is our front runner."

My eyes scan the racks of weapons available for us to choose from. My mind flicks back to the weird sword hidden beneath my floorboard, as if it's calling my name. I shake it off and focus on what's provided.

Standing back, I wait to see what Jade chooses so I can make my decision based on her weapon. She drags her fingers over each blade and spike until they settle on a spiked hammer small enough for her to swing around easily.

Sauntering up to the weapons, Jade's shoulder bumps into mine as she passes me. Turning my head, I glare at her, and she just smiles back tauntingly.

"I hope you're counting down the last minutes of your life, *sweetie*," she spits viciously. "They won't even be able to recognize you after I'm done with you, just like that little boy you got killed. *Poof*, turned to dust." She pretends to blow smoke from her hand, and it takes everything in me to hold myself back, gritting my teeth and denying her the satisfaction. I know she's just trying to mess with my head, and I won't stoop to her level.

"Seems like everyone who struck an alliance with you is now *dead*, how fitting. You kill everything you touch, but you won't be killing me today." She sticks her fingers out, counting them down. "Hudson, Aeron, and sweet Rayah are all dead because of *you*," she seethes. "Fear not, though. Today is your end, and they will all cheer me on when I claim your last pathetic breath."

She mockingly pats my shoulder, then saunters away with a skip in her step and a gleam in her eyes.

Someone needs a snack.

Quickly, I reach up, plucking a simple dagger off the rack, my gut telling me to grab *something simple* and slip it into my boot. It's lightweight and easy to wield. I can use it like a small sword or throw it if necessary. It's short, so I'll have to get close to Jade if I want to use it, which is a slight disadvantage, but it's a much better choice than the awkward hammer she chose.

Lining back up, I notice Tank sporting no weapons as he slams his fists together, cracking his knuckles. His bleached hair shines bright under the sun, and his baby blues shine even brighter with malice. Next to him, Cartwell trembles subtly while white knuckling a long scythe almost as tall as him. I don't blame him for grabbing a massive, long weapon when he's up against a human who could be classified as a giant.

"Ladies and gentlemen, who's ready to see these competitors fight to the death?" the Empress bellows, throwing her arms out wide. The crowd's screams are deafening, making me flinch.

"As a reminder, the game will not finish until one competitor is left standing. There is no tapping out or ties. Today will prove who amongst you are the strongest and most deserving to ascend to the final round of the Crucible!"

Swooping her arm, the Empress points towards a small circle drawn in the sand, directly in the center of the Bubble. "Tank,

Cartwell, you're up first. Please step into the ring with your chosen weapon."

They both saunter forward, Tank looking excited and Cartwell looking sickly and petrified. Stepping into the tight circle, they turn to face each other.

"Up first, we have Tank from Sweat sector. His weapon of choice…" She trails off, not spotting any weapons in Tank's grasp. Tank lifts his fists, banging them down on his shirtless, tanned chest like an animal, making the Empress blink in shock. "It appears Tank will be utilizing his fists for weapons. Points for confidence, I guess," she mutters. "He will be facing off against Cartwell from Enlightened Sector. His weapon of choice, Scythe."

Turning, she whispers something to the Vanquisher who entered with Hade. He nods and steps up next to her, his hand raised in front of him. Red magic bursts from his hands, igniting the circle around my competitors until it bursts into flames. The flames lick up out of the sand in the perfect shape of a circle around them, growing a few feet off the ground, high enough not to step over but not tall enough to block our view.

My heart races at the new added element. There's no escaping this fight. You either fight, or you cower and burn. One way or another, only one person is stepping back out of that ring, and I'll be damned if this is how fate finally captures my soul. I'm too stubborn to die at the hands of an unworthy enemy.

Clearing her throat, the Empress says her final remarks. "The only rule of this game is there are no rules. Nothing is off the table. Nothing is considered cheating or dirty fighting. Do what you must to win, and most importantly, give us a good show." Smiling, she cups her hands, backing up to sit on her gaudy throne.

"Let the games begin," she shouts, and all hell breaks loose.

Charging forward, Tank slams his body into Cartwell's small frame, taking him by surprise. They both slam into the wall of fire, but neither falls through, a magical barrier holding them in.

Flames lick up the back of Cartwell's legs, making him scream out in agony as Tank holds his body against the fire with a wicked smile, thoroughly enjoying this.

Blowing his blue hair out of his chocolate eyes, Cartwell slams his scythe into Tank's toes with a crunch. Tank sputters, loosening his grip on Cartwell, who takes the chance to duck under his arm and run to the other side of the small ring.

Screaming, Tank turns with fury burning in his eyes. I don't see this going well for Cartwell, but maybe he can outsmart his way through this challenge.

Yelling a war cry, Cartwell charges forward, slashing his long scythe through the air with all his strength, aimed right at Tank's giant chest. The blade *whooshes*, but Tank side steps at the last second, slamming his elbow into the wooden snath, deflecting its course.

Tank lets out an angry grunt when the blade slices his upper arm instead, creating a sizable gash and drawing a steady stream of blood. Swiping his hand across the cut, he coats his hand in blood and rubs it between his palms, turning them both bright red. He swipes two fingers across each of his cheeks, marking himself in war paint.

Coated in his own blood with a promise of death on his face, he looks *terrifying*.

Defiantly, Cartwell lifts his scythe above his head, readying himself for a killing blow. He looks like he's expelling every bad thing that's ever happened to him and channeling it into this one, lifesaving blow.

Before he can swipe down with his blade, Tank's long arm whips out, gripping him tightly around his neck. Cartwell's once pale face instantly goes red, coughing for a sliver of air. Tank swings him around like a doll, slamming him into the wall of fire next to them.

Cartwell's body flings around like he has no bones, rattling him so hard, the scythe is knocked out of his grasp. His eyes go wide with realization.

The one thing giving him a chance of walking out of this alive is gone.

Cartwell thrashes in Tank's grip, but it only fuels him more. Clawing wildly, Cartwell attempts to pry Tank's giant hand from his throat, but Tank presses Cartwell further into the fire, making him scream in pain.

Bile rises in the back of my throat when the smell of burning flesh hits my nose. I gag, attempting to keep my breakfast down while watching the life snuff out of my competitor's eyes. Reality settles deep in his bones as he comes to terms with his outcome.

There's no way out of his life ending.

Blood drips from Tank's arms from deep gouges Catwell makes with his nails. Reaching back, Tank slams his fist into Cartwell's face with a loud *crunch* with an explosion of blood. Throwing him to the sand, Tank pounces on top of Cartwell, straddling his chest and holding him tightly between his large thighs.

Like a rabid animal, Tank's fists fly through the air, pummeling into Cartwell's face in a fury of lethal punches. Each punch makes his face a little less recognizable as blood coats his fists, his knuckles gliding across Cartwell's slick face with each jab.

Cartwell's body has long since stopped moving, but Tank continues his pursuit until one last, sickening crunch rings out, and Cartwell's skull finally fractures, caving his face into a flatten pile of bones and gore in the sand.

A silent sob escapes my throat at the same time as Jade hollers excitedly next to me, like this is all some fun game and not one human taking a life.

And just like that, it's over.

That painful realization has my reality sitting heavily in my chest.

Now, it's my turn.

"TANK! TANK! TANK! TANK!" the crowd chants in time to the beat of my racing heart. I'm sickened by their lack of compassion and humanity for this poor, lost soul.

Did Cartwell know this could very well be the outcome when entering the Crucible?

Yes.

Does that mean this gruesome and inhumane mutilation of his life should be celebrated?

No.

Gritting my teeth, I dig deep within myself to calm my racing thoughts. I block out the crowd. I wash away the pressure of staying alive for those I've met up here counting on my survival. I clear my mind of every life altering moment I've shared with Hade, because none of those matter if I lose today.

If I *die.*

I open my eyes when all the weight of the world is finally lifted from my shoulders, until all that's left is a deadly weapon forged from an unjust life. Now I'm a disease, planning on infecting anything in my path of seeking the justice not owed to me, but I will take forcefully anyways.

Because life is unfair, but…

I will *not* die today.

Today, I will be *reborn* in the blood of my enemies. May the gods send them right to Hade's doorstep in the afterlife so the ruining may continue for an eternity.

"Your first winner of today's game is…Tank from Sweat Sector."

The Empress strides over, grabbing his giant arm in her small grasp and raising it above her head, marking his victory. I spot an Illuminist walking around Cartwell's butchered and bloodied body, getting a closer look at all the gore to commit to memory and replay for the masses later.

Turning to face us, the Empress announces, "Jade. Nyxi. You're up. Give us your worst and try to make it longer than thirty seconds this time, for our sake." She gestures to a second circle marked in the sand next to the one Cartwell's dead body still lies in.

I step over the line of the ring, and instantly, my mind goes blissfully blank. There's nothing left inside but a blinding will to fight for my life. Squaring my shoulders, I lock eyes with Jade, and she laughs maniacally while swinging her hammer in a figure eight.

Taunting me.

Playing with her prey.

She will soon learn I'm no one's prey, least of all hers. Today, I'm the monster lurking below her bed in the shadows, ready to trap her in my jaws of death.

"Two Vagrants, fighting for the final spot in the final round of the Crucible. I have no doubt they will provide us with anything short of a vicious bloodbath." She laughs to herself wickedly, clapping her hands in enjoyment.

"Jade's weapon of choice, a spiked maul. Nyxi has chosen to wield a dagger," she recites plainly. "Ladies, as a reminder, there are no rules. Only one of you will step out of this ring."

The Empress' words are abruptly cut off by raging flames licking up from the sand, rising to just above my waist. The flames warm my skin through the black diamond bodysuit Des designed for me when I first arrived in Lunaria. It allows me to move around seamlessly like a second skin, providing extra protection against deep gashes on my limbs and lower torso, but my chest and head remain exposed for deadly blows.

Theo's dagger necklace burns blissfully in the secret pocket Des created, giving me the extra strength to get through today.

"BEGIN!" the Empress screams from the comfort of her throne.

Narrowing my eyes, I start to slowly circle Jade's small frame, who does the same in return. I've watched Jade over the weeks while she trains, taking note of her habits and weaknesses. She's a fierce competitor around my same age, and her size makes people underestimate her, which is her greatest strength. She's smart and calculated with her moves. She's fast and always prepared.

I've also noticed how she's right handed but is currently using her left to hold her hammer, leading me to believe she's injured on her right. She also has a habit of tapping her left foot before she attacks. It's so subtle, most competitors would miss the tell, but growing up being a spy has honed my skills for noticing and studying people's habits.

And just like that, a plan forms in my head with every way I can use her weaknesses to my advantage. Just as the thought settles, a welcoming pressure settles over my shoulders, draping behind my neck like a snake. To the naked eye, it may look like a shadow over me, but to me, it means *everything*.

Hade's magic rests supportively on my shoulders, creating a connection between us, letting me know he's here with me. He doesn't talk to me through it, knowing any distractions could mean sure death.

Jade continues to circle me, her blonde hair bobbing around. Her vicious green eyes zone in on me, the crowd growing louder and louder with each step we take. I spot her subtly rolling her right shoulder back in discomfort, and I smile to myself internally.

Flipping my dagger casually in my hand, I finally draw Jade's interest enough for her to think she can make a move. She attempts to catch me off guard as my hand goes to swipe my dagger, just like I hoped she would.

Checkmate.

She screams, charging me at full speed, her hammer outstretched. I wait for her to get close, letting her think she's got me beat. Using her signature move, she drops to one knee at the last second, swiping her hammer at my ankles.

I jump over her hammer easily, turning around swiftly as her momentum keeps her body falling forward, and slam the hilt of my dagger into her right shoulder. She lets out a muffled cry, caught by surprise, but she jumps up immediately, just as I suspected she would.

Jade is a fighter. Growing up in Vagrant, we learned to grow up and fend for ourselves at a young age. Vagrant toughens the weak and kills the inept. It feasts with an insatiable appetite, cleaning the streets of those who can't make a life within its belly.

I plan to slowly weaken and slow Jade before I attempt any killing blows. It's my best bet with an opponent as scrappy as her, who will just get more feisty the angrier she gets. I'm here to play the long game until she can no longer stand to make another move against me.

Then, I will claim my prey.

"That's all you got, *killer*?" Jade taunts while smiling through the pain in her shoulder that I know she's feeling heavily. "Did your small brain forget which end of the weapon you're supposed to wield?" she spits, full of venom.

I ignore her, tracking each of her movements and readying for another attack. On cue, she lunges forward, swinging her hammer while laughing like a lunatic. Abruptly, she latches her hands on each end of the long wooden handle, putting her arms straight out in front of her, aimed right at my neck, shoving me back towards the fire.

Ducking, I elbow her in the gut and slip under her shoulder at the last minute, making her buckle forward in pain. Her hands fall as she leans forward, letting out a hiss of pain when her knuckles connect with the fire in front of her.

I take the opportunity to rush her from behind while she's down. The demon inside her seeps out when she turns quickly on her heels, expecting my arrival, and I curse myself for falling into her trap. Before I can stop my momentum, the wind is knocked out of me from my side.

Jade looks at her hammer in confusion, likely wondering why none of the small spikes around the head drew any blood. My suit succeeded in keeping my skin intact, but it definitely didn't prevent the likely bruised or broken ribs from the impact of her swing.

Gritting my teeth, I hiss through my teeth, trying to catch my breath. Sharp pain explodes from my side each time I inhale. I push it down, forgotten and lost amongst the rest of the pain that brutalizes my body and soul daily. Squaring my stance, I bounce on the balls of my feet, hyped up on adrenaline and a life full of enough heartache to flood an overflowing reserve of burning vengeance.

"Maybe try swinging a little harder next time," I taunt, attempting to rattle her enough to force her into being sloppy and rushed. "I know you're used to making Tank do all your heavy lifting."

A spark ignites behind her eyes, and I watch the bomb explode within her, setting her in motion. I catch her left foot tap the smallest amount, and I ready myself for the incoming blow. A guttural scream rips from her throat, and she charges me with death in her gaze. She swings angrily at my head from the side, but I'm prepared for it.

I duck easily under her arm and quickly swipe my dagger across her stomach, aiming to maim but not kill. It rips through her shirt, creating a shallow incision a few inches across. Her white shirt turns a deep red, soaking up the blood running from her wound.

Swiveling on my heels, I spin in time to see the hatred dripping from her features. She ignores her wound altogether, squaring up against me once again.

I'll give her points for perseverance.

"You're a dead woman!" she screams. I smirk in return, tightening my grip on the handle of my dagger, never letting my eyes stray from hers.

"Show me your worst," I say, my tone low while I circle her again.

Nothing else exists in this moment. The crowd and chants melt away to a blur until all I see are her and the ruining about to take place.

I embrace it with welcome arms today.

I *thrive* in it.

Grunting, I lunge forward, launching us back into vicious combat. I swipe my dagger through the air, aimed at her face, but she uses the handle of her hammer to deflect it. I drop immediately, kicking out my foot and connecting with hers. She stumbles sideways, falling to her knees. Throwing my body, I knock her onto her back and jump on top of her. Her hammer is knocked from her hand and falls beside us. Seizing the opportunity, I swing my right fist, connecting with her face with a sickening *crunch*. She screams, wrapping both her hands around my neck, cutting my airways off.

Blood rushes to my head, turning me dizzy and disoriented; I lose my dagger in the sand next to us, so I resort to raining down blow after blow with my fists. Quickly, she turns into a bruised and bloody mess. Through it all, she never lets up on my throat, and I can feel myself growing weaker by the second as my punches slow in their assault.

One of Jade's hands slips from my throat, landing in the sand next to us, and I gasp my first deep breath. Prickling at the edge of my brain makes me *look left*, and just as I turn, I spot something moving through the air towards me.

I try to bring my hands up to protect my head, but I'm too late, only deflecting the blow slightly, just enough to make a difference. Jade's hammer connects with my head, knocking me sideways.

My brain rattles in my skull, but luckily, Jade's growing weakness meant the blow wasn't at her full strength.

Warm liquid drips down the side of my face while I gain my bearings. Before I can collect myself, Jade's face comes into view above me—she straddles me and presses the handle of her hammer against my throat, cutting off my airway once again.

I can already feel the bruises forming around my throat, and I wince as my eyes grow fuzzy. My bloodied hands claw desperately at the wooden handle, trying to pry it away for another breath.

Jade's bloodied smile and swollen, bruised eyes grow darker with each second she has me pinned below her, deprived of any air. My hands grow weaker until one falls slack next to my side. Finality flickers within Jade's eyes as she celebrates her impending win. I try to push through the pain and everything stacked against me, for Theo...for Hade. This is not how we meet again.

I won't allow it.

"*I believe in you*," Hade's strong voice whispers against my ear as the final moments of my life flicker by. A small light of hope illuminates deep within me, careening me towards my will to fight for my life until my very last breath.

I am Nyxi, born from Vagrant, rebirthed by survival, and I will not succumb to my enemies today.

I repeat the chant inside my head, growing louder each time until it's etched within my very fate, rewriting the stars depicting my life.

My hand connects with something smooth and cold buried in the sand next to me. That flicker of hope turns into a full-fledged fire raging beneath my skin, like a phoenix rising from the ashes of its enemies.

"This is more satisfying than I thought," Jade grunts above me, bloodied spit flying from her mouth. She looks like a rabid beast plaguing the lands and feasting on lost souls.

She is everything I stand against.

She is everything I wish to eradicate from this world.

She is first on my hit list of purging all evil from this world.

"Hey, Jade?" I choke out between strangled breaths. "Say hi to Aeron for me."

I plunge my dagger deep into the side of her neck, all the way to the hilt in one final, killing blow. Life drains from her eyes above me, a ghostly look taking over her features. Shock is frozen on her face, permanently etching her haunted look into my memory forever. She chokes on blood, making a gurgling noise as blood sprays from her mouth.

I rip my dagger from her throat, and her lifeless body falls on top of me, trapping me below her. I draw my first full breath into my lungs, over and over again until I'm hyperventilating.

I *killed* her.

My weak arms try to shove her deadweight off me frantically as my breaths get louder and choppier. Sickness takes over my stomach, and I dry heave between frantic breaths.

"Breathe, Nyxi," Hade whispers against the side of my face, gently pushing Jade off me. "You did good."

The weight of her body off mine feels like a slice of heaven for the briefest moment before reality comes tumbling back at me in full force.

"I killed her," I choke quietly.

He reaches out, pressing his thumb against the pulse of my neck, reassuring himself I'm still alive, a habit I've noticed of his. "You did what you needed to *survive*," he says calmly, reassuringly.

I nod numbly, my breaths now almost calm. The adrenaline of the fight floats away, leaving me hollow and aching. I slowly stand, my eyes never blinking as Hade lets me lean on him for support.

My face, a mask of indifference.

My soul, a swirling mixture of every emotion.

My body, still *alive*.

"What a wonderful performance!" the Empress's shrill voice registers somewhere in the distance, but I'm checked out. "There you have it. Our second and final contestant moving on to the final round of the Crucible. Nyxi from Vagrant Sector," she chants.

I barely register my hand being raised for me above my head in victory, as life is playing out in slow motion. Taunting laughter and chants come in and out of my hearing like blips in time. My body shakes slightly as I stare with blurred vision at nothing in particular, the world becoming one large blob in front of me.

I have no idea how long I stand there, not until a familiar rough hand clasps around mine, gently pulling me into their side. I go willingly, like an animal being led around by its master. Smoke and sandalwood wrap around me in a comforting blanket, and I sigh heavily as I'm led back to the castle.

I *survived* another day.

I just had to bargain my soul in the process.

Chapter
Forty

"Let me help you," Hade says softly next to me.

I'm fumbling with my bodysuit, trying to rip it from my skin but failing miserably. My arms feel lead filled as I try to get my blood-soaked clothes as far away from me as possible. Each wet piece touching me feels like a brand of sin against my cold flesh.

My arms fall for the fourth time before I give up and let Hade take over for me. He gently drags the zipper farther down my chest, slipping one arm out at a time for me. Kneeling, he slowly drags the suit down my torso, revealing my black lace undergarments beneath.

His touch is soft, respectful and precise. Skillfully, he drags the material down each leg, bunching it as he goes, and then slips each foot out until I'm barely covered before him. My eyes are zoned out on the wall in front of me, shock holding a firm grip over my body.

A soft touch to the side of my head breaks my trancelike state. Blinking a few times, I turn my neck to look at Hade prodding my head for injuries. Pain registers where he presses, but I remain still, letting it consume me. I use it as a reminder that I'm still alive.

"You have a nasty laceration on the side of your head, and between the bruising on your ribs and your shallow breathing, I assume you could have a broken rib or two," he says while looking me over. "I've already called for a healer, and they should be here soon. Let's get you cleaned up before they get here."

Scooping me up, he walks me to the ensuite washroom and gently plops me down in the bath already full of steaming and bubbly water. It's only now I register he brought me to his room and not my own.

I zone out as he washes my body, scrubbing all the blood and dirt from my skin. Unfortunately, no amount of scrubbing could clean my soul of today's events. I relax back, letting him take care of me while my mind swirls like a vortex of survival and disgust.

Two wet hands grip my cheeks, dragging my face up to look at him. His scar glows in the dim lighting, and my eyes trace the jagged white line through his glowing eye from his temple across to his nose. I yearn to drag my finger across it, my pain calling to his, but I remain relaxed as I take him and all his lethal beauty in.

"Jade's death is not on your hands. She chose to enter this game, and fate finally caught up to her." He gently presses a kiss to my forehead, so at odds with his serious tone. "Do you understand me?" he whispers against my flesh.

I nod slowly in response before Jade's lifeless eyes flicker back in my memory, making me tense in his hold.

"I keep seeing her face every time I close my eyes," I admit defeatedly. "I see my dagger in the side of her neck and then her lifeless eyes staring back at me." I choke the words. "I know I should be happy I beat her. I know she would have enjoyed seeing the light leave my eyes. But no matter how many times I try to remind myself of those things, I can't shake the uncomfortable feeling just beneath my skin. I cannot scrub away the blood I can no longer see on my skin but still feel all the same."

"That is your humanity, love," he says with a soft smile. He reaches forward, placing his palm on my skin just over my heart. "It may feel like a curse to harbor a bleeding heart, but to me, it just proves how nothing in this world could ever compare to the beauty you radiate." Stroking his thumb across my flesh, he adds, "I fear too much time around you will eventually make me go blind from the radiance you exuberate."

My breath hitches in my throat at his unguarded words. I mull them over in my head, committing them to memory and easing my heart slightly.

I look up at him as he continues to wash me of my sins. "How come you don't call me nightmare anymore?"

Smiling down at me with the most genuine smile I've ever seen from him, he responds, "Because you're more of a *dream* now."

Hade finished washing me just before the healer arrived. Trina, the healer who worked on me before, quickly mended my head and ribs with her magic while Hade watched. Of course Hade would order one of the best healers in Lunaria to tend to my wounds. It seems this man has no bounds or limits when it comes to me.

After finishing, Trina ordered me to take it easy for a couple days but informed me I should be good as new thanks to her magic. I can't imagine the things she's seen and had to heal. It must feel good to have magic that can make such a difference.

My thoughts wander to all the possibilities of the magic I could possess if I win the Crucible. I honestly haven't taken a second to even think about the possibility of wielding magic. My sole focus has been on getting through each day at a time.

The thought of that leaves an uncomfortable feeling under my skin as I look over at Hade in conversation with Trina. He knows nothing of the reason I entered myself in the Crucible, and to my surprise, he's never asked. It feels wrong to keep my motives to myself at this point, and if I can truly trust him with my secret like I think I can, then maybe he can help me.

Hade escorts Trina out his door then strides back to me while I stand next to his floating bed in one of his oversized t-shirts, nervously spinning my thumbs. Brushing past me, he pulls back his sheets and gestures for me to get in.

"You can sleep here tonight," he says, patting the bed behind me. I jump in without hesitation, sinking into the abundance of giant fluffy pillows against the headboard. "I'll just be right over there in my chair if you need anything," he says before swiveling on his heels.

I quickly reach out, snagging his wrist before he can walk away. "Stay with me," I whisper, an invitation floating between us. He just nods, dragging my hand up to place a soft kiss to my knuckles.

The floating bed dips slightly, bouncing softly after he slides in on the other side. There's almost a full person's length between us in his giant bed. Slowly, I inch closer to him, seeking out his warmth and comfort. Before I realize how far I've scooted, I'm nuzzled up against him. He happily scoops me under his arm and draws me into his warm body.

Melting into him, I tentatively rest my hand on his bare chest, lazily tracing circles on his skin. Chewing my lip, I finally gather my nerves to speak.

"I have to get something off my chest," I admit.

"It would be my honor to burden the weight for you, dream," he responds without hesitation. His hand connects with mine on his chest, weaving our fingers together like they yearned to touch me. His thumb lazily strokes the soft skin on top of my hand.

"How come you've never asked me why I entered the Crucible?" I ask softly.

He hums to himself and then answers honestly. "It is none of my business, and I figured when you were ready to tell me, you would. I will never pressure you to tell me things you aren't ready to share, Nyxi."

My heart swells in my chest, the warmth spreading throughout my body like a blanket until it reaches the tips of my toes and fingers. I hum to myself happily at his response and then carry on.

"I guess I'm ready to tell you." I respond in a sure tone.

"I'm all ears," he replies and gives me a quick, reassuring squeeze.

"Theo," I blurt, trying to decide exactly how to inform Hade of everything. He remains quiet, allowing me to sort through my thoughts. If I were a boat freely floating about a choppy ocean, Hade would be my anchor, allowing me to find solid ground and stability.

"When he died," I continue, "I made a promise to myself that I would do anything to extract my revenge. I feel so guilty for not being there to protect him when he most needed it after years of him protecting me."

Hade nods in understanding, a story written behind his eyes of similar pain and guilt, two souls forged from pain seeing eye to eye in familiarity.

"Rouge Necroshrieks are known to plague the skies of Vagrant Sector frequently. They mostly just like to taunt and scare us, but sometimes, they liked to take a life or two of stray drunks or abandoned children." Choking on my words, I continue with pain laced in each word, painting them into existence. "I've never seen such violence and destruction from one of them, not like what occurred that day. The day Theo died," I say defeatedly.

I spot Hade's jaw hardening through my watery eyes as I fight to keep my tears from spilling down my face.

"It was pure chaos. Shattered windows. People screaming and running for their lives. Kids getting trampled by the masses. Gore and madness every turn I took. It was sickening, and deep down in my gut, I knew something was wrong. I raced home as fast as I could, but it wasn't enough."

Pausing to catch my breath and calm my heart, I finally say the words aloud.

"I found him dead and unrecognizably battered, sitting in our house, clutching a pail of purple paint he had been out fetching for *me*. I'd been begging him for so long to paint the house a pathetically bright purple, just to see if he would agree. I made a promise that day to myself: I would do everything in my power to make it up here and get justice for what happened to him."

Sobs finally take over, letting my tears run free and purging my heartache out with them. Guilt vibrates through my body as I'm taken back to that day. The what ifs circle my mind like a never-ending tornado. If he hadn't been out getting the paint I begged of him daily, would he still be alive? If I had not lounged about my work that day and had gotten home sooner, could I have saved him?

The *unknown* is one of the most dangerous drugs in existence. Its addictive quality sinks its fangs far under your skin, becoming a permanent limb for eternity. It eats away at someone until they are left hollow, down to just their bones.

The unknown is a sickness, the only disease in the world with no a cure. It's mind numbing and life altering, and it takes and takes until it drives someone to insanity.

The unknown was my *undoing*.

It changed me chemically and spit me out something completely different.

"I am so sorry, Nyxi," Hade says sincerely, pulling me from my swirling thoughts. He leans up on his elbow so he can look down at me with his full, undivided attention.

"What happened that day is unacceptable, and I'm ashamed it occurred under my watch without my knowledge." Resting his hand on my cheek, he pleads, "You have my word that I will personally speak with every Vanquisher under my guard and make sure they know an attack on any sector will be punishable by death. And once you win this competition, I will help you find who's responsible, and you will get the justice that's due."

My lip trembles at his promise, a small whimper escaping my throat with all the emotions racking my body. I may not have been able to save Theo, but by talking to Hade, I may have just saved someone else's Theo.

His death was not for nothing. My sweet Theo, always saving others, even in death.

"Thank you," I whisper, pushing my cheek further into his warm palm. A tear slowly falls down my cheek, but Hade scoops it up with his finger, wiping it away and all the pain that came with it.

Hade, the man I never knew I needed but quickly learned I couldn't live without. He's no longer Hade to me. No, now, he's my *home*.

I ponder one last thought and decide now is the time to ask. "Are you bonded to a Necroshriek?" I ask him hesitantly.

He nibbles his lip, lost in thought before settling on his words. "I am…or was. My bonded is retired, so to speak. We are still connected, but I have not tugged on that thread in a long time. My Necroshriek grew unwell in her head, and I thought it was best to relinquish her of her duty."

He speaks so intimately about the beast, as if they have thoughts and feelings. I'm curious to ask more, but exhaustion is coming for me with a tight grip as I let out a loud yawn.

Wiping the last of my tears away, Hade settles back into bed next to me and draws me into his embrace, making sure every inch of his skin makes contact with mine, letting me know he's here with me, like always.

I feared after losing Theo, no other soul would ever truly know me. I think Hade understood me from the second we laid eyes on each other. Not every fact about me, but the essence of what makes me, me.

The pain. The heartache. The need to fight for survival every single day to keep the darkness at bay.

Two of the same, separated by air alone.

Hade feels like looking into a mirror and seeing your reflection staring back at you. Every piece of darkness reflected in the same places. Every scar perfectly depicted. Every flaw laid bare before my eyes like a badge instead of dishonor.

I like me when I'm around him.

I feel *seen*.

"Have you ever heard the term *eternals*?" I ask the last question sitting in the back of my brain since reading about it for the first time. It's been like a nagging feeling constantly sitting on my shoulders. I've never heard of such a thing in Fallout, but we know little about Lunaria and the Magicals who live here.

His face goes unnaturally pale for the briefest second, but then he clears his throat and gives me an unconvincing smile.

"Yes," he responds quietly.

"Do you believe in it?"

"Yes," he replies quietly, lost in his beautiful head.

I think over his response, an abundance of questions flicking to the end of my tongue, but one outweighs the rest.

"Do you think you have an eternal out there somewhere?" I phrase the words hesitantly.

"Having an eternal is the greatest honor one could receive," is all he says before tucking my head under his chin and pulling me closer. "Goodnight, *dream*."

Chapter
Forty-One

"MORE!" HADE GRUNTS FROM ABOVE ME. I'M PANTING LIKE A DOG IN heat, squirming under his hard body pinning me down.

"Do you have to be so rough?" I force out between harsh breaths.

"You like it when I'm rough," he says, his tone low.

He's right…I do, but goddamn, I don't know how much more my weak body can take. I feel like I've been run through by a horse. And not just any horse—the biggest, baddest horse you could find, then double it. He's just so…big. I honestly don't know why I thought I could handle him. Leave it to my giant ego to bite off more than she can take.

"Maybe I don't want you to be rough right now?"

"Where's the fun in that?" he quips back, lightning fast as he presses down harder into my body.

I think I'm going to have a rash on my back from his body grinding into mine for the past hour. He's a beast, truly. It's unfair how he never tires while I'm lying like a ragdoll under him. If there are any gods out there, I'm begging for mercy.

"Think you can take more?" Hade grunts from above me. The ends of his long dark curls are soaked with sweat, and his skin sparkles with a light sheen. Damn him for looking so sexy right now.

"You're just so...big!" I wheeze out while shoving my body into his. Smirking down at me, he applies more pressure, which has me screaming. "Fuck, Hade!" My body tenses under him until it's too much to take.

"Mercy!" I scream, tapping his shoulder desperately. Hade lets out a satisfied moan before sliding off my body and falling next to me in a pile of limp limbs.

Breathlessly, he sighs. "That was—"

"Awful," I reply, cutting him off.

He chuckles, his deep, rumbly tenor making my insides flip. "I was going to say exhilarating, but I guess I wasn't the one who just got their ass beat in sparring."

His face is so smug, I want to wipe his shit-eating grin from existence. The more I stare at him, though, with how the sun makes his beautifully sculpted body glow, other thoughts start to circle my mind, and none of them originate from my brain...

Why does he have to be so captivating? He's like an addiction. I'm okay being hooked on this drug for the rest of my life, though. I will avoid all interventions held in my honor. I plan to ride this addiction to the grave.

Dragging myself up to sit, I rest my elbows on my knees, attempting to catch my breath after putting my body through the ringer for the past hour. Hade has never been one to go easy on me, and I'm grateful for that. He knows it will only hinder instead of help me.

Don't get me wrong, I would rather not collect the bruises and aching limbs, but each time we spar, I get a little stronger and learn a new technique that could potentially save my life. It's a fair trade off.

Do I wish my body was being pushed to its limits under different circumstances? I mean, a girl has needs, but honestly, no. I cherish the time I get to spend in the sand, letting the darkness flow through my limbs, purging the toxins beneath my skin.

It feels good to hold my own against him. It feels good to take back power over my life. It feels good to *feel* again.

Sometimes, we talk while we spar, giving each other tips or praises, and other times, we talk with only our bodies. No words, just silence and our pain being forced from our beings with each jab or punch we make.

Healing the hurt, that's what we do.

Hade knocks his shoulder into mine. "You did good today."

"That's not what I would call it, but I'll take the compliment all the same. I'm a greedy bitch, it seems."

"You should be proud of yourself," he responds earnestly. "You held your own, even had me pinned a few times. I wasn't making it easy on you. I've been training my entire life, and I'm easily double your size." He says the last part with a smirk, and I slam my shoulder into his, knocking him off balance. I laugh and go to help him up, but he grabs my wrist and pulls me down onto him, our chests crashing together in the sand.

Time slows for a second as I study the man under me who only weeks ago was a stranger. An enemy. Now, he's carved his name into my heart with a branding iron, burning me thoroughly in the process. But nothing worth having in life is ever painless.

I like the pain he's brought. It compliments my own.

Catching his glimmering eyes, I smirk down at him and playfully flick the tip of his nose. He laughs, a deep, toe curling sound that has my insides purring. He lashes out, grasping the side of my neck, slightly pressing into the side of my throat. His thumb indents right above my pulse point, where a steady beat calls back to him.

Smiling to himself, he whispers under his breath, "Alive."

"Alive," I breathe back, throwing him a wink in return.

As he licks his lips, his eyes slightly darken. The light one turns an ashy gray, the black one almost disappearing completely. His hand travels from my neck over to my lips, dragging his thumb across them, making the lower one pop out.

Licking my lips, I lean down, slowly hovering my mouth directly above his, sharing breath. His hand travels to the back of my neck, slightly tightening. I throw him a wicked look, leaning in the rest of the way until our lips are barely pressed together. His smile falters when he feels the pressure of something cold and sharp against his throat.

Pressing my dagger lightly against his skin, I shoot him another wink. "What was it you told me before? Never underestimate an opponent?"

He grumbles to himself, but he can't hold back the smile that replaces his grouchy tendencies. "The fight was over," he mumbles, lifting his hand to envelope mine wrapped around the dagger pressed to him.

I innocently bat my eyelashes at him. "I have no idea what you're talking about."

"I seem to recall you were the one yelling 'mercy' and begging for it to be over."

Raising an eyebrow at him, I pretend to ponder his words. "Hmmm, nope. I don't recall saying that."

"Then you said I was the strongest male in Lunaria, and you could never compete against my giant muscles and striking features that steal your breath away every time you look at me."

I gasp dramatically, followed by a small giggle. "I most definitely *never* said that."

Quicker than I expected, he rips the dagger from my hand, launching it across the sand before flipping us over so he's straddling me. Gripping my face in both his hands, he forcefully crashes his lips to mine in a pleasant surprise.

Pulling away just as fast, he smiles down at me, and my heart warms with the taste of him lingering on my lips, adding to my addiction. I can't help the blush that creeps up my throat. This man never ceases to make my body react to him.

"I'm taking you out tonight," he states abruptly.

I look up at him, confused, but he shoots me a look that says *don't ask questions, just go with it.* I nod, which satisfies him as he drags me up to stand.

"I have some business to tend to first, so I'll come grab you after dinner. Winston will escort you in my absence."

"DES, I THINK I MIGHT BE HAVING A PANIC ATTACK," I HUFF WHILE throwing yet another pair of pants in a pile on my bed. It's slowly growing over her body as she reads Theo's journal. "Are you even listening to me?" I whine.

Snapping the journal shut, she gives me the stink eye. "You seem to be breathing just fine, sparkles, and you're digging into my hopeless romantic reading time."

Closing my eyes, I grip my throat, pretending to choke, and she huffs loudly in response. "I'm." *Cough.* "Not." *Cough.* "Fine." Peeling one eye open, I spot an unimpressed Des glaring at me. "I need your help," I plead. "That's what friends do. They help each other when they are in need instead of snooping in private journals."

Rolling her eyes, she pins be with a glare. "I did help you. Five times, to be exact, and you shot down every outfit I picked for you. You're *impossible* to please."

Wincing, I try to come up with a reasonable response. "They—they just didn't feel...*right*," I drag out while nervously nibbling my nails.

"You're overthinking it," she says plainly. "You are the main accessory, not the clothes. They are just there to enhance you." Pausing, she asks, "What exactly were his words again?"

"He said, 'I'm taking you out tonight.'" I do my best to impersonate his deep voice. "And then he mentioned he would grab me after dinner."

"Well, that's not much to go off. We'll have to work on his communication skills for the future. He's not taking you to dinner, so I'm sure what he has planned is more casual."

"Casual," I repeat.

Looking through the growing pile of clothes on my bed, the five outfits Des picked out included, she drags her arm out, scooping the clothes up and throwing them off the edge onto the floor.

Clapping her hands together, she sighs. "You're right. None of those were it."

I can't help the laugh that explodes from my throat at the ridiculousness of this whole thing. Des joins in on my laughter and playfully bumps her shoulder into mine. "I'm overthinking it, aren't I?"

"Maybe," she says in a high pitched tone. "But...that just means you care...a lot," she adds.

I do. I care a lot, for some reason unbeknownst to me. This feels important, like a change in the tides between me and Hade. We've spent plenty of time together in the library or sparring in the Bubble, but this feels *different*.

"Butter me up and call me a biscuit! I have the perfect idea!" Des shouts so loud, it feels like talons dragging down my insides. Covering my ears, I shoot her wide eyes, urging her to explain herself while protecting my ears from further hearing loss.

Shoving herself into my armoire, she practically disappears into the clothes as she rummages around in the back. Clothes go flying as she digs for the perfect piece. I narrowly dodge a shoe she blindly hucks over her shoulder, and it bangs loudly against the wall behind me.

"Watch it," I warn, but there's no malice behind my tone.

"No time!" she shouts back, but it's muffled by all the clothes swallowing her body. "C'mon, I know you're in here," she mumbles to herself. "Holy Aunt Susan, I found it!" she screeches excitedly while backpedaling out of the chaos she created.

Huffing and with reddened cheeks, she shoves her arms out in front of her, presenting me her treasure.

"What..." I stare in both disbelief and shock. I don't understand how this could be possible.

"Theo's leather jacket!" Des confirms with a smile.

"I don't understand?"

"I didn't need his entire jacket to make your dress for the ball since it was so oversized. I knew I could just chop some off the bottom and still have plenty left over for you to keep. I cropped it so it will fit your frame now and maybe added a few things to give it character." Shrugging, she adds, "I honestly totally forgot about it until now, or I would have given it to you sooner."

Rushing forward, I throw my body into hers, enveloping her in a giant hug. She chirps excitedly in my arms like a bird, loving the attention, as always.

Stepping back, I take the jacket and look it over, rubbing the soft leather between my fingers. "I love it, Des. It's perfect, thank you!"

It truly is a work of art, and getting to keep a part of Theo makes it even more special. I was okay with her cutting his jacket to make a beautiful dress for me, but now, I realize how much I've missed having it.

With the bottom trimmed, it falls perfectly at my hips, with little black diamonds sewn across the hem. Des' signature flare, I've decided. The sleeves are cuffed and sewn in place, more black diamonds rimming the edges. She's lined the inside with a black fleece that goes all the way up to the collar folded at the top. It's finished off with a dagger made of diamonds sewn down the center of the back, in honor of the dagger I wear around my neck.

Sliding it on, I look at my reflection in the mirror while spinning, devouring every inch. It fits perfectly and allows me to move around without feeling restricted.

"I just knew it!" Des beams beside me. "This is definitely what you're wearing."

Sifting through the piles of clothes scattered throughout the room, she pulls out a pair of black flare pants to pair with the jacket, a simple white tank, and black boots. After getting dressed, she twists back my front two curls, joining them in the back and tying them off. We both decide against any makeup, comfortable with my natural features and freckles.

Just when I finish getting ready, a knock sounds on my door, and my nerves decide to make an appearance. Striding over, I open the door and come face to face with a very casual looking, but still just as handsome, Hade.

"*Ready?*"

Chapter
Forty-Two

"Chug! Chug! Chug! Chug!"

Well, Des was right. This is definitely…casual. Hade pushes me along with his hand on the small of my back towards a rugged looking, but very lively, tavern nestled in the heart of the city. The night sky casts a blanket of shadow across the tops of the unique buildings in contrast to the bright light and rowdy cheers streaming through the front window.

"The Hammered Nail…" I read aloud from the rusted sign literally hammered with a single nail into the crooked wooden door.

"I promise, you will love it," Hade reassures me. "She may not be the prettiest tavern in Lunaria, but she provides the liveliest company and best tasting ale." Pausing, Hade scratches the side of his head while wrinkling his nose. "Scratch that last part. The ale tastes like piss, but for some reason, we always come back for more…so that has to count for something."

Laughing, I nod and usher him to take the lead. "Well then, let's go drink some *pale!*" He looks at me confused, and I can't help the small giggle that escapes at how adorable he looks like this, relaxed and *living*. "Piss ale…*pale*," I repeat, shrugging.

His confused face morphs into amusement, and his shoulders start the hike up in a deep, warm chuckle. "I can't wait to tell the others, especially *Harry!*"

"Harry?"

"You'll see." He throws me a wink and strides towards the door, stopping briefly to drag his palm across the top of a tall, deep blue crystalized rock plopped next to the door. The top looks worn down where his hand touches compared to the shiny lower half.

"Why did you do that?" He looks over his shoulder, and I point to the oddly placed rock to his right.

"It's tradition to touch it before entering the tavern," he says casually. "I honestly didn't even realize I did it; it's just second nature now. The rock was here before they built. They tried to move it, but it seems to be spelled in place. There's an old wise tale that it brings good luck if you touch it. That's why the top is rubbed away. It seems everyone is in need of some good luck these days."

Hade throws open the door, and I quickly rush behind him, throwing my hand out to drag across the so-called "good luck rock", which sends a tingle over my hand before I step in after him.

Cheers assault my ears as I follow directly behind Hade, weaving through the giant mass of citizens filling every inch of the tavern. My shoe squelches when I try to take a step from sticky ale holding it hostage. A bead of sweat forms on my forehead from the heat enveloping me. If I could assign one word to this tavern, it would be *alive*.

An older man bumps into me from the side, making me lose sight of Hade for a moment before a hand reaches back through a group of people, gripping my arm and pulling me through until my chest crashes into his. He smirks before pulling me along behind him to the bar counter nestled in the back.

An older lady stands behind the counter, filling five mugs full of ale until foam sloshes over the edges. Without looking, she floats all five down the length of the bar with her magic to a group of men sitting at the end, who salute her in thanks.

Hade whistles, getting her attention, and throws up two fingers to her. She rolls her dark blue eyes but grabs two mugs with her leathery tan hands, filling them up extra full and slamming them down in front of us.

"There you go, asshole," she grumbles under her breath, making her short white hair swoosh across the tops of her shoulders. It's then I notice her shirt, "Pour Decisions Only" stitched into it.

"Thanks, old bitch," he responds.

I suck in a breath, looking back and forth between the two, ready for a fist fight. They scowl at each other like it's some competition, and right as I'm about to leap in between them, they double over laughing the way old friends would.

"Haven't seen you around here in a while, old fart."

"I got tired of looking at your crusty face," he banters back with a smirk.

Reaching over the bar, she tugs the neck of Hade's shirt, dragging his face down while digging her knuckles into his hair as if he's a child she's scolding. He could easily pull out of her grasp, but he lets her have her fun, laughing the entire time.

It's mesmerizing seeing him like this, relaxed and in his element. He has a whole life outside of being the Cardinal. Out here, he gets to be *Hade*.

Smiling to myself, I grab one of the mugs and take a big swig of ale. As soon as it hits my tongue, without thought, I spray it out of my mouth all over the countertop and quickly cover my mouth with my hands in shock.

"Holy shit, that tastes worse than piss!"

Hade looks utterly amused beside me, picking up his mug and downing half of it in one swig. He winces slightly as it glides down his throat, and then he throws the barmaid a thumbs up.

"The tavern should be named pale, not The Hammered Nail." I wheeze, trying to scrape the remaining sour taste of ale from my tongue with my teeth.

"Pale?" the barmaid questions.

Nodding, I shrug. "Pale, short for piss ale." Hade winces beside me, and I grow concerned.

"Why are you making that face? I'm Nyxi, by the way." Reaching over the counter, I shake the barmaid's hand.

"Harry," she responds with a wicked smile. "Short for Harriet," she adds with a wink.

My smile immediately drops.

This is why you have no friends, Nyxi.

"Harry owns this tavern and even brews the ale herself!" Hade says excitedly. I want to crumble into myself and disappear from Lunaria forever.

"It's delicious," I shout, too high pitched, with a smile that isn't convincing. "Award winning, even." I tack on for good measure.

"Don't lie to my face, kid." She scowls.

I'm in deep shit, so I might as well stand in said deep shit with dignity. Sighing, I look her dead in the eyes. "That's the worst thing I've ever tasted, Harry. I'm pretty sure I got a chunk of mold in my gulp, I won't lie to you."

I hold my breath for the colorful words and maybe fists flying at me. Bracing my core and closing my eyes, knowing I deserve every moment of what's to come. A deep earthy cackle unlike anything I've ever heard has me slowly peeling one of my eyes open. Harry's cheeks are bright red, and she's laughing so hard, her large breasts are bouncing with each gritty laugh.

"I like her," she shouts over to Hade, and what looks like… pride shines back in his warm eyes to her. That can't be right… can it?

Looking back to me, she shoots me a smirk. "I know the shit tastes nasty. I won't even touch the stuff myself, honestly, but it's cheap, so the tavern stays packed wall to wall every night, and that's all I could ever wish for in life."

I nod in understanding, a genuine smile forming on my lips. This place is her home, and seeing all the happy smiling faces around me, I can tell this is a home for a lot of people.

It's a refuge for the lost and broken.

Hade slides a generous amount of coppers her way, clearly more than the two ales cost, and she places her hand over his, giving it a firm squeeze. They share a moment in silence, and I sit back in fascination. Each new layer I peel back of Hade only cuts the fissure in my heart a little deeper with the imprint of his soul marred across mine.

She mouths thank you to him and then throws her finger up, pointing to the opposite side of the tavern in the corner. "The animals are over there, playing Jezzle." Hade dips his head in thanks and then grips his ale in one hand and my hand in his other, whisking me away through the overpacked crowd.

"BULLSHIT!" A woman slams her fists down on the table, making it rattle.

"Sorry, *darlin'*, the Jezzle gods just love me more it seems."

"You have to be cheating. That's like four wins in a row." She scowls.

He shrugs. "Six, actually, but who's counting?"

Huffing, the woman swiftly gets up, her empty mug in hand, and vanishes in the growing crowd.

"*Women,*" he jokes to himself while blowing out a puff of air.

"Women what…?" I question boldly, stepping up to the table with raised brows. Hade chokes next to me, biting his fist, clearly amused and ready to see what unfolds next.

"Are the greatest gift from the gods." The words effortlessly roll off his tongue, and I have to give the man some credit for the balls to not even flinch or stutter before me. As I take him in further, a sense of familiarity falls over me. I realize I've seen this man before. A pang of sadness washes over me, but I force it back down, not wanting to ruin the night.

A night of living.

He was the Vanquisher tasked to watch over Rayah, my little ball of *sunshine*.

Taking a deep breath, I silently mourn a lost friendship that hadn't even really bloomed yet, still growth and nourishing, ripped too soon from the soil giving it life. I mourn the memories that hadn't come yet. I mourn the face of perseverance in its rawest and strongest form. I mourn the girl who just wanted to be seen and loved for what she was. I mourn for the change she represent-ed. I mourn for myself in losing another precious thing.

I file it all away, and a sense of calm seeps deep within me, knowing she would want me to keep moving, keep living in her honor.

"Zale," he announces, reaching over to grab my hand, placing a soft kiss atop my knuckles. His thick, light blonde curls fall over his brows as he dips forward. Freckles dot his nose and cheekbones subtly, and his sky blue eyes pin me in place.

"Nyxi," I mumble back, quickly pulling my hand away. "I call next game," I say in a tone that brokers no room for argument.

His eyebrows shoot up in surprise and amusement at the same time Hade's deep chuckle crawls up my back. "Do you even know how to play Jezzle?" he questions curiously, but not in a rude manner.

Shrugging, I respond casually. "No, but if you can win six times in a row, it can't be too hard, can it? You can teach me the rules, and then I'll beat your ass. Simple as that."

An infectious smile grows across his face, and he points to the empty chair across from him for me to join. A few others sit around the sides of the table, clearly here with the group, all offering me inviting smiles.

"It would be my pleasure, *darlin'*," he coos.

A pair of dice sit on the table between us, but no board or cards are present. Looking over the dice more closely, I notice they are not matching. Both are six sided, but while one has the numbers one through six etched on it, the other has different symbols.

Casually leaning back in my chair, I kick my feet up on the edge of the table and plant my hands in my lap, giving him my undivided attention. "I'm all ears, *darlin'*," I sing back. A slight blush rises to his cheeks, clearly thrown off by my boldness, but his pearly whites gleam back at me in challenge.

He lays out the rules, which are simple enough to follow. The numbered die is rolled first to decide how many rounds will need to be won by a player for the game to be over. Once a number is decided, we each take turns rolling the Jezzle die etched with symbols. Each player gets one roll per round, and whatever symbol it lands on is the decided power for that player to use during that single round against their opponent's magic.

There's a hierarchy to each of the six powers, which he explains in detail. "This die here is where the magic happens...literally." He shoots me an excited zap of energy with his eyes, and my skin prickles with anticipation.

Turning the die, he taps the first face, showing off the symbol. "Sitting at the bottom of the totem pole is the Pegasus, representing Air magic. She's cute, but she can't really cause much damage." Rotating the die, he points to the second face. "Octopus for

Shapeshifting magic, obviously. Still a great power to have, but weak compared to the others in deadliness."

Flipping the die again, he points to two squiggles carved deep within the face. "Eels for Electricity magic. May hurt like a bitch but still survivable. Dragon for Fire magic, and that most definitely *can* kill you. Sea Snakes for Poison manipulation magic. A couple drops of that stuff, and you're a goner." He rotates the die to the very last face and shoots Hade a knowing smirk, which I track over to his red growing face before I slide my eyes back to the die. "And the last, and, for obvious reasons, most deadly of them all...The Grim Reaper to symbolize Death magic."

Heat rises to my cheeks at the memory of that exact magic exploring my body like something worth worshipping. Tilting my head to the side, I try and fail to hide what those two words are doing to my body. Clearing my throat, I drop my feet to the ground and plant my elbows on the sticky table.

"So, I just need to roll a power greater than the one you roll, and I win that round?" Sounds like this game is very much luck based. It almost sounds like a glorified game of rock paper scissors, if you ask me.

"Precisely, but there's a little more to it than that."

"Do tell, because so far, it sounds like you've gloated about being *lucky* six times instead of actually winning due to any sort of skills you may possess."

His warm chuckle bounces across the table over to me, and I can't help the sly smirk I throw back. "If it was all luck, I would have ran out by now. Seeing as I'm undefeated, that seems unlikely. The dice just love me."

Scoffing, I pin him with my stare. "You act as if the dice talk to you."

His smile unnerves me. "*They do.*"

I stare at him, waiting for everyone at the table to laugh at his absurdity, but the table stays silent. "Are you trying to tell me you have voices in your head, *Zale*? Because if that's the case, I happen to know one of the best healers in Lunaria who I'm sure would gladly rummage around in that pretty head of yours to find the loose screw."

The entire table bursts into rambunctious laughter, Zale and Hade included. I look around dumbfounded, clearly missing whatever conversation they are all having with their eyes.

"You may be onto something about the loose screw part, but no, I'm not crazy." Reaching forward, he grasps both dice in his hands and tosses them over to me. Instinctively, I reach out, catching them before they can go tumbling to the ground. As soon as my hand makes contact with the smooth, cold dice, a humming buzzes over my skin.

They feel...*alive*.

Dragging my eyes up to Zale, he gives me a knowing smile. "They are imbued with ancient magic. It isn't known whose magic lies within them, but it is strong."

As I roll them in my hand, a zap of magic tickles across my palm in response, making goose bumps rise along my arms and spine.

"Nyxi, divine one. What a welcome surprise."

I jolt, instinctively chucking the dice across the table as the remnants of its slithering, whispering voice sinks its teeth into my skin. Zale scoops the dice back up and returns them to my frozen, upturned palm while giving my shoulder a reassuring pat. *Listen*, his eyes seem to tell me. Closing my fist around the dice again, I close my eyes and focus back on the thrumming of magic.

"Clearly, the welcome surprise is one sided," the dice hiss into my mind with a hint of amusement.

How is this possible? I think to myself.

"All your questions will be answered in due time, my child." I jolt again, not realizing it could hear my thoughts. I keep the dice planted firmly in my grasp this time.

Who are you?

"That is unimportant for now, change bringer. Are you interested in playing a game of Jezzle, my child?"

Yes. My voice comes out strong in my head, like a command.

"You must first offer me something invaluable in exchange to play. A rule asked of all players, of course."

An offering? I mumble in my head, trying to come up with something.

"A secret for an answer." It hisses back in one long, drawn out sentence. *"If you would like to play with my magic, you must first offer me a secret no one knows. If you are to win the game, I will grant you one answer to any question you may have, as long as I know the answer."*

So you steal people's secrets and sell them?

"No one is forced to play this game or give me their secrets. They do so to lift a weight off their shoulders. They know the risk of telling me their secret, that it may be told to another, but that is how I am able to answer questions asked of me by winners. It is how I gain my knowledge."

Nodding to myself, I squeeze the dice a little tighter. If I can win against Zale, I could potentially get an answer to the question burning a hole in my brain since the start of the Crucible. It could potentially save my life.

"Do you still want to play, my catalyst?"

Yes, I want to play, I think immediately.

"And what secret would you like to offer me in payment?" it hisses loudly.

I involuntarily tense, thinking over what I could offer the dice that I wouldn't mind being reshared. I doubt anyone would be asking anything about me anyways, but I'm still hesitant. Gulping, I set my heart on a silver platter.

I am afraid of living. I think the heavy thought that is always nagging my brain at all times of the day, as permanent as the tattoos marking Hade's skin.

"Explain," it hisses calmly.

Taking a deep breath, I decide to let one thing inside the impenetrable force field around my aching heart. *I am afraid to live without him. I am afraid to move on when he can no longer move with me. I am afraid if I open my heart again, he could be forgotten and left behind. I am afraid to live and be happy without him, because it makes me feel guilty. It should be him here still walking these lands instead of me. So yes, I am deathly afraid of living because that means he's really gone.*

"Do you truly believe those words, my spark?"

I don't know, I sigh back.

"I think you know deep down, but you need to forgive yourself before you can truly answer truthfully. Thank you for your secret, young one. Enjoy playing with my magic."

The dice glow in my hand, a tendril of magic looping itself around my wrist, linking me to the game. Zale smiles at the glowing magic, clearly happy with my decision to play. Hade gives my shoulder a squeeze as I settle into my chair, ready to destroy Zale in a game of Jezzle so I can win an answer.

"It is time to roll for the number of rounds played, my players," the dice hisses between us, and I assume Zale can now hear its voice in his head too, since he leans forward and scoops up the dice.

"Ladies first," he shouts at the same time he chucks me the numbered die.

Catching it, I close my fist around the die, shaking it around a few times before launching it across the wooden table. It tumbles loudly until it lands in the center of the table. Leaning forward, I read the number aloud.

"Three!" I shout with a smirk. I just need to have three better rolls than him, and I'm one step closer to solving the riddle.

"Kick his ass," Hade whispers maliciously into my ear.

Gesturing to the Jezzle die, Zale says smoothly, "Have at it, darlin'. Let's see what those hands can do."

Taking a swig of my ale for liquid courage, I hold back the wince as I scoop up the die, looking it over more closely. "Let's see if the die loves you as much as you claim it does, *darlin'*."

"*Round one, commence,*" the die hisses at the same time a thin magical barrier appears between us on the table top. Closing my eyes, I give the Jezzle die a good shake and open my eyes right as it explodes out of my hand, barreling onto the table. It flips many times, clanking the whole way until it finally lands right in front of the barrier, so Zale can't see.

A buzzing hums from the die at the same time a bright blue light explodes from the top, where a glowing blue orb in the shape of a...miniature octopus crawls across the table, using its tentacles to glide while a thin blue light acting like a rope tethers it to my wrist.

Staring at the creation in front of me, I'm frozen in astonishment. Now I understand what the Jezzle die meant when it said have fun playing with my magic. The little octopus sits ready and waiting at the magical barrier, bouncing up and down on its tentacles.

Shaking myself from the initial shock, I pick up the die and toss it over the barrier to Zale to roll. I hear the die tumble on the other side of the table as it leaves his hand, and a faint humming vibrates from just beyond the barrier, the magic making his eyes glow.

The barrier melts away to nothing, showing us the entirety of the table again. A faint giggle accidently slips up my throat that I have to quickly muffle with my palm as I take in the adorable purple miniature Pegasus tethered to Zale's wrist. The thing doesn't look like it could hurt a fly, and to prove my point, a burst of glitter shoots from its nose.

The smile falters on my face when my octopus' tentacle lashes out, stretching longer then should be possible, making me understand why it symbolizes shapeshifting magic. It wraps around the

Pegasus' neck, choking it to death. Zale's Pegasus tries to use its wings to fly away to safety, but as soon as my octopus wraps its entire body for the fourth loop around its neck, its head falls to the side, completing the first round.

I gasp in shock, suddenly not in the mood to laugh. Zale's cute magical creature lies limp and dead on the table. Sensing my unease, Hade moves a little closer behind me, sharing his body heat with me in comfort.

"It's only magic. It's not real, and it doesn't hurt them," Zale says softly, also noticing my shock. On cue, both creatures fizzle away into a blue and purple mass of magic, until they are sucked back into the Jezzle die, ready for the start of round two as the magical barrier settles itself between us.

That seems to relax my shoulders again, knowing this is just a fun game and no one is actually dying or being harmed here. My life has too much death in it for my liking, and it's nice to know this isn't permanent for once.

"*One point, Nyxi.*" The die's snakey voice slithers up my spine. "*Round two, commence.*"

"I'll go first this time, and we will rotate starting each round," Zale states. "You ready to see what these hands are actually capable of now that they are warmed up?" He shoots me a wink and then lets the die float through the air down to the table. He lets the magic explode out of the die before tossing it over to me for my turn.

"I hope they age like fine wine, because so far, they seem rather...*lacking*." I draw out the last word as I let the die tumble from my hand. The die lands with the eels facing up, and a bright white glow comes from within until two zappy little things slither out onto the table. They look like lightning bolts as electricity dances over their slithering bodies.

The barrier vanishes, and two yellow sea snakes launch immediately, trying to sink their fangs into my eels. The eels zap the snakes a few times, trying to warn them off, but as soon as the snake's poisonous fangs sink into my eels, the fight is over.

"One point, Zale," the die's haunting voices calls to us.

Zale's shit-eating grin beams at me from across the table, his dimples on full display. "Better luck next time, darlin'. It seems these fingers are indeed capable of making magic happen." He twinkles his fingers at me while raising his eyebrows suggestively, and I choke out a laugh at the same time I hear a faint, disapproving grunt from Hade behind me.

Rolling my eyes playfully, I pick up the die again as the barrier constructs itself between us. "Even a blind squirrel can find a nut once in a while," I quip back. I release the die in front of me, and it rolls a few times before landing on the dragon. Red light erupts from the top, and the cutest red dragon barrels out of the face, stomping its little feet across the table as steam billows out his nostrils.

Satisfied with my roll, I pick up the die and throw it over to Zale. He rolls quickly, the faint glow of magic casting on his face right before the barrier melts away. Two eels try to slither across to my half of the table, but before they even make it two inches, my dragon unhinges his jaw. Red hot fire erupts from deep inside him, turning both eels to a pile of ash.

Efficient—I like it. I want to scoop him up and slip him in my pocket so he can incinerate all my enemies to come. Just as the thought leaves my brain, my little dragon friend dissolves into a blob of red magic, sucked back into the die along with the eels.

"Another point to Nyxi. One more and she wins."

The Jezzle die puts reality at the forefront of my brain with just how close I am to the answers I need. One more win, and I could potentially have my ticket to solving the riddle. To saving my life. With only one trial left, it truly is life or death for me. If the trial has anything to do with strength, Tank has a major advantage over me, and I don't like those odds.

With the barrier back between us, Zale rolls for his turn and then tosses the die back over to me. Closing my eyes, I send Theo a quick prayer, hoping my plea for luck is answered, and then release the die from my palm. It rolls so hard, it knocks into the barrier, wedging itself there. I swear I catch the faintest shadow whip out and knock it a touch so it tips right instead of left, finally landing on a face.

Dark black magic bursts from its face, and my eyes grow wide as a grim reaper holding a scythe gallops out of it, riding a mini horse.

Death magic.

Hade's magic, to be exact.

The barrier dissolves between us, and my grim reaper wastes no time, running at full speed right into battle against Zale's… Pegasus. The poor thing trembles slightly, not even trying to find a way to escape. If it wasn't so cute, I would be howling with laughter over how pathetic his Pegasus roll is compared to my grim reaper for someone who is apparently an *undefeated champ*.

A *swoosh* rings out as my grim slices his scythe through the air, fully decapitating Zale's Pegasus, easy as butter. The grim trots his horse in a circle around the head, marking his victory before all the magic is sucked back into the die, signaling the end of the game.

"Game well played," I say casually while kicking my feet up on the table again. I pretend to pick dirt from under my nail, as if winning the game means nothing, while secretly waiting to see what Zale has to say in return. I try to wait as long as possible, which is precisely one second before I launch out of my chair a little too eagerly, the ale aiding my outburst. "Empress, that was embarrassing. What was your name again?"

Of course, I remember his name.

"Zale," he says with a slight edge, but he's too prince charming to really crack his confident shell, which is now my new priority challenge to meddle with. Life is utterly too boring if you aren't trying to push your finger in every crack you find and dig around a bit.

"Hmm, are you sure? I could have sworn it was Zeke?" His eye slightly twitches, but he says nothing, and I smile internally at the newest crack I've whittled. "I guess it doesn't matter, because your name is last week's news after that performance." Turning, I look over my shoulder, gesturing for Hade to look at my lower back. "Do you think you could rub out this knot I have from carrying that entire game on my back?"

The most glorious thing happens then, and it plays out in slow motion in my head on loop. Hade lets out the loudest, most heart stopping laugh I have ever had the pleasure of hearing. It's warm and infectious—quite honestly my new favorite thing. His eyes wrinkle at the corners when his lips grow into a full smile as the most carefree laugh sings out around us, and I can't help staring, stunned at this beautiful creature.

A smile touches my lips just from taking in this moment at the same time Zale joins in with Hade, who still can't control his laughter. It's a forever moment, one I will think about when the hard days come.

"I like her," Zale says authentically over to Hade, who has recovered from his laughter assault and nods back with a panty dropping smile.

"That's two in one night," he says under his breath, more to himself, but I catch it all the same. "She's one of a kind, that's for sure."

The ale has definitely altered my ego, but I'm still right minded enough to know how to treat a person, or maybe a new…friend? Striding over to Zale, I grin at him sincerely and offer him my hand. "Good game," I say honestly. "Apparently, the odds were in my favor tonight, but six wins in a row is very impressive. One might say it's your *lucky* number."

He shakes my hand and once again brings it to his lips, kissing my knuckles gently with a smirk on his face. "A pleasure, *darlin'*. Hade will just have to bring you back another night so we can even the score."

Squeezing his hand back, I drop it to my side and look over to Hade. "I would love that." Hade gives me a weak smile I catch from the corner of my eye. It looks slightly pained, and I know exactly why. He's concerned I will run out of days.

Just as the Crucible grazes my mind, a slithering, eerie voice claws against the inside of my skull again. *"Congratulations, my meta-morphosis. As promised for winning, one answer to any question will be grant-ed within realistic parameters. I cannot tell you answers to the future, nor can I tell you the answers to your destiny, but I can grant you my knowledge. Choose wisely, because you only get one question."*

There are so many questions I would love to ask, but one is more important than all the rest, no matter how badly I would love the answers to everything. Taking a moment to think, I choose carefully exactly how I want to phrase my question for the best outcome to help aid my search for the answer to the riddle.

Going with the most up front one, I think my question. *Can the answer to the Empress' riddle be found in the personal journal collection inside the Castle library?*

The dice's snakelike voice answers immediately, giving me a lifeline to grasp for dear life. *"All the answers you seek, my child, are within your grasp. Follow your intuition, and all will be righted again. Find the answers and force the world to listen. It must be you. It has always been you."*

I'm left with so many questions, and just as I scramble to ask what the heck that all means, the Jezzle dice disappear complete-ly. I'm left staring at the now-empty table in complete shock and confusion.

Force the world to listen? I have nothing to say to the world. All I want to do is solve the riddle and get on with my revenge so I can live out the rest of my life in peace. I come to the conclusion someone must have fed the magical dice false secrets, because no way he meant to say I am the answer to…to what?

What the hell am I the answer to?

I feel a soft weight on my shoulder, and I drag my eyes up to be entrapped between two pools of night and day. He gives me a concerned look that I shrug away, forcing a smile that doesn't quite reach my eyes.

"Did you get the answer you were seeking?" he says gently.

"Yes and no," I huff, annoyed but still grateful I have a good plan in place to solve the riddle. I think it's time for a date with the rest of the journals, starting immediately.

We say goodbye to the group of friends Hade is oddly very comfortable around, and I make a mental note to get to know the others better if I get the chance to meet them again. Hade finished off his second ale before planting a kiss on Harry's wrinkled cheek when returning his mug to the counter, the thoughtful gentleman he is.

Harry waves goodbye as Hade grabs my hand. She looks down at our joined hands and shoots me a wink, like she's in on some secret I have no clue about.

Shuffling through the still-packed crowd, we sneak out the door behind a large, rowdy group calling it a night. I find it funny that not a single one rubs a hand over the rock, but I chalk it up to them being too drunk to remember. Hade, of course, mindlessly glides his hand over the smooth surface, and I follow suit, looking for all the extra luck I can get, soaking in the warm comfort that dances over my skin at the contact.

Now it's time to find the winning answer that balances my destiny between life and death.

Chapter
Forty-Three

Journal Entry

Age 15

Tomorrow is my sixteenth birthday. Mama and Papa are hosting a coming of age ball in my honor today that will last all the way until the clock strikes midnight, marking me one year older. All I can think about is how I get to see my eternal today and celebrate with him by my side. That was my one wish. He told me down the bond that he would travel to hell and back to see me. I still can't fathom why people fear him when he's sweeter to me than the candy I'm currently chewing on.

As excited as I am for today, an uneasy nervousness has been prickling the back of my neck after the talk Mama had with me this morning. I had to take a trip to the crystal Papa and I made from our combined magic to calm myself. An indestructible constant for you to seek, Papa had told me when creating it together. I've lost count how many times I've sought out its solace over the years, loving the familiar hum of our magic.

I've been trying to shake the uncomfortable feeling all day and focus on all the fun to come, but the way she spoke to my soul today still has me wavering. She kept telling me how much she loved me and to always remember that, as if she was going somewhere. I asked her if everything was okay, and she assured me everything is as it should be. I wasn't sure if she was referring to my celebration or something much bigger.

She told me she left a secret birthday present under the floorboards of the library, and that I will know when the time comes for me to retrieve it, that it will open my eyes to the world and help forge me into the woman I am destined to be. I asked her how I would know when to retrieve it, and she tapped my heart with soft fingers and said once again how much she loved me, how, deep in my soul, I will know when the right time comes. I'm not sure why I would ever <u>need</u> a birthday present, but it must be important.

It's silly to say, but it felt like she put the world on my shoulders with that one conversation. I'm not sure I'm ready to bear the weight of it just yet. For now, I will focus on celebrating another year older, surrounded by the people I love most.

Celebrations are meant to be exciting, right? What could go <u>wrong</u>?

Chapter
Forty-Four

I JOLT AWAKE WHEN A HEAVY WEIGHT COLLIDES WITH MY BODY, NEAR-ly knocking the wind from my lungs.

What the heck?

It's pitch dark—so dark, I can't see a damn thing, meaning it still has to be the middle of the night.

Disoriented and half asleep, I feel around, realizing I can't even see my hand in front of my face. That is…odd. Someone grabs said invisible hand, which I'm now convinced is cast in some invisible magic, and throws me off my bed to the floor.

Rude!

"Did your mother teach you no manners?" I shout through gritted teeth. "This is no way to wake a lady. Haven't you heard of beauty sleep, and what did you do with my hands?" Looking around more, I realize everything must be cast in the same invisible magic, because where in all the lands did everything go?

"This is rather boring for me." I pout, still half out of it and clearly delirious. "Can you just give me my hands back and let me go back to sleep?" Realizing I probably need to offer something in return, I add, "I'll refrain from putting my fist through your teeth if you do so," I say in a sickly sweet voice, even though that's the last feeling I'm having right now.

No one messes with my beauty sleep and lives to talk about it. Rule number one in the Nyxi Code of Conduct handbook.

Instead of a verbal response, I'm answered with the back of their knuckles against my cheek.

"Shit... I..." He trails off, seeming shocked by his outburst.

"*Ouch!* Could you at least *un-invisible* everything so I have a fighting chance against your bony ass hands? There's literally no padding on those things. You have to be at least seventy."

I'm greeted with a swift, "Shut up, *woman!* Do you ever stop talking?"

Now, I'm fully heated—no one talks to me like that and gets away with it. "Now I know your mother didn't teach you *that*. You can make it up to me by helping scratch this itch on my ankle, seeing as I still can't find my invisible hands."

I hear him shuffle closer, probably only humoring me to shut me up. I wait until he's close enough that I can hear and smell his putrid breath. In the blink of an eye, I rear my arm back and throw it full speed at the sleep-stealing culprit's face. I know I've made solid contact when I hear a crunching noise and a faint *clink* of what I assume is a rouge tooth cascades across the floor.

Check mate!

"*Fuck!*" he bellows while letting out a few pained grunts through labored breaths.

"Well I could have itched my own ankle, but you had to go and turn everything invisible," I say thoughtfully.

"You're not invisible!" he hisses, sounding a bit lisp-y due to the missing tooth, courtesy of yours truly.

Atta girl!

"Tell that to my invisible hands!" I flail the missing things around wildly, making my point.

"You're blindfolded, *woman*," he says, thoroughly annoyed. Under his breath, more to himself than me, he mutters, "Shit, when he said you would be trouble, he wasn't kidding."

Blindfolded? Oh... Maybe I did overreact a bit with the whole magic accusation, but when someone startles you awake in the night with their body on top of yours—and not in the fun kind of way—wild accusations are the only correct response...right?

Right!

"Wait, who warned you?" Thinking about it for two seconds, I answer my own question. Hade, obviously, which brings me to my second question. "Scratch that. Why the hell am I blindfolded? This isn't some kinky part of the Crucible I'm unaware of, is it? Because I wasn't forewarned, and to be fair, I was so tired from reading late last night, I sort of skipped washing off, and let's just say no one wants to get anywhere near me right now."

I hear him choke on his own tongue, shocking him speechless, which is exactly what I was going for. Going for my killing blow, I add, "Unless maybe you're into that sort of thing? Is that why you itched my ankle for me? To get closer? Are you trying to hit on me, sir? Whatever happened to wine and dine first? Now it's assault them in their sleep, blindfold them, and itch smelly ankles to get a whiff?" I scoff to myself. "What is with men these days?"

"Can you please just stop talking!" he rushes out, but it's shaky and unsure.

"Gladly," I say with a smile. "As soon as you remove the bag from my head."

"Not happening," he responds solidly, leaving no room for argument.

Damn, he bounces back fast. "I guess I will have to acquaint you with my other fist, then, because she's feeling rather left out at the moment."

"You will do no such thing. We are already late, so you're going to shut up and not put up a fight, or I will have to knock you out. Contrary to your belief, I don't want to hurt you. I would like to keep my head attached to my body."

Now that does bring a genuine smile to my face.

"Where are you taking me?" I resort to pouting again. "Can we rain check it until I at least get a couple more hours of sleep? Seeing as it's still the middle of the night."

I feel him grab my arm, dragging me up to stand. "It's eight in the morning. You've had plenty of sleep."

"Eight? Did you fail school or something? Since when is the night sky still out at eight in the morning?" This man has lost his marbles.

He sighs, clearly thoroughly over me. "It's bright out; you just can't see it due to the blindfold," he replies in a clipped tone.

Oh, right…the blindfold. *Whoopsies.*

"Well…if you took the blindfold off, I wouldn't be so confused about what time it is, would I? So why don't you do us both a favor and just take it off…*please.*"

"No."

"Brute!" I grumble.

Tugging me to follow him, I suddenly panic, realizing I have no idea who this man is and what he plans to do with me. Why the hell have I just been sitting here doing nothing about it? I chalk it up to tiredness, and honestly, I can smell the anxiety pouring off him, like he's scared to touch a single hair on my head. If I were in true danger, I would sense it. So far, all the man has done is timidly acquaint me with the back of his hand, and I think it shocked him more than it did me.

Digging my heels into the floor, I do my best to slow us down. Even though I think I could take this man blindfolded and half-asleep, I still have an uneasy feeling about this.

"Stop that!"

"Tell me where we're going, and maybe I'll oblige. Do you even workout? It feels like I'm pulling against a child right now." I gasp dramatically. "You're elderly, I forgot. Brittle bones and all that. We wouldn't want you to snap a femur trying to take another step out my door."

"I'm taking you to the Bubble for the final round of the Crucible. There, are you happy?"

"No."

"You are insufferable, woman!"

I sigh. "So I've been told. Hate to break it to you, but that's last week's news." I think it over, his words finally hitting me as hives spread over my body.

The Crucible.

Today is the final round of the Crucible, meaning it could very well be my last day alive. An array of questions rack my head. Why is it starting so early? Why am I blindfolded? Where is Hade? Who is this man? Will I get to say goodbye to Des or Winston before I potentially die? What will today's game entail?

The questions are a never-ending tide swirling around my head in a dizzying manner, and my body slickens with sweat. I had a plan in place for today, and this puts a major, life-altering wrench right in the center of it.

After finishing the last of the journal entries last night, I was left with even more questions and avenues to chase down. Why did the journals abruptly stop at age fifteen? Did I miss some of them in the library, or did something happen at that birthday ball? I still have no idea who the journals belong to, but I know they are important to solving this riddle.

I was planning on heading to the library first thing this morning and checking for loose floorboards, praying whatever mysterious gift hidden within them was still there. Clearly, fate laughed in my face and had other plans. That was my last ticket to solving the riddle before the last round of the Crucible, and now, it's gone.

There's no getting out of this, and like every other moment in my life, I will have to fight my way out to survive. Nothing I'm unfamiliar with. So far, my track record for staying alive is on a twenty year winning streak, so I'll take my odds.

Count your days, Tank, because they are about to be over.

"I didn't want to have to do this, but you leave me no choice."

I'm about to ask him what exactly he's talking about right as I feel a small prick in the side of my neck, and then, everything truly goes dark.

GROANING, I SLOWLY PEEL ONE EYE OPEN WHILE STRETCHING MY neck, feeling a giant, uncomfortable kink in the side. Once I'm coherent again, I register chanting around me, but once again, I see nothing.

I see black. I see him, dark as death itself, the hazy abyss calling to me akin to how it feels to be wrapped in his dark, blissful magic.

Except it's not him. It's just a blindfold, and reality comes crashing back.

The Crucible.

Licking my chapped lips, I swipe a tongue full of sand that must have snuck into the bag around my head, swiftly sputtering and spitting.

We're in the Bubble.

This is it. Life or death. Strangely, I'm not as nervous as I should be. Instead, a small pit of excitement festers deep in my stomach, a small ball of hope for today being the first obstacle to check off my list in my *oath of vengeance* for Theo. A smaller part of me is also buzzing at the thought of being able to wield magic.

Magic had zero sway in my decision to enter the competition, contrary to my opponents, but now that I can practically reach out and grab it, it's exhilarating. I push the thoughts away and ready my mind and body for this last test.

The chants grow louder, signaling someone's arrival. I try to push myself up to sit, but I realize my hands are tied behind my back.

Rude!

"Lunaria, my magical citizens, I am pleased to announce the final round of the Reaper Crucible!" The crowd erupts into a fit of screams and hollers, ready for the blood bath to commence. I'm glad my life on the line is amusing to them.

"Our final two contestants have battled for their life to get to this very moment. It hasn't been easy or full of rainbows and butterflies, that's for sure, but we have been provided with the utmost entertainment. Give a round of applause for your finalists!"

I hear a mixture of chants screaming our names, shocked I have any fans rooting for me at this point. That definitely won't be good for my ego. The chants finally die down, and an eerie silence slips into its place.

Sand shuffles next to me, and then blinding light sears my eyes when the bag around my head is ripped away. I slam my eyes shut to dull the burning pain.

Rapidly blinking away the tears and now grains of gritty sand sticking to my wet face, I slowly take in my surroundings. The crowd surrounding the Bubble is one giant, screaming blur, the Empress dressed to the nines per usual.

And then, there's *him*.

Hade stands stoic as ever, an unmoving, double enforced statue dressed in full black, a deadly weapon forged to be unbreakable. Tension runs through his entire body, wound tight and ready to attack at a moment's notice.

Tanned muscle bulges from under his fighting gear, all muscle and thick veins honed for killing. Still on my side, I keep my eyes glued to him, a common occurrence I've learned to not fight anymore. His fists clench by his sides, but he stays looking forward, an impenetrable wall bound by duty and devotion.

His face falls out of vision when a hand grips me from behind and spins me until I'm sitting up in the sand. My head spins from the change of gravity and whatever lingering sedative was unwillingly injected into my neck. My throat is raw and dry as I peel my tongue off the roof of my mouth, wincing through the headache resting at the front of my temple.

An angry grunt grabs my attention to the left, and when I turn, I find a very angry Tank elbowing a Vanquisher away from him, who no doubt just ripped a bag off his head, if his tousled hair is anything to go by. I feel bad for the poor soul who was tasked with sneaking into his room and kidnapping that giant brute. How did they even pick him up?

"Congratulations my finalists," the Empress' condescending voice shines through, but at a much quieter level. The Enhancer next to her dropped his amplifying magic so we are the only ones who can hear her. "Though I'm quite saddened no one has yet to solve my riddle. What a shame." She practically pouts. "Though I guess you still have one last opportunity to impress me. So, what will it be? Anyone have any news to share with me, or are you both still as incompetent as I suspected from day one?"

I grit my teeth at the insult, both angered by her harsh words and disappointed in myself for failing. First, I failed saving Theo, and now, I failed at getting revenge for him. Like hell I'll lose today and fail him in that as well.

The Empress bores into Tank, and surprisingly, I spot him twitch under her thick scrutiny. Not so tough anymore are you, big boy? He pretends to think to himself, trying to come up with an answer, and I use the extra second to think over the riddle one last time.

Where three meet, one left behind. A sacrifice greater than mankind. A piercing cry from the one black eye. For that shall reset time before the ultimate crime.

Each time I think it over, the more confused I get. I keep getting stuck on the one black eye part. The obvious answer would be Hade, but he hasn't always had one black eye, as I've recently learned. My next obstacle is the crime. What giant crime has been committed? My thoughts go to the separation of Magicals and those of us who grew up on the ground, but still, I don't see a huge crime in that. If I had just had a few minutes to search the library this morning for that hidden birthday gift, maybe everything would make more sense.

Maybe I could have ended this competition before the madness ensued.

"Pity," the Empress coos to Tank's empty response before turning her glaring eyes towards me. Not wanting to draw it out and make a scene, I quickly shake my head. I swear, I see the slightest ounce of sadness or pain underneath her cold indifference, but at this point, I wouldn't put it past my mind to play tricks on me.

With a snap of her fingers, the Enhancers magic falls over her voice once again, amplifying it for all to hear. "You are all in for an extra special treat for the final round of the Crucible!"

There go the cheers and chants again for my impending death. I will never understand the appeal of seeing someone cling for dear life and praying they indeed fall. Unless their names start with a T, J, or A—then I would be rooting alongside them.

"What kind of Empress would I be if I didn't provide my citizens with the utmost entertainment? Think big and deadly, and then double that, and you will find what our finalist will be facing today." She laughs to herself, seeming totally amused with what she's conjured up.

Lovely.

"With a little imagination and a skilled Fabricant," she gestures to another Vanquisher standing next to her, "I present to you the final challenge standing between you and winning the Reaper Crucible."

The Fabricant raises his hands, swirling until a ball of magic grows within his palms. When he harshly shoves his hands in the air, magic explodes from his palms, shooting in all directions until two, oddly-shaped platforms float high above our heads, sitting at the top of the bubble.

It looks to be a bunch of squares abstractly shoved together to make some sort of long obstacle course. What it entails and why it's so high in the air escapes me.

Quickly, I glance over at Hade, trying to plead with my eyes for any foresight, but the only answer I get is his teeth gnashing as he grinds his jaw, trying to remain calm. Clearly, he is not happy about whatever is about to happen.

That makes two of us, buddy.

"Who doesn't love a little game of Hopscotch?" The Empress' wicked smile sets my body on edge. "It's a simple game, really. Jump on the respective squares with the correct feet and race to the end. What could go wrong?"

Steadying my heart, I wait for the ball to inevitably drop.

"Oh, I should mention this isn't just any hopscotch course. No, that would be too boring." And there goes the ball. "Obviously, there's the height. If either contestant were to lose their balance, they would no doubt fall to their death. Instant elimination. Though that would make it easier on our part, I would rather not have boring entertainment today. So please try and stay on course."

I would hate to be an inconvenience, I almost retort back, but luckily, my lips are solid as metal today. Gritting my teeth to keep from lashing out, I wait for her to continue to spout off all the evilness she has planned for us today.

"Then there's the hidden traps within the obstacle, of course." Now that does raise the hair on my skin. "Hidden beneath certain squares lie deadly traps that will be triggered with the simplest misstep. It should be easy enough to avoid them, since I've been gracious enough to mark each trap square with a giant X. As long as you make it through the course the fastest, without falling or stepping on any of the dangerous spaces, then you will be crowned our winner. If, however, one of you shall fall or succumb to fatal injuries from one of the marked squares, the surviving contestant will be crowned victorious. If both finalists fail to make it through today's challenge alive, then there will be no winner for this year's Crucible."

She makes it sound simple enough, which leaves an uncomfortable feeling beneath my skin. It cannot be as simple as jumping over a few spaces marked with giant Xs. She has to be leaving something out. The last round of each Crucible is known to be one of the most violent and deadly. I've heard some contestants' heads have been blown off in past years during the last round, so this simple little game of hopscotch isn't adding up to me.

"Ahh, I almost forgot. There will be an advantage for our leading finalist, as is tradition." Snapping her fingers, a leaderboard beams into the air, only showing two names this time.

"After his swift and brutal performance last week, sitting in first place, we have Tank from Sweat Sector." An ungodly number of cheers erupt, mostly men, which I find funny. "Which means sitting in our second place spot, after a much more exciting performance last week, is Nyxi from Vagrant Sector. Her performance was exhilarating to watch, but she was lacking control throughout, and if a few things would have fallen differently, we would have had a much different contestant sitting here today."

Internally rolling my eyes, I slap on a smile.

"Settle down now," the Empress bellows. "As reward for being in first place, Tank will choose which hopscotch course he would like to tackle. Each course is unique. Tank may choose to tackle the shorter course, but you will notice it is also riddled with more squares marked with Xs. Or he can choose to take on the longer, more time consuming course, but that course has fewer danger squares marked to avoid stepping on. Each has their advantages and disadvantages, and the choice is up to you, Tank."

I still don't understand where the catch with this is. One course has to have obvious advantages, but looking at how large the squares are, I'm confused on how this could be that dangerous. This is supposed to be the grand finale, and to be quite frank, this seems laughable. I could jump through this course with my eyes closed and in my sleep. So where does the true danger lie?

Clearing his throat, Tank grunts, "I'll take the shorter course."

"As you wish!" the Empress purrs. Flicking her fingers, Hade strides up to her side, passing over two small clear vials. He lets them go reluctantly, his body physically recoiling at being an accomplice to whatever is inside them. My body mirrors his unease for what's to come.

"There is *one* last thing I should mention." She walks closer, a smile that could only be described as the devil incarnate shines brightly across her smug face. "Before each of you begin, you must both drink the contents in these vials. They are of crucial importance to this final game to test your strength and willpower to persevere through the toughest of trials. These," she taps the clear small vials, "will decipher who has what it takes to be the toughest of this year's contestants and take it all."

I don't like the sound of that one bit. I assume some type of drug is in the vials, but to what extent? Will it knock me out?

Weaken me? Turn me vicious? Make me sick? I really would rather not find out, but if I refuse, it's a sure death sentence.

Reaching forward, I pluck a vial from her hands. Here's to hoping this option won't also be a death sentence. Pulling the cork, it pops out easily, and a faint floral scent rises to my nose. Hand slightly shaking, I wait for Tank to grab his and the Empress to nod for us to continue. In one swift movement, I shoot the drug back like alcohol, the cool liquid burning the back of my throat. Dropping the vial to the sand, I stomp my foot, shattering the glass. Lifting my gaze, I stare the Empress straight in the eyes, not a lick of fear to be seen.

Today, I'm staring death straight in the face, making it fear me instead.

"Very well." She claps happily. "Let the final round of the Crucible commence! Good luck to you both, and may death not claim your soul today."

Cheers erupt again as a float flanks us, flying us into the air up onto our respective hopscotch courses. Landing with a heavy thud, my head spins slightly. Harshly, I blink to catch up with reality.

Turning to thank the Vanquisher, his face starts to morph, his mouth suddenly in the place his nose should be. Rubbing my eyes, I open them again to find he's back to normal. I find it weird but decide to move on, having more important things to worry about right now.

"Thank you," I mumble. My lips are slightly slower to react than the signals my brain is sending them, so it comes out a little slurred. He shoots me a worried look then nods and floats back down to the sand.

Turning to face the obstacle in front of me, my head dances, as if jumping from cloud to cloud. I grit my teeth, trying extra hard to focus until the course comes into perfect view.

Peering over at Tank's course to my left, I notice his is at least half the length of mine. A queasy feeling lurches in my stomach, but my muscles slightly relax when I notice over half of his spaces are marked with Xs.

Looking back to my own course, it seems about only a quarter of the squares are marked as dangerous. I like those odds. I may have to travel further, but I like my odds of avoiding the danger. One wrong step could mean life of death, and I like having more options to misstep and avoid hitting an X, unlike Tank. His size alone is a giant disadvantage; his large feet will most likely take up almost the entire length of each square.

Movement catches my eye as the Empress comes into view between our two courses, escorted by a float.

This is it, Nyxi. Just one last challenge. One more obstacle to prove your worth and extract your revenge. For Theo, I can do this. For Theo I can do *anything*.

"Lunaria, my citizens, are you ready to witness *the* entertainment of the year? Who will take it all? And who will perish in the others' success, ripped away for the rest of eternity? A race of life or death. A game of luck and skill. The final test to decide this year's Reaper Crucible champion."

Looking us both in the eyes with a sickening seriousness, she finishes with, "Let the final round of the Crucible commence!"

Grunting, Tank takes off at full speed, jumping onto his first square as the Empress floats back down, leaving an Illuminist in her place.

Taking in my course, I map out a clean path to weave between the scattered Xs. Satisfied, I leap to the first row of three squares, the one in the center marked with an x. Spreading my legs, I plant each foot in the outside spaces, avoiding the danger in the center.

"Nyxi!"

I would recognize that voice the same as the feel of my own skin. Gasping, I drag my eyes up and spot… No, that can't be right.

Theo stands at the end of my course. My Theo, alive and here with me. He smiles, jumping up and down while waving his hands like a maniac. Everything fades away, and the permanent frost surrounding my heart melts with *one single smile*. His smile is a remedy I so desperately was looking for. His smile could solve world peace. That one smile single-handedly fused every fissure and ache riddled into my dying corpse of a heart.

Happy tears spring to my eyes, and a laugh bubbles up my throat. "Theo, you came back to me!" I gasp. He came for me like he always has.

My protector.

My *home.*

All the air leaves my lungs, and a blood curdling scream rips from my throat as the giant flaps of black tattered wings sail in from behind him.

Necroshriek.

I try to warn him to turn around. To run. To not let history repeat itself.

"Run, Theo!" I scream. "Please, I can't lose you again."

My feet move on instinct, and I launch into a run with only one thing on my mind. I have to save him this time. I need him. I won't survive losing him a second time. My heart couldn't bear it.

"THEO!" It feels like my throat is bleeding from how hard I'm screaming. The Necroshriek is only a foot behind him now and I feel like I'm having déjà vu. I'm living out my worst nightmare over again, except this time, the Necroshriek flies straight through him, as if he was nothing but a cloud in the air.

"Theo?" I gasp. Clutching my throat, my lungs seize, unsure how to work anymore. Where did he go? Falling to my knees, I drop my face in my hands but spread my fingers when I hear a faint *click*. What comes into view between my spread fingers has my heart lurching in my chest.

My knees are planted on one *giant* black X.

Smoke slowly billows up out of the square, and as soon as it makes contact with me, a burning like I've never felt melts my skin and has me shooting up. I wince and whimper when the smoke burns through my cargo pants and hits my ankle, where I can feel a blister bubbling instantly.

I fell asleep in my training clothes last night by accident after reading late. I didn't have time to change into Des' protective suit, since I was dragged here by force, but I'm thankful I at least went to bed in my sparring gear and not a nightgown. However, right now, I could really use the extra protection.

Whipping my head up, I look to the next row of squares to find only one, and it happens to be another black X. Breathing through the pain, I launch myself as hard as possible over the next row with the single X and onto the following row, using all the force in my body to make it there. It feels as if the shadows around me give me the extra boost I need to make it.

I land, wincing after falling directly on my shoulder. I feel a slight pop, then searing pain, and decide I most likely dislocated it.

Points for style, I guess.

Holding my shoulder with my hand, I scan my eyes left and right, looking for any danger. I sort of launched myself to this row, trying to get as far away from the acid as soon as possible before seeing where the danger lay on this row.

There are three squares in this row. I happened to have landed in the center one, which is safe but bordered by one X on each side. It seems luck was on my side with this one.

I take a moment to check over my wounds, rolling up my pants to spot two vicious red ankles riddled with small white blisters. The boots rub them, making them ooze and spread like fire across my skin.

Hissing through the pain, I roll my pants back down carefully, then look over to see how far along Tank is. He hasn't made it very far and is sporting a few cuts and bruises. He's shouting at nothing, like he's out of his damn mind.

Deciding I have enough time, I assess my shoulder next. Prodding, I instantly recoil from the pain and the way my arm hangs limp by my side. It's definitely dislocated. Lethargy seeps over my body, but I push through, knowing what comes next is a necessary evil.

Raising my bad arm above my head, I bend my elbow as if I'm trying to itch my back and slowly inch it over towards my other shoulder behind my neck. Screaming through the pain, I keep pushing it until a loud pop sounds and provides me instant relief.

Now that it's back in place, the pain is much more tolerable. I look over the course that seems to sway, or maybe it's me. I don't know at this point, and my eyes seem to grow fuzzier by the second.

The majority of the course still lies ahead, but there are plenty of spaces for me to have an easy route if I just stay the course and keep my wits. I hop through the next two rows easily, even with my ankles screaming in pain with each step.

Landing in a crouch, I balance on a single square row with nothing but air on each side of me. Boots come into view in front of me, my eyes slowly dragging up. Hade stands directly in front of me with a grin that could melt snow.

Confused, I blink up at him. He knows he can't interfere with the Crucible.

"Hade?" He just blinks back and keeps smiling. "W-what are you doing here?" I mumble, struggling to make my lips work. Still, he just stares at me, unwavering. Finding it odd, I slowly push myself up, wobbling until I'm fully balanced.

Out of nowhere, Aeron appears behind him, a blade poised right at Hade's throat. In one swift movement, he slices the blade across Hade's flesh, cutting from side to side. Blood immediately pours out, an endless red river. His eyes turn lifeless, but his smile remains as he tips forward and starts to freefall.

"No!" I scream. "You can't leave me too."

Without thought, I lunge for him, trying to catch him before he falls off the platform. My arms go to wrap around him, but instead, they glide through him like mist. He disappears, and reality tumbles back as I fall towards my impending death.

At the last second, I throw my hands out, my shoulder screaming in protest when my fingers barely catch on the edge of a square two rows up. I dig my nails in, trying to hold all my weight with them.

Click.

The square trembles under my hands as I slowly try and wedge myself more onto the square. Something pricks my palm at the same time I see hundreds of tiny needles rise from below the giant black X marking the spot I'm clinging to for dear life.

Having no other options, I swing my leg up, landing on the sharp needles, my pants taking most of the impact. I slowly drag my body up and onto the square. Spotting the space next to me showing no X, I grunt through the pain and roll my body until I land on my back in the center of it. I swear I see a dark shadow follow slightly behind me again.

Cuts mar my hands, blood trickling between my fingers, back, and legs, but I'm *alive*. That is all that matters right now. One square at a time, and I can survive this.

I *will* survive this.

Standing, I notice my vision has significantly plummeted. The course spins and moves around like the pieces are dancing in front of me. I attempt to take a step forward, but I end up falling slightly backwards before catching myself.

"Fuck!" a male voice screams in the distance. My head turns at a snail's pace until it lands on Tank across from me. Blood pours from his leg, what looks like a trap with spiked teeth clamped tight around his ankle. Ripping his fingers to shreds, he pries the mouth of the trap open and slides his mangled leg out. Part of his flesh catches on the trap and tears away, dragging another scream from him.

He looks to be in worse shape than the last time I looked over at him, but I have no room to talk. His left eye has a blooming dark bruise around it. He looks to be missing a finger, and his leg looks like it was personally acquainted with a shark's mouth.

Swaying my head forward, I realize I'm around halfway through my course. I just need to finish the second half before my legs give out, and it will all be *over*. This is the last test to prove myself before getting my revenge, and it's by far the hardest to persevere through.

Not only does this test strength physically, but mentally as well. My head has never been so mangled and confused while my limbs scream for reprieve. How easy it would be to just call it quits and lie down in the grave of my own making.

It's enticing to just let go. I can taste freedom on the tip of my tongue—freedom to finish this final test, freedom to let go of it all and finally live among the stars.

But which freedom calls to me more?

A familiar sensation caresses against my ear like an embrace, and I lean into it. I know my brain is playing tricks on me, but it feels so real, and I accept it all the same.

"It is not our time yet, Princess. You must fight for me."

My brain is most definitely playing tricks on me now, because there's no mistaking the sound of his warm, familiar voice as it dances across my skin.

"It's me, *love*. You have to keep fighting. *Promise me!*" he pleads. *Theo?*

"Is it really you?" I sob on a hopeful breath. My heart cannot take losing him again. That pain will permanently dig the grave where I will lie my heart to rest for good.

"I'm real. I'm here with you."

Sobbing hysterically, I throw my hand up to muffle my cries. The faint sensation of a shadow still tickles the edge of my ear, and it all makes sense.

Hade.

The man who has been looking out for me since day one. The man who forced me to eat when he saw me withering away. The man who helped train me and never went easy on me. The man who spent his free time letting me scavenge the library for answers. The man who saved my life and forced the gods to keep me here when he could have easily let me bleed to death in my bed. The man who provided countless distractions from my self-imploding just to put a smile on my face and dull the endless ache within the walls of my chest.

It's him. It's always been him. His shadow caressing me provides an extension of himself, helping me get through this last hurdle. He's using his death magic to let me speak to the one person I *need* in this moment, the reason why I'm doing all of this.

It's really Theo.

"I miss you." It comes out as a whisper.

"I miss you too, my love. Promise me, *please*. This is not your end."

My lips tremble. "I promise."

"You would have made the most beautiful bride." His voice shines with pride, and it's my undoing.

I'm unraveling at the seams, flaying and breaking but more whole than I have been in a long time. Another sob racks my body as I hold on to this moment for as long as possible.

"I don't want to say goodbye."

"I have never left your side. I've been with you through it all, and I couldn't be prouder of the woman you are today. You are the key to it all, and now, you have to fight for me. Fight and then *live*. Truly live in every sense of the word. Words cannot describe the privilege of being yours for even just a blip in time. You are my greatest achievement, Nyxi. Always you."

His voice grows fainter with each word, and I realize Hade is struggling to keep the door open between here and the veil beyond.

The final moments of *us*.

"Love you now and in every life to follow," I whisper into the tendril of shadow that now caresses my cheek, providing me strength.

"Love you now and in every life to follow," he echoes back, but it sounds distant until his voice fades into the abyss.

The tendril scoops up a rogue tear sliding down my cheek, leaving love and strength in its wake, my anchor to lean on.

I can do this.

I *will* do this.

"I've never doubted you." The voice is deeper this time, filled with adoration.

Hade.

With one last drag across my cheek, the shadow withdraws back to the corners of the Bubble.

"Thank you," I whisper as I watch them disappear.

Wiping my tear-streaked face, I ready myself again for one last battle. There are eight rows left between me and the finish platform, between me and my revenge. Looking to my side, I count four rows left for Tank to get through, but his are mostly spaces marked with Xs.

Wasting no time, I launch back into motion, leaping to my next row of three. One X sits in the center, which I avoid by spreading my feet and planting them in the squares that bracket it. Wobbling, I throw my arms out wide, trying to regain my balance. The squares dance again in my vision, and the row containing one square in front of me turns to three and then back to one in a dizzying manner.

Braving it, I wobble forward with my arms still out, leaping and hoping my eyes stay true, praying there actually is one safe square in front of me. I collide with the square, but my fall isn't graceful, and I end up rolling my ankle in the process.

The muscle strains but holds true. I don't hear or feel any popping, but it throbs like a heartbeat, probably sporting a small sprain. It's the least of my worries, though, as I check my progress compared to Tank. He only has three rows left.

"Fuck!" Tank bellows next to me. I don't have time to look as I map out my next step at the same time my body sways heavily with fatigue, pain, and a dizzy spell. I can no longer tell which way is up or down, forward or back. It's all a jumble of moving pieces, and I can't keep up.

Something *thumps* a space behind me, and I turn, looking over my shoulder to spot a glowing red orb of light. I can't tell if this is another hallucination or real life. Seeing the smug smirk on Tank's face as he looks between me and the glowing orb behind me, makes me think it very much is real life, and I need to get moving. Looking below him, I notice he's standing on a giant X, and there's a hole missing from the center of the square, where I assume this thing he so graciously gifted me came from.

This *motherfucker* really just threw his mistake at me.

Light grows bigger behind me, and I scream, launching my-self forward at the same time I feel a hot explosion at my back, propelling me further through the air until colliding with a square three spaces up.

I land harshly, the air whooshing from my lungs. I wheeze and cough until the first trickle of air seeps back into my lungs. I feel blood trickle down my forehead, and my back is scorched to shreds. The course behind me is now charred black, burnt to a crisp.

But I'm *alive*.

"You can't kill something already dead inside!" I scream to Tank, but it comes out slurred and wobbly as I try to regain my bearings.

My back protests in red hot pain, the old burns beneath hissing to life. Whoever said wear your scars like badges of honor is not my favorite human at the moment. I'm holding on by my last thread, barely able to put one foot in front of the other.

Three rows left between me and my freedom.

I push the pain of my throbbing, bleeding head, blistered ankles, rolled ankle, scorched back, distorted shoulder, and tattered hands into a nice, neat box, leaving it there to deal with later. There's no time for pain right now, only *winning*.

Screaming out a war cry, I grit my teeth and push on, commanding the squares to stay put and quit their little dancing charade.

I will not die today.

I leap to the next row easily, planting my feet sturdy within the spaces, each foot bracketing the center space marked with an X. Two more. The next row contains only one space, and unfortunately, it's marked with an X. I'll have to launch myself over it onto the last row of spaces, which I realize now has three, all marked with Xs. There's no avoiding them.

It's a trap.

I could pick the single dangerous space now and pray it's the lesser of the two evils, then try to launch myself over the last row of three Xs onto the finishing platform. Or, I hop over the single space X and land on one of the three Xs on the final row. Surely, one has to be better than the other. If I jump and land on the final row, then I can try and scurry to the finish line before one of the three goes off and pray they aren't lethal.

Deciding that's my best bet, I bend my knees, readying myself to make the giant leap, but I freeze in my tracks when a bloodcurdling scream shreds my ears. I can't believe what my eyes see. Tank freefalls from his course, just one row away from the finish line, a giant blade protruding from his gut.

He tumbles through the air, his back getting closer to the ground as his arms and legs flail helplessly for purchase he won't find. His wide eyes find me, and it's the first time I've truly seen fear in his eyes. He looks like he's seen a ghost, and as he gets eerily close to the ground, I avert my eyes before I see him splat to a million pieces.

A loud thump sounds, and then his screams turn silent.

Tank's *dead*.

Gulping, I turn back to my course, staring down the final two rows. Just because Tank is out of the competition doesn't mean I have a free ticket. I still have to finish the course.

Sending one last prayer to Theo, which I know now he's been hearing, a phantom wind brushes against my cheek in answer, and it's all the strength I need. I know what I have to do, and my intuition tells me I need to land on the *left square*. Throwing my body into the air, I careen onto the X on the left of the three provided on the final row.

Click.

The space starts to rattle and shake. Quickly, I stumble onto my hands and knees as my consciousness fades in and out. I can't take any more. I'm losing too much blood, and I don't think the swaying of my head and hallucinations are due to the drugs alone anymore. With the last ounce of energy I can muster, I drag my battered, bleeding body across to the finish platform and collapse in a heap of limp limbs just as the square I was on snaps away and tumbles to the ground.

My eyes dance with spots, and everything around me quiets as all the pain I had locked away batters against my body. It's too much to bear, sinking its sharp teeth in me, attempting to drag me under.

A large body scoops me up and cradles me in their warm embrace. I'm holding on to the cusp of consciousness as I dance in the in-between, begging for mercy from the pain lancing my body.

"You cannot leave me. I won't allow it. Stay awake for me, please! I *need* you." A feather light caress sweeps across my cheek at the same time wetness lands on my face, and I find it odd it could rain inside the Bubble. I wiggle deeper into the embrace, loving how the warmth feels against my skin that is slowly starting to go numb. Yes, this feels nice, and I welcome the pain fizzling away as my body goes light.

I'm ready for sleep.

"I would give up every last drop of my magic this instant if it meant spending one more day with you, if it promised I could hear that beautiful siren laugh of yours that's the illogical reason behind mending my irreparable heart. You hold all my favorite memories in your delicate grasp, you know that? Your hands might even have a claim on my heart too." A strand of hair is brushed from my face. "What have you done to me, dream? I never stood a chance, did I?"

Dream. Yes, that sounds so nice right now. I finally let go and drift off into a peaceful, welcoming sleep.

Chapter
Forty-Five

A HEAVINESS SITS ON MY CHEST, MAKING IT DIFFICULT TO BREATHE. I try to push through the thickness in my lungs, shoving as much air into them as possible. I startle when the heaviness in my chest... shifts.

Using all the energy I can muster, I peel one eye open. Sunlight assaults my eye, making it sting as I squint my surroundings into focus. The heaviness in my chest stirs again. No, not in my chest—*on* my chest.

Black, unruly curls come into view, splayed in a pile of madness across my chest, and I yearn to run my fingers through them. Even, deep breaths fan from his lips, the same plump lips that currently sit *inches* from my face.

Trailing my eyes up, I trace the white lightning bolt scar from his nose up through his pale eye, ending just before his hairline before it disappears underneath his obsidian curls.

I take a moment to study him, enjoying this peaceful moment for myself. I soak it up, every scar, mark, and feature etched within his skin that make up this unique beast. I'm lost in the moment, enjoying a second of quiet for the first time in weeks.

"Perfection," I whisper under my breath as I grip one of his unruly curls between my thumb and finger.

"Are you done stripping me bare with your eyes?" His voice comes out gruff, like he hasn't used it in a very long time.

I jolt, shocked I didn't notice he was awake. "How did you know I was awake?"

Grunting, he shuffles, lifting his head to brace his chin on his fists, his elbows on the edge of the bed. Slowly, he drags his eyes down my entire body, looking me over for any wounds, I'm sure. "I notice everything when it comes to you, *Nyxi*."

Empress, the way he says my name sends a jolt straight to my heart, threatening to stop it completely and revive it wholly in the same beat.

"You're making it a habit of walking death's door." It's a statement, not a question, flooding me with a million emotions.

"As long as you stand on the other side of that door to catch me, I don't see the problem. What is it Winston called you? *Daddy Death?*"

"It's a nasty habit you need to break," he threatens, but it holds no malice, only an underlying tone of concern.

"As long as you keep saving me, I will make it my life's mission to never stop."

Rolling his eyes playfully, he looks me over once more, satisfied with my intact limbs and healed skin. He leans back in his chair, pulled close to his bed where I'm currently lying, and pins me with his stare.

After an intense moment of locked eyes, I manage to speak. "What happened?"

"You won the Crucible," he replies simply.

I nod in understanding, remembering the last moment of dragging my battered body across to the finish before being devoured wholly by pain and nothingness. "How long have I been out?"

"A week. The blessing ceremony is set for tonight, but you don't have to attend if you aren't feeling up to it. It took a lot of mending to get you healed, and clearly, your body needed time to recuperate, seeing as you've been out cold for a week now."

"I want to go." The answer comes out firm, leaving no room for doubt. I've made it this far. This is the last step between me and my freedom, and then my revenge. I'm suddenly whipped in the face by the reality of what tonight's events entail.

I will be granted *magic*.

"What does it feel like?" I question, nervously chewing on my bottom lip. His eyes track the movement before going back up to my eyes in understanding.

"Like a steady hum beneath your skin, a pool of untapped potential at the tips of your fingers, ready to use and shape as you please. It's overwhelming and can corrupt someone if they are overtaken." Thinking to himself, he continues, "To me, it's always felt like a weapon, like I'm the definition of death, which I guess I am. Others who have lesser magic say it feels freeing, like floating on a cloud, but I've never experienced that side of magic. It takes everything in me to control the power threatening to escape and destroy. It is why I always must stay in control. If I let one ounce slip between my fingers, I could corrupt everything in my path."

"You are no weapon to me. You are light. You are healing."

He searches my face desperately for any deception, but he won't find any. He means every sense of the word to me and has shown me what it's like to live again, to see beyond the dark veil clouding my vision, opening my eyes to all the light around me.

Reaching forward, he dusts his knuckles gently across my cheek. "Do you think you got your freckles from your mom or dad? Or maybe the gods blessed you with their touch, each hand placing their mark upon your porcelain skin." He hums to himself happily.

Did he just compliment me? This is uncharted territory, and I don't know how to respond. I open my mouth, and he smirks at my malfunction, chuckling to himself.

"Did I leave you speechless, *dream?*"

"No," I rush out. "I'm still recovering, is all." Attempting to shove the attention on him, I ask, "Why does it look like you're in the same clothes as the last time I saw you?"

"Because they are. I haven't left your side since the Crucible."

I recoil. "But that was a week ago."

"Is that a question or a statement?"

"You mean to tell me you sat in that chair by my side for seven days straight?" I look at him like he's gone mad.

"No. I also held your hand for most of it and ate once when my body protested."

That's it—he's definitely gone mad on me. No one in their right mind would waste seven days of their life sitting in a chair, especially for someone like me.

Reading me like a book, he grunts. "Stop that."

"What?"

"Acting as if you are not worthy of my time or attention. You were hurt badly, and I was there to make sure air remained in your lungs. End of story."

Is that why his head was on my chest? Was he listening to make sure I was still breathing? That is... Well, that is... What the fuck do I even say back to that? Thanks for making sure there was sufficient air in my lungs for the last seven days, even though it meant sleeping in a chair and not washing or eating property? It's too much.

Once again, he reads the emotions flitting across my face, as if we share the same head. "I am right where I *wanted* to be, Nyxi. Lunaria could be crumbling, falling from the damn sky, and I still wouldn't have left your side. Nothing could have pried me from your healing body until I knew you were okay." I go to protest, but he halts me with a single finger to my lips. "You have no idea how long I've waited for someone like you."

"You've waited for damaged goods?" I whisper around his finger.

"More like *perfection*. In every sense of the word. I could not find a better entity to represent the word. You are *perfection* and nothing less."

I drag air into my lungs, trying to remind myself how to breathe. This softer side of Hade is a lot, but it's also healing parts of me that have been dark for far too long. I think back to my conversation with Theo and the promises I made him.

Fight and live. Truly live in every sense of the word.

He made me promise to use this life I have to be happy, to continue without him by my side but always in my heart. To live and to love again. To be free. All of this has been for him. Once I finish what I came here to do, I will fulfill my promise.

I will continue to live in every sense of the word. For him, but also for myself.

"Thank you," is all I can bring myself to respond with, because how does one respond to a man serving compliments like that on a silver platter, as if I personally hung Lunaria in the sky for him? "Now that you've confirmed there is indeed air in my lungs, maybe you could go wash up. You positively *stink*." I'm only playing with him, because this man could walk out of battle and still smell like a smokey dream, but I also know he needs to take care of himself after dedicating a week to taking care of me.

That deep chuckle I love so much washes over my skin as he pulls the back of my hand up to his lips. "I'm glad to see you're back to your annoying, attitude-filled self."

The door swings open at the same time Hade moves to stand. "I still don't understand why you placed her here and not her room. It's like you purposely did it to make me walk a million extra steps to see her."

Stretching my neck, I peer behind Hade's tall frame and collide with a stunned pair of forest green eyes. Des is dressed in a blush pink dress with red hearts stitched into the fabric that I'm sure she sewed herself. She paired it with a black leather corset, red hearts clipped in her light gray locks.

"*Always and tomorrow,*" she gasps between hysterical sobs. She breaks into a full sprint and tackles me in bed. My muscles groan on impact, still sore from being mended.

"Shit, sorry. Are you hurt?" Turning as if I'm not capable of answering myself, she asks Hade, "Is she okay?"

"I'm right here, you know. I can answer for myself."

"Shhh, not now. Is. She. Okay?" she asks Hade with a deadly seriousness I've never heard from her. I sigh, rolling my eyes and trying to pull away, but she just moves along with me.

"She's okay," he says thoughtfully, and I swear, a silent conversation passes them.

Satisfied, Des scoops me up into the tightest hug that threatens to remove the air from my lungs after Hade made it his life mission to make sure they stayed filled. "I knew you would come back to me. You're too much of a badass to die. That would be so beneath you. Plus, who would dress you to perfection in the afterlife? That would be truly criminal."

"I missed you too," I giggle into her hair.

"Don't ever give me a heart attack like that again," she threatens. Peeling her body from mine, she pins me with her pleading stare that hurts my heart a touch, spotting the pain I've caused her. "Promise me," she whispers.

"I promise. Always and tomorrow, remember?"

She grips my pinkie in hers and then tugs me forward, planting a sloppy, wet kiss on my cheek. "I have to catch you up on all the castle drama!" she exclaims excitedly, back to her over the top, chipper self. "Oh, Empress, what is that god awful smell?" She pinches her nose, making a show of it, and Hade takes it as his cue to dismiss himself to the ensuite washroom.

Sinking back into the bed, Des slides in next to me and strokes my hair while she spills all the drama. We laugh, we cry, she tells me about the romance book she's reading, and we just enjoy each other's company and this life we are blessed to live. I feel happily content.

"I almost forgot," she screams. "I have a surprise for you we've been working on!"

We?

Chapter
Forty-Six

My knees threaten to buckle at the reflection staring back at me. I don't even recognize the woman in front of me. It's me, but it's also a fighter. A warrior. A symbol of perseverance and defiance.

I've never felt more beautiful and powerful in my life.

"Des…" I breathe.

Smacking my arm, she warns, "Nope, I told you, no crying. You'll ruin my masterpiece, and I'm not humble enough to refrain from saying this is my best work to date. So keep it together for the both of us, because I did not just slave away for hours for nothing." She harrumphs.

No words could describe the immense pride I have at the outfit Des has created. It's truly a work of art, hands down the most beautiful thing I have ever laid witness to. It embodies every emotion I feel, and I feel unstoppable.

I glide my hands down the material, snaking through my fingers like liquid gold mixed with an airy embrace, sending chills down my spine. I don't know how she got him to help, but Hade is woven into every inch of the outfit.

The night sky stares back at me, glittering and swirling in a hypnotizing madness gloved to my body. When Des told me Hade *gifted* her a portion of his shadow magic as a material to weave and work into the very fiber of my Blessing Ceremony outfit, my ass about hit the floor.

I had no idea one could even give away a chunk of their magic. Des told me it is not something she has ever seen anyone do, but it is possible. It can be painful, like losing a part of your very being, a limb. For most, it could be draining and detrimental, but Des assured me Hade is one of the strongest Magicals in all of Lunaria. His magical reserves are practically endless. To him, it would feel like losing a single hair from his head.

Each detail is hand woven and designed to utter perfection. The entire outfit floats about like a fluid wave, swirling around me in a veil of sparkling obsidian. Long, tapered, wispy sleeves drape to the floor like torn, shadowed fabric.

The bodice is made from sparkling black shadows, woven together to make a lacey pattern over my chest and stomach, letting parts of my skin shine through. A waterfall of black fabric swooshes out from the bottom of the bodice, layered with shadow magic to create a wave-like flowing mass around me. They fall to the floor but float just an inch above, slithering like restless snakes. There's a slit on each side where each leg slips through, almost all the way up to my hip bone, where a sheet of fabric drapes between them.

Every inch of the dress glitters like a million stars. I feel safe and protected with him wrapped around me, as if he's actually here.

A long, black shadow-infused veil drags behind me on the floor, attached to my long black curls that cascade down my back.

Des used her Luster magic to paint my eyes dark and glittery to match my dress, making my steel-forged eyes glow in harsh contrast. My porcelain skin glitters subtly, making my glittering black lips stand out like the dead. To finish the look, Des marked the center of my forehead with an abstract, black glittering moon and star symbol.

If the night sky was a person, I would be her, and I feel like I could take over the world in this outfit.

"Oh, one last thing." She reaches into my vanity, pulling out a dainty black necklace. The air whooshes from my lungs. I haven't worn it in a week, and my neck has felt naked without it.

Standing behind me, she drapes the dagger necklace over my front and easily clasps it at the back, letting it flow down my cleavage. Now, the outfit feels whole, having both the men who saved me with me.

"I thought you said no crying," I scold playfully.

Biting her quivering lip, she shakes her finger at me. "I said you couldn't cry. I never made any promises about myself. Now, give me a spin and let mama see her masterpiece in its full glory."

Giggling, I twirl for her as she smiles and dabs the tears from her happy weeping eyes. The material floats like waves crashing against a cove with no rhyme or reason, just shadows slithering around me.

"Perfection," she chokes out and scoops me into a hug.

Pulling away, I kiss her forehead and thank her for working her magic on me once again. She tries to fluff my dress for the eighth time, even though it's already perfect. "Stop fussing over me and go, or you're not gonna have enough time to get yourself ready for the ceremony." She looks me up and down, ready to protest, but I shove her towards the door. "I look perfect. Now go before I shove you out the door myself."

Throwing a playful glare over her shoulder, she disappears out the door and down the hall. As soon as the door shuts, I let out one, long breath as nerves and anticipation take over.

Looking at the clock, I note I have exactly twenty minutes until Hade promised to collect me from my room for the ceremony, which is enough time to conduct my plan. I silently slip out into the hallway, towards the one place I've been dying to visit, born from pure curiosity and unease.

It won't help me now, but I'm still dying to know if it's still there and what it could be. As I approach the hidden library, my heart threatens to rip from my chest to the floor.

I stop at the door, apparently not thinking this plan through when I realize I'm locked out without Hade. One of the tendrils of Hade's magic woven into my dress slithers up, wrapping around the handle and pushing it open. The door recognizes his magical signature; it opens with ease, allowing me access.

My lungs deflate as the anxiety buzzing under my skin dissipates a fraction, but not completely. Walking through the door, it closes behind me, and I take in the dark, empty space riddled with old and new books.

Getting onto my hands and knees, I knock on each wooden floorboard, listening to any that sound hollow beneath. After ten minutes of crawling around, I stop dead in my tracks when one knock vibrates with a different tune, as if there's a pocket beneath it.

Wedging my nails in the crack, I pry the floorboard up, and my eyes widen when I note a single leather bound book placed within.

The birthday gift the journals mentioned.

Carefully, I snatch it out of the cavity and stride over to the worn leather chair Hade favors. Settling into the indent he's made, I drag my finger across the weathered cover.

"The Tale of Gods," I whisper, dragging my finger over each letter of the title.

A fable book? Why would a book of fables be so important to hide within the floorboards, only to be found when the time is right? Seeing as it's covered in dust and cobwebs, I conclude it was never found or retrieved until now.

Why was the mother referenced in the journals so intent on this gift? Did she leave a special note hidden within? Is it a family heirloom passed down through the generations? I try not to be discouraged, but I'm slightly disappointed in my findings.

Even though the Crucible is over, the riddle the Empress gave us has been sitting at the forefront of my brain, nagging me to find the answer. It feels too important to ignore, even now, when it won't save me from anything except my annoyingly overbearing need to know the answer.

My curiosity gets the best of me, and I open to page one, reading over the table of contents. *Family Tree, Creation, Checks and Balances, Legacy, Recorded Powers,* and finally, *The Corruption of Dark Magic.*

Opening it to the section titled *Creation,* I start reading.

The creation of a god is set forth long before one is birthed into power. It is a complex and widely unknown system created by Mother Nature herself and is up to her sole discretion. No one knows why she chooses who she does, only the patterns of her maternal giftings.

Every five thousand years, god blood runs true in one person of her choosing. A drop of it runs through their very veins, starting from birth, and grows with them over time. Mother Nature will test her new subject with trials and tribulations, studying their decisions and moral compass.

If they pass each of her trials, in their sixteenth year of life, exactly five thousand years after the previous blessing, she will bless them with the ability to become one of the ruling gods. Their full magical abilities will bloom in that year, granting them immortality and the official knowledge of their new title.

Each god is widely known to be stronger and more powerful than the last, as Mother Nature herself has become pickier over the years, stringent on only turning out perfection. The hierarchy of gods govern in a faraway land called Ouranos that has never been studied due to its classified and unattainable nature. There is no knowledge of where this land sits, or what it entails.

No one is perfect, even Mother Nature herself, and as such, there may be unprecedented times when a faulty god is chosen and starts as something almighty and pure but turns towards evil temptation. While this is rare and few and far between, it is not entirely ruled out.

Gods are born from raw power, and as such, crave the very being that make them up. They are picked to strive and be the best, and being the best means having an abundance of power to manipulate and rule over the mortals.

While Mother Nature creates and molds her gods, she does not govern them. They are to be perfect children, and fall into a hierarchy best fit to mold and support the mortals in their need for endless guidance.

When a new god emerges, they are to mentor under the wing of the current top god and take over as the superior god with their abundance of raw power, as they will always be gifted with more power than the last. The gods are ever evolving, learning from past endeavors and remaining superior above all else.

They are to guide and mold society to success, each god handpicked to support in each role needed to mold society into a working, unbreakable system.

My mind whirls with this new information, an uneasiness settling deep in the pit of my stomach. Is this really a fable, or is there some truth behind the text? Deciding to dig further, I flip to the front of the book, looking over the family tree. My finger drags down each name, all branching to fill the page until I get to the last recorded god.

Airestol Stacardi.

Looking at the date etched next to his name, I do the math and notice he was blessed into an immortal five thousand and four years ago. Under his name is a blank space that should have been filled out four years ago, marking a new god's emergence. The line sits empty and waiting, as if forgotten over time.

Maybe they forgot to fill it out. Maybe it truly is a fable. Maybe the new god did not pass the tests. Or maybe this text was transcribed and has not been updated in a long time.

I go to flip to the next section, curious to dive into the world of the gods, but then my attention catches on the clock on the wall, and I curse under my breath. I have exactly two minutes before Hade knocks impatiently at my door; if I know anything about him, it's that he is always punctual and *hates* being late.

I quickly stuff the book back under the floor, shoving the boards back down for a later date, and rush out of the room like my feet are on fire. My dress swooshes aggressively as if the shadows are agitated at me, or maybe they are just missing their daddy.

Collecting the moving abundance of material in each fist, I rush down the last hallway into my room just in time to catch my breath and fix my rogue frizzy curls poking out from under my veil from running so fast.

Just as I'm satisfied with the woman staring back at me in the mirror, I hear a steady three knocks on the other side of my door, and my heart flutters with anticipation. Striding over to my door, I take one deep, steadying breath and swing it open, just for all the air to whoosh out of my lungs in less than a second.

I consciously try to hold my jaw firmly shut from the devastatingly handsome man standing opposite me. Hade is dressed to the nines in an immaculate white suit, the opposite of me in every way. His usual all black getup is gone to the wind, and frankly, he's never looked better.

Don't get me wrong, his fighting uniform does things to me no sane woman could survive, but seeing him in a simple, bright white suit paired with accents of black has me on the verge of a real life heart attack. His dark eye swirls with malice while his light eye seems to brighten when paired with the suit, and I cannot take my eyes off him.

Gulping slowly, he looks me over from head to toe at an excruciatingly slow pace that has my pulse hammering in my neck. "*My gods*, Nyxi." He drops to his knees in front of me, my eyes about to bulge out of my goddamn head.

This man, this beast, this powerful killing machine, is on his knees before me as if I am his sole god to worship.

"You are magnificent, *dream*," he whispers to himself.

I try to reach forward, attempting to pull him back to his feet, but he only snatches my hand and places the softest kiss on my skin. "I'm exactly where I belong, worshiping at the altar of the goddess who has blessed me with viewing privileges of the rarest piece of art in all of Lunaria. *Fuck that*, in the entire universe. I would pray at your feet for the rest of my days if it meant I never had to take my eyes off you."

I think I might just die right here and now, because nothing could ever top the high I am riding, and I'm afraid nothing ever will.

Chapter
Forty-Seven

THE BALLROOM IS DECORATED EXTRAVAGANTLY, EXPENSIVE DECOR dripping from every inch. It's bright and fresh, white and silver painted throughout. It seems the Empress has gone for a sky theme in homage to Lunaria.

Guests mingle, packed from wall to wall for the blessing that will commence shortly. They chat, drink, and dance with the anticipation of what power will be imparted to me by the Empress, and I won't lie—that is exactly what has taken occupancy in my head as well.

Hade gracefully maneuvers us into the ballroom and through the boisterous crowd, leading me with my arm linked through his. A waiter walks by with a tray of drinks, and he snatches two off before thanking the man.

"For the nerves, my lady." He hands me one of the glass flutes, which looks to have champagne in it. I can't help the faint, anxious blush creeping up my cheeks.

"Such a gentleman," I tease.

"Only for you," he hums.

I eagerly lift the glass to my lips, downing one large gulp that bubbles down my throat, drowning a sliver of my nerves with it. I take a second sip for good measure, which makes Hade lift a quizzical eyebrow.

"Positively parched." I throw the words over my shoulder as I take the lead, dragging him towards the dance floor. He moves with me seamlessly, and I think at this point, he would let me drag him all the way to the edge of Lunaria without a single fuss.

I turn to face him and crash into his large chest pressed close behind me. Tipping my chin up with his finger, he smiles down at me. "Dance with me, *dream*."

We each finish off the last of our drinks and abandon them on a nearby table. Gripping my hand softly, he drags me to the center of the dance floor. This side of Hade is dizzying in the best way possible. Every inch of this hard man has slowly softened into a puddle of malleable mush each time he's in my vicinity. I'm not sure if it's from almost witnessing me die on multiple occasions, or if he's slowly learning to drop his walls around me. Either way, as long as he keeps showing me these softer sides, I'm content.

Pulling me close, we sway to the slow music, couples moving in tandem to the beat. His body heat seeps into me, a warm, unmoving wall to latch myself to.

"Last time I was here, I was in another man's arms," I tease, breaking the silence.

Leaning down, he growls into my hair, "Don't fucking remind me. And never speak of another man while you're in my arms, *nightmare*."

My breath hitches. "I thought you were done with that little nickname?"

"I thought you were done being a brat, but it seems we're both sorely mistaken."

"Brute," I mumble playfully under my breath.

He draws our bodies closer. "*Your* brute."

Both of our shocked gazes collide with his outright admission. He's never said something like that so openly before, or labeled what this is between us. So far, we have been clinging to each other as a way to survive each round of the Crucible. Now that's all over, what does this mean between us?

He searches my eyes—for what, I don't know. Maybe to see if I'm scared, or repulsed, or if I'm about to run and flee after practically handing me a sliver of his heart, but if anything, it only pushes me closer to him.

Slowly, moving up on the tips of my toes, I plant a soft, innocent kiss to his lips to smooth over the emotions taking war over his worried gaze. It seems to do the trick as a slow, long breath fans over me from his stunned lips.

His large, rough hands engulf my face, angling me to look up at him. "Do you know what you do to me, Nyxi? Your gorgeous fucking eyes, *good lord*. One look from you could bring an entire army to their knees. You *decimate* me every time those silver orbs grace my skin."

In one fluid, sure movement, he crashes his greedy lips to mine, not giving a damn where we are or who's watching. He's ravishing me like it will be the last time, desperate to taste all of me. I lean into the kiss, letting him take all he wants and reveling in the way my body hums to life under his burning touch.

Pulling back, we take deep breaths, trying to calm our racing hearts and heaving lungs. His eyes bore into mine, a plea and a promise shining within them, a plea to take a risk and a promise for tomorrow and forever.

I smile back at the man in front of me, a genuine full smile, and pull him close again. I mold my body to his, joining us as one. We sway to the music, more upbeat than the last song.

Squealing, my feet lift off the ground as Hade drops me to stand on his shoes so he can take the lead. I playfully slap his chest but stay put, enjoying this little slice of fun. It's light, it's easy, and it's something I could get used to for the rest of my days.

"Are you going to do that little darkness trick again if another man asks to dance with me?"

He chews the inside of his cheek. "I have no clue what you are referencing, *woman*."

"So you wouldn't be an overprotective jealous brute if I were to say…" Looking around the room, I find the tallest man standing on the perimeter of the ballroom and point his way. "Ask that man if he would fancy a dance with the Crucible champion?"

Hade's fingers dig possessively into my hip, and he leans down so his lips brush the shell of my ear. "You can go ahead and try, Nyxi, but it would be his life you are forfeiting. I dare you to walk over there, but I fear by the time you make it to his side, there won't be an ounce of air left trickling through his pathetically weak lungs."

His deadly calm threat washes over my skin; I don't doubt that if I were to take two steps in his direction, he wouldn't hesitate to strangle the life out of that man with his shadows. Weirdly, I don't feel put off by his comments. No, instead, I feel wanted.

Important.

"So you admit you're a jealous man?"

"I would have to be envious of him to be a jealous man, and that man has nothing of value." Leaning over me, he drags his finger possessively down the bodice of my dress, sending chills scattering in every direction. "The only thing I truly envy right now is how my shadows are currently wrapped around your bare flesh instead of me."

I am well and truly *fucked*.

"Oh," I breathe, trying to find the right words to respond to that bomb he just left in my lap. I think I would prefer the one

Tank threw at me during the Crucible to this one that has my lungs heaving for air under this tight dress and his even more suffocating gaze. I swear, I feel Hade's shadows weaved into my dress squeeze me tighter. I'm suddenly overheating, squirming under his half-lidded gaze crawling across my skin and leaving permanent marks in its wake.

"Oh," he repeats in a gravely tone.

Trying to break this tension I swear I could grip between my fingers, I reply sarcastically, "So that's a no to going over there, then?"

"Negative." He warns in a deadly low tone.

"Was just double checking," I say sweetly, booping his nose with my finger.

He growls under his breath but loosens his hold on me slightly, spinning us to the beat again. Both of our moods lighten instantly, to the point I start to giggle as he throws me out and spins me back to him, my dress billowing like a cloud of mist.

Des and Winston eventually join the chaos as we dance and laugh. Odessa downs her fourth glass of alcohol while Winston nurses a glass of orange juice, trying to savor it. They begin to dance to a beat that doesn't line up with the music, and I can't help the boisterous laugh while watching them trip over each other.

Des' immaculate, sparkling silver cloud dress catches on Winston's feet, and they topple into each other while laughing the entire time. We are becoming quite the spectacle, and with my second glass of champagne sitting deep in my belly, I welcome the attention with open arms.

"*Attention! Attention!*" Empress Gwyn stands center stage, clinking a knife to her glass. "Welcome, my citizens, to another wonderful Blessing Ceremony." Cheers and claps erupt, and she lets them play out for a moment. "Can we please have our guest of honor join us on stage?"

I gulp thickly, dragging my suddenly clammy hands down my dress. Hade grabs my arm firmly in his and leads the way to the stage, anchoring me the whole way. He gives my hand one firm, supportive squeeze before gesturing me up to join the Empress.

She reaches out for me, pulling me up next to her. Weirdly, her grip feels warm and comforting, which I find odd, but I don't pull away.

Swinging my arm above my head, she announces, "Ladies and gentleman, this year's Reaper Crucible winner, Nyxi from Vagrant Sector." Another round of shouts and whistles ring out, louder this time, and I look out over the crowd, feeling a pang of pride for once.

We did it, Theo.

Dropping my arm, she continues. "Now, the fun part. The blessing. As you all should know, I'm an Impart, meaning I can pull from the very ground below me and grant someone the ability to wield magic. While I can grant magic, I cannot choose the type they are blessed with. That is solely decided by who they are at their core and what the universe deems they can handle." Pausing for dramatics, she says excitedly, "Shall we see what magic the universe has decided to bless our dear Nyxi with?"

The crowd goes silent, and I close my eyes, committing this last moment of peace to memory.

Opening my eyes, I feel steadier than I have in a very long time. The Empress points her palms down towards the ground, closing her eyes. Her fingers curl as bright light erupts from the ground, her hands moving slowly as if she's plucking the magic through the floor.

The light grows until it snaps from the ground and forms one giant, glowing orb. Opening her eyes, she floats the orb in front of my chest. "Nyxi, it is time to see what fate has destined for you."

In one, swift movement, she shoves the orb into my chest. It clashes harshly with my body, knocking me back slightly until it becomes one with me. I feel a heavy pressure in my chest as it slides inside me, learning its new home.

It's an uncomfortable pressure at first, until it slowly seeps into every inch of my body, a heavy hum beneath my skin. I'm vibrating, and it's overwhelming as my body fights this foreign entity inside it. I breathe through the pressure, air seizing my lungs each time I try to take too deep of a breath. My eyes burn, and my body becomes heavy and dizzy with the sheer power running through my veins.

Whispers of anticipation break out, but I can't hear any of them as I fight to stay conscious. My fingers tingle and itch, as if they are begging to release an ounce of this heaviness within me. My back aches, a pressure sitting between my shoulder blades, begging to be released.

Without thought, I flex my buzzing hands while closing my eyes, startling when deathly screams rupture my eardrums. My body feels light as a feather, the buzzing under my skin now a manageable hum, and the ache between my shoulders has dissipated.

Opening my eyes, I panic when I notice the entire ballroom is plunged in pure darkness, nothing in sight. Something feels like it's nudging at me...no, at my *magic*, as if trying to wrangle it into submission.

The darkness surrounding us is coming from *me*.

The nudging feels cold and dark...familiar in a way. I stop fighting it, letting it invade my senses and brush against me, urging me to fall under its command. It pushes against my magic, and my magic responds, easing its way back inside me where it belongs.

When I feel a single tendril snake across my cheek, I realize why it feels familiar. It's Hade, helping me gain control, coaching me through it. I close my eyes again and open myself to him fully, allowing him to take control.

Gasps ring out, making me open my eyes once more. I'm met with hundreds of stunned eyes staring back at me. The room is no longer plunged in darkness, and my feet are no longer touching the floor. Every citizen drops to their knees, bowing before me.

Looking to my left and right, I realize why the ache between my shoulder blades has resolved. Two beautiful black wings jut out from my back, flapping lazily to keep me afloat. My gaze sweeps to my right again, and I can physically feel all the color drain from my face when my eyes land on the giant black sword from under my floorboards grasped tightly in my shaking hand. My head is thrown back as I'm assaulted with a flashback that has my body convulsing.

A young Hade kneels in front of me, presenting me with his personal black sword with owl eyes carved just above the handle. He stares at me with knee-wobbling intensity, promising it will protect me in his absence. It is imbued with his magic, and as his Eternal, it will recognize a part of him within me.

I'm launched back into the present, gasping for air as my wings vanish, and I fall to the floor. Getting to my feet, I snatch my dress up and take off, sprinting out of the ballroom.

My whole life is a lie.

Chapter
Forty-Eight

My body can barely keep up with my feet as I race down the hallway. I have no idea where I'm headed, just that I needed to get out of there. I don't let myself stop, or everything will come crashing down, and I don't think I'm ready for that.

"Nyxi!" Hade shouts.

I don't stop, my feet push me harder, and I realize I'm headed towards my room. I round the last corner and crash inside. I fall to my hands and knees, heaving and begging for air to enter my lungs.

A crash thuds, like my door has been ripped off its hinges. A large presence kneels next to me, and a soft embrace rubs down my back. "Breathe," he whispers. I manage to drag one shaky breath into my lungs. "That's it. Again."

I gasp again, less shaky this time, and he continues stroking my back until I'm able to gain control of my breathing enough to speak. "I don't understand." I try to speak again, but a searing sensation rips across my back, and I gasp, my back bowing.

Standing, I rush to my vanity, ripping the veil from my hair and turning my back to face the mirror. "Oh my gods." Staring back at me is a large marking sitting in the center of my back. A delicate, abstract, black swirl wraps around a ball of fire.

My Eternal marking with Hade.

When I look up, my eyes crash with his wide ones in the mirror. He takes one slow, painful gulp.

"Hade?" I whisper shakily.

"You came back to me," he says, trembling through his words.

The magic humming through my body pushes at the permanent fog around my mind, slowly melting it away. Every repressed memory of my entire life since birth plays out in my head.

I see myself growing up in the castle. Learning to wield my night magic. Meeting Hade for the first time. My mother...oh gods, *Mama*. The Empress is my mother. My loving, sweet mother, who would never harm a hair on a single person's head but is somehow now corrupt. And Papa... Where is my father?

What happened that changed it all? The last thing I remember is the day before my sixteenth birthday, getting ready for my coming of age celebration. Mother told me how much she loved me. She mentioned the birthday gift she hid in the library for me, that it would forge me into the woman I was destined to be when the time was right.

A nagging feeling itches the back of my brain. What am I missing? One glaring question zaps me straight in the heart.

What happened to all the magic? There was never a Crucible growing up, and citizens in Fallout were originally sent there from Lunaria as punishment until they started their own civilization, growing families and breaking off into sectors. That means they would all have magic down there as well. How did I end up down there...with Theo?

I think over everything I know, and then I'm reminded of one important thing.

The riddle.

Where three meet, one left behind. A sacrifice greater than mankind. A piercing cry from the one black eye. For that shall reset time before the ultimate crime.

"Hade?" I whisper.

"Yes, dream?" He takes a hesitant step, as if trying not to frighten me but needing to be closer.

"Remind me what you nicknamed the sword you gifted me?"

"*Black eye.*"

I blanch.

"I don't understand," I whisper defeatedly. Hade takes another hesitant step towards me, and I raise my heavy eyes up to meet his. He stands inches from me, and I can tell his heart is racing inside his chest. He looks devastated but also more complete than I've ever witnessed. He looks lost but hopeful. He looks like he's seen a ghost.

"Did you know?"

"No," he rushes out then nibbles his lip nervously. "Yes. Well, no, not entirely." Running his hands through his hair, he sighs. "At first, no. When I arrived at your house to collect you for the Crucible, I had no idea who you were. I was so offput and negative towards you because I felt this uncontrollable pull to wrap you in my arms and never let you go. I didn't understand why. So I was mean, trying to push you away because being around you was unbearable. A piece of my heart has always felt like it's been missing, a piece of me ripped away, but I could never understand why." Dropping his forehead to mine, he breathes a sigh. "Now, I know. The missing piece was you. It's always been you, Nyxi. It seems nothing can keep us apart."

I nod, knowing the feeling. From the beginning, I never should have felt a pull towards him, not with Theo so present in my mind, but I did. I didn't understand it, but he felt familiar. He felt like home, same as Theo.

"I tried to keep my distance, get you a new guard. I couldn't control my need to take care of you, be near you, *protect* you. I couldn't stand the thought of another man looking at you, let alone talking to you. The night Aeron tried to assassinate you, I had this feeling pulling me towards your room. It's like the bond knew you needed me, and so it called me."

Gripping the back of my neck, he rubs his thumb down to my pulse point and presses lightly. "I've never felt such rage as the scene I walked in on. Seeing him over your bleeding dying body...I snapped. I pride myself for my control, but that night, all I saw was black, death, and revenge. I was physically shaking to control my power so I wouldn't blow the whole damn castle to shreds, you included. My only regret is that I didn't draw out his torture. Death was too easy for the things he made me feel, for the things he did to you."

Pulling back, he pins me with his haunted gaze. "That night, when you asked me to join you in the bath, my whole world flipped upside down. When I saw your back, I wasn't only haunted by the burns etched into your perfect skin. I also saw your Eternal mark that matched the twin one on my back. I didn't understand how it was possible. You had no idea it was there, but I could see it all the same. You just broke the glamour and found your memories by regaining your magic."

His next words come out pained as he presses our foreheads closer. "I still had no memories of you, but I knew you were my Eternal, my one true match in life, and you had no idea. It pained me, but I knew I couldn't tell you. You wouldn't understand, especially if you couldn't see your own mark. I didn't want to push you, not with everything you had been through with Theo, how heavily you loved and missed him.

"I knew I would never be able to fill the shoes he left behind. You talked about him as if he was the only important thing you've ever had in your life. The more you told me about him, the more I fell in love with him too, with the way he treated and loved you. I died inside when I found out who you were to me, knowing I couldn't tell you. I most likely would never have you the way my soul begged for. You may never feel the same way back."

His words come out hurt but hold no malice. This bond between us runs deep within our blood, our very souls. There is no escaping it. There is no avoiding it. There is no forgetting it.

"You once told me you never needed anyone in life," I whisper softly.

He grunts, a soft laugh following. "I am a liar, Nyxi. But if I am a liar, that makes you a thief, because you stole my heart from the moment those beautiful eyes landed on me. I knew that because you didn't have magic, the bond would never snap in place for you. You were still heart-shatteringly glamoured, and there was nothing in the world I could do about it. I screamed inside for you to see me, the real me."

He pulls back to stare me dead in the eyes. "So I knew right then and there, with every inch of my trapped and tortured soul, I had to make you see me for me without the bond, as long as you would allow your heart to be vulnerable again. I had to make you fall in love with me for me, not the bond aiding you along the way. I would have burned the entire castle to the ground to gain an ounce of your attention, to feed my starved soul with your presence."

Cupping his cheek softly, I lean into him. "Little did you know, you were chasing a love that was already there. You were trying to get me to fall *back* in love with you."

"And did it work, dream?" he says hopefully.

"You tell me." Leaning forward, I crash my lips to his. He scoops me up and drags our bodies together, and it feels like running home again. It's a kiss full of lost time and love. It's an answer and a plea wrapped in one. His lips don't devour mine; instead, they take their time memorizing every inch of lost skin pressed to his. They eagerly welcome me home, where I've always belonged.

Our bodies finally part but stay connected by our souls. Shifting my tear-filled eyes up at him, I ask, "Was any of it real?" By the expression on his face, he knows exactly what I'm referencing. It feels like this man has his hand wrapped around my heart, able to burst it with his next words.

"Yes, of course, it was real. The love you two shared was raw and powerful. You may have not spent all your years growing up with Theo like you thought, but the love you shared is as real as the love I have for you. Immense, endless, unbreakable."

I drag one wobbly lip between my teeth, hanging on to every word this man preaches, mending my heart back together piece by piece. "Are you upset at me?"

Pulling me in for a hug, he whispers into my hair, "I could never be upset with you, love. I'm so thankful you had Theo to love and look after you in my absence. The only thing keeping me sane after learning I've missed out on four years with you is knowing Theo was there taking care of you. My life will forever be indebted to him for keeping the single most important thing to me alive and loved."

I press my face into his warm chest, trembling in his hold as silent tears stream down my face. It's a bittersweet feeling, knowing I get one love but having to lose the other in the process. Except, it isn't lost. It will always live on in my heart, traveling alongside me.

"Hade?" I whisper. He pulls away just an inch so our faces are inches from touching, so much yearning and hope shining on his face. "*I love you.*"

The smile that takes over his face could level the entire continent. He takes a deep breath to respond when a knock thuds on the other side of my door.

I have a feeling my world is about to flip upside down again.

Chapter
Forty-Nine

CLEARING HIS THROAT, THE VANQUISHER STANDING ON THE OTHER side of my door slightly bows. "Miss, the Empress has requested your presence in her private chambers."

My pulse hammers in my neck, and I give the man a curt nod. Hade saddles up next to me protectively and links his arm in mine, always my rock when I'm feeling anxious.

"*I've got you.*"

My shocked eyes collide with Hade's already staring back at me. He just spoke in my head...the bond. I forgot the Eternal bond allows you to speak in each other's mind. I didn't realize how much I've missed hearing his voice in my head, having a constant line of connection to him until this very moment.

"*We've got each other,*" I send down the bond to him, pouring as much love as I can with it. He squeezes my arm as we walk down the endless hallways to my mother's chambers.

The grand doors open to showcase an opulent room. We walk into a sitting room at the front, where a giant black velvet couch sits in the center, bracketed by two chairs and a short table.

The Empress lounges on the couch, sipping a glass of champagne, while a lady I don't recognize sits expectedly next to her. I notice her bright blue eyes first, her soft black curls floating about covered by a veil. She has a certain glow to her light skin that has my eyes snagging for a couple extra seconds. I hesitantly enter the room, and both of their eyes snap up to meet mine.

When my eyes clash with the Empress', a million repressed emotions simmer to a breaking point. "Mama?" I gasp.

"My baby," she breathes lovingly, gesturing me forward. I run towards her as she scoops me up into one of her healing hugs I've missed so much. She drags her palm down the back of my head in a maternal way that makes me want to ball up in her lap.

"I don't understand," I whisper into her neck.

"That's what I'm here for, my child. It will all make sense, love. You just have to trust me. Can you do that for me?" I nod, and she strokes my hair one last time. "Good girl. You have always been the key to a brighter tomorrow, and now is the time to begin."

We part, and I settle into one of the chairs next to the couch. I would expect Hade to settle in the other across from me, but his protective nature takes over. He moves to stand behind my chair, like a gargoyle looking over me to scare away my enemies.

"Alright, let's begin," my mother says. "What's the last thing you remember, Nyxi?"

I nervously nibble my lip as my mind rewinds to my last lucid memories of living here in Lunaria. "My coming of age celebration. You kept telling me how much you loved me. You told me you hid a birthday present under the floorboards of the library and to only seek it out when I knew the time was right."

She nods once. "And did you seek out that gift?"

It's me who nods this time. "I did. Although at the time, I did not know I was looking for my own gift. Before the blessing ceremony, I snuck away because I kept feeling this curiosity as to what the gift could be, this pull to the riddle even though the Crucible was over. I found my old diaries in the library a while back and have been reading them over for answers. In the last one, I wrote about a gift left for me in the library, and I haven't been able to stop thinking about it since."

"You found it exactly when you should have, just as I asked. Fate has a way of pushing things into action. I'm proud of the woman you've become."

"What do the journals or my gift have to do with any of this? How did I end up in Fallout? Why did I not remember you or Hade or living up here?"

"There is one more important question. It is the key to it all."

I know the question she's begging me to ask, because it's also been at the forefront of my mind and the thing I'm most confused about.

"Where did all the magic go?" I question.

"Exactly, my dear. I'm glad you asked." She smiles at me with such pride. My heart feels funny trying to divide my mother from the cruel Empress I've endured.

My mother gestures over to the quiet lady next to her, who has been observing every detail. "This is Hesti. She has helped guide you in times when I could not."

I look over at the soft, quiet lady next to my mother in confusion. "I don't understand. No offense, but I've never seen this woman in my life." She shines me a sweet, understanding smile, and it eases my nerves an ounce.

"Just because you've never laid eyes on her, dear, does not mean she hasn't helped guide you in times of need."

My eyebrows furrow in confusion. Now that I think about it, I've always felt like I had a sixth sense guiding me through life decisions. I always thought it was my gut getting me through tough times, but maybe it was *her.*

"You helped me during the Crucible?" She nods once with a genuine smile. "You helped me escape Tank and Jade in the first round, pushed me towards certain blocks to pull for round two. You even shoved me towards the boat to sit in for round three."

Oh gods, *Rayah.* I was shoved towards the boat that would ensure my survival while simultaneously sentencing my friend to death. It's not fair; it isn't right.

"You, my youngling, are what's most important. You are the key to it all, and your survival is crucial," Hesti responds in a firm but loving tone.

"I don't want to be the key. I don't want any of this. I just want my friend back." My heart seizes at the thought of Rayah, with her bright hair and even brighter smile.

"All will be righted in due time, just as long as you stick to the plan. You are capable of big things. You just have to stay strong, same as you have this entire journey to a better tomorrow. The world is counting on you."

Well, no pressure there. How can someone as minuscule as me be the key to everything?

"You are the strongest person I've known in all my years. Never discredit your worth, Nyxi." His voice comes down the bond, unwavering and full of pride. I reach up and squeeze the hand he has resting on my shoulder.

"So you've helped me survive, but what does that have to do with where all the magic went?" I look between the two women next to me.

"The day before your sixteenth birthday, Hesti came to me. She is one of the ruling gods of our land, and she came with a warning and a gift. She gave me *The Tale of Gods*, transcribed by the magical who tracks the birth of new gods. She informed me that at midnight, you would have officially passed all the trials put forth by Mother Nature, and as such, would be transformed into the next ruling god."

I think my eyes might fall out of my head. How could someone like me become…a god? They have to be mistaken.

I am *minuscule*.

I am *weak*.

I am not *fit* to be a god.

"Gods are not blessed with the knowledge of their future until the moment they are about to transition, so your father and I had no idea what was in store for you that night. Hesti came as an act of good faith to warn us. If you read the book gifted to you, you will know each god is born stronger than the last. The last god was not happy to give up his title. He tapped into dark magic, which is forbidden. He planned to kill you the night of your celebration before you were to turn, trapping all the other gods on their island so they couldn't stop him."

My mother takes a deep breath to gather herself then gestures next to her. "Hesti found out and snuck away to warn us before she could be trapped along with the other gods. We came up with a plan to save you in hopes that one day, when you were ready and strong enough, you could save us all."

The more my mother talks, the more confused I become. How did I have no knowledge of any of this? I knew she was acting weird that day, but I chalked it up to her being anxious over me growing up, becoming a woman.

"What was this plan that uprooted my entire life?"

My mother grimaces, looking like she's in pain, trying to fight the demons in her head. She grits her teeth while closing her eyes, collecting herself before she relaxes and looks up at me again.

"Hesti walked in on Airestol channeling dark magic one evening without him noticing. He was being corrupted by it, turning evil right before her eyes. She snuck into his chambers to read through his personal diaries, where she found his entire plan detailed out. He planned to take out the next god before they transitioned and then use dark magic to curse the lands and steal all the magic for himself."

Dark magic? I saw there was a section in the book about it, but I didn't have time to read it. I still don't understand—how can the existence of our people rest on my miniscule shoulders?

"Your father and I made a plan. He was to fight off Airestol while I snuck you away. With the help of Hesti, I placed a glamour on you so if anyone looked at you, they would be spelled to forget who you once were, even though your features did not change. We wiped your memories along with it. Hesti had been watching over a boy in Fallout with no home. He was desperately in need of a family and love, and we needed someone we could trust to take care of you, to love you. We placed you together in the orphanage."

Theo. My heart squeezes. I have memories of us as children growing up in the orphanage together, him protecting me, taking care of me. They are all lies? My heart feels like I've known Theo my whole life, when in reality, I only shared four years with him. Hade squeezes my shoulder again, comforting me.

"But I have memories growing up in the orphanage with Theo. How is that possible?"

"We had to place false memories to fill the gaps. I am so sorry."

"Your love with him was real. The memories you shared for the last four years are real. Theo will always be a part of you. I promise, Nyxi."

I soak up the comforting words from Hade down the bond and use them as armor. He's right. Even though we didn't have as many years together as I thought, we still had four very real ones, full of love and memories, and that will never change.

"After Hesti dropped you at the orphanage, she came back to finish our plan. By the time she returned..." My mother pauses, choking on her words. She looks like a shell of a woman, and my heart aches for her. "It was too late. Airestol killed your father and was looking for you."

Papa is dead? No, that can't be true. I never got to say good-bye, never got to hug him one last time and tell him how much I loved him. I was his miniature in every way. We shared our dark hair and our night magic.

My mother gives me a knowing look. "It has been difficult without your father, but I had to hold on for you. Now is that time, my dear. I wish we had more time, but I'm afraid time is a currency we run low on."

I file away another painful ache in a neat box to unravel later and focus back on my mother. She looks so weak and tired, and I can tell being alive without Papa has been taxing on her.

"All magic requires balance. As such, there must be checks and balances put in place, even in regards to dark magic. One must give in order to take, especially the amount Airestol was channeling. So, I struck a deal with him."

My eyes go wide in horror. Why would she make a deal with the devil? My heart hammers in my chest, waiting for the ball to drop and my life to do a one-eighty again.

"What did you promise him?" I ask hesitantly, waiting for the impending doom to strike its blow.

"My life for yours." My mother gathers herself. "Airestol linked the curse to my life. I am the balance. I am what's standing between the life we live now and the life everyone deserves."

My brows pucker in confusion. This is all too much for me to process and handle after weeks of brutally fighting to stay alive. I had one mission: fight, stay alive, and get my revenge. Now, I have…and I'm on to the next.

Life never stops, it seems.

"Airestol was furious you had disappeared, afraid you would return one day and retaliate. To steal all the magic, the curse required a tether. I am that tether. He was more than willing to use me as the balance in his plan, thinking it would stop you from ever trying to break the curse. He had no idea I glamoured you and wiped your memories. I had Hesti watch over you, guide you through life, eventually guiding you back to me when the time was right."

Each word out of my mother's mouth only scrambles my brain further. How can this be real life? I struggle to breathe and keep pace with the never ending words.

"The deal I struck with Airestol ensured a way for you to make it back to me. I created the Reaper Crucible and conjured up the riddle as a failsafe. I spun the idea to Airestol as a way to control our citizens and hold power over their heads. How else would we explain why some citizens had magic up here while others below did not? I would be the face, and he would be the brains behind the scenes. He was to start by taking all the magic from Fallout, and then, after getting used to the abundance of magic within his possession, he would start tapping into Lunaria's reserves. I bargained that too much magic would overwhelm him."

Sighing, she nibbles her lip as she looks over to Hesti for support, who gives her a single reassuring nod. "As you now remember, I am no Impart. I am a Scorch disguised as an Impart. Airestol granted me a small chuck of the magic he stole from Fallout each year to gift the winner of the Crucible. Truly, it was just removing the curse preventing their magic from surfacing. The curse not only stripped all citizens of their magic below, but it also planted a false memory that magic never existed. They no longer remembered that everyone once had magic, or that I was their loving queen with a doting family. I was spun to be their evil Empress, who ruled over both Fallout and Lunaria, so that the once compassionate Lunarians were now hateful and excited to watch members of Fallout fight to the death. I spent so much time living down in Fallout as a way to watch over you."

She grits her teeth, hissing for a moment with her eyes closed before looking back at me. "The only thing I didn't account for was the curse tethered to me, slowly taking over my body and soul. At first, it felt like nothing, but over the past four years, it has slowly seeped more into my soul, corrupting chunks of me, leaving behind the vile Empress you have been acquainted with. I have moments like right now, when I'm lucid enough to take control of my body, but I have to fight hard to remain in control. It is painful, but I can manage for short periods. The rest of the time, I'm afraid it is the curse controlling my body and actions. I was losing all hope until my beautiful, storm cloud-eyed daughter showed up at my doorstep with vengeance in her eyes, and I knew I had made the right decision."

She leans forward slowly, gripping my hand in hers. "You are a force of nature. You are the tide that washes away the evil to make way for a brighter future, full of justice and change. You are going to make a wonderful queen to our people. Words will never be able to truly express the immense pride I have in being able to call you my daughter. You, my dear, are the roots that will bind us all together again. You will fight, you will not cower in the face of evil, and you will resurrect the injustice ripped away from our people."

She grips my cheeks in a way that almost feels like a goodbye while she looks at me with the last fraction of light shining through her eyes.

"Take back what is rightfully yours and make all who stand in your way bow before the holy ground you leave in your wake. Do not let them think you are anything less than what Mother Nature has deemed you, because you are the *god of all gods*. Make them bow at your holy throne."

I blink through the tears slowly cascading down my face. My mother pulls our foreheads together as the tremble in her hands slowly takes over her body. She's fighting so hard to stay in this moment with me as my mother and not the evil taking over her body.

My mother has sacrificed so much for me and this kingdom. She keeps saying how strong I am, but at this moment, the only strength worth admiring is the woman fighting to remain pure in front of me, no matter how painful it may be. She has been fighting for me this entire time.

There's one last piece I'm still scrambling for answers to. I look up into my mother's dulling eyes that no longer show any ounce of light, a shadow casted across them. I'm losing her.

"And the riddle?" I ask her on a gasp.

She nods against my forehead sadly as I replay her words from all those weeks ago.

Where three meet, one left behind. A sacrifice greater than mankind. A piercing cry from the one black eye. For that shall reset time before the ultimate crime.

My wide, pleading eyes clash with my mother's, who just smiles back while wrapping her hand around my other hand. Our hands move together as one, a single tear dribbling down her cheek while my brain processes the reality of the riddle's answer. I put the pieces together right before my mother speaks in a strangled tone. "I would have sacrificed myself a thousand times over if it meant keeping you safe. *I love you, Nyxi.*"

A slicing echoes around us, and I scream when I notice what she's done. I hadn't realized I still had Hade's sword clutched in my grasp, the same hand my mother had wrapped hers around and slowly moved towards her labored chest. She pushes our conjoined hands a little harder until it fully sheathes itself into her heart while simultaneously shattering mine.

Her *death* is the answer to the riddle.

She slouches on the couch, and I scream again, jumping to kneel over her. "MAMA? No, you can't leave me too. I cannot do this without you. I just got you back." I try to press my hands around the protruding sword to stifle the blood, but there's too much.

A haunting peace takes over her face, looking as if she is finally accepting her fate and welcoming the soft bliss about to sweep her away.

"Please don't leave me," I beg, sobbing above my mother.

"This w-was the only way to break the curse, love. Do not mourn my loss. I have co-completed my journey here, and you are ready to take over. I am able to finally reunite with your father, who has b-been waiting for me." I sob on her chest as she grips my bloody hands. "You must be s-strong now in the face of these new trials. You are the only one who can defeat Airestol. Hesti will guide you in my absence." With one last, strangled breath, she looks behind my shoulder where Hade now stands. "Take care of *our* girl."

My mother's eyes close, and her chest refuses to rise again, even with the immense pressure I still hold over her wound. I collapse onto her chest, screaming and crying until my throat goes raw.

"Please don't leave me. I will not allow it. Do you hear me, Mama? You can't leave me here alone to deal with this mess. I am not capable. I cannot do this without you."

I wait and wait for her eyes to open again, for her chest to rise and fall, but it doesn't and it won't.

She's dead, and so is Papa.

I am all that remains.

I am our last hope for freedom.

Hade rubs my back as I cry, mourning the mother I just got back. My body shakes, but as the vibrations become more intense, I realize it's not me, but the air around me.

Magic... It's back. I feel it all around me. The curse is broken at the price of my mother sacrificing herself. I hear shouts and commotion is the distance, but I pay them no heed as a tingling sensation buzzes over my body. It's strange and unfamiliar.

Pulling my body off my mother's, I'm met with two pairs of wide eyes. They look at me as if they've never seen me before. Hade is rendered speechless, and Hesti looks at me in awe.

Rushing to the closest mirror, I gasp when I see bright red flames licking over the roots of half my hair. I'm about to sprint to the nearest washroom to put it out, but I stop as I see the flame slowly travel down half my head, leaving bright red hair in its wake all the way to the tips.

My skin begins to sparkle and glow like Hesti's, and when I lift my hands to examine it, a dark ball of magic appears in one hand while a bright ball of fire appears in the other.

Half black, half red.

Half night magic, half fire magic.

Half my father, half my mother.

All god.

This was what Airestol was afraid of. Each god is stronger than the last.

Two abilities is unheard of, but magic loves its balance. I spin around and almost lose my footing when Hade comes into view, down on his knees before me, bowing deeply. He's looking at me like I'm his savior, his deity.

"You are the most majestic thing I've ever laid witness to, the only god I will worship every sunrise and sunset. Make no mistake, I am a greedy man, Nyxi. You are a rarity I intend to hide from the rest of the world." He swears under his breath. "My *lungs* only breathe for you. My *heart* only beats for you. My *love* only lives on in my heart for you. *I am yours*," he growls.

"Same as I am yours," I breathe. "You own every piece of me, Hade." Choking on a sob, I grasp his hand. With a shaky hand, he pulls my knuckles to his lips and takes his time kissing each one, worshiping my skin.

"I have something I need to show you," Hade says, and I'm afraid my world is about to spin once again.

Chapter
Fifty

Hade grabs my hand firmly, leaving Hesti behind with my mother while we barrel down the endless hallways. Pure chaos erupts around us, screams of fear, bewilderment, and excitement at their resurfaced memories.

It dawns on me that they will be looking for their queen to lead them, to answer their burning questions. They need someone to look to for guidance, and seeing as my mother is no longer with us, that role now falls on my shoulders. I feel the weight of it settle heavy over me, its roots wrapping around my legs and dragging me under.

I will need to gather them and explain everything, make them trust in me even if I don't fully trust in myself for the job. I have to fuse the gap between Fallout and Lunaria and create a better society for us all. There's also the issue of Aire, who, by now, has to be aware of my reappearance, magic buzzing back to life around us.

I follow dutifully behind Hade, making a mental note to address my people first thing after this little excursion. Dodging citizens left and right, we make it to the castle's front doors and continue through them to gods knows where.

Especially not this *god*.

"Where we are going is a place I have kept hidden for years." Hade's deep timber pushes at the walls of my head through the bond.

"Four years, to be exact?"

"Smart girl." His dominating personality reflects authentically in my head, and it's an overwhelming experience to get used to again. *"The queen—your mother, when she was first cursed, came to me, made me make her a promise. Ever since then, I have done everything in my power to uphold that promise for this very day. I did not know at the time what it was all for, but now, it all makes sense. She was preparing for war. She was preparing for you."*

We blend into the madness taking over the streets, walking for what seems like ages before making it almost to the very edge of Lunaria. I haven't visited this area before, seeing as it mostly looks rundown and abandoned at the edge of civilization.

I'm about to question Hade if he's feeling okay, to ask what the heck is going on, when he waves his hand in front of us. A ripple glitters in the air, and my eyes threaten to stay permanently wide when the glamour vanishes, revealing a small, makeshift camp.

"They've been waiting for you, dream."

Hissing through my teeth, I try to keep the sob inching up my throat from spilling over. *"Rayah?"* My voice cracks. "Is it really you?"

"Flowers! Are you trying to steal my colored hair, Nyxi?" she teases.

I rush forward, scooping her into my arms and holding tight, afraid to let go, only to see her vanish again.

"How is this possible?" I whisper into her bright pink hair.

Do you trust me? Hade's words from that day rush back to me. He kept telling me everything would be okay, to trust him. He kept her safe. Looking around and spotting Sierra and Yazi, I realize he's saved them *all*.

Hudson's small body disintegrating to a pile of ash pushes against my memories, and I'm struck harshly with the reality that not all of us were saved. I distinctly remember Hade strangling these two with his shadows until they went limp in front of me, so I'm not sure how they are currently pushing oxygen through their supposed burst lungs.

As I pull away from Rayah, a warm embrace saddles up to my back, towering over me. Looking over my shoulder, I find Hade studying me. Whether he's waiting for me to either snap, or break down, I'm not sure. The others decide to dismiss themselves, giving us a moment alone.

"I have tried to save as many of them as I could over the past four years. When your mother was fully lucid, she showed me this abandoned war camp. We fixed it up, and she asked me to save as many as possible. I had no idea why, seeing as my memories were wiped as well, but I never asked questions. I think, deep down in my gut, I knew."

His hand moves then, landing lightly on my shoulders and spinning me to face him. "I couldn't save them all for you, and for that, I am sorry. I did everything in my power to build you an army. Not everyone wanted to be saved or was worthy of a life fighting for you. Those who were, I saved and brought here. Some of the Vanquishes I trust come here daily to help train them and bring supplies, weapons, and food."

Pointing to Yazi and Sierra, he states, "I never killed them. I had to make it look like I did, but I only cut off their airways long enough to make them pass out so I could move them. Once they woke, I gave them a choice: to live and fight, or die a coward."

I stroke my thumb lightly across the scar dissecting his discolored eye. "What happened?" I whisper on a jagged breath.

He tries to turn his face to hide, but my hand is faster, and I grip the side of his cheek to face me again. Taking a deep sigh, he presses his warm cheek further into my palm.

"Airestol is what happened. I couldn't save him." His face breaks at the same time my brain puts the pieces together. He chokes. "Gods, Nyxi, I tried so hard to save him, but I failed you. I will never forgive myself for being the reason you no longer have a father. Because of me, you no longer have a family. I wear this scar as a reminder of that failure, so I may never forget the wreckage I've brought you."

Eyes watery, I smile softly. "I have *you*. You are my family, Hade. *You* are enough. You have always been enough." He tries to shake his head, rejecting my plea, but I look him dead in the eyes so he can see the truth in my words.

My voice never wavers. "There is no me without you. There is no life beyond you. There is no plan in my head that doesn't involve you beside me. A life without you is a tragedy greater than the loss of magic, because *I* cannot live on with only the memory of you. You are more than family to me—you are the very life that runs under my skin."

A single beat of silence crackles between us before Hade's giant hands engulf my face and he crashes his lips to mine. It's an answer. A plea for forever. A sealing of a declaration stronger than the magic holding Lunaria in the sky. It's an unbreakable bond between two souls so intertwined, you cannot find one without discovering the other.

"I hate to be the one to break up this sweet little family reunion."

Hade rips his lips away a deathly low growl of warning leaving his throat. He instinctively grips my hand while trying to drag me behind him. I hold my ground, preparing to fight this battle by his side.

"Aire." Hade's voice is more a warning than a statement.

"No need to stop all the fun on my account. Please, do continue. I was loving the sweet declarations." He turns to look at me. "Except you forgot something—one of you will vastly outlive the other. Isn't that right, *Nyxi?*"

I grit my teeth, vibrating with the need to attack, but Hade squeezes my hand tightly. "What do you want?" I spit each word like venom.

Splaying his arms out wide, he smiles condescendingly. "Now, now, little ghost. Is that any way to speak to a god?"

I sink my teeth into my bottom lip to refrain from spewing a slew of hateful words. This man is no god to me.

"You are no ghost, though, are you? Imagine my surprise when I discover the missing heir to the throne has been hiding under my nose the entire time. You really went and fucked everything up, didn't you? That's okay, though—you're going to fix it for me."

Hearing enough of his bullshit, I take a step towards him, slipping my hand from Hade's. "The only thing I'm going to fix is removing your presence from *my* kingdom."

In a flash, wind whips me in the face as Aire appears behind Hade, pressing a single finger to his temple. Volts of electricity skitter through Hade's body, making him seize. His other hand lashes out, creating a vortex bubble, keeping us isolated. I swivel on my feet, flexing my hand to bring my own magic to the surface when his words halt me in my tracks.

"Take one more step, and his eye color won't be the only thing plucked from his body."

I hold my hands up in surrender, pleading with him to stop while trying to come up with a plan. Hade's body continues to shake from the magic frying him from the inside out, and I break a little. His eyes plead with me to stay strong, but I can't live seeing him like this. He won't last much longer with the amount of magic coursing through him. It's simply unbearable to watch, and I would do anything to make it stop.

Hade must read the surrender on my face, because his choppy words stream down the bond. *"Please don't do this. I will not survive losing you a second time. My heart cannot take it."*

Turning my head to the side, I try to ignore his words full of so much heartbreak, it's almost too much to bear. Hade grunts loudly in pain, and my eyes shoot to where Aire's finger presses harder against his flesh, shoving an impossible amount of magic into him. Hade can't even use any of his own magic to protect himself.

"I think I'm having a case of déjà vu," Aire says comically.

"Okay, enough!" I scream.

Aire's wicked smile sends shivers down my spine. *"Beg me* to save his pathetic life."

"Please, stop. Please spare his life in exchange for mine. It's me you want, and if you kill him, you will kill any chance of me ever working with you."

"Nyxi, please." Hade's words are a whisper down the bond, his energy almost fully drained. He's fading fast, and it's killing me.

Aire shoves his finger one more time harshly against Hade's temple, making him gasp for air he can't find, and I lose all control. Both my hands whip out, black and red magic sitting ready in each of my palms.

"I said ENOUGH! You have my attention now, so what do you want?"

Looking between my hands as I harness two types of magic, he smiles, satisfied. "I want you. It seems the rumors were true. Of course, each new god will be born of magic stronger than the last. That is the magic of evolution. But two powers? Well *that* is unheard of."

My hands twitch, the magic dancing wildly while Hade's body trembles, though a bit softer now that Aire has let up a fraction. "I thought you wanted me dead?"

Shrugging, he states, "Plans change, my little goddess. Now that I've seen what you can do, I want you for myself. The strongest god to date, born of two powers, in my back pocket? I would be unstoppable. *We* would be unstoppable."

"*I'm sorry. Please forgive me. You must live on without me, or this will all be for nothing. Live that beautiful life we talked about. Promise me.*" I send the words down the bond to a barely coherent Hade before locking Aire in an intense gaze. "Let him go. Let them all go. Promise you will not harm them, and I will give myself to you."

"Deal!" His words feel thick and sticky across my skin, making me uncomfortable, but I keep my face blank and devoid of any emotions until I know Hade is safe. "I have big plans for us in Ouranos."

In another flash, Hade falls to the ground, and Aire appears by my side, gripping my hand possessively. I try to pull away, but his grip tightens painfully, making me hiss.

Hade screams a guttural sound that shatters my heart. He blinks heavily, trying to stay awake as he, inch by inch, tries to drag his limp body to crawl to me. "You c-cannot have h-her." He does not stop. He does not waver. Determination flames across his face as he desperately grasps the remaining light slowly fading from him. Every place his trembling fingertips touch the grass below him, his Death magic weakly seeps out, draining the ground of life.

"*I told you, dream. My heart only beats for you. Without you, there is no me. I will not face a life without you in it. My life was gray before you brought the color. I will not go back to a life of black and white when I can have the whole damn rainbow.*"

As he lifts one trembling hand, black shadows snake down his arm. Pointing one threatening finger at Aire, he looks me painfully in the eyes. I feel every aspect of his next words as he says down the bond, "*I love you, Nyxi.*"

Before Hade's magic gets a chance to blast towards us, Aire zaps a single bolt of electricity right at Hade's battered body, hitting him directly in the chest. With a scream, I jolt forward, but Aire wraps his arms around me from behind, restraining me as Hade crumples to the ground.

Hade's lifeless body is the last thing I see before clouds envelop us, and we slam through time and space at a nauseating speed. I don't react when my feet hit the ground once again, or when a new land I don't recognize comes into view. I don't react when Aire announces, "Welcome to Ouranos, your new home."

I don't react because all I can think is, *if Hade is truly dead, then so am I.* And if he's not, I will tear every realm apart until I have him again. I am a demon disguised as a god, ready to destroy her enemy from behind territory lines.

My love does not live on without you, Hade.

A new god is in town, and this time, she's getting her vengeance.

To be continued...

Acknowledgments

WHEW. HOW'S EVERYONE FEELING AFTER THAT ENDING? HOPEFULLY you're not *too* mad at me—and that you're ready to stick around for book two in the series!

If you've made it all the way to this point, I hope that means you enjoyed the emotional roller coaster I put you through. What started as a silly little fantasy idea in my head quickly grew into something raw, deep, and incredibly personal. My goal for this book was to create something real—flawed, complex, and relatable characters that readers could connect with. For this being my debut novel, I'm beyond proud of what I've created and how deeply I fell in love with this story and these characters.

So, from the bottom of my heart, thank you for taking a chance on this newbie indie author. It means the world to me that anyone would want to read something I dreamed up.

This book would not exist without the amazing support system I have behind me.

To my entire family—grandma, aunts, uncles, in-laws—thank you for cheering me on, supporting me endlessly, and helping spread the word on social media. Your excitement helped fuel my own.

To my parents (all of you): thank you for always pushing me to chase my dreams, no matter how wild or impossible they may have seemed. Your constant support and belief in me over this past year kept me going. I truly couldn't have done this without your love and encouragement.

To my sister—the real MVP of this story. You're the reason this book exists. When I told you it would be fun to write a book someday and you responded, *"You can,"* something clicked in my brain and the mental barriers melted away. Your belief in me gave me the final shove I needed. You've always been my role model, and thanks to you, I've found my dream career. Your support while reading along—texting me reactions and hype—kept me going chapter after chapter. I love you more than words can say.

To my alpha readers: Brianna, Cara, Delaney, and Gabi—thank you for riding this wave with me. Your texts, your emotional reactions (even the angry ones hehe), and your excitement lit a fire under me every time I sat down to write. You made this journey joyful, and I'm so grateful to have each of you in my life.

To my husband—my rock. Thank you for supporting this crazy dream without hesitation. We joke that I pick up a new hobby every month, but when I told you I was actually going to write a book, you didn't even blink or act surprised. You just stood beside me, encouraging me every step of the way. Thank you for making dinner so I could write late into the night, for celebrating each finished chapter, and for being the inspiration behind the love story woven into this fantasy world. Our love story is my favorite one—and yes, I *did* sneak some of your long-distance texts into Hades' dialogue. I love loving you, and I know our story is only just beginning.

And to you—the reader. Thank you for taking a chance on me. I know how many incredible books are out there (trust me, my TBR is out of control too), so the fact that you chose to spend your time with my story is life-changing. You mean more to me than I can express, and I hope you've fallen for these characters as deeply as I have. I hope this story gave you a place to escape to, even just for a little while.

If you've made it this far, you're a true trooper. I *love* hearing reader reactions, so please don't hesitate to reach out and slide into my DMs. I live for your messages.

Now, it's time for me to dive back into the trenches and keep this story going. Buckle up—the emotional whiplash from book one is far from over.

With all my love,
-Alexis Morgan

About the Author

ALEXIS MORGAN WAS BORN AND RAISED in the beautiful rainy state of Washington. She discovered her love for reading and writing later in life—thanks to a bout of boredom while her husband was deployed overseas. Since then, books have become her passion (and, admittedly, her whole personality).

When she's not curled up with a good book, accompanied by her Frenchie, Enzo, and cat, Evie, you'll likely find her at the gym, spending time with family, or—more often than not—browsing the aisles of her favorite bookstore.

Follow me on socials:
Instagram: @authoralexismorgan